NORTHWEST
VISTA
COLLEGE

D1570539

34009001100982

THE BATTLE OF THE SEXES IN SCIENCE FICTION

THE WESLEYAN
EARLY CLASSICS OF
SCIENCE FICTION
SERIES

GENERAL EDITOR
ARTHUR B. EVANS

Invasion of the Sea Jules Verne
The Mysterious Island Jules Verne
Lumen Camille Flammarion

THE BATTLE OF THE SEXES IN SCIENCE FICTION

JUSTINE LARBALESTIER

Wesleyan University Press Middletown, Connecticut

Published by

Wesleyan University Press

Middletown, CT 06459

ISBN 0-8195-6526-1 cloth

ISBN 0-8195-6527-x paper

Printed in the United States of America

Design by Rich Hendel

Set in Electra type by B. Williams & Associates

5 4 3 2 1

Cataloging-in-Publication Data appear at the end of the book

FOR JAN LARBALESTIER,

for inspiring me with a love

of fiction and feminism

CONTENTS

ILLUSTRATIONS

ACKNOWLEDGMENTS

This book is part of a journey, a part of the process of my becoming "plugged in" to the field of science fiction. In 1992, when I began this book, I would have said that I was well versed in science fiction, yet I had never read any histories of the field nor any critical accounts of it. I did not know that many considered the appearance of the first issue of the magazine *Amazing Stories* to be the beginning of science fiction. I had never heard of *Amazing* or any other science fiction magazine. I read mostly books that were published at the time I was reading them. I had never heard of fanzines and had no sense of the people who produced the texts I loved. In short, science fiction, for me, was neither field nor community, but books alone. In the course of writing this book I have become increasingly aware of and engaged with a science fiction that consists not only of texts but also of people: writers, readers, fans, artists, critics, and editors.

The history of science fiction that had formed around my reading was almost completely at odds with the histories of the genre that I read in the course of producing this book. The sf I had read while growing up was almost entirely written by women and often had strong female protagonists. I had heard of Isaac Asimov and Robert Heinlein, but I had never read them. I had no idea that science fiction was generally considered to be a "boy's own" genre. However, I did not start reading science fiction until the 1970s, by which time, it is generally considered, feminism had begun to have a considerable impact on the field. The more I read, discussed, and participated in the sf community, the more I was surprised to learn that in many of the histories of the genre women appear only on the peripheries, and that fantasy is the other side of the dichotomy from science fiction, at least as frequently as mundane fiction.

This book is greatly indebted to Joanna Russ's 1980 article "*Amor Vincit Foeminam*: The Battle of the Sexes in Science Fiction." What struck me about Russ's article and the texts she explores therein was that they illustrated that science fiction's engagement with feminism, sexual difference, and sex and sexuality was not a recent development. Science fiction, it appeared, had a *tradition* of engaging with these issues. The increase in feminist engagements with science fiction in the 1960s and 1970s was made possible not only by the increase in consciousness of feminism generally and in the science fiction world in particular but also by science fiction's prior engagement with feminism. This is demonstrated by the many battle-of-the-sexes stories, as well as by debates about the place of women in the field. I discovered these debates in the letters pages of prozines such as *Astounding* and *Thrilling Wonder Stories* of the 1930s and 1950s.

There is considerable debate about what constitutes science fiction. In the entry "Definitions of Science Fiction" in *The Encyclopedia of Science Fiction* (1993) there are seven columns of discussion of just a few of these definitions. In this book I am not concerned with boundary delineation or maintenance of the genre. Any text published as science fiction, claimed by those engaged with science fiction to be science fiction (regardless of what else it may be), is, for my purposes, science fiction. My rationale is that the focus of my book is on those who produce and consume texts, as well as those texts themselves. I use "science fiction" to refer to a community or, rather, communities. These communities' physical location is centered on the United States of America, although there are community members, like myself, who are located outside the United States.

In 1993–1994 I spent five months doing research in North America, first in Toronto, then in New York City and San Francisco. My "fieldwork" had the dual purpose of accessing texts that are unavailable in Australia and making connections with science fiction communities. I interviewed writers, publishers, editors, fans, and agents, as well as the sf buyers for two of what were then the major book chains in the United States—Dalton's and Walden's. I also went to my first sf conventions: the 1993 World Fantasy Convention in Minneapolis and the 1993 ArmadilloCon in Austin, Texas. These two conventions, coming early in my trip, while I was still based in Toronto, allowed me to meet many people in the community before I went to New York City and San Francisco. I was able to meet with and interview almost everyone I needed to talk to. I am grateful to the science fiction community in North America for being so welcoming and supportive.

Like any other theorist, student or scholar, I am engaged in the process of constructing the object of my investigations. At the same time my object, in this case, the field of science fiction, reconstructs the subject—me. Becoming part of the science fiction field and conversant in its language was a process that began before I thought of writing a book about science fiction. However, in the process of producing this book I have found myself much more overtly a part of the science fiction community as a practitioner and creator of this field.

In calling this book *The Battle of the Sexes in Science Fiction*, I create an object—the battle of the sexes in science fiction; to tell a story about something is to shape that something. The story I tell in this book is also an interested story. By beginning in 1926 with the advent of *Amazing Science Fiction* and ending with the James Tiptree Jr. Memorial Award, I make the development of the Tiptree Award from the mostly antifeminist battle-of-the-sexes stories from the 1920s onward look both natural and inevitable. It begins to look like evolution. Yet my creation of "the battle of the sexes" does not take place in a vacuum. It is constrained by the historical knowledge that Joanna Russ set out such a genre in her 1980 article of the same name, and she did so knowing that Sam Moskowitz had published an anthology of this genre of science fiction in 1972.

I began my survey of sf criticism in the traditional manner, by reading articles published in the academic sf journals *Extrapolation*, *Science Fiction Studies*, and *Foundation*, as well as with book-length studies. At the same time, however, I began to read fanzines. It soon became apparent that they and other forms of "informal criticism" were essential sources for this book. I am indebted to Pauline Dickinson, who first showed me around the science fiction collection in the Rare Books Collection of the University of Sydney Library. The core of this collection consists of the enormous bequest made to the library by longtime Sydney collector and fan, Ronald E. Graham. Because of this bequest, the University of Sydney has one of the largest public collections of science fiction material in the world. The collection includes a very sizable proportion of *all* the science fiction novels and magazines published up until Ron Graham's death in 1978. There are complete or near complete runs of famous early magazines such as *Amazing*, *Astounding*, and *Weird Tales*. The collection has been crucial to this book. Without it I would not have discovered so quickly what Samuel R. Delany calls a "vast tributary system of informal criticism, comprised of 'apas' (amateur press associations), fanzines, reviews, and assorted commentary" (Delany 1984: 238).

I would like to thank Pauline Dickinson along with the other librarians of the University of Sydney Library Rare Books section, who helped me in more ways than I can enumerate. Working with them has been not only educative but an absolute pleasure. Their patience, understanding, and helpfulness knows no bounds. Many thanks to the late Bruce Belden, Neil Boness, Linden Fairbairn, Sara Hilder, and Richard Ratajczak.

Several people have read and commented on this book in manuscript. I thank Samuel R. Delany, John Docker, L. Timmel Duchamp, Rosemary Huisman, Sylvia Kelso, Jan Larbalestier, Kelly Link, Helen Merrick, and the two anonymous readers for Wesleyan University Press for their comments and suggestions.

Without the advice and knowledge of longtime fan and science fiction expert, Graham Stone, this book would have been infinitely poorer. I am grateful to Graham for bringing to my attention books, stories, and articles I would never have seen otherwise, for allowing me access to his own enormous science fiction collection, and for all his suggestions and answers to my many, many questions.

This book would not have been possible without the support of an Australian Postgraduate Award scholarship. I am grateful also to the University of Sydney for awarding me a G. H. S. and I. R. Lightoller Travel Scholarship as well as a Conference Travel Grant.

Also I'd like to thank the following for their help and support via email: Brian Attebery, Chantal Bourgault, Yvette Christianse, Ray Davis, Karen Joy Fowler, Joan Haran, Judith Merril, Julie Phillips, Jeff Smith, Grant Stone, Susanna Sturgis, Lucy Sussex, Elisabeth Vonarburg, Elizabeth Willey, Delia Sherman, and everyone on the fem-sf discussion group.

Thank you to Julie Phillips, Jeff Smith, and Gordon Van Gelder for supplying me with Tiptree material and talking Tiptree with me. Thanks to Bruce Pelz and the many others who responded to my various requests to rec.arts.sf.lovers, fem-sf, rec.arts.sf.fandom, and the Timebinders list. Thank you also to the marvellous organizing committees of WisCons 20, 24, and 25 (May 1996, 2000, and 2001) for providing the perfect site—a four day feminist utopia—in which to meet so many of my virtual friends.

Thanks to everyone associated with the Tiptree Award for all their help—especially Karen Joy Fowler and Jeanne Gomoll. Thanks also to Brian Attebery, Freddie Baer, Nicola Griffith, Elizabeth Hand, Richard Kadrey, Ellen Klages, Ellen Kushner, Janet M. Lafler, Pat Murphy, Debbie Notkin, Delia Sherman, Susanna Sturgis, and Lucy Sussex.

Thanks also to my nonvirtual Sydney friends for support intellectual and otherwise, Joelle Chenoweth, Yvette Christianse, Louise D'Arcens, Jennifer Ford, Brigid Gaffikin, Karen Horne, Luisa Manfredini, Jeannie Messer, Jane Pritchard, Nina Puren, Mandy Sayer, George Sheridan, and Catherine Waters.

The University of Sydney English Department helped me in areas both intellectual and administrative. Thank you Judith Barbour, Marion Flynn,

Simon French, Helen Fulton, Margaret Harris, Kate Lilley, Adrian Mitchell, Judy Quinn, Pat Ricketts, Margaret Clunies Ross, Milly Vranes, Geoff Williams, and Maree Williams.

Thanks also to Meg Luxton of Women's Studies, York University, Canada, and Andrew Ross of American Studies at New York University for arranging my time as a visiting scholar at their respective institutions.

Mary Cannings, Annette Mocek, and Lorna Toolis at the Merril Collection of Science Fiction, Speculation and Fantasy in Toronto, Canada, were marvelous, providing me not only with help and guidance with the collection but also with the city of Toronto.

Thanks to the University of Sydney Arts IT Support Unit who in the face of my overwhelming computer ignorance still managed to smile, be helpful, and tell really dreadful jokes. Thanks to John Couani, Jim Dwyer, Nigel Oram, and Lawrence Wong.

Many kind people extended hospitality on my research trip to North America: Marlea Clarke, Paul Clift, Shelly Clift, Ellen Datlow, Ray Davis, Karen Joy Fowler, Miriam Jones, the Kane family, Donald Keller, Kitt Kerr, Robert Killheffer, Ellie Lang, Meg Luxton, Linzi Manicom, Paul Campbell, Nicola Nixon, Debbie Notkin, Andrew Ross, Lawrence Schimel, Martha Soukup, Caroline Spector, Gordon Van Gelder, and Elizabeth Willey.

My thanks go also to Johanne Knowles, Stephanie Tall, and all the staff at Galaxy Books, Sydney, to Justin Ackroyd of Slow Glass Books, Melbourne, and Ron Serdiuk of Pulp Fiction, Brisbane. I'd also like to thank everybody at Bakka Books in Toronto, The Other Change of Hobbit, Berkeley, and Dark Harvest Books, Berkeley.

I thank my editor at Wesleyan, Suzanna Tamminen, for believing in the book, enjoying the grammar (!), answering all my endless questions, and for being a really fine editor.

It's a risky business to be thanked for manuscript preparation and technical help, but the work of Niki Bern, Geoff Horne, Helen Merrick, Jeannie Messer, and Scott Westerfeld was astounding. Thank you! Any remaining mistakes are mine.

The science fiction editor Jenna Felice died in March 2001. She helped me with this book, both directly and indirectly, from manuscript preparation and helping me with my research to being a warm and wonderful friend from the time of my first research trip to the United States in 1993. I miss her.

Special thanks and love to Jan Larbalestier, John Bern, and Niki Bern for their patient support and love over the years.

INTRODUCTION

This book is about a type of sf story, the battle-of-the-sexes story, and how such stories provide insight into the role of women in science fiction, literally and textually, from the mid-1920s until the present. It is equally about the battle of the sexes as it was played out in what Samuel R. Delany calls "the vast tributary system of informal criticism" (Delany 1984: 238). In the pages that follow, you will see that letters, reviews, fanzines, and marketing blurbs are as important as the stories themselves in understanding the evolving relationship between men and women in sf.

I take the term "battle of the sexes" as it applies to sf from Joanna Russ's 1980 article "*Amor Vincit Foeminam*: The Battle of the Sexes in Science Fiction".[1] Russ uses the term to refer to sf texts that are explicitly about the "sex war" between men and women and which posit as a solution to this conflict that women accept their position as subordinate to men. Many of the battle-of-the-sexes texts are overtly antifeminist, and frequently comically so. In her foreword to the reprint of "*Amor Vincit Foeminam*," Russ discusses how bad they are:

> Samuel Delany told me the stories were too idiotic to bother with, but they would not leave me alone until I gave them their place in the sun. Their crudity and silliness were worse than my representation of them, honestly; they were terrible. But it was fun. As a critic, a reviewer, and a teacher, I have spent my life reading a huge amount of extraordinarily bad fiction; sometimes the only way to discharge the emotion aroused by the incessant production of gurry is to beat the gurry to death, especially when it's as marvellously foolish as this was. (Russ 1995: 41)

Russ discusses ten stories published in the United States between 1926 and 1973. I have concentrated on the same period but have broadened my study to include many texts not examined by Russ: those that fit her rubric as well as others that posit a range of different "solutions" to the battle of the sexes, including characters that are neither male nor female but hermaphroditic. I then take the discussion further, from the formation of the James Tiptree Jr. Memorial Award in 1991, to the year 2000.

The period from 1926 to 1973 is absolutely crucial to the formation of contemporary feminist science fiction, and yet very little critical work has been undertaken on that period. For example, almost all feminist accounts of the field concentrate on the period from the 1970s onward. The importance of the seventies to feminist science fiction has been convincingly demonstrated (Rosinsky 1984; Lefanu 1988; Cortiel 1999), but the importance of the earlier period needs explication; this book aims to do just that. In chapters 2 through 5 the complex relationships among sf and women, men, sex, and sexuality are mapped out. In chapters 7 and 8 I demonstrate the links between the earlier period, 1926–1973, and contemporary feminist science fiction by examining the career of James Tiptree Jr., a science fiction writer who began publishing in 1968. Tiptree, revealed in mid-career as Alice Sheldon, writing under a pseudonym, was the winner of multiple Nebula Awards and helped break down the imaginary barrier between "women's writing" and "men's writing." To emphasize the connections I make among James Tiptree Jr., the award named after him/her, and the battle of the sexes in science fiction, each chapter of this book is named after a short story by James Tiptree Jr. Since 1991 the James Tiptree Jr. Memorial Award, named in her/his honor, has been awarded annually to a fictional work that explores and expands the roles of women and men in the field of science fiction.

The genre of science fiction has always contained some kind of engagement with the terrain of sex and sexual difference. Science fiction engaging with feminism, and feminist science fiction, however, are not necessarily the same thing. Russ's article allowed me to engage with feminism and science fiction, feminist science fiction, and women and science fiction. These distinctions are important. There are as many feminist science fictions as there are feminisms and science fictions. Feminist science fiction is both a reading practice and a writing practice. For example, on the on-line discussion group fem-sf, heated debates arise when we try to delineate exactly what we mean by "feminist science fiction." One of the few things we can agree about is that although there were women engaged with science fiction as early as the 1920s and 1930s, and although there have always been women fans, that does not necessarily mean that women have always felt welcome within the field or that these women were all feminists.

While not all of the women who have been part of the field of science fiction would identify as feminists, the fact of their participation has become a feminist issue. The mere fact of their presence created a tradition that other women could then become a part of. Connie Willis in her article "The Women SF Doesn't See" discusses stories by women she read while growing up: "It never occurred to me that SF was a man's field that had to be broken into. How could it be with all those women writers? How could it be when Judith Merril was the one editing all those *Year's Best SFs*?" (Willis 1992: 8).

Another tradition of women's writing is created by Jane L. Donawerth and Carol A. Kolmerten, the editors of *Utopian and Science Fiction by Women: Worlds of Difference*, who argue that "utopias and science fiction by women—women's 'literatures of estrangement'—constitute a continuous literary tradition in the West from the seventeenth century to the present day" (Donawerth and Kolmerten 1994: 1). While I concur with the argument that a writer can be part of many different traditions, the problem with locating women science fiction writers in such an expansive definition of utopian literature is that it tends to ignore the importance of the field of science fiction. To read Joanna Russ's *The Female Man* (1975) as a utopia, and only in relation to Charlotte Perkins Gilman's *Herland* (1915) or Margaret Cavendish's *The Description of a New World, Called the Blazing World* (1668), ignores the ways in which it rewrites various battle-of-the-sexes texts within science fiction, where worlds of all women are presented as dystopias not utopias. Russ's familiarity with both the utopian and the science fiction fields is a crucial force in the texts she produces. Her two articles, "*Amor Vincit Foeminam:* The Battle of the Sexes in Science Fiction" (1980) and "Recent Feminist Utopias" (1981), make this clear.

In the 1980s there was talk within the feminist science fiction community of an erasure of the overtly feminist science fiction culture that had emerged in the previous two decades and particularly in the 1970s. This sense of unease about the ways in which the feminist science fiction of the 1970s was being devalued and even sometimes erased was part of the background to Pat Murphy's 1991 announcement of a new award, the James Tiptree Jr. Memorial Award. Murphy, and her coconspirator, Karen Joy Fowler, felt that feminism generally, and within science fiction in particular, had a long way to go. Murphy had "come to believe that to change the way that people think about women and men, we need to show people in different roles" (Murphy [1991] 1992: 8). It was hoped that the new award would encourage new work that challenged sexual stereotypes.

Many of the quotations you will see in the chapters to follow are drawn from fanzines, amateur publications put together by lovers of science fiction, who call themselves fans. Fandom (as fans call it) began with letters to the editors of professional science fiction magazines such as *Amazing*. Their letters frequently concerned the stories published, the covers of the magazines, and science. Addresses were printed with these letters, and before long letter writers who lived in the same area were contacting each other and forming friendships and loose-knit communities and talking, among other things, about science fiction.

The fanzines that I worked with date from the mid 1930s to the late 1970s and were from the United States, Australia, England, and Canada. Very few of them are professional looking. They are stapled-together pieces of paper with or without covers, often almost illegibly printed on a hektograph machine. An example of a one-page fanzine put together by the New York Futurian fan group is reproduced in figure 1. Most of the fanzines were full of reports of fan activity, meetings, conventions, feuds, reviews and some debate about science fiction, though frequently discussion of science fiction is minimal. The fanzines are also full of their own language, and I soon became familiar with terms like "gafiate," derived from the acronym for "get away from it all," meaning to leave fandom; "fen," the plural of "fan"; and "prozine," a professional science fiction magazine like *Amazing*.

Although fandom grew out of the letter column of *Amazing*, and following it, other science fiction magazines, by 1944 the entry on "fan" in *The Fancyclopedia* claims that although the term is "used by the scientifictionists who *merely* write letters to the editor and collect pro mags . . . the fen of fandom have a more restricted meaning in mind" (my italics; Speer 1944: 29). By this time "merely" writing to prozines is not enough for authentic fanhood. The entry then goes on to elaborate some of the more "restricted meanings": "The IPO made no attempt to isolate an essential characteristic by which all fans mite *[sic]* be distinguished, but said that 'A *real* fan fulfils practically all of the following requirements: He *[sic]* buys and reads most of the professional fantasy magazines (this was when there were less than half a dozen), collects them, and writes the editors. He subscribes to at least one fan magazine. He corresponds with other fans. S-f fandom is his ruling passion. He has probably tried his hand at writing, either for fan or pro magazines or both'" (my italics; Speer 1944: 29–30).[2] A discourse of fan authenticity was already in operation. Though, as this entry demonstrates, the term "fan" was contested. It is also clear that fans during this period were assumed to be male. By far the majority of the fanzines I looked at were produced by men and contained letters and articles by men. There

FUTURIAN NEWS

Published by the FUTURIAN SOCIETY OF NEW YORK to carry news and announcements of Futurians to their members and friends. (Member, Futurian Publishers Group)
Volume 1, Number 5 January 4th, 1939

WHO ARE THE FUTURIANS?
The Futurian Society of New York is an organization of imaginative young people in New York and vicinity who enjoy meeting together once in a while (specifically, twice a month) in order to discuss literature, art, science, progress, poetry and the world at large and to enjoy each others company and controversy. They are bound together by a mutual desire for betterment both of this world and of their prowess and appreciation of it. They believe that the future holds much in store for all and that the "futurian outlook" is well worth cultivating. Science-fiction is a hobby and interest of most of them and that particular subject is often on deck, especially since most of the Futurians are old time fans and internationally-accepted authorities on that subject.

There is nothing aloof or suspicious about the Futurians. They are always glad to see newcomers and welcome them as friends regardless of their views or previous opinions. Meetings vary from small groups to large, formal ones. At a meeting you may find anything from a formal debate to jovial socialities (p.s. we do not blackball people on one vote. We trust our friends.)

FUTURIANS IN PRINT
This month's issue (February) of Amazing Stories features "Marooned Off Vesta" by Isaac Asimov. This young man is a member of the Futurians and a promising young writer. This story marks the first he has had accepted but we suspect, far from his last. John W. Campbell remarked of Asimov that he expects him to go far as a writer. His works, as far as that editor has seen, being very, very good. We suspect that it will not be long before our Futurian is accepted in all the magazines.

In the past many of the Futurians have broken into print in various publications. The future will undoubtedly see many more of them successful.

XMAS MEETING A GREAT SUCCESS
A large and interesting meeting was held December 26th when almost the full membership of the Society turned up at the Pohl-Michel apartment. The meeting was to have been held at a hall, but it seemed that at the last minute it would not be available. In spite of this, the members were not daunted and showed up at the Futurian H.G. Among those present were Dick Wilson, Harry Dockweiler, Donald Wollheim, Jack Rubinson, John Michel, Jack Gillespie, Sylvia Rubin, Robert W. Lowndos, Daniel Burford, Gertrude Lee Winters, Herman Leventman, Cyril Kornbluth, Isaac Asimov, Abraham Oshinsky, Edward Landberg and many others. Leslie Perry [*sic*] and Terry M. Roth showed up later. The meeting was featured by a heated debate between Pohl and Kornbluth on the subject of "Is There a Science-

Fiction Poetry?" Pohl won when Kornbluth fled as Fred started reading one of Cyril's earlier indiscriminations from JEDDARA. Discussions too numerous to list were also indulged in and threshed out by the members.

NEXT MEETING TO BE SUNDAY, JANUARY 8th.
The Futurian Society's first meeting of the new year will take place this Sunday afternoon at about 3 p.m. The place this time is to be the home of Cyril Kornbluth, 506 West 213th Street, New York City, (Manhattan). The nearest subway station is the 215th St. station of the Bway IRT line, This house is about a half block from the subway lines. DON'T FAIL TO SHOW UP.

1. Futurian fanzine, *Futurian News*, 4 January 1939

were, however, women fans, and I found letters from them in the prozines as early as the 1920s and in fanzines as early as the 1930s.

The entry gives other definitions of a "fan" citing well-known fans, or BNFs (big-name fans) as sources: "Widner said he thinks the essential thing about fans is that they have an ideal of a better way of life and want to change things; but this hardly sets them apart from millions of non-fans. [illegible] well received is Norman Stanley's 'sense of fantasy', a taste for the imaginative analogous to the sense of humour" (Speer 1944: 29).

Fans began writing their own history and naming their own periods very early. The *Fancyclopedia* appeared in 1944, only fourteen years after the appearance of the first fanzine, Ray Palmer's *The Comet*.[3] In the *Fancyclopedia* there are entries for the various historical periods, First Fandom, Second Fandom and so forth that were already in use at the time. The *Fancyclopedia* was produced in association with NFFF (National Fantasy Fan Federation) and LASFS (Los Angeles Science Fiction Society) and also vetted and corrected by the New York Futurians and other well-known fan organizations of the period.

An important part of the discourse of fandom was the idea that it could lead to a professional engagement with science fiction. The transition of fan into pro (professional) is the process of the accumulation of cultural capital within the field. A number of the names I came across in prozine letter columns and fanzines—Isaac Asimov, Ray Bradbury, Lee Hoffman, Judith Merril, and Frederik Pohl—become pros. This notion of the fluidity of the science fiction community, where you could go from being a fan to being a BNF to being a professional writer or artist or editor, is no longer as important an aspect of fandom as it once was. Far fewer contemporary pros were once fans. Kim Stanley Robinson, Karen Joy Fowler, and Nalo Hop-

FUTURIAN NEWS

Published by the FUTURIAN SOCIETY OF NEW YORK to carry news and announcements of Futurians to their members and friends. (Member, Futurian Publishers Group)
Volume 1, Number 3 January 4th, 1939

WHO ARE THE FUTURIANS?

The Futurian Society of New York is an organization of imaginative young people in New York and vicinity who enjoy meeting together once in a while (specifically, twice a month) in order to discuss literature, art, science, progress, poetry and the world at large and to enjoy each others company and controversy. They are bound together by a mutual desire for betterment both of this world and of their prowess and appreciation of ir. They believe that the future holds much in store for all and that the "futurian outlook" is well worth cultivating. Science-fiction is a hobby and interest of most of them and that particular subject is often on deck, especially since many of the Futurians are old time fans and internationally-accepted authorities on that subject.

There is nothing aloof or suspicious about the Futurians. They are always glad to see newcomers and welcome them as friends regardless of their views or previous opinions. Meetings vary from small groups to large, formal ones. At a meeting you may find anything from a formal debate to jovial socialities (p.s. we do not blackball people on one vote. We trust our friends.)

FUTURIANS IN PRINT

This month's issue (February) of Amazing Stories features "Marooned Off Vesta" by Isaac Asimov. This young man is a member of the Futurians and a promising young writer. This story marks the first he has had accepted but we suspect, far from his last. John W. Campbell remarked of Asimov that he expects him to go far as a writer. His works, as far as that editor has seen ,being very, very good. We suspect that it will not be long before our Futurian is accepted in all the magazines.

In the past many of the Futurians have broken into print in various publications. The future will undoubtedly see many more of them successful.

XMAS MEETING A GREAT SUCCESS

A large and interesting meeting was held December 26th when almost the full membership of the Society turned up at the Pohl-Michel apartment. The meeting was to have been held at a hall, but it seemed that at the last minute it would not be available. In spite of this, the members were not daunted and showed up at the Futurian H.Q. Among those present were Dick Wilson, Harry Dockweiler, Donald Wollheim, Jack Rubinson, John Michel, Jack Gillespie, Sylvia Rubin, Robert W. Lowndes, Daniel Burford, Gertrude Lee Winters, Herman Leventman, Cyril Kornbluth, Isaac Asimov Abraham Oshinsky, Edward Landberg and many others. Leslie Perry and Terry M Roth showed up later. The meeting was featured by a heated debate between Pohl and Kornbluth on the subject of "Is There a Science-Fiction Poetry?" Pohl won when Kornbluth fled as Fred started reading one of Cyril's earlier indiscriminations from JEDDARA. Discussions too numerous to list were also indulged in and threshed out by the members.

NEXT MEETING TO BE SUNDAY, JANUARY 8th

The Futurian Society's first meeting of the new year will take place this Sunday afternoon at about 3 p.m. The place this time is to be the home of Cyril Kornbluth, 506, West 213th Street, New York City, (Manhattan). The nearest subway station is the 215th St. station of the Bway IRT line. This house is about a half block from the subway lines. DON'T FAIL TO SHOW UP.

kinson, for example, had never heard of fandom until becoming professional science fiction writers. However, most science fiction writers, even if they were never fans, go at least occasionally to science fiction conventions. At the same time there have always been fans who were uninterested in becoming pros, as well as fans who were more interested in fandom than in science fiction—fans for whom the motto "fiawol ("fandom is a way of life") is most apt.

While fandom is tremendously important to the formation of the field of science fiction and endlessly fascinating in its own right, it has been estimated that at most only 5 percent of the population who read science fiction are active fans (Hartwell [1984] 1985: 158). Fandom and science fiction are overlapping fields rather than one being a subset of the other. Fandom has also changed over time. In the 1930s and 1940s it was possible to say that there was only one science fiction fandom[4] and that almost every fan in the United States at least knew of every other active fan. Today that would be impossible, and there are many different fandoms. For example, media fandom (which in itself consists of many different fandoms for the different shows such as *Doctor Who*, all the different *Star Treks* from the original to *Voyager*, and *Buffy the Vampire Slayer*—all of which have their different fanzines and conventions) is now vastly larger than written science fiction fandom.

My book draws on, and is also a contribution to, a variety of fields, most especially feminist theory, semiotics, American studies, cultural studies, literary theory, science fiction, and histories of sexuality. I do not view these fields as being discrete or as consisting only of a body of written texts. I argue that science fiction texts, and indeed all texts, are engaged in a series of discourses about sexuality, knowledge, subjectivity, and power—in short, social relations and the world. Texts are not merely examples of the operations of these discourses; they *are* those discourses. My approach involves moving away from a treatment of "fictional" texts as the raw material of analysis and "theoretical" texts as the means of explicating such texts. In this light I view semiotics, literary theory, and work on the history of sexuality as engaging in dialogue with the science fiction texts that are the focus of my book. The book emerges from this dialogue. Reading science fiction texts and talking and meeting with science fiction practitioners has shaped my readings of Judith Butler, Michel Foucault, M. A. K. Halliday, Katie King, Thomas Laqueur, Eve Kosofsky Sedgwick, and Terry Threadgold, as much as my readings of these theorists have influenced the way I have engaged with the field of science fiction.

All fiction is engaged in both theory and practice, indeed all writing, all speech, is doing both/and rather than either/or. All language *is* metalanguage. However, I am making here a special claim for science fiction. Science fiction is more overt about its place within discourses of knowledge than other literary genres are. For example, both the battle-of-the-sexes texts in science fiction and the romance genre are concerned with relations between the sexes, and hence both engage with discourses of sex, sexuality, and gender. In romance, the traces of these discourses are typically visible as part of the narrative pattern. In the battle-of-the-sexes texts there are more overt, often didactic contributions to these discourses. Questions such as, What would happen if a society were controlled by women? What would happen if there were few or no men? are explicitly raised and answered.

That science fiction overtly engages with discourses of knowledge (stereotypically science) is not a new claim. In 1960 Kingsley Amis argued that this is precisely what marks science fiction as being different from other genres. Amis suggests that this would not work in other genres: "[O]ne imagines how a reader of Westerns would take to a twenty-page discussion of frontier ethics" (Amis 1960: 79). The same point had been made by Bernard DeVoto in a 1939 *Harper's Magazine* article about science fiction: "A cowboy story could not possibly interrupt a stage robbery with a page of rhetoric about sunrise in Raton Pass, but the writer of science fiction can hold his audience enraptured with pages of talk about the FitzGerald Contraction, quanta, the temperature of distant stars, the molecular structure of minerals, and other matters which one would suppose to be far over the heads of the people addressed in the advertisements" (DeVoto 1939: 446). Indeed, many of the battle-of-the-sexes texts from 1926 to 1973 routinely include large sections of exposition and philosophical explication. I want to emphasize that the battle-of-the-sexes stories' engagement with debates about the social constructions of women and men and the organization of relations between them is made possible by science fiction's generic rules. Science fiction is not tied to a "mimetic faithfulness to the world as it is" (Jackson 1995: 95). The process of imagining a world in which women are the dominant sex immediately exposes many of the processes that normally operate to keep women subordinate; it renders these processes of power *visible*.

Science fiction's lack of "mimetic faithfulness" operates even at the level of its grammar. Samuel R. Delany argues that there are "clear and sharp differences" between science fiction and mundane fiction[5] "right down to the way we read individual sentences" (Delany 1984: 88). Delany gives a number of examples of this difference in reading practices, such as, "[H]e turned on his left side" (88).[6] In the mundane sense this means that he turned over on to his left side; in the science-fictional sense it means that he flicked a switch and his left side lit up.[7] M. A. K. Halliday developed a systemic functional grammar that illustrates well the difference in lexical and grammatical meaning (Halliday 1994):

MUNDANE ANALYSIS

He	*turned*	*on his left side*
Actor	Process	Circumstance: location

SCIENCE FICTIONAL ANALYSIS

He	*turned on*	*his left side*
Actor	Process	Goal

We see in this example the differences in meaning between two clauses with exactly the same wording.

What do I mean by the terms "sex," "gender," and "sexuality"? The distinction between "sex" and "gender" has typically understood "sex" as a "biological given and gender as a social construction which overlays this biology" (Gatens 1996: 31). Charting the moment at which the one begins and the other ends has proven elusive. Indeed, the very notion that "the body" and its sex *are* biological givens and have remained so throughout history is no longer tenable (Martin 1987; Laqueur 1990; Oudshoorn 1994; Hird 2000). Eve Kosofsky Sedgwick argues that "even usages involving 'the sex/gender system' within feminist theory are able to use 'sex/gender' only to delineate a problematical *space* rather than a crisp distinction." She says of her own usage that it "will be to denominate that problematized space of the sex/gender system, the whole package of physical and cultural distinctions between women and men, more simply under the rubric 'gender.' I do this in order to reduce the likelihood of confusion between 'sex' in the sense of 'the space of differences between male and female' (what I'll be grouping under 'gender') and 'sex' in the sense of sexuality" (Sedgwick 1990: 29). I find Sedgwick convincing on this point. I will, however, reverse her practice and use the term "sex" to refer to this "problematized space." I do this for two reasons: (1) for consistency—because in the battle-of-the-sexes texts the term "sex" is used in this way, and (2) because, as Sedgwick notes above, there is a confusion between "sex" meaning "the space of differences between male and female" and "sex" meaning sexuality and acts of sexual intimacy including intercourse (Sedgwick 1990: 29). Confusion and blurring between the two is another characteristic of many of the battle-of-the-sexes texts, where a person's sexuality is one of the most important aspects of what makes that individual either man or woman. This is also a central component of subjectivity. Learning the categories that constitute your sense of self includes knowing that you are a man or a woman.

The discourse of romance is a crucial shaping force in many of the battle-of-the-sexes texts of the period 1926–1973. In debates about the role of women in science fiction, the process of heterosexual exchange taking place between hero and heroine, and the woman's role in it, is designated "the love interest." In these debates, as I show in chapter 6, the terms "love interest," "romance," "sex," and "women" are used interchangeably.[8] They become one and the same. On the whole this equivalence between "women" and "love interest" disqualifies women from the field of science fiction, since love belongs to the field of romance or, rather, literature for "sentimental old maids who like a bit of 'slop'" (from a letter by David McIlwain in *Astounding Science Fiction* [November 1938]: 158).[9] The battle-of-the-sexes stories are an area of science fiction where the two fields, of science fiction and of romance, are overtly in operation. The discourse of romance, and of heterosexual relations upon which the discourse is predicated, is built upon the differences between the sexes. The romance discourse is part of the heterosexual economy and is a primary site "where gender difference is re-produced" (Holloway 1984: 228).

The violence of romance has been frequently observed, from the Middle Ages and the invention of romantic love until the present day.[10] Indeed, the formation of Western romantic love is said to be predicated on the antifeminist and misogynist discourses of the Middle Ages. R. Howard Bloch claims that the "asceticism of the earlier [Christian] period, synonymous with the deprecation of the feminine, was, in the High Middle Ages, simply transformed into an idealization both of woman and of love" (Bloch 1991: 10). He argues that "courtliness . . . is a much more effective tool even than misogyny for the possession and repossession of women in what Julia Kristeva terms 'the eternal war of the sexes'" (196). John Wyndham's battle-of-the-sexes story "Consider Her Ways" (1956), also makes this argument. The women in his matriarchal world are happy and peaceful without men and recognize that romantic love was invented to subjugate women and make them love their chains: "They were caught up in a process, and everything conspired against their escape. It was a long process, going right back to the eleventh century, in Southern France. The Romantic conception started there as an elegant and amusing fashion for the leisured classes" (Wyndham [1956] 1965: 49).

The coercive violence of the "Romantic conception" or discourse of romance is played out in many texts. Love stories are replete with metaphors of war alongside those of love. It is arguable that the discourse of romance is *produced* through the conjunction of war and love. Certainly the title of some of the battle-of-the-sexes texts and the phrase itself are suggestive of such a conjunction: "The War of the Sexes" (1933), "The Priestess Who Rebelled" (1939), "Amazons of a Weird Creation" (1941), *The Sex War* (1960), "The Masculinist Revolt" (1965), "War against the Yukks" (1965), and *Sex and the High Command* (1970).

The hegemonic force of the romance discourse can be seen in Leslie F. Stone's "The Conquest of Gola" (1931). Stone was one of the earliest women writers of science fiction (see figure 2). Her story is told from the point of view of the Golans, a race ruled by women. The Golans are invaded by an all-male force from earth, and because of their technological superiority the Golans are easily able to deal with the invaders. The Golans find the human men ugly: "Never before have I seen such a poorly organized body, so unlike our own highly developed organisms. How nice it is to be able to call forth any organ at will, and dispense with it when its usefulness is over!" (Stone [1931] 1994: 33). However, the human men, enlisting the aid of the Golan men, rebel against their captors and seize the Golan women in their beds. The Golan narrator, despite her amusement with the "poorly organized" human body, responds to the male human body in typical romance style: "I started up only to find his arms about me, embracing me. And how strong he was! For the moment a new emotion swept me, for the first time I knew the pleasure to be had in the arms of a strong man" (40). In this brief moment, the romance discourse finds its way into the text only to be dispelled almost immediately, as the Golans soon expel the would-be invaders from their planet permanently.

I saw many connections between the battle-of-the-sexes texts and later, overtly feminist science fiction texts. Many of the battle-of-the-sexes texts differ markedly from the later texts in that they seek to contain the threat of change to the relationships between men and women. However, in attempting to do so they make these processes of constructing maleness and femaleness and the relationships between the two more visible. Many of the battle-of-the-sexes texts make explicit the ways in which romantic heterosexual love and sexual intercourse are crucial to the shaping of "real"

THE CONQUEST OF GOLA 1281

things of our world bow their heads, and so she recognized these visitors for what they were, nothing more than the despicable males of the species! And what creatures they were!

Imagine a short almost flat body set high upon two slender legs, the body tapering in the middle, several times as broad across as it is through the center, with two arms almost as long as the legs attached to the upper part of the torso. A small column-like neck of only a few inches divides the head of oval shape from the body, and in this head only are set the organs of sight, hearing, and scent. Their bodies were like a patch work of a misguided nature.

Yes, strange as it is, my daughters, practically all of the creature's faculties had their base in the small ungainly head, and each organ was perforce pressed into serving for several functions. For instance, the breathing nostrils also served for scenting out odors, nor was this organ able to exclude any disagreeable odors that might come its way, but had to dispense to the brain both pleasant and unpleasant odors at the same time.

Then there was the mouth, set directly beneath the nose, and here again we had an example of one organ doing the work of two for the creature not only used the mouth with which to take in the food for its body, but it also used the mouth to enunciate the excruciatingly ugly sounds of its language forthwith.

Guests From Detaxal

NEVER before have I seen such a poorly organized body, so unlike our own highly developed organisms. How much nicer it is to be able to call forth any organ at will, and dispense with it when its usefulness is over! Instead these poor Detaxalans had to carry theirs about in physical being all the time so that always was the surface of their bodies entirely marred.

Yet that was not the only part of their ugliness, and proof of the lowliness of their origin, for whereas our fine bodies support themselves by muscular development, these poor creatures were dependent entirely upon a strange structure to keep them in their proper shape.

Imagine if you can a bony skeleton somewhat like the foundations upon which we build our edifices, laying stone and cement over the steel framework. But this skeleton instead is inside a body which the flesh, muscle and skin overlay. Everywhere in their bodies are these cartilaginous structures—hard, heavy, bony structures developed by the chemicals of the being for its use. Even the hands, feet and head of the creatures were underlaid with these bones, ugh, it was terrible when we dissected one of the fellows for study. I shudder to think of it.

Yet again there was stil another feature of the Detaxalans that was equally as horrifying as the rest, namely their outer covering. As we viewed them for the first time out there in the square we discovered that parts of the body, that is the part of the head which they called the face, and the bony hands were entirely naked without any sort of covering, neither fur nor feathers, just the raw, pinkish-brown skin looking as if it had been recently plucked.

Later we found a few specimens that had a type of fur on the lower part of the face, but these were rare. And when they doffed the head coverings which we had first taken for some sort of natural covering, we saw that the top of the head was overlaid with a very fine fuzz of fur several inches long.

We did not know in the beginning that the strange covering on the bodies of the

LESLIE F. STONE

2. Sketch of Leslie F. Stone, accompanying her story "The Conquest of Gola" in the April 1931 issue of *Wonder Stories*, p. 1281. Artist unknown.

women's subjectivities and their integration into an economy of compulsory heterosexuality (see Rich 1980; Wittig 1992).

Looking at the way the battle-of-the-sexes texts theorize sexual difference is part of the work of historicizing sex and examining questions of difference. In these texts there are often many more sexes than two or even three. Being a man or a woman is not a given; it is always unstable—as it is in the mundane world outside science fiction. But many of the battle-of-the-sexes texts insist that male and female characters act according to their true sex and act that sex *properly*. These texts offer the possibility, however, of being something other than a proper man or woman, and thus they problematize the notion of a true sex in the same way that the existence of hermaphrodites and transsexuals in the "real" world do.

Some of the battle-of-the-sexes texts can be read in terms of the one-sex model discussed in Laqueur's 1990 *Making Sex*. Laqueur argues that from the eighteenth century onward, a two-sex oppositional model gradually came to be the dominant way of seeing sex, but until then a one-sex model, "where the boundaries between men and women are of degree and not of kind," dominated (Laqueur 1990: 25). Women and men, in this model, are not opposites. They are composed of the same liquids, they both excrete sperm and have the same genitalia, except that the woman's is hidden—her vagina is a penis (later the correlation is made between clitoris and penis) and her ovaries are testicles. Women are "inverted, and hence less perfect men" (26). In *Making Sex*, Laqueur writes of the one-sex world: "In this world, the body with its one elastic sex was far freer to express theatrical gender and the anxieties thereby produced than it would be when it came to be regarded as the foundation of gender. The body is written about and drawn as if it represented the realm of gender and desire. . . . An open body in which sexual differences were matters of degree rather than kind confronted a world of real men and woman and of the clear juridical, social, and cultural distinctions between them" (125).

Both Foucault's and Laqueur's understandings of the historical changes in the shaping of the category of sex are central to my book. However, my understandings of their theses about the category of sex is shaped by my readings of the battle-of-the-sexes texts, rather than vice versa. This is an extremely important distinction, one that Simon Goldhill makes in his book *Foucault's Virginity*. Goldhill argues there that Foucault's focus on philosophical writing and medical treatises in the classical world leads him to ignore or minimize contemporaneous literary texts that might have complicated his arguments. Goldhill is worth quoting at some length:

> A recent critic [Lois McNay in *Foucault and Feminism* (1992)] has commented, however, that there hasn't been much criticism of these later volumes [of the *History of Sexuality*], except, she adds somewhat sniffily, for the occasional classicist complaining of Foucault's inaccuracies of interpretation (as if mere (mis)reading was unimportant when there are Big Ideas to be discussed). She herself goes on to analyse Foucault's concept of the self and sexuality with barely a reference to the texts from which his conceptualization is developed. This is paradigmatic, it seems, of a difficulty in maintaining the balance between an engagement with the sweep of Foucault's vision, and an engagement with the series of individual readings from which that sweeping vision is formulated. I will in my classicist hat sometimes point to places where systematic misreading seems to me to be more than usually debilitating to an argument. (Goldhill 1995: xi–xii)

Sexuality and sex are negotiated in a variety of discourses, although it seems in most histories of sexuality, like Foucault's and Laqueur's, that their sweeping panoramas are privileged over the texts from which these panoramas are developed. This is part and parcel of the worship of Big Ideas to which Goldhill refers. As I hope to show in the chapters that follow, the battle-of-the-sexes texts also negotiate questions of sex and sexuality in ways that contribute to these broader understandings.

1 FAITHFUL TO THEE, TERRA, IN OUR FASHION

Stories about Science Fiction, Fandom, and Community

1926: Gernsback and *Amazing Stories*

If Hugo Gernsback had stayed home, everything would have been different. (Knight 1977: 1)

Science fiction as a community, and certainly science fiction as a publishing category, begins in the United States in 1926 with the first English-language science fiction magazine, *Amazing Stories.*[1] Scholar Frank Cioffi argues for *Amazing*'s importance: "Starting with Hugo Gernsback's publication of *Amazing Stories* in 1926, the science fiction pulps gradually assumed a position of importance in the pulp fiction market. . . . What before had been isolated stories, curios, or, more often, original ways of approaching fairly traditional literary endeavors, became in the thirties a self-conscious and discrete genre" (Cioffi 1982: 6).

Samuel R. Delany also argues strongly for the 1920s and 1930s as the beginning of the science fiction field, as opposed to much longer science fiction genealogies that have been proposed (Aldiss 1973; del Rey 1979). However, Delany broadens Cioffi's notion of "genre" to include the practices of reading and writing texts as well as the texts themselves:

> By "science fiction" I don't mean the 19th-century didactic fables that include not only Victorian utopian writing but also the scientific romances Verne and Wells wrote in response to the 19th-century information explosion. I don't mean the "fayned histories" and "fayned voyages" of the 15th, 16th, and 17th centuries, before bourgeois science separated themselves out from another set of discourses differently organized—discourses primarily concerned with instruction, moral or factual. I mean the first intrusion of the modern 20th-century scientific imagina-

> tion into the very texture and rhetoric of a pre-existing fictive field in the pulp magazines of the '20s and '30s, which, taking advantage of that fiction's paraliterary status, developed a new way of reading language—a new way of writing it to take advantage of this new way of reading, i.e., a practice of writing, a discourse. (Delany 1984: 165)

This practice of reading and writing, this discourse, begins to be articulated in the editorials and letter columns, as well as the stories, of *Amazing Stories, Air Wonder Stories,* and *Science Wonder Stories* in the 1920s, and in what the *Fancyclopedia* refers to as the "big three" of the 1930s: *Amazing Stories, Wonder Stories,* and *Astounding Science Fiction* (Speer 1944: 7).[2] In the 1930s this discourse of science fiction flows into fanzines and conventions, and fandom generally. In fact, one effect of emphasizing the importance of 1926 and *Amazing* as the site of the emergence of the new discourse of science fiction is to make fandom a part of the emerging field of science fiction. This is what many histories of the field do *not* do. For example, Brian Aldiss and David Wingrove, in *Trillion Year Spree: The History of Science Fiction,* are explicit about writing a history of written texts—"[O]ur concern is to present SF as a literature, not as social activity" (Aldiss and Wingrove 1988: 346).[3] My concern, however, is to present science fiction as a "social activity," or rather a series of social activities.

Amazing Stories was published and edited by Hugo Gernsback. For many members of the early science fiction community, Gernsback was the inventor of science fiction; Sam Moskowitz has called him "the Father of Science Fiction" (Moskowitz [1963] 1974: 225–42). The centrality of Hugo Gernsback is reflected in the amateur or fan awards for science fiction, which are given in his honor.[4] Officially they are called the Science Fiction Achievement Awards, but they are universally known as the Hugos. Awarded every year since 1955 at the World Science Fiction Convention (WorldCon), they are the oldest and best-known science fiction awards (Clute and Nicholls 1993: 595-600).

Gernsback's science fiction magazine publishing and editing career lasted from 1926 until 1953. During that period *Amazing* was not the only professional sf magazine (prozine) that Gernsback published. Gernsback was, in fact, *Amazing*'s editor for only three years, losing control of it in 1929. But he went on to found other science fiction magazines, including *Science Wonder Stories Quarterly, Scientific Detective Monthly, Air Wonder Stories,* and *Science Wonder Stories*; the last two were amalgamated in 1930 to form *Wonder Stories*. Gernsback remained in control of *Wonder Stories* until 1936. His publishing endeavors after that date had far less influence on the field, and throughout the 1920s and 1930s he delegated the editorial work on these magazines to T. O'Conor Sloane, C. A. Brandt, and Wilbur C. Whitehead (Clute and Nicholls 1993: 490–91; Tymn and Ashley 1985: 14–57). This means that Gernsback did not necessarily write all or even the majority of the editorial comments during the periods in which he was the publisher and editor of such magazines as *Amazing Stories* and *Wonder Stories*. However, such is the mythic force of Gernsback, the founding father, that in the majority of the work I have read on this period he is spoken of as though he wrote every word of editorial comment in the magazines he published. "Gernsback" has come to operate as synonymous with the magazines he founded, whether he was actively contributing to them or not. I will continue this practice, allowing "Gernsback" to stand for the house editorial voice.

Amazing Stories and the other early science fiction magazines did not come out of nowhere. There had been a long publishing history in the United States of general fiction magazines as well as science, technical, and mechanical magazines that had published what Gernsback refers to as "scientifiction." Gernsback opens his first editorial for *Amazing* by referring to the overwhelming number of fiction magazines at the time: "Another fiction magazine!" (Gernsback 1926a: 3) (see figure 3).

The pulps—as many of these magazines were called because of the poor quality of their paper[5]—were very popular. There were, among others, western, detective, crime, occult, sex, true confessions, as well as boys' and girls' adventure pulps (Ashley 1974; Tymn and Ashley 1985; Clute and Nicholls 1993). Gernsback makes several claims for his new magazine in this first editorial. He explicitly distinguishes the magazine from other magazines, which he refers to as the "usual fiction magazine, the love story and the sex-appeal type of magazine, the adventure type and so on." His magazine is not "usual" but "different" or "new." The word "new" appears seven times in the editorial, along with phrases such as "entirely different," "never been done before in this country," "a pioneer in its field," "the new romancers,"[6] "blazing a new trail," "the first time." Once the newness of *Amazing Stories* is established, Gernsback then explains scientifiction. His explanation underlines the indeterminacy and slipperiness of what he is trying to name. He slides among a variety of phrases as he tries to explicate just what scientifiction is and what this new magazine will be concerned with. The limits of the discourse are not yet overdetermined; they are, in fact, being shaped as he writes. "Scientifiction," he states, consists of "the Jules Verne, H. G. Wells

Volume 1

THE MAGAZINE OF SCIENTIFICTION

April, 1926 No. 1.

HUGO GERNSBACK, F.R.S., *Editor*
DR. T. O'CONOR SLOANE, M.A., Ph.D.; *Managing Editor*
Editorial and General Offices - - - 53 Park Place, New York, N. Y.

Extravagant Fiction Today - - - - - - - Cold Fact Tomorrow

A NEW SORT OF MAGAZINE

By HUGO GERNSBACK, F.R.S.

NOTHER fiction magazine!

At first thought it does seem impossible that there could be room for another fiction magazine in this country. The reader may well wonder, "Aren't there enough already, with the several hundreds now being published?" True. But this is not "another fiction magazine," AMAZING STORIES is a *new* kind of fiction magazine! It is entirely new—entirely different—something that has never been done before in this country. Therefore, AMAZING STORIES deserves your attention and interest.

There is the usual fiction magazine, the love story and the sex-appeal type of magazine, the adventure type, and so on, but a magazine of "Scientifiction" is a pioneer in its field in America.

By "scientifiction" I mean the Jules Verne, H. G. Wells, and Edgar Allan Poe type of story—a charming romance intermingled with scientific fact and prophetic vision. For many years stories of this nature were published in the sister magazines of AMAZING STORIES—"SCIENCE & INVENTION" and "RADIO NEWS."

But with the ever increasing demands on us for this sort of story, and more of it, there was only one thing to do—publish a magazine in which the scientific fiction type of story will hold forth exclusively. Toward that end we have laid elaborate plans, sparing neither time nor money.

Edgar Allan Poe may well be called the father of "scientifiction." It was he who really originated the romance, cleverly weaving into and around the story, a scientific thread. Jules Verne, with his amazing romances, also cleverly interwoven with a scientific thread, came next. A little later came H. G. Wells, whose scientifiction stories, like those of his forerunners, have become famous and immortal.

It must be remembered that we live in an entirely new world. Two hundred years ago, stories of this kind were not possible. Science, through its various branches of mechanics, electricity, astronomy, etc., enters so intimately into all our lives today, and we are so much immersed in this science, that we have become rather prone to take new inventions and discoveries for granted. Our entire mode of living has changed with the present progress, and it is little wonder, therefore, that many fantastic situations—impossible 100 years ago—are brought about today. It is in these situations that the new romancers find their great inspiration.

Not only do these amazing tales make tremendously interesting reading—they are also always instructive. They supply knowledge that we might not otherwise obtain—and they supply it in a very palatable form. For the best of these modern writers of scientifiction have the knack of imparting knowledge, and even inspiration, without once making us aware that we are being taught.

And not only that! Poe, Verne, Wells, Bellamy, and many others have proved themselves real prophets. Prophesies made in many of their most amazing stories are being realized—and have been realized. Take the fantastic submarine of Jules Verne's most famous story, "Twenty Thousand Leagues Under the Sea" for instance. He predicted the present day submarine almost down to the last bolt! New inventions pictured for us in the scientifiction of today are not at all impossible of realization tomorrow. Many great science stories destined to be of an historical interest are still to be written, and AMAZING STORIES magazine will be the medium through which such stories will come to you. Posterity will point to them as having blazed a new trail, not only in literature and fiction, but in progress as well.

We who are publishing AMAZING STORIES realize the great responsibility of this undertaking, and will spare no energy in presenting to you, each month, the very best of this sort of literature there is to offer.

Exclusive arrangements have already been made with the copyright holders of the entire voluminous works of ALL of Jules Verne's immortal stories. Many of these stories are not known to the general American public yet. For the first time they will be within easy reach of every reader through AMAZING STORIES. A number of German, French and English stories of this kind by the best writers in their respective countries, have already been contracted for and we hope very shortly to be able to enlarge the magazine and in that way present always more material to our readers.

How good this magazine will be in the future is up to you. Read AMAZING STORIES—get your friends to read it and then write us what you think of it. We will welcome constructive criticism—for only in this way will we know how to satisfy you.

3. The first *Amazing Stories* editorial, April 1926, p. 1, by Hugo Gernsback

type of story," "a charming romance intermingled with scientific fact and prophetic vision," "clever romance [with] a scientific thread," "amazing romances," "scientifiction stories," "stories of this kind," "amazing tales," "science stories," "this sort of literature," and "stories of this kind." Scientifiction, it seems, can be located in a body of preexisting texts by writers such as Poe, Verne, and Wells. Poe, Gernsback claims, "may well be called the father of 'scientifiction,'" though his choice of modality here ("may well be called") undermines his claim.

After providing his scientifiction with a lineage, Gernsback then points to the shaping force of modernity: "[W]e live in an entirely new world. Two hundred years ago, stories of this kind were not possible." This new world, according to Gernsback, has been made possible by science. Treating the two words as synonyms, Gernsback states that "science and progress" are directly responsible for "stories of this kind" because "[i]t is in these situations that the new romancers find their great inspiration." Gernsback's next claim is a critical one to the discourse of science fiction as it would develop in the next few decades. This "sort of literature," he says, is not only entertaining but also "instructive," "supplying knowledge that we might not otherwise obtain . . . in a very palatable form." (I examine this idea of science as being good for us, and science fiction as the ideal way to instruct us in its merits, in more detail in the third section of this chapter, "The Science in Science Fiction.")

For Gernsback, while the discourse of science and scientific knowledge enables scientifiction, scientifiction in its turn enables scientific change—in the form of prophecy. He cites as proof Verne's prediction of "the present day submarine almost down to the last bolt!" This idea of prophecy and prophets shapes the new field of scientifiction as a quasi-religion of science fiction locked into a magical union with science proper. The knowledge that "these modern writers of scientifiction" impart thus is divinely inspired, and it is passed on to disciples, in the form of the readership of *Amazing*. Gernsback is well aware of "the great responsibility of this undertaking." Its centrality to his project is underlined in the motto that appears above each editorial: "Extravagant Fiction Today—Cold Fact Tomorrow."

The editorial ends with a call to its prospective readership to "get your friends to read [the magazine] and then write us what you think of it." Many readers did, and in their letters they took up many of the claims that Gernsback makes for scientifiction in his first editorial. All become part of the shaping of the discourses of science fiction and of fandom.

Many of the claims of Gernsback's editorial are taken up in subsequent editorial comment. For example, his method of defining scientifiction by pointing to predecessors like Verne and Wells is one he returns to in later editorials. The word "scientifiction" might be new, but its referent, Gernsback wants to say, is not. In an editorial titled "The Lure of Scientifiction" Gernsback declares:

> Scientifiction is not a new thing on this planet. While Edgar Allan Poe probably was one of the first to conceive the idea of a scientific story, there are suspicions that there were other scientifiction authors before him. Perhaps they were not such outstanding figures in literature, and perhaps they did not write what we understand today as scientifiction at all. Leonardo da Vinci (1452–1519), a great genius, while he was not really an author of scientifiction, nevertheless had enough prophetic vision to create a number of machines in his own mind that were only to materialize centuries later. He described a number of machines, seemingly fantastic in those days, which would have done credit to Jules Verne. (Gernsback 1926c: 195)

However, his claims are tentative: "suspicions" modified with "perhaps" and "probably" and the statement that Da Vinci "was not really an author of scientifiction." This is an unstable genealogy, but one that Gernsback attempts to shore up with his choice of stories and serialized novels in his new magazine. The first issue of *Amazing* consisted entirely of reprints, including a story each from the three fathers—Jules Verne, H. G. Wells, and Edgar Allan Poe—invoked by Gernsback in the first editorial.

While Gernsback maintained that scientifiction was "not a new thing on this planet" (Gernsback 1926c: 195) and that it had its antecedents in Poe, Verne, and Wells, the newness of it was also part of the discourse. As early as 1930 one reader, Hegory Joywater of Brooklyn, New York, writes that "[s]cience fiction is a new endeavor. Until the advent of Mr. Gernsback, it was strongly individualized, resting in such luminaries as Wells, Verne, Poe etc. But Mr. Gernsback knew that imagination was inherent in everyone; that suitable expression could be molded by just a little coaxing or incentive. So from all America he culled the outposts of science fiction writers" (Joywater 1930: 1142–43). Gernsback responds: "It is true that Science Fiction is in its infancy, and that the publishers of this, and our sister magazines, spend hundreds, perhaps thousands of dollars in advertising for Science Fiction writers, advising them, often teaching them the finer points and sometimes the fundamentals of their craft. But to a great extent we are aided by the readers of these magazines, amongst whom are many well-known scientists, and all of whom are above the average in mentality and intelligence" (Gernsback 1930: 1143).

Sam Moskowitz notes the effect that such pronouncements had on fans: "Hugo Gernsback did something for the science fiction fan that had never been attempted before: he gave him self-respect. He preached that those who followed this sort of reading-matter avidly were not possessed of a queer taste, but actually represented a higher type of intellect" (Moskowitz 1954: 4). According to Malcolm Edwards, in his entry on Gernsback in *The Encyclopedia of Science Fiction*, Gernsback also "gave the genre a local habitation and a name" (Clute and Nicholls 1993: 491). To be precise, Gersback gave the genre two names: scientifiction and science fiction. In the first few issues of *Amazing*, Gernsback's editorials refer to the material he would publish as "scientifiction." He says that he nurses a "secret hope that some day it [the word "scientifiction"] might appear in a standard dictionary" (Gernsback 1928d: 5). When he first aired the possibility of a fiction magazine devoted to this kind of fiction in 1923 he planned to call it just that—*Scientifiction.*[7] In Gernsback's editorial in the first issue of *Science Wonder Stories*, dated June 1929, however, he refers to "science fiction."[8] Mike Ashley suggests that Gernsback coined "science fiction" in an effort to disassociate himself from his old magazine *(Amazing Stories)* and thus avoided the term "scientifiction" that he had used before (Tymn and Ashley 1985: 746–47). The two terms "science fiction" and "scientifiction" remained interchangeable for many years, with "science fiction" eventually gaining the ascendancy.[9]

The place that Gernsback gave the genre was his magazines, *Amazing Stories* and *Wonder Stories*. In the pages of *Amazing Stories* fans begin to discuss their longing for this particular kind of writing, which was unnamed before *Amazing*. The existence of the magazine allowed them to *speak* their desire as well as fulfill it. In this way the discourse of science fiction formed around these magazines and their readers and the interactions between the two. Before the existence of *Amazing*, regular readers had to look for these stories in such popular all-fiction magazines as *Argosy*[10] and *All-Story*,[11] in more specialized fiction magazines such as *Weird Tales*,[12] in the fiction of Gernsback's earlier, primarily nonfiction, technical magazines *Radio News* and *Science and Invention*, or in the books of such writers as H. G. Wells and Jules Verne. But while these readers may have found stories they could retrospectively label "scientifiction," until the advent of *Amazing Stories*, they did not have the discourse that enabled them to talk about these stories.

The place Gernsback provided grew into the set of complex relations comprising and constituting science fiction communities. Jack Williamson, who began writing and publishing science fiction in the late 1920s, talks about this process:

> My own way into it [science fiction] wasn't opened until 1926, when Hugo Gernsback launched *Amazing Stories*, the first magazine that was all science fiction. . . . A friend loaned me a copy of it that fall, but it was the next spring before I wrote for and received a free sample copy of my own. Money was scarce, but Jo [his sister] helped me pay for a subscription. It was a cheaply printed pulp with lurid but wonderful covers, the early issues filled with the reprinted classics of Poe and Verne and Wells and Merritt. Completely infatuated, I began dreaming up and writing my own. (Williamson 1979: 10)

Frederik Pohl, science fiction writer, editor, and New York Futurian,[13] expresses similar sentiments: "[A]t some point in that year of 1930 I came across a magazine named *Science Wonder Stories Quarterly*, with a picture of a scaly green monster on the cover. I opened it up. The irremediable virus entered my veins" (Pohl 1979: 1).

Science Fiction Communities

> *Oh, yes, letters, lots of letters, and probably they were the most interesting things in many of the magazines. Some fanzines, like the long-lasting West Coast* Voices of the Imagi-Nation, *printed nothing else. (Pohl 1979: 33)*

The most important space *Amazing Stories* provided for its readers was its appropriately named letter column, "Discussions." The column was launched in the January 1927 issue with the following announcement: "In this department we shall discuss, every month, topics of interest to all our readers. The editors invite correspondence on all subjects directly or indirectly related to the stories appearing in this magazine. Only letters of interest to all of our readers will be published, and discussed by the editors" (Gernsback 1927a: 970).

Readers had begun to take up a visible space in the magazine as early as the second issue, when Gernsback discusses their letters in an editorial headed "Thank You!": "The first issue of *Amazing Stories* has been on the newsstands only about a week, as we go to press with this, the second issue of the magazine; yet, even during this short time, we have been deluged with an avalanche of letters of approval and constructive criticism from practically every section of the country" (Gernsback 1926b: 99). In the third issue Gernsback uses the word "fan" for the first time to refer to the passionate readers of his magazine. This may well be the first recorded use of the word to refer to science fiction readers. Fans thus became part of the field of science fiction, by virtue of having their letters published in *Amazing Stories.* Once part of the field, they were part of the process of constituting that field. One instance of this is the search for antecedents that Gernsback refers to; in finding "old scientifiction tales," they helped construct a history of scientifiction.

In the sixth issue Gernsback has this to say about *Amazing*'s readership.

> We knew that once we could make a new reader pick up *Amazing Stories* and read only one story, our cause was won with that reader, and this is indeed what happened. Although the magazine is not as yet six months old, we are already printing 100,000 copies per month, and it also seems that whenever we get a new reader we keep him. A totally unforeseen result of the name, strange to say, was that a great many women are already reading the new magazine. This is most encouraging. We know that they must have picked up *Amazing Stories* out of curiosity more than anything else, and found it to their liking, and we are certain that if the name of the magazine had been "Scientifiction" they would not have been attracted to it at a newsstand. (Gernsback 1926f: 483)

This extract is typical of the editorials: the authoritative tone, the emphasis on the literature being discussed as more than mere entertainment but as serious, important, and educational. Gernsback views his readers as disciples and continues the evangelical tenor of the first editorial when he writes of "capturing" readers. He shows gratitude for even the most "unlikely" converts: "strange to say . . . a great many women are . . . reading the new magazine."

This reference to women readers of *Amazing* is not the only evidence of a female readership. Gernsback quotes readers, such as Michael H. Kay of Brooklyn, New York, who share their magazine with daughters and wives: "You will generally find that when one has read your magazine he will become so enthusiastic, so elated over his discovery, that he will deem it a pleasure to extol its virtues to his friends. Even now my wife is anxiously waiting for me to finish this first issue, so that she may read it herself" (Gernsback 1926b: 99).

Women were part of *Amazing* from the first issue, though their participation was tenuous. On the cover of the first issue there are skating figures, clad in fur, some of whom appear to be women. This is a marginal presence, just a possibility, and all the figures are overwhelmed by the looming presence of the huge planet, Saturn, and by the huge *Amazing Stories* logo.

Less tenuously, there were also letters by women published in "Discussions." These are clearly signaled as anomalies with titles such as the following, "A Kind Letter from a Lady Friend and Reader," by Mrs. H. O. De Hart of Anderson, Indiana, who ends her letter: "Well, I've written Mr. Wastebasket a rather lengthy letter this time, but I do not really expect you to clutter up your columns with it. I am only a comparatively uneducated young (is twenty-six young? Thank you!) wife and mother of two babies, so about the only chance I get to travel beyond the four walls of my home is when I pick up your magazine" (De Hart 1928: 277). The editorial response focuses on the fact that this "very interesting letter is from a member of the fair sex" (Gernsback 1928m: 277). But marking the letter in this way makes it appear that it is "interesting" *because* it is by a woman and undermines Gernsback's earlier claim that there are "a great many women" readers of the magazine.

Mrs. L. Silverberg of Augusta, Georgia,[14] states flatly that she thought she was the only woman reading *Amazing*. Again, her letter is signaled as being from one of "the fair sex" with the heading, "A Lady Reader's Criticisms": "It is the letter of Mrs. H. O. De Hart in the June issue of your publication that is the cause of my writing my little say. For more than a year I have been a reader of this magazine, and this is the first time I have seen a letter from a woman reader. In fact I was somewhat surprised as I had believed that I was the only feminine reader of your publication. However, it is with pleasure that I note that another of my sex is interested in scientifiction"(Silverberg 1928: 667). The editorial response is almost identical to that which Mrs. De Hart received: "We are very glad to hear from one of the fair sex and would be glad if more of the weaker (?) sex were contributors to our Discussions Column" (Gernsback 1928n: 667).

A further letter comes from Mrs. Lovina S. Johnson of Lysite, Wyoming: "In the October issue of AMAZING STORIES, I noticed that a woman reader is heard from. I was glad to know that there are other women readers of my favorite magazine, than myself. Glad, also, to hear her reactions to the magazine" (Johnson 1929: 1140). Again, the editorial response reassures her that she is "not the only member of the fair (and voting) sex who writes us nice letters and contributes to our discussion columns" (Gernsback 1929f: 1140).

In a similar vein is a letter in the January 1930 *Science Wonder Stories*, one of the magazines Hugo Gernsback started after he lost control of *Amazing*. The letter is titled "No Discrimination against Women." Mrs. Verna Pullen of Lincoln, Nebraska, writes: "I have noticed that you print more letters written by men than by women, so I suppose this won't get in. Nevertheless, I wished to let you know how much I enjoyed your new magazine" (Pullen 1930: 765). Gernsback is horrified: "As you see, we are printing your letter. We have no discrimination against women. Perish the thought—we want them! As a matter of fact, there are almost as many women among our readers as there are men. The only difference is that our male readers usually bring up some point of scientific interest, while the ladies content themselves with general expression of approval or disapproval. We are always glad to hear from our feminine readers" (Gernsback 1930a: 765).[15]

Gernsback claims that he had as many female readers as male, but far fewer women became actively involved with fandom than men. Despite their numbers, the main route to fandom—having your letters published—was blocked to them, perhaps, as Gernsback implies, because they were less interested in engaging with the science of science fiction than men. At least one reader of the period, Lula B. Stewart of Harmony, Pennsylvania, is frank about what she thinks is the problem. Her letter, which appears as figure 4, gives a history of one woman fan's involvement with fandom. In it, she figures the letters columns of the professional sf magazines (prozines) as a battlefield (Stewart 1953: 133) in which women are not equal and are only accepted on sufferance. Her experience of fandom is echoed in Robin White's much later "Are Femme Fans Human?" where a femme fan's humanity depends on how male fans "accept her and treat her" (White 1968: 53). It was across this battlefield that the two sexes engaged in an uneven battle in which the women were outgunned until the 1950s. (I examine the letter columns as the battlefield for the war of the sexes in more detail in chapter 4.)

Stewart begins her letter by talking about her "infection" with science fiction, an infection presumably contracted through reading a science fiction magazine. In writing to a prozine she risks entering "the virulent stage"—of becoming a fan. Letters to prozines were the beginnings of fandom, because readers' addresses were printed with their letters, and on the basis of that, many of them started corresponding and meeting. By 1929 these informal connections had developed into science fiction clubs, and by the late thirties science fiction conventions were beginning to be held.

I REMEMBER MAMA
By LULA B. STEWART

Dear Sam: Way back thar, circa 1928, I read a science-fiction mag, and was infected. This chronic derangement might have culminated in the virulent stage known as actifandom at a very early date had not fate intervened to save me. While I was madly cerebrating over my first epistle—it had to be both significant and scintillating—another damsel sent in a missive to ye ed.

That dawdling undoubtedly saved my hide, but, Ooooo! what happened to the other poor maiden! It shouldn't be done to a diploid! I can still hear the primitive screams of the man-pack echoing down the corridors of time. The rage of that mob was something awful to behold. Not only was I witness to that early kill, but cowered in my cave as other foolish females tried to run the gauntlet. (You male fans who wail plaintively, "I can't see why the gals are so belligerent," hunt up a few copies of those early reader columns. G'wan, I dare ya.) Yes, I listened, shivered, and hastily swallowed back all those witticisms and criticisms that are the birthright of a stf fan.

For, the First Law is– SURVIVAL!

Now, at last, in the dawn of a new era, I dare creep forth, and claim my heritage of egoboo. In the interim I have entered wedlock, produced two offspring, and survived the arrows of outrageous fortune accruing to such states. This Spartan training welded a will of iron, and hammered out a hide impervious to attack. So, at last, backed by a formidable phalange of femfans, I dare speak up, brave lassie that I am.

Permit me one last look at the long, thin line of both gems and grislies that have flowed from the pens of our splendid staff authors through the years, and afforded hours of incomparable reading pleasure. There was Leigh Brackett's DANCING GIRL OF GANYMEDE, wonderful memory-stirring mood piece – and so many whose titles are lost in the mist of time.

Oh, to think of all the praise I might have meted out – and didn't! Ah, to remember the unuttered howls of protest (quit kissing my hand, boy – stop thanking me). 'Tis true, the saddest words of tongue or pen—

(A hankie, please, Sammy, that I may wipe the dewy drops from these dim old orbs – after you, dear boy, after you.)

Ah, well,. Frustrations gone, I, too, am a genuine, *tin carrot* neo-fan, and contributor to that great, new, all-female Femzine (who's trying to sneak in a plug?). Once fandom appeared over the far horizon as a strange, uncharted land, but all that is changed, and I feel *so* at home. This familiarity was bred the moment I learned, with unholy glee, that fandom, like all the rest of good old aberrated humanity, has its rigid social structure, too – a pyramid of subtle gradations that culminates in that awesome capstone, the mighty BNF (Big Name Fans, to you igerunt uninitiates).

Remember the Big Name in kindergarten – the kid who always hit and bit the firstest with the mostest? Or, the Jackson in high school who sported the loud attire, and louder larynx? Of course, we older and wiser adults use no such trifling yardstick in electing our Big NOise [*sic*] – pardon, Name – a BN of the suburbs is judged strictly by the intricacy of his TV antennae these days!

THE READER SPEAKS

(Continued from page 6)

touch with someone who can construct a good story, but lacks the story material. We could bounce a story back and forth through the mails and maybe come up with something. I can supply outlined plots on everything from humor and murder to cowboys and rockets.

Do you think anyone would care to try it? I have read that some writers use mechanical gadgets to obtain plots. I have a drawer full.

Any help you care to give to this matter will be greatly appreciated.—*643 Robinson Courts, Texarkana, Texas*

Your problem is now a world-wide problem. Writers everywhere are hereby invited to worry with you or to collaborate with you as they may choose. Just one of the services supplied as part of the entrance fee by this incredible column.

I REMEMBER MAMA

by Lula B. Stewart

Dear Sam: Way back thar, circa 1928, I read a science-fiction mag, and was infected. This chronic derangement might have culminated in the virulent stage known as actifandom at a very early date had not fate intervened to save me. While I was madly cerebrating over my first epistle—it had to be both significant and scintillating—another damsel sent in a missive to ye ed.

That dawdling undoubtedly saved my hide, but, Oooo! what happened to the other poor maiden! It shouldn't be done to a diploid! I can still hear the primitive screams of the man-pack echoing down the corridors of time. The rage of that mob was something awful to behold. Not only was I witness to that early kill, but cowered in my cave as other foolish females tried to run the gauntlet. (You male fans who wail plaintively, "I can't see why the gals are so belligerent," hunt up a few copies of those early reader columns. G'wan, I dare ya.) Yes, I listened, shivered, and hastily swallowed back all those witticisms and criticisms that are the birthright of a stf fan.

For, the First Law is—SURVIVAL!

Now, at last, in the dawn of a new era, I dare creep forth, and claim my heritage of egoboo. In the interim I have entered wedlock, produced two offspring, and survived the arrows of outrageous fortune accruing to such states. This Spartan training welded a will of iron, and hammered out a hide impervious to attack. So, at last, backed by a formidable phalange of femfans, I dare speak up, brave lassie that I am.

Permit me one last look at the long, thin line of both gems and grislies that have flowed from the pens of our splendid staff authors through the years, and afforded hours of incomparable reading pleasure. There was Leigh Brackett's DANCING GIRL OF GANYMEDE, wonderful, memory-stirring mood piece—and so many whose titles are lost in the mist of time.

Oh, to think of all the praise I might have meted out—and didn't! Ah, to remember the unuttered howls of protest (quit kissing my hand, boy—stop thanking me). 'Tis true, the saddest words of tongue, or pen—

(A hankie, please Sammy, that I may wipe the dewy drops from these dim old orbs—after you, dear boy, after you.)

Ah, well, frustrations gone, I, too, am a genuine, *tin carrot* neo-fan, and contributor to that great, new, all-female Femzine (who's trying to sneak in a plug?). Once fandom appeared over the far horizon as a strange, uncharted land, but all that is changed, and I feel *so* at home. This familiarity was bred the moment I learned, with unholy glee, that fandom, like all the rest of good old aberrated humanity, has its rigid social structure, too—a pyramid of subtle gradations that culminates in that awesome capstone, the mighty BNF (Big Name Fans, to you igerunt uninitiates).

Remember the Big Name back in kindergarten—the kid who always hit and bit the firstest with the mostest? Or, the Jackson in high school who sported the loud attire, and louder larynx? Of course, we older and wiser adults use no such trifling yardstick in electing our Big NOise—pardon, Name—a BN of the suburbs is judged strictly by the intri-

cacy of his TV antennae these days!

So, here's to fandom's BNFs—be it him or her (especially if her name ends in Bradley):

> I've never captured a BNF (pronounced B'niff)
> And if I did, I'd free one
> They got rights, too,
> Tho', still 'tis true,
> I'd druther see th'n be one!

You may not print this one, Sam, you misled old misogynist, but just the same, you'll be seein' me around. This feudin', frolicin' fan-fun is mighty heady stuff for us old timers.—*%Osmond, R. D. #1, Harmony, Penna.*

This fascinating bit of tribal history has touched us upon a tender spot—one of the few tender spots we have left. The days when the occasional femfan cowered in fear of the wolf pack are only part of our wistful folklore. Now the once lordly male takes to cover as the Amazons ride. And drunk with power hammer out the deadly cacophony with which the female has, from time immemorial, subdued the surly male. Ah, yes, power corrupts and hell hath no fury like a woman scorned and—by the way, have you dug slit trenches and rigged up the barbed wire around your post office yet?

So, here's to fandom's BNFs – be it him or her (especially if her name ends in Bradley):

I've never captured a BNF (pronounced B'niff)
And if I did, I'd free one
They got rights, too,
Tho', still 'tis true,
I'd druther see th'n be one!

You may not print this one, Sam, you misled old misogynist, but just the same, you'll be seein' me around. This feudin', frolicin', fan-fun is mighty heady stuff for us old timers. - *% Osmond, R. D. #1, Harmony, Penna.*

This fascinating bit of tribal history has touched us upon a tender spot – one of the few tender spots we have left. The days when the occasional femfan cowered in fear of the wolf pack are only part of our wistful folklore. Now the once lordly male takes to cover as the Amazons ride. And drunk with power hammer out the deadly cacophony with which the female has, from time immemorial, subdued the surly male. Ah, yes, power corrupts, and hell hath no fury like a woman scorned and – by the way, have you dug slit trenches and rigged up the barbed wire around your post office yet?

4. Letter from Lula B. Stewart, *Thrilling Wonder Stories*, August 1953, p. 133

These kinds of activities and, indeed, fandom itself demonstrate how active fans are in their involvement with sf, confirming the truth of a remark by the writer Michel de Certeau: "[W]hereas the scientific apparatus (ours) is led to share the illusion of the powers it necessarily supports, that is, to assume that the masses are transformed by the conquests and victories of expansionist production, it is always good to remind ourselves that we mustn't take people for fools" (de Certeau 1984: 176). Fans are not passive consumers. Many of the letters I have read in prozines and fanzines constitute reading as creation, compulsion, consumption, and belonging. Fandom begins with the act of reading. It was, and is, at once an articulation of a passionate involvement with texts, as well as being that passionate involvement. The letters to *Amazing Stories* and other science fiction magazines like *Astounding*, whose first issue appeared in 1930, give flesh to de Certeau's observation.

Fandom is a shifting set of complex relationships: the science fiction reader who becomes a fan who becomes a professional, and who frequently remains all three, and the relationship of that reader to consumption of sf. Marion Zimmer Bradley discusses her own involvement with the field thus:

> Letters from the readers. Pages and pages of intelligent discussions of the stories, the authors, the science in the stories . . . and a column of reviews of fanzines. Little magazines published by readers, fans in my new language. . . . Within a week I had written off for a dozen of the little magazines, within six months I had started my own, and was writing voluminously to fans all over the United States. My pocket money went for magazines—yes, and sometimes my lunch money too. I took the train to New York City, all by myself on the spur of the moment, called up a fan I'd exchanged letters with, and he took me to a conference where a hundred fans sat in a room and listened to a group of scientists talk about the possibility of man on the Moon before the year 2000 A.D. (Bradley 1977–78: 13)

Marion Zimmer Bradley became an extremely successful science fiction and fantasy writer.

Until very recently the story of a comfortable transition from fandom to a professional engagement with science fiction has been a dominant one, so much so that there is a slight tone of annoyance when someone does not follow this transition. For example, longtime active fan, Jeffrey Smith, in his interview with James Tiptree Jr. in his fanzine *Phantasmicom,* writes this about Tiptree's unusual path to pro-dom.: "Not only do you have a magical sf place, but you find yourself in one of the upper echelons. You are a respected writer. . . . You never even spent your apprenticeship as a fan, but as a non-fan reader. It smacks of fantasy, Tiptree" (Smith 1971: 12). By skipping fandom altogether Tiptree is going against what was, in 1971, still the accepted story of how an sf writer emerges. The overwhelming impression that I received from reading accounts by pros in fanzines and prozines and books of the period was of an almost effortless slide from fan to pro. This impression supports Smith's idea that fandom is a kind of professional apprenticeship, an apprenticeship that Tiptree failed to serve. At the same time "fan" and "pro" are placed in an oppositional relationship, as characterized by the well-known term "filthy pro," with its implication that to become a pro is to abandon and betray fandom.

Evidence of sf professionals serving their apprenticeships in fandom is thick in the professional science fiction magazines of the period. There are letters from people who went on to become well-known science fiction practitioners. I read letters by Isaac Asimov from the late 1930s (which I discuss in more detail in Chapter 4). I found letters from Ray Bradbury—including one to *Astounding Science Fiction* [April 1939]: 159), where he confesses parenthetically, "Yes, I'm a writer myself—amateur, so far; give me time—you'll get a barrage of manuscripts before long"). I found other letters to *Astounding* from well-known sf writers such as Damon Knight (1939) and an extremely long letter from Australian sf writer George Turner, which says he has been reading "stf" since he was nine years old (Turner 1940: 155–57). Harlan Ellison had letters published in *Thrilling Wonder Stories* and elsewhere (Ellison 1952). There is a letter from Marion Zimmer (who became Marion Zimmer Bradley) in almost every issue of *Startling Stories* throughout the late 1940s and early 1950s. In the December 1952 issue of *Thrilling Wonder Stories* she refers to her-self as a BNF (big name fan), with six years of fandom to her credit (130). There are many other examples of letters from fans who went on to be professionally engaged in science fiction as writers and editors and publishers. Many continued to write to science fiction magazines and fanzines even after they had become "filthy pros."

In the 1930s and 1940s, collecting professional science fiction magazines and writing in to their letters columns was an essential part of being a fan. In *Startling Stories* Langley Searles of New York writes a typical letter: "I got to thinking the other day. I do little correspondence with fellow fans, but almost without exception—when I do, that is—the fans mention in their reminiscences something like this: 'Say, remember the reader's columns in the old *Wonder*?' or: 'Now take the old *Wonder Stories*; *they* had a reader's department to be proud of!'" (Searles 1940: 110). By the late sixties some readers were nostalgic for the readers' columns of the 1940s. Edward M. Osachie of Vancouver, Canada, asks that an entire issue of the magazine be devoted to letters: "Can you see the idea? Well, if not, let's have some fun like that in the old *Thrilling Wonder* and *Startling Stories*. They had grand old letter departments" (Osachie 1969: 157). The importance of the letter columns for the formation of science fiction fandom became more apparent as fandom grew. By 1952 letters like this one by Marion Mallinger of Pittsburgh, Pennsylvania, appear regularly (Mallinger is explicit about the recruitist potential for fandom of the letters column):

> The letter department of your magazine is good. I may go so far as to say as good as some of the stories. Instead of finding the stories rehashed, I find good, interesting letters that are worth reading. This is a good drawing card to people who have only now started reading S.F. If they find letters that talk about previous stories (this was good, that was bad) they lose interest and skip the section. Here maybe someone who would have turned into an active fan is lost. But in writing letters to the editor that actually discuss interesting questions a lot of people get pleasantly

excited, talk about it and so spread the growth of S.F. a little faster. (Mallinger 1952: 134)

At the same time, however, many fans were ceasing to read prozines altogether. The *Fancyclopedia* argues that the relationship between fandom and the prozines is a changing one: "Quite a few long-time fans have at times completely given up reading the pros thru disgust, or preoccupation with fan and other activities. The course of fan history has varied from close to slite connexion [*sic*] with the pros, and the wish has often been expressed that we could get along without the pros as a recruiting medium. This is principally a fanationalistic manifestation, however; the average stefnist eats up good stfantasy, has an exaggerated idea of its literary merit, and will leap to defend it against detractors" (Speer 1944: 68–69).[16]

Another place created to accommodate fandom was the convention. Conventions were and are places where the communities of sf fans can make themselves visible. In convention spaces the fan's sense of being one of many ceases to be imaginary and becomes actual. Conventions are a visible manifestation of what is, for the most part, a virtual community that stays in touch via written texts—although with the advent of the Internet that communication is substantially faster. The first convention was held about ten years after the appearance of *Amazing*, though it is a matter of dispute which one was first. Fan-historian Joe Siclari writes that the "so-called" first sf convention was held on 22 October 1936, when some New York fans, including Frederik Pohl and John Michel, caught the train to meet with some Philadelphia fans (Siclari 1981: 91–92).[17] The entry on conventions in *The Encyclopedia of Science Fiction* by Peter Roberts and Rob Hansen states that "the first formally planned sf convention took place in Leeds, UK, in 1937" (Clute and Nicholls 1993: 261). From those beginnings, conventions rapidly became very important. In 1939 the first WorldCon was held in New York in conjunction with the World's Fair. The WorldCon is now the biggest science fiction convention in the world and is held annually.

Conventions became so important that by the fifties there were fans who were interested only in conventions. By 1940 the form of the science fiction convention was more or less set: "One of the principal features of sf fandom, conventions are usually weekend gatherings of fans and authors, frequently with a program of sf discussion and events. In fan language conventions are usually referred to as cons. They are informal not professionally organised, and with no delegated attendants or, usually, paid speakers. Typical activities include talks, auctions, films, panel discussions, masquerades and banquets" (Clute and Nicholls 1993: 261). Del Rey describes the WorldCons thus: "[A]uction, banquet, masquerade—and numerous speeches from fans and professional. . . . More than any other activity, the worldcons gave a feeling of unity and common goal to all the elements of the world of science fiction" (del Rey 1979: 147–48). Or, as was said on many occasions at WisCon 20, held in May 1996, the convention was "a coming together of the tribe," the tribe being on that occasion not just del Rey's "world of science fiction" but the world of feminist science fiction.

The Science in Science Fiction

Fans are Slans! (Fan slogan)

Science was simply an accumulation of facts, and the deductions of conclusions from those facts. And who better could bring divine order from intricate reality than the mighty-brained, full-grown, mature slan? (van Vogt 1953: 95)

As I noted in the introduction, the notion of "science" has always been one of the constraints within which science fiction texts are produced. "Science" itself was a contested issue. Arguments about the relationships among science, science fiction, and readers and fans were an important part of the discourse. The June 1926 editorial of *Amazing Stories* points to some of them: "Scientifiction . . . furnishes a tremendous amount of scientific education and fires the reader's imagination more perhaps than anything else of which we know" (Gernsback 1926c: 195). In other words, the reason to read scientifiction was to educate yourself scientifically and perhaps become a scientist. Andrew Ross argues that "in Gernsback's view, sf was more a social than a literary movement" (Ross 1991: 103). Gernsback was particularly keen to proselytize to the young: "If we can make the youngsters think, we feel that we are accomplishing our mission, and that the future of the magazine, and, to a degree, the future of progress through the younger generation, is in excellent hands. Once upon a time the youngsters read Indian stories, which were not at all educational; nowadays it is scientifiction, which is an education in itself. All we can say therefore is 'More power to the young men, and let's have more of them'" (Gernsback 1927j: 625). *Amazing*'s rhetoric was about progress and improving the world, which was inextricably linked with science.

That this was a religious project is clear from Gernsback's phrase "our mission." Fandom, growing out of its pages, would create a space in which "fans" could find others who were interested in (fictional) representations of scientific inquiry and endeavor. Gernsback's pronouncements on the subject begin in the first issue of *Amazing*, where he stresses the connection between this kind of fiction and science: "Not only do these amazing tales make tremendously interesting reading—they are also always instructive. They supply knowledge that we might not otherwise obtain—and they supply it in a very palatable form. For the best of these modern writers of scientifiction have the knack of imparting knowledge, and even inspiration, without once making us aware that we are being taught" (1926a: 3). And later in the same issue he writes: "There are few things written by our scientifiction writers, frankly impossible today, that may not become a reality tomorrow. Frequently the author himself does not realize that his very fantastic yarn may come true in the future, and often he, himself, does not take his prediction seriously. But the seriously-minded scientifiction reader absorbs the knowledge contained in such stories with avidity, with the result that such stories prove an incentive in starting someone to work on a device or invention suggested by some author of scientifiction" (195).

Gernsback and his magazine have been frequently identified with an idealist, naive science worship, and certainly he published many letters that supported his views of science and reinforced his vision of science fiction as a recruiting tool for the scientists of tomorrow. One of his readers, Ted Mason of Los Angeles, California, writes that the "science in most of the stories is an inspiration to me in my studies in electrical engineering" (Mason 1929: 467). Gernsback responds: "We are glad to get this letter from a student, and to learn the value to him of the science contained in our stories. He will find that the stories are written by men who are not only well-trained in science but who have a mastery of it. The instinctive understanding of scientific principles is necessary to a writer of science fiction. For his lack of understanding becomes painfully apparent to our critical readers" (1929g: 467).

Indeed, the bulk of letters received are from readers pointing out the improbability of the science in a given story. The accuracy of the science in a story is, in these debates, the sole criterion for whether it is a good story or not. A large part of these readers' pleasure in science fiction is in debating the plausibility of the stories with other readers. The obsession with scientific "accuracy" is spoofed by *Astounding* reader John Wasso Jr. of Pen Argyl, Pennsylvania, who threatens that "[o]ne of these days I'm going to write a yarn so chockful of deliberate errors, flaws, contradictions and impossible science that it will drive all you error-mad hunters NUTS!!!" (Wasso 1940: 152).

There were also many letters published that echoed Gernsback's recruitist hopes for science fiction. The following, from Earl B. Brown of Amesbury, Massachusetts, is typical: "Science is good for everyone. If everyone knows a little science, the world will be better off, and will advance more quickly. But, if everyone delved a little into science, something else will happen. They will begin to think. My high school chemistry professor, when I first began that course, said to me, and to the class, 'You are taking chemistry to learn how to think.' I have never forgotten that. And I have found that he was right. There are too few people in this world who do a little thinking" (Brown 1927: 1078).

The linking of science and progress and the strong belief in the onward upward impulse into a glorious future is often imputed to the early fans of science fiction—and indeed to many current fans. Henry Jenkins, in his work on MIT *Star Trek* fans, argues that they are part of "a long tradition of science fiction fans acting as arbiters of the scientific validity of popular fictions" (Tulloch and Jenkins 1995: 217). This tradition began with *Amazing Stories*.

In the early years of pulp science fiction magazines in the 1920s and 1930s there are not many letters that discuss what science fiction or scientifiction is. Everyone knew what "it" was—it had something to do with "science"—but everyone seemed to have a different notion of what constituted "science," what does and does not belong to the universe of science fiction and who has the rights to make these decisions. What science fiction is, the genre, is taken for granted in the letters, but the texts, the instances of this genre, are not so defined, so that attempts to limit the field become a series of test cases about which there is not always agreement. By the 1950s, however, definitions of science are expanding, and letters such as the following from Virginia Winchester of Grimsby, Ontario, are much more common. In it she asks, "Has any criterion been established to determine if a story is 'Science Fiction'? What takes a story out of the pure fantasy category and gives it the title 'science'? Science embraces many fields: physiology, archeology, history, crime detection etc. that this very diversity prompts this question" (*Thrilling Wonder Stories* [August 1952]: 128).

In the 1930s and 1940s there were raging arguments among some members of fandom about the nature of science and progress and what kind of future was being and should be shaped. The connections among science, technology, and progress were not unproblematic ones (and continue to be disputed). The proponents of science and technology as the way of remaking the future were of a variety of political persuasions. There were anarchists, communists, and fascists within fandom, who all subscribed to the idea of science as humanity's savior. One of these debates is summed up in this entry from the *Fancyclopedia*:

> Gernsback delusion—(Michelists)—The purpose, imputed to Gernsy, of making scientifiction fans into scientists by putting accurate scientific information into stf stories—sugarcoating it. This was proved wrong, said the Michelists, by the failure of the ISA, the purpose of science-fiction should be to make active idealists. Some fans who were working in or studying science replied that they believed s-f had stimulated their interest in science a great deal. Another reply was that Uncle Hugo never expected his readers to turn scientist wholesale, but that reading s-f puts the scientifictionist well ahead of the average man in understanding science. (Speer 1944: 42–43)[18]

The debates within fandom among the mostly very young and very male membership were part of debates taking part in the wider community. In his book, the critic Andrew Ross argues in a chapter titled "Getting Out of the Gernsback Continuum" that "many of its [early pulp fiction's] salient features, often considered to be 'naive,' were linked to central elements of progressive thought in the first three decades of this century" (1991: 102). Ross argues that "the national cults of science, engineering, and invention, [and] . . . technocracy's role in the social thought of the day" were crucial to "North American SF genre formation" (103). His attempt to historicize the emergence of science fiction as a socially located genre in the United States stands in stark contrast to accounts like that of Aldiss and Wingrove's *Trillion Year Spree* (1986), which construct the genre as primarily a collection of books having almost no interaction with the social context in which they were produced.

By the 1950s, however, many longtime fans of science fiction felt that the centrality of their notion of science to the field was being eroded. Critic William Atheling Jr.[19] wonders why John W. Campbell, editor of *Astounding,* finds it necessary to print an article about the science background of a story he had earlier published:

> Why does Campbell want his readers to know that writing a long science-fiction story takes careful preparation before the more obviously fictional elements of the story are filled in? First, because he assumes that his readers don't know it. In itself this is a revolutionary assumption. There was a time in the development of magazine science fiction when the most vo-

> cal part of the readership insisted upon minute attention to detail, and as much accuracy as the known facts of a given would permit. This is not a prejudice fostered by Campbell. It was implicit in T. O'Conor Sloane's delight in listing every degree and academic honour his authors (or he himself) had ever earned. . . . It was equally visible in Gernsback's practice, and in Gernsback's last magazine, *Science Fiction Plus*, the emphasis upon the scientific qualification was even more nakedly paraded, and sometimes even more dishonestly. Everybody once knew that to be a good science-fiction writer you had to Know Your Science. (Atheling [1964] 1973: 46)[20]

Many fans saw their engagement with science fiction and with science as marking them as different and more intelligent than those in the mundane world. Atheling's comments quoted above are a lament for the way science fiction once was.

The discourse of difference was an important one in the emergence of the science fiction community. While science fiction is a marker of the sf person's difference, that very difference is the reason that person turns to science fiction in the first place:

> Damon Knight says that, as children, all we science-fiction writers were toads. We didn't get along with our peers. We had no close friends and were thus thrown on our internal resources. Reading, particularly science fiction, filled the gaps. A more charitable explanation might be that most science-fiction readers were precocious kids who got little reward from the chatter of their subteen schoolmates and looked for more stimulating companionship in print. Either way Damon was hooked and so was I, and so were some ten or twenty thousand people all over the world who comprise the great collective family called "science fiction." (Pohl 1979: 2)

This sense of difference was summed up in the well-known fan slogan that serves as an epigraph to this section, "Fans are slans." The *Fancyclopedia* describes the importance of this notion of "slanhood": "Because the central character in the story was a youth in unsympathetic surroundings, and because of the obvious similarities to fans' dreams of greatness, the unserious claim to slanhood has become the Third Fandom parallel to the Second Fandom's half-serious Star-Begotten claim" (Speer 1944: 81).[21] The term comes from the novel *Slan* by A. E. van Vogt, which first appeared in serialized form in *Astounding Science Fiction* in the September, October, November, and December 1940 issues, and which became a firm part of the early fans' conception of themselves. The jacket blurb from the 1953 English edition reads:

> Jommy Cross was a Slan. Human beings had killed his mother, fearing the whole race of Slans as freaks, artificially created monsters.
>
> Alone and friendless, Jommy set out to solve the mystery of his own existence. He knew that his own kind had been almost wiped out in the Slan wars, which had left civilisation in the grip of an autocratic world-wide police state. Only by the slim tentacles that gleamed, half-concealed, in the hair of Slans, could Jommy recognise his race.
>
> How to organise resistance, how to free the world from the frightening hold of the police, these were Jommy's problems

The text engages with ideas of science, and it is Jommy's mastery of various different technologies, as much as his physical superiority, that sets him apart. Many fans read this as an analogy for the way in which their engagement with science fiction set them apart. The blurb goes on to say that "*Slan* is recognised as one of the major classics of modern Science Fiction. First published in 1945, it was so much in demand that readers were willing to pay many times the published price to obtain a copy. Now A. E. van Vogt has somewhat revised his story—although he found his earlier predictions about the uses of atomic energy had proved amazingly accurate."

In the thirteen years between its first appearance in *Astounding* and the appearance of the 1953 edition, *Slan* has become a "classic" and has proven to be prophetic—one of Gernsback's marks for identifying the "most amazing" scientifiction stories. The volume of mail received by *Astounding* after *Slan* appeared was phenomenal. All four parts (the first part tied with "Blowups Happen" by Robert A. Heinlein) were voted first in the "Analytical Laboratory" (*Astounding Science Fiction* [November 1940]: 63; [December 1940]: 112; [January 1941]: 73; [February 1941]: 67).[22] The vote on the last part occasioned the following editorial comment: "As of noon, December 2nd, at which time this issue went to press, 'Slan' had set a definite and unchallenged record. The whole December issue of *Astounding* had drawn an unusually heavy number of reader votes, with 'Slan' itself apparently the reason for the unusual number. The record lies in this: every voter had placed 'Slan' in number-one position. . . . I expect to wait a considerable time before another story comes along on which there is such surprising unanimity of opinion; apparently 'Slan' merited the praise I gave it" (Campbell 1941: 67).

The following letter from Carl H. Anderson of Traverse City, Michigan is typical of the responses generated by the story:

> There is, it seems, a man named Van Vogt. The fellow apparently owns a type-writer, ten fingers well-skilled in its operation and a mind of a brilliance that has not been directed at the field of science-fiction since the halcyon era of Weinbaum-Smith-Campbell-Williamson and the zenith of imaginative writing.
>
> This chap, who, within a single twelve months had written three or four of that year's ten best, had apparently finished a thing called, "Slan." Again the effusive blurb—the extravagant promise—the kind of thing we've grown used to in a year of such tactics. "Ah, yes, the bonnie Campbell laddie is awa' again."
>
> Ah, yes, and the bonnie Campbell laddie was right again.
>
> "Slan" is good. It is definitely great stuff. It is the stuff which is called classic. It is the unforgettable—the brilliant—the ultimate. It is the kind of thing that justifies science-fiction. (Anderson 1941: 156).

All the letters in the February 1941 issue have extravagant things to say about *Slan*, though there are some letters in earlier issues that are less enthusiastic. Edward Sumers of Long Beach, New York, for example, writes that "Slan is not living up to all the advance publicity you have given it" (Sumers 1940]: 113).

The discourses of science fiction precede, condition, and constrain fandom so that it is difficult to separate the two. The slan-fan emerges from the fan's engagements with a particular science fiction text. The slogan "Fans are slans" is a recognition of their difference from the mundane world, and it is a location of this difference in the world of science fiction. These superior fans have priveleged access to scientific knowledges, which open for them discourses that allow the fans to speak, as well as a position from which to speak.[23] Discourses of science thus become particularly enabling.

Science fiction, however, never attained universally high standards of scientific accuracy. Although many fans who identify strongly with the science in science fiction articulate a dissatisfaction with the woeful scientific standards of the majority of science fiction, they also demonstrate a great deal of pleasure in pointing out in minute detail the many scientific inaccuracies. Their pleasures in science fiction are not just in discovering the rare scientifically accurate stories—though this is a very real pleasure—but also in pointing out their absence.

There were other fans who did not take up these particular discourses.

The scientific authenticity of science fiction was not the crucial shaping factor for them. In the midst of all the letters criticizing the inaccuracy or praising the accuracy of the science of particular stories in *Amazing*, there are letters praising stories for being a cracking good read. Bradford Butler, a "Counsellor at Law"[24] of New York, writes: "Once a month it [*Amazing Stories*] turns an otherwise amiable and attractive household into an inferno of selfishness—son against father, daughter against mother, and each against the field—each seeking to pre-empt the copy of the magazine to learn how Gerald got out of the mountains of Mars or how Octavius saved the fair Olivia from the machinations of the super-heterodyne monster of the Moon" (Butler 1927: 1077). Indeed, a strict definition of science fiction in which a story is not considered to be science fiction unless the science is accurate would mean that few of the stories in *Amazing* or *Astounding* were science fiction at all.[25] Most of the stories offend against the known science of their time and are full of faster-than-light interplanetary travel, of humans being able to breathe unhindered on Mars or Venus, and of humans who in just a few centuries have evolved wings. Edgar Rice Burroughs was regularly reprinted in *Amazing*, and many of his stories would today be classified as fantasy.[26]

Many fans had an obsessional engagement with the kind of fiction published in *Weird Tales* and other magazines that had little or no interest in science and its benefits for "mankind." In the *Fancyclopedia* science fiction is, in fact, lumped in with two other subgenres under the broad category of fantasy, which is divided into the trinity of "science-fiction, weird fiction, and pure fantasy" (Speer 1944: 33). All three areas were of interest to the fan, and there were many fans who were more interested in weird fiction and pure fantasy than science fiction.

9 MAMA COME HOME

Introducing the Battle of the Sexes

In the field of science fiction there is a body of stories explicitly about relations between men and women. Some are predicated on an unequal relationship between the sexes in which male rule is naturalized and female rule is demonized; others negotiate a less unequal relationship between the sexes. These so-called battle-of-the-sexes texts raise many issues concerning men and women and sex and sexuality and form a genre where the negotiations that produce and shape heterosexual subjectivities are explicitly realized.

The title of Robert Wentworth's story "World without Sex" (1940) sums up the dominant-male texts neatly,[1] because sex in these texts actually has a very limited reference. This is not a world in which no sex acts take place but one in which a specific heterosexual engagement of a dominant man and a submissive woman is (at first) absent. That engagement is symbolized by particular kinds of female bodies, the kind of desirable female bodies that were commonly represented on the covers of many sf magazines. But a world where desirable female bodies are not available to men is a world without sex. For a woman to become a part of the heterosexual economy, she must learn to perform her sex properly so that she can then *be* sex: "One is not born, but rather becomes, a woman" (de Beauvoir [1949] 1972: 295). Neither is one born a real man.

The majority of the battle-of-the-sexes texts I consider in this chapter are of the kind that Joanna Russ refers to in her essay "The Image of Women in Science Fiction": "The strangest and most fascinating oddities in science fiction occur not in the stories that try to abolish differences in gender-roles but in those which attempt to reverse the roles themselves. Unfortunately, only a handful of writers have treated this theme seriously. Into a world of cold, cruel, domineering women who are openly contemptuous of their cringing, servile men. . . . [Then] arrive(s) men (a man) from our present world. With a minimum of trouble, these normal men succeed in overthrowing the matriarchy, which although strong and warlike, is also completely inefficient" (Russ 1974: 56). This role reversal serves to demonstrate that female rule is misrule.[2] At the heart of these texts is the struggle to restore male rule and the "natural order of things." A central aspect of the natural order is a heterosexuality predicated on the romance discourse, which I call the heterosexual economy. The matriarchal worlds of the texts are heterosexual, yet they are outside this economy—men there exist only for reproduction, and if there are no men, then there is no sex. The matriarchal women must be reincorporated into the heterosexual economy that they were a part of in their patriarchal past. For the women of these matriarchal worlds, reincorporation is a return, as a class, to the rule of the father. In many of these texts there is both a literal war between men as a class and women as a class and also a metaphorical war between two individual representatives of their class: the hero and heroine. In the process of rescuing the heroine from her matriarchal existence, the hero transforms her into a real woman. The process of the woman's incorporation (not reincorporation, because for the heroine this is her first encounter with patriarchy) to the heterosexual economy is achieved through some kind of heterosexual penetration, usually a kiss.

The field of science fiction was not the only site during this period in which debates about women, sex, sexuality, and feminism were taking place. In 1928 Virginia Woolf was struck by the number of books written about women: "One went to the counter; one took a slip of paper; one opened a volume of the catalogue, and . . . . . the five dots here indicate five separate minutes of stupefaction, wonder and bewilderment. Have you any notion of how many books are written about women in the course of one year? Have you any notion how many are written by men? Are you aware that you are, perhaps, the most discussed animal in the universe?" (Woolf [1929] 1977: 27).

Wallace G. West's battle-of-the-sexes story, "The Last Man" (1929), which I discuss below, begins with an epigram from Thomas M. Ludovici's *Lysistrata, or Woman's Future and Future Woman* (1923—one of the books by men about women contributing to Woolf's "wonder and bewilderment"). Ludovici's treatise concerns the degeneracy the human race has fallen into because of Woman. Ignoring the fact that there were very good reasons why women outnumbered men in the workforce immediately after World War 1, Ludovici extrapolates from the sad state of contemporary affairs two scenarios for the development of the future world. In one, women take over and eliminate all men, and it is from this version of the future that "The Last Man" takes its epigram: "By that time, however, a significant precedent will have been established and a lesson learnt that will not easily be forgotten. The superfluousness of men above a certain minimum will have become recognized officially and unofficially as a social fact . . . in a very short while it will become a mere matter of routine to proceed to an annual slaughter of males who have either outlived their prime or else have failed to fulfil the promise of their youth in meekness, general emasculateness *[sic]* and stupidity" (Ludovici 1923: 95). He continues: "[T]here is still a fight to be fought with Feminism. . . . [W]e ourselves, though heart and soul pro-feminine, still remain active anti-Feminists . . . if anti-Feminism means resisting the further development of Feminism, to prevent it from culminating in some or all of the changes outlined . . . ; if it means a struggle to maintain the natural functioning of male and female in reproduction; and if it also means the retention of the family, the home, and some beauty in our social scheme, then it certainly cannot yet be a lost cause" (101).

These ideas about what the natural relations between the sexes should be are central to the majority of the battle-of-the-sexes texts I examine in this chapter. Indeed the title of my chapter, taken from Tiptree's story "Mama Come Home" ([1968] 1973), is a direct reference to this desire to make the relations between women and men return to an imagined past when there was no feminism and all the mamas were at home.

The Battle of the Sexes in Science Fiction, 1926–1973

The two main accounts of the battle of the sexes in science fiction during this period are Sam Moskowitz's collection *When Women Rule* (1972)[3] and Joanna Russ's essay "*Amor Vincit Foeminam:* The Battle of the Sexes in Science Fiction" (1980). Although Moskowitz's book is titled *When Women Rule*, he includes two stories in which women do not rule. In "The Last Woman" (1932) there is only one woman left in the world, and in David H. Keller's story "The Feminine Metamorphosis" (1929) women are thwarted in their attempts to seize power. Moskowitz locates the stories in his anthology within the genre of science fiction to show how inclusive the genre is despite claims to the contrary. He argues that the theme of "woman dominant . . . spotlight[ed] the female sex" and notes that it has "since the beginning . . . been regarded as legitimately within the province of science fiction" (1972: 1). Russ, on the other hand, is concerned to show how appalling the typical battle-of-the-sexes texts are and contrasts them with a more recent genre, which she calls feminist utopias. Part of the process of writing about the battle of the sexes is to decide which texts belong in this category. Russ excludes feminist utopias from the battle-of-the-sexes type, although she notes that most of them are "concerned with the battle of the sexes" (Russ 1980: 13). She also briefly mentions some texts by men that she deems to be possibly profeminist, though she excludes them from the designation "battle of the sexes" (13).

For my purposes, any text concerned with relations between the sexes is a battle-of-the-sexes text, including Russ's "feminist utopias" and "profeminist" texts by men, texts where men rule, and texts where women rule, as well as less typical battle-of-the-sexes stories such as H. O. Dickinson's "The Sex Serum" (1935) and Philip Wylie's *The Disappearance* (1951).[4]

That the battle of the sexes was a known subgenre or theme of science fiction is highlighted by the intertextualities of the stories. Along with the unconscious intertextualities that occur because writers are immersed in the same discourses and fields of knowledge, there is also a great deal of conscious rewriting of earlier texts in science fiction. For example, according to Moskowitz, Thomas S. Gardner's "The Last Woman," first published in the April 1932 issue of *Wonder Stories*, was "deliberate[ly]" written as a counter to West's "The Last Man," first published in the February 1929 issue of *Amazing Stories* (Moskowitz 1972: 13).[5] In "The Last Man," all men have been destroyed except for one, M-1, the Last Man, who is kept on permanent display in a museum. He is rescued by a woman who is a throwback to the time when the world was bisexual, and they escape to the mountains. In "The Last Woman," all women have been destroyed except for one, the Last Woman, who is kept on permanent display in a museum. She is rescued by a man who is a throwback to the time when the world was bisexual, and they attempt to escape into outer space. Richard Wilson's *The Girls from Planet Five* (1955) has a series of short "Vox Pop" sections where Joan and George, Mr. and Mrs. Everyman, gradually discover that the matriarchal world is abnormal and that George is meant to be the man of the house and undertake paid work to take care of his wife. In *Venus Plus X* (1960) by Theodore Sturgeon, there are a series of "Vox Pop" sections about Herb and Jeanette (Mr. and Mrs. Everyman) where they—though mostly Herb—consider questions of sex and gender and misogyny. *Venus Plus X* also refers specifically to *The Disappearance* (Sturgeon 1960: 71–72). Battle-of-the-sexes stories also share many motifs, such as the use of role reversals, matriarchal worlds modeled on insects, and parthenogenesis.

Real Men and Real Women

In her article "Gendering the Body: Beauvoir's Philosophical Contribution," Judith Butler writes that "there has been a great deal of popular and scientific thinking that has tacitly subscribed to gender as a kind of being. We speak quite often of someone being a real or true man or woman, being 'manly' or 'womanly' as if participating in an ideal Form of man or woman, and here we tend to assume that man and woman are substances that not only exist but are causally responsible for certain kinds of behavior" (1989: 258). The majority of the battle-of-the-sexes texts that I discuss in this chapter are predicated on an ideal form of manliness and womanliness and show ways in which woman and man are distinct substances whose manliness and womanliness cause them to engage in certain behaviors. These behaviors mean that they *are* real women and real men; those who do not engage in these behaviors are *not* real men or women.

Gardner's "The Last Woman" (1932), for example, is set in a world entirely populated—with the exception of one woman—by real men. Men have become the dominant sex since they defeated women's attempt to "femin[ize] civilization" (Gardner [1932] 1972: 135). The story ends with the last woman being executed and an all-male "Science Civilization" triumphing. Russ (1980) discusses "The Last Woman" and its all-male scientific utopia, but by the end of her article she seems to have forgotten the narrative resolution that results in a world without women: "[N]o Flasher book [Russ's alternative name for the battle-of-the-sexes texts] I was able to find envisioned a womanless world (or dared to say so); about half the feminist Utopias matter-of-factly excluded men" (14).

The all-male world of "The Last Woman" is a world of real men not homosexuals. The world is achieved through the discovery of "the Elixir," as "[a]ll the energies that had been turned toward sex and the emotional side of life were released for thought and work. Every branch of science advanced and the Scientists began to control the money and power resources of the Earth" (134). The Elixir keeps mankind "intensely masculine"; they do not become "thin-chested neuters" (133). However, the invention of the Elixir is not enough for the triumph of the Science Empire. Women have to be eliminated, because "the female bred truest to type and held the primitive characteristics longer than the male and . . . she reverted to the primitive type the quicker" (135). The elimination of sex means the elimination of creatures who divert man from his true role as scientist.[6]

"The Last Woman" notwithstanding, there is no need to envision a world without women, as there has always been science fiction that "matter-of-factly excluded" women. A letter written by Isaac Asimov to the editor of *Startling Stories* makes this point: "There is a great deal of significance, I think, in the fact that the four stories of the September issue of *Startling Stories* did not contain a single female character. . . . [T]he September issue goes to prove that good stories can be written even with the total absence of the weaker sex" (Asimov 1939c: 115).

That there is more than one sex in other sf texts is obvious: after all, they are about the battle of the *sexes*. In the majority of the texts the explicit assumption is that the battle takes place between two opposite sexes, male and female. However, while many texts tell of two sexes engaged in warfare, many also tell a story in which there is a multiplicity of sexed bodies. Some posit at least four: real women, real men, not-real men, and not-real women. Consider, for example, Nelson S. Bond's sequel to "The Priestess Who Rebelled," "The Judging of the Priestess" (1940), in which the heroine, Meg, says of the hero, Daiv: "It is no Man-*thing*, Mother. It is a Man; a real Man such as were the Gods! Not a scrimping parody like our breeders, nor a foul brute like the Wild Ones—but a Man. He is Daiv, my mate!" (46).[7] Edmund Cooper, in his novel *Who Needs Men?* ([1972] 1974), provides another example: The heroine, Rura, after she is captured by the renegade men, asks, "What do you usually do with women you take prisoner?" Her captor, Diarmid, responds, "Ah, well, that is a double question, you see. Usually we divide them into two classes—women and exterminators" (87). Later Diarmid tells her that she will "be seen not as an exterminator but as a free woman." Rura asks, "Are your women free, then?" and Diarmid responds, "They are free to be women" (94).

Joanna Russ argues that these texts are built around a central contradiction: "When women fight men, the battle is won by men because women are loyal to men" (1980: 12). On the one hand, men and women do come into conflict with each other; and on the other hand, women are not really opposed to men. In other words, women and men—women and men acting according to their true natures—are perfect complements to each other.

However, within the heterosexual economy of real men and real women there is no such contradiction. In worlds where there is more than one kind of woman, the real women are those who are always loyal, and the not-real women are those who fight against men. This is clearest in the texts where the women who work to wipe out the men are, in fact, aliens. There are a number of battle-of-the-sexes stories where an alien race of women is intent on wiping out the men. In Jerry Sohl's *The Haploids*, for example, the haploids look exactly like women except that they are unnaturally cold ([1952] 1953: 81). They are a parthenogenetic race created by an insane female scientist, Dr. Gardner. Gardner has also created a deadly radiation device that kills all men who are exposed to it except those who have AB blood. She is defeated because her daughter turns against her to help the hero, who has AB blood. The daughter turns out to have been brainwashed into believing that she too is a haploid, when she is, in fact, the doctor's "natural" daughter. She is therefore a real woman and, once she overcomes her brainwashing, loyal to the male cause.

This idea of alien women forming a secret conspiracy against men is also the center of *The White Widows* (1953) by Sam Merwin Jr.[8] In this story, the hero, Larry Finlay, has written a thesis on hemophilia examining the female carriers of the disease. In the process he accidentally uncovers a centuries-old conspiracy among certain superhuman women to wipe out men, develop a way of reproducing without them, and rule the world:

> There had been a number of definite characteristics, some physical, some physiological. For one thing, haemophilia carriers tended to be women of a driving dominant type, which he had termed the "Empress Type" in his thesis—their drive intensified by their ability, with or without great native beauty, to make themselves attractive to men.
>
> They were strongly erotic, with a tendency towards lesbianism, basically heterosexual. Physically, in most cases they tended towards unusual length of limb, coupled to longevity and extranormal strength, and speed of reflex.
>
> . . . [B]asically these women are believers in a world of one sex. Amazons if you will. (63)

Marriage and love, he implies, are a trap to destroy men. Finlay prevents the women's conspiracy to launch germ warfare over Asia and so begin the destruction of mankind. The novel ends, however, with Finlay married to one of the Amazon women and aware that the conspiracy against men has been stalled, not defeated.

In *The Haploids* and *The White Widows* the women involved in the conspiracy against men are not real women; they are "haploids" or "Amazons." There are real women in these texts who are loyal to their men. By contrast, in "The Misogynist" (1952) by James E. Gunn, all women are aliens.[9] The narrator and his friend Harry sit and talk; or rather, Harry talks and the narrator listens. The narrator says that "nobody tells stories like Harry," though "women don't think Harry is funny" ([1952] 1955: 16). According to Harry, women, "[t]he alien race," are involved in a conspiracy to wipe out men (17):

> What better way . . . to conquer a race than to breed it out of existence? The Chinese learned that a long time ago. Conqueror after conqueror took the country and each one was passively accepted, allowed to intermarry. . . and eventually was absorbed. Only this case is the reverse. Conquest by marriage might be a good term for it. Breed in the conqueror, breed out the slave. Breed in the alien, breed out the human. . . .
>
> . . . It's only in the last few generations that their plans have been coming closer to success. They have the vote, equal rights without giving up any of their privileges, and so forth. They're outliving men—and it's men, of course, who are extending the life span for them. . . . And there's something else men are doing for them. . . . We're experimenting with fertilization by salt water, electrical stimulus, that sort of thing. Once we work it out properly. . . .
>
> . . . They'll just refuse to marry, use prenatal sex determination to produce nothing but girls, and then you'll have a single race—the female race. (17–20)

Harry's account includes many of the elements of other battle-of-the-sexes texts, including matriarchies (18) and parthenogenesis (20). As in Sohl's *Haploids*, marriage is a conspiracy to destroy men by breeding them out. As proof of his theory Harry quotes and recites a litany of misogynist sentiment: Homer, Ovid, Swift ("A dead wife under the table is the best goods in a man's house"), Antiphanes, Menander, Cato, Shakespeare, Lord Chesterfield, Nietzsche, and others (20). Misogyny is transformed into reason. At the end of the story Harry is dead and the narrator is about to go down to the cellar where his wife is banging about with a poker (24).

The coldness of the haploids and these other alien women and their conspiracies against men fit stereotypes of lesbians, and indeed in *The White Widows* women are even said to have a "tendency towards lesbianism" (Merwin 1953: 63). There are undisguised lesbians in other sexbattle texts, such as *The Disappearance* (1951), *Virgin Planet* (1957), *World without Men/Alph* (1958, revised 1972), and *Who Needs Men?* (1972). However, as in *The Haploids*, the main function of lesbianism is to show how infinitely preferable heterosexuality is, and to mark those women who do not instantly become heterosexual on seeing a man or being kissed by him as not-real women. Monique Wittig has argued that lesbians are seen as not women because they cannot be incorporated into the heterosexual order (1992). I found no mention of male homosexuality in any of the texts I discuss in this chapter, particularly not in Gardner's story "The Last Woman" ([1932] 1972), where an all-male world is made possible by the eradication of "sex and the emotional side of life" (134).[10]

In these stories there is always only one kind of real man and real woman. However, there are sometimes several types of not-real women and not-real men. In Nelson S. Bond's "The Priestess Who Rebelled" ([1939] 1972) there are three different kinds of not-real women: the warriors with "corded legs, the grim, set jaws. The cold eyes. The brawny arms, scarred to the elbow with ill-healed cicatrices. The tiny, thwarted breasts, flat and hard beneath harness-plates. Fighters they were, nothing else" (198); the mothers, who were "full-lipped, flabby-breasted bearers of children. . . . Those eyes were humid; washed barren of all expression by desires too oft aroused, too often sated. The bodies bulged at hip and thigh, swayed when they walked like ripe grain billowing in a lush and fertile field. They lived only that the tribe might continue to exist. They reproduced" (199); and the workers: "Their bodies retained a vestige of womankind's inherent grace and nobility. But if their waists were thin, their hands were blunt-fingered and thick. Their shoulders were bent with the weight of labor; coarsened. . . . Their faces were grim from the eternal struggle with an unyielding earth. . . . The workers' skin was browned with soil, their bodies stank of dirt and grime and unwashed perspiration" (199).

The description of the workers' bodies as having "retained a vestige of womankind's inherent grace and nobility" clearly implies that women are naturally graceful and noble. If the workers retain "a vestige" of these qualities and the warriors and mothers have none, the implication is that they are not really women at all. The same array of sexed female bodies is present in John Wyndham's "Consider Her Ways" ([1956] 1965), which is mostly set in a far future world where all men have been extinct for generations (14).

In Bond's "The Priestess Who Rebelled" there are also two different kinds of not-real men. There are those kept for breeding purposes in the matriarchal communities: they have "pale, pitifully hairless bodies" and "soft, futile hands and weak mouths"; they "loll" about and make "small enticing" gestures (198). Then there are the Wild Ones, who "roam the land . . . [s]earching for food" and "most of all for mates." The Wild Ones have "shaggy bodies," "thick, brutish faces," and "hard, gnarled muscles" (207); the Wild Ones are male, but they are not real men either.

As I have shown, an identifiably male or female body does not, in these textual worlds, automatically grant the person the status of man or woman. The distinction is not new. Elizabeth Spelman, in *Inessential Woman* (1988), argues that in "Plato's proposal for a kind of 'equality' between men and women . . . he is referring to a very small group of men and women" (80). In Plato's view, males with womanly souls or females with womanly souls—who are almost invariably those of the lower classes—are excluded from the potential equality shared by the manly-souled philosopher elite.

In the real men/real women sf texts, bodies are pared down to a bare minimum. There are, with few exceptions, only white, heterosexual, middle-class, and mostly North American bodies—and *even* among these there are people that do not qualify as real men and women. In the sexbattle world, bodies and behaviors rather than souls are the grounds of admittance to the exclusive caste of the real. What sort of bodies and behaviors qualify? In Bond's "The Priestess Who Rebelled," Meg, the heroine, who by the text's end has become a real woman, is described thus: "[H]er legs were long and firm and straight as a warrior's spear. Her body was supple; bronzed by sunlight save where her doeskin breech-cloth kept the skin white. Unbound her hair could have trailed the earth . . . her skin was golden-brown, and pure gold where the sunlight burnished the fine down on her arms and legs; between her high, firm breasts" (Bond [1939] 1972: 204).

Compare this to the warriors, mothers, and workers above. Bond's hero Daiv's "body is smooth and almost as hairless as [Meg's] own. Bronzed by the sun. But it was not the pale, soft body of a [lowercase] man. It was muscular, hard, firm; taller and stronger than a warrior" (208). The two are linked together by the language of the description: "smooth," "hairless," "firm," bodies "bronzed" by the sun. Daiv is more masculine than the women warriors of Meg's tribe, and Meg is as straight and firm as one of their spears.

The different categories of not-real man and woman and real man and woman are fixed. However, the sexed bodies are fluid and can be transformed, moving from one category to another. An example of such a transformation occurs at the end of Richard Wilson's *Girls from Planet Five* (1955): the beautiful and tall non-Earth women, the Lyru, learn that their men—whom they have never taken seriously because they are shorter and less brave than the women are—have been secretly working against the evil Crones for generations. After this revelation one of the Lyru, Lori, "look[s] happily at Iason, who seem[s] almost as tall as she [is] as he stands beside her" (180).

The wide range of sexed bodies in these texts is not a static one. All of the bodies discussed here, although (literally) textual bodies, are historically contingent. The philosopher Moira Gatens argues that the "qualitative difference in the way we live out our particular balances (or imbalances) of masculine and feminine traits is crucially connected to our bodies" and this cannot be separated from "the meaning and significance of the sexed body in culture" ([1989] 1996: 30). Culture is not ahistorical. For instance, in West's story "The Last Man" the women of the matriarchal world are described as "tall, angular, narrow-hipped, flat-breasted" ([1929] 1972: 109), which sounds like a description of a high-fashion catwalk model—one of the late twentieth–early twenty-first-century ideal womanly bodies. In the context of the story, however, it is a description of a kind of body that women developed once all the world's men disappeared: "In the ages which followed, great physiological changes took place. Women, no longer having need of sex, dropped it, like a worn-out cloak, and became sexless, tall, angular, narrow-hipped, flat-breasted and *unbeautiful* (my emphasis; 108–9). These "tall, angular, narrow-hipped, flat-breasted" unwomen are contrasted with the heroine, who has "[h]air red as a slumberous [*sic*] fire—eyes blue as the heavens. . . . Unafraid she wrinkled her nose at him, then wrapping about her a long black robe which but half concealed her deep breasts and the forgotten womanly grace of her carriage" (110).

Some of these stories are more overt about their historical context than others. For instance, in "The Feminine Metamorphosis" by David Keller, published in the August 1929 issue of *Science Wonder Stories*, the sexual inequality of the contemporary world is foregrounded. Unlike many of the other sexbattle texts, the women who wish to take over the world in "The Feminine Metamorphosis" have a clearly stated reason for doing so. Their dissatisfaction is put in the context of the erosion of the gains won by American women in the workforce during the First World War:

> During the World War the feminine sex had tasted the sweetness of responsibility with increasing incomes, so that at the close of the war they were reluctant to return to their former humble positions. Well educated, capable, and hard working women were striving to occupy positions on a par with men, and the situation had become so acute that many corporations had passed regulations, strictly limiting the advancement of women in their employ. . . .
>
> The result had not been a happy one. More and more women were preparing themselves for positions of trust and large salaries. Every phase of business activity, especially those requiring brain power, was being handled by the members of the fair sex, who, by their constant application to work, their ability to look after the smallest details, and their one-track minds, were far more capable of holding positions of trust than was the average business man. ([1929] 1972: 151)

The story begins when a Miss Martha Belzer is told that she will not be promoted because she is a woman. This despite being "brilliant," "capable," "shrewd," and "intelligent" (149–50). The male business leaders of America have decided that Miss Belzer, and other women like her, must be prevented from "gain[ing] control of the great corporations of the nation. . . . So, the word passed from the President of one great concern to the Chief Executive of the next that under no circumstances should a woman be promoted to certain positions in these companies" (153). Miss Belzer forms a conspiracy with other women to take over the United States and the rest of the world using a drug made from diseased gonads removed from Chinese men. They transform five thousand of their number into men and these men take over the business world. They also start investigating parthenogenesis and invent a formula that causes women to have only female children. Unfortunately for the women's conspiracy a detective, Taine of the Secret Service, uncovers their plans. At the same time the disease that was in the gonads, which seems to be syphilis, starts to drive the five thousand female men mad.

The justice of the women's complaints is irrelevant. They are unnatural power-seekers and their intelligence, which had allowed them to prosper in the workforce until their promotion was blocked, is marked as unnatural. The other women in the text who are not part of the conspiracy are not clever. Taine lectures the unnatural women: "You went on with your plans, but you forgot God. He had certain plans for the human race, and it was no part of His plan that women should live . . . without men. . . . You took . . .

loving wives and wonderful mothers—you took the best that we have bred, and through your desires to rule, you have changed them into . . . insane women" (194–95). The women have attempted to change the natural order of things, whereby men work in the public sphere and women in the private as "loving wives and wonderful mothers." To go outside the heterosexual order is to go insane, and a mad woman, like a lesbian, is not a woman. Further, when the women have become men, they are unnatural men; they are described in terms that imply homosexuality, they refuse to play "a real man's game, like golf" (171), and the way they dress is suspicious: "Their clothing was masculine, but at the same time, it had a dash of color to it, a peculiar something that was different. When one of this group walked down on Fifth Avenue, his general appearance was such as to make passing women, and men also, turn to look again at him" (169).

The initial desire by Miss Martha Belzer and other women to be promoted because of their ability soon becomes a "dream of a manless world. . . . We do not want two sexes in this fair world of ours, not as long as one sex can run it so efficiently" (186). This equation between a desire for equality and a desire for power and dominion over men and their eradication is made frequently. Some examples are "The Last Man" (West 1929), *The Haploids* (Sohl 1952), *The White Widows* (Merwin 1953, reprinted as *The Sex War* in 1960), "For Sacred San Francisco" (Coppel 1969), *Sex and the High Command* (Boyd 1970), and *Who Needs Men?* (Cooper [1972] 1974).

Parthenogenesis is a key element in these texts. Once this method of reproduction is discovered, as in *Who Needs Men?* and many other texts, men become redundant. This is an old notion. Laqueur notes that this is a "question with which two-seed theorists were plagued for millenia: if the female has such powerful seed, then why can she not engender within herself alone: who needs men?" (1990 [1992]: 40). Once the women in these stories discover the secret to parthenogensis men's days are numbered. The battle-of-the-sexes texts take place in a universe in which nonsexual interaction, friendship, and affection between men and women cannot exist because their relationships are constructed across a bridge of biology (Russ 1980: 3). Once the biological necessity for their interaction is removed, that is, reproduction of the species, women and men cease to have any need of each other. If a society produces artificial ova and incubators as in "The Last Woman" (Gardner [1932] 1972: 135–36), then who needs women? And if parthenogenesis is achieved, as in *Who Needs Men?* (Cooper [1972] 1974) and many other texts, then, indeed, who needs men?

Sex and Science

A page from David Keller's story "The Feminine Metamorphosis" (figure 5) reproduces a newspaper cutting that is meant to legitimate Keller's story and illustrates how "fiction becomes fact." The story is not merely a fiction but a *science* fiction.

Examples such as this from the real world of science were often used in sf magazines of the 1920s and 1930s to legitimate science fiction. The editorial blurbs that accompanies the stories frequently draw attention to the scientific accuracy or relevance of a story before pointing out its merits as an entertainment. Indeed, the blurb for "The Feminine Metamorphosis" follows this format:

> When a physician-author writes a story on a biological subject, you may be sure that it will be more than interesting. Only during recent years, have the functions of the various glands in the human body assumed a tremendous importance. It seems that the glands are responsible for almost everything imaginable in our mental and physical make-up. It is also true, very frequently, that these functions can be interfered with by altering or otherwise influencing the glands.
>
> It has been known for some time, that extracts from various glands can be used as a stimulant to the live glands of human beings, although the extract has been secured from animals or human beings.
>
> It may be safely said that the wonderful field of gland surgery and medicine is as yet practically untouched. Some of the most surprising and far-reaching discoveries will come when we know more about them.
>
> In the present story Dr. Keller, with his usual insight, has written a most original story that is as good as it is amazing. And incidentally, he has given us a most clever O. Henry ending—a climax as surprising as it is unique. (*Science Wonder Stories* [April 1929]: 247)

It transforms the story into a serious engagement with recent discoveries about glands.

The blurb accompanying "The Last Woman" (Gardner 1932) also legitimates the story by claiming a relationship between it and recent discoveries about glands (in this case, the glands are explicitly described as "sex glands":

> Despite its title, this story is not calculated to appeal especially to our feminine readers. For it is a red-blooded story, and a bizarre one; yet it deals with events that are well within the limits of probability.

gave you all a piece of expensive jewelry. She gave you a piece of jade, Dr. Hamilton, and she gave the doctor whom you call Lucy this ring. Lucy thought the little China girl rather nice. Well, to make a long story short, I was that little girl. I lived in the hospital with you for some months. The Government sent me over to find out what you girls were doing there. I had some ideas then and during all these years those ideas have been slowly working into definite form. I suspected some of the things you spoke of tonight, yet, at the same time, you went a lot further than I thought sensible people would go. I know a lot about women, but I cannot understand what's the matter with you—unless you really are insane."

Dr. Hamilton shook her head gravely.

"I guess he is right, girls. I remember that little Chinese girl, and he did give me the jade. He would not have known about that unless he had been there. I have heard about him, but I had no idea that he was so damn clever. But is he clever? To get the best of Lucy and come here dressed to impersonate her? And then this chorus girl. Well, he says he is Taine, and I really do not think he has harmed Lucy—just locked her up somewhere. So, the best thing we can do with him is to kill him right away. He knows too much—we can handle this chorus girl, but this man—the only way to keep him quiet is to kill him. I hate to commit murder, but I have been working on this plan for years and I am not going to have it go to pieces just on account of a man."

Miss Patricia Powers agreed with the Doctor.

"You are right, Hamilton," she said. "He knows too much. If he is dead, we will put through our financial coup, and in a week it will not make any difference if they do find out he died here at the Club."

Suddenly the San Francisco doctor, Lucy, who was really Taine, seemed to change. His face grew hard, and his hands, within his coat pockets, twitched.

"Now, you sit down, ladies, and listen to me talk. You are not going to kill me or anybody tonight. There are about five hundred policemen around this building. If I am not out safely by midnight, they are going to find out why. No one is going to leave. You women have played a great game, but it was a selfish, inhuman sort of a game, and you are going to lose out and it's not your fault or my fault, but just one of those happenings that make me believe in predestination. You want to run this world, and have all the men die off and make it a female Paradise, and you forgot there was a God and that He made man just the same as He made woman. I admit that some men are rather bad sort of fools, but some of us are really rather good sorts — take me, for example. My wife thinks I am wonderful—of course, all my boys are girls, but, at the same time, she would have been tickled had the last one been a boy. You go and change your bodies, and try and make men out of yourselves, and all the rest of what you call your programme, and now you think that you are going to win out by killing me. If it were not for the Missus and the kids, I would not mind much if you did, but even if you were able to, what good would it do you?

"I think your Dr. Hamilton is a rather bright expert. I always shall be indebted to her for operating on Ming Foo. She had a wonderful plan and she has worked it out in a wonderful way—but she did not know the Chinese people—not the way I do. I have lived with them and slept with them and I know a little more about them than you would think, just by looking at me. During these last two weeks I have been having long talks with scientists from all over the East. Perhaps your detectives know who they were, though they could not tell what we talked about. But I wanted to learn all I could about that medicine Dr. Hamilton prepared in that hospital, and these men told me. I said so and so and they agreed with me that my idea might be right. What you have said tonight convinces me that I was right.

... over the great victory democracy has obtained in England, which in these times of Fascism and bolshevism is comforting."

TELLS OF A TUMOR THAT MODIFIED SEX

Medical Journal Tells of Woman Who Began to Grow Beard—Operation Restored Her.

Special to The New York Times.

BALTIMORE, May 31.—Introducing evidence that the ductless glands may change the sex, Dr. Oscar Riddle of the Carnegie Institute, in an article in the current number of The Journal of the American Medical Association quotes Dr. John Abel, Professor of Pharmacology at the Johns Hopkins University, in connection with the case of a young woman who developed a mustache and a beard and many characteristics of the male and had her sex restored by an operation.

The case of the young woman occurred in England. When her characteristics changed toward male, an investigation revealed a tumor which was making certain glands function in an abnormal manner. It was removed and her restoration to her own sex followed in the course of time.

An illustration how fiction becomes fact.
From the New York Times, May 31.

Taine Explains

"YOU went on with your plans, but you forgot God. He had certain plans for the human race, and it was no part of His plan that women should live on, century after century, without men, as you were preparing them to do. So, this is what

(*Concluded on page* 274)

5. Page 263 of David H. Keller's "The Feminine Metamorphosis," *Science Wonder Stories,* August 1929

> The understanding of how our sex glands function, and their effect upon us is just beginning to be understood. When we finally do understand, certainly a new era will dawn in the history of the race.
>
> Some men already predict that women will eventually rule the world, and they will at least make the attempt to overthrow masculine domination. But suppose they lose, and man holds the undisputed sway, with but one woman left. Will men idolize her; will they fight over her like wild beasts; or will they enslave her? The answer that our author gives is much different than you will think. This is a distinctly original story, and deals with an absorbing idea. (*Wonder Stories* [April 1932]: 1239)

Both "The Feminine Metamorphosis" and "The Last Woman" were published during the period Nelly Oudshoorn discusses in her 1994 book *Beyond the Natural Body: An Archaeology of Sex Hormones*. Oudshoorn focuses on the period of the "1920s and 1930s in which scientists became confused by their own assumptions about sex and the body" (1). She investigates the scientists who were engaged at the time in understanding, as the blurb to "The Last Woman" puts it, "how our sex glands function, and their effect upon us." Outside science fiction, scientists such as Samuel Elzevier de Jongh in 1936 were struggling "to define which observed characteristics can be considered decisive for our judgement [of the sex of a hormone]: male or female" (Oudshoorn 1994: 1), and others like William Blair Bell in 1916 were discovering that "there are many individuals with ovaries who are not women in the strict sense of the word and many with testes who are really feminine in many other respects" (Oudshoorn 1994: 37). Within science fiction these struggles were being translated unproblematically into "understanding . . . how our sex glands function." The struggles and negotiations Oudshoorn documents were popularly understood as scientific endeavor and, therefore, as a series of discovered facts that could become the scientific basis for some of the battle-of-the-sexes texts.

The editorial introduction to H. O. Dickinson's story "The Sex Serum" (1935) appears as figure 6. Science in this passage is animate and has agency. It can solve mysteries and make discoveries—the kinds of discoveries that will lead to a story such as "The Sex Serum" being transformed from science fiction to "actual" science.

This rhetoric is also present in the comments that accompanied Wallace West's "The Last Man" in the February 1929 issue of *Amazing Stories:*

THE SEX SERUM
By H. O. DICKINSON

*I think that my vanity is forcing me to write, although I know as I set down the words in this almost illegible handwriting that it will get no farther than the bottom drawer of my desk. Yes, it will be fortunate if it ends there, for I am a very impulsive person and the wastepaper basket is nearby.

But when I reflect, it seems hardly fair—back to myself and all those people who were cheated out of the answer to a first-class mystery. Consider too that eminent man, Sir John Norton. I think the satisfaction he would have derived from this manuscript would more than compensate him for the inconvenience caused by the striking out at least one case from his latest volume: "Unsolved Mysteries of the Twentieth Century."

I have read his fourth problem, "The Manor House Murders," with a smile upon my lips and that aloof and superior feeling which comes to a man who knows the truth. And why should I not smile? It is the only reward I will ever obtain from my knowledge. For you do not realize that I am the only person alive to-day who knows the real solution of a crime which baffled, and is still baffling, a whole country—a unique position to be in, you will agree, and one that arouses all man's latent vanity.

I have kept the secret for a long time now and no one would suffer from the telling of it not that I think it would be believed, but it will pass as another of one of the more fantastic and imaginative theories that have often been advanced as explanations of a mystery which has for so long defied logical solution.

And again, further excuse for my vain and babbling tongue. Unusual stories are the fashion these days when every normal plot has fallen prey of the modern literary mass-production machine, dealt with as a cow does its cud—chewed, twisted, turned about, contracted, reversed, dished up in a thousand different ways, then swallowed in disgust. And now it turns, with despairing howls, to Frankensteins, covered freaks, and mummified horrors for its sustenance.

You remember the Mount House murders, non-existent reader?—the strange disappearance of both Professor Neville, the famous biologist, and his daughter Jeanette. Then there was the finding of the dead and battered body of an old lady in Neville's study and the half-dead body of a young man, since thought to be the Professor's son, lying by her side.

*What makes a male and what makes a female human being?
Science so far has not been able to solve the mystery. It is known, however, that during the first weeks of conception, the human fetus (unborn child) is neither female nor male; it has the characteristics of both male and female. Only later on the predominate sex begins to develop, and at birth usually the child is either male or female, but not necessarily always. There are even exceptions here, and not so infrequently it is impossible to tell whether the child is male or female because it may be both—the so-called hermaphrodite types.

Sooner or later, science will develop means by which it will be possible to change human characteristics, as to sex, at will. As a matter of fact, science is coming nearer to the solution every day.

You will find the present story—an entirely new solution in science-fiction—particularly absorbing, because there is no question that in the future it may happen. It is for the first time that this subject has been used in science-fiction, and we congratulate our English author for having brought to us not only a novelty in science-fiction, but a masterful story as well.

6. Editorial blurb by Hugo Gernsback, accompanying H. O. Dickinson's "The Sex Serum," *Wonder Stories*, October 1935, p. 589

According to Kipling, "The female of the species is always more deadly." By that, he means that she is stronger in her own way, and we know that she usually is more numerous. Even among human beings, there are more females than males. Perhaps in thousands of years, evolution will have progressed in such a manner that the world will be entirely peopled by females. This is not so impossible as it would seem to be, because with many insects, the female of the species already predominates.

The present story then is founded upon an excellent scientific basis and the story itself is excellent as it is original and unusual. You will not forget it for a long time. (1030)

The leaps of logic here, from Kipling's comment to there being more women than men, to women taking over because amongst insects the "female of the species already predominates," are fairly breathtaking. All these leaps, however, constitute an "excellent scientific basis" for the story. The writer asserts that there is a core of "truth" to this story, therefore it is science fiction.

As I demonstrated in the previous chapter, the idea of scientific accuracy was central to discussions of science fiction stories in the letter columns of these magazines. Sexbattle stories were also debated in these terms. For instance, John J. Kelly Jr. of St. Paul, Minnesota, wrote a long response to David Keller's "The Feminine Metamorphosis," headed "Is Man Made the Same as Woman?"[11] Kelly writes that "The Feminine Metamorphosis" is "unfair and one-sided" because the women were "merely striving for economic liberation. Due to the intolerance of the male sex, the only way that the women could secure their freedom in this instance was by

THE SEX SERUM

By H. O. DICKINSON

● What makes a male, and what makes a female human being?

Science, so far, has not been able to solve the mystery. It is known, however, that during the first weeks of conception, the human fetus (unborn child) is neither female nor male; it has the characteristics of both male and female. Only later on the predominate sex begins to develop, and at birth usually the child is either male or female, but not necessarily always. There are even exceptions here, and not so infrequently it is impossible to tell whether the child is male or female because it may be both—the so-called hermaphrodite types.

Sooner or later, science will discover means by which it will be possible to change human characteristics, as to sex, at will. As a matter of fact, science is coming nearer to the solution every day.

You will find the present story—an entirely new solution in science-fiction—particularly absorbing, because there is no question that in the future it may happen. It is the first time that this subject has been used in science-fiction, and we congratulate our English author for having brought to us not only a novelty in science-fiction, but a masterful story as well.

● I think that my vanity is forcing me to write, although I know as I set down the words in this almost illegible handwriting that it will get no farther than the bottom drawer of my desk. Yes, it will be fortunate if it ends there, for I am a very impulsive person and the wastepaper basket is nearby.

But when I reflect, it seems hardly fair—back to myself and all those people who were cheated out of the answer to a first-class mystery. Consider too that eminent man, Sir John Norton. I think the satisfaction he would derive from this manuscript would more than compensate him for the inconvenience caused by striking out at least one case from his latest volume: "Unsolved Mysteries of the Twentieth Century."

I have read his fourth problem, "The Manor House Murders," with a smile upon my lips and that aloof and superior feeling which comes to a man who knows the truth. And why should I not smile? It is the only reward I will ever obtain from my knowledge. For you do not realize that I am the only person alive to-day who knows the real solution of a crime which baffled, and is still baffling, a whole country—a unique position to be in, you will agree, and one that arouses all man's latent vanity.

I have kept the secret for a long time now and no one would suffer from the telling of it—not that I think it would be believed, but it will pass as another of one of the more fantastic and imaginative theories that have often been advanced as explanations of a mystery which has for so long defied logical solution.

And again, further excuse for my vain and babbling tongue. Unusual stories are the fashion these days when every normal plot has fallen the prey of the modern literary mass-production machine, dealt with as a cow does its cud—chewed, twisted, turned about, contracted, reversed, dished up in a thousand different ways, then swallowed in disgust. And now it turns, with despairing howls, to Frankensteins, covered freaks, and mummified horrors for its sustenance.

You remember the Mount House murders, non-existent reader?—the strange disappearance of both Professor Neville, the famous biologist, and his daughter Jeanette. Then there was the finding of the dead and battered body of an old lady in Neville's study and the half-dead body of a young man, since thought to be the Professor's son, lying by her side.

the annihilation of the men" (*Science Wonder Stories* 1, no. 6 [November 1929]: 563). Worse than being unfair, the story is "unscientific":

> Detective Taine when he had the women trapped at their conference . . . aid, "—and you forgot that he (God) made man just the same as he made woman." Is this science? If it is, I am not acquainted with it. I have made the study of scientific subjects my hobby for years, but never came in contact with a statement like that.
>
> Is not Dr. Keller familiar with the fact that at one time the female was the only animal in existence on earth? . . . [T]he female organism alone existed as such but was fertilized by the male sperm cell, and that this cell was a part of the female organism. According to this, it would appear untrue that "man was made the same" as woman. The male organism (which characterizes the sex) was of later derivation by the processes of evolution. When Dr. Keller states that man was made the same as woman he is . . . making a scientific error. (563)

Kelly does not argue with the misogyny of "The Feminist Metamorphosis" but with its inaccuracy, with Keller's "scientific error."

Real Man Makes Real Woman

"The Feminine Metamorphosis" (Keller 1929) is unusual amongst the sexbattle texts because it has no central pairing of hero and heroine. The unnatural order of things is not resolved through a "romance" between this pairing but by the will of God. The more usual romance pairing is very close to the one Lacan describes in his description of hysteria (conveniently summarized in this passage by Monique Plaza): "[T]he hysteric is a woman who is struggling against men, and who doesn't know if she is a man or a woman . . . [S]he will emerge from her revolt when she meets the master she seeks, who will give her the desire to be a woman" (1984: 81). If we amend this slightly to read "who will make her a woman" then the description covers a group of sf texts in which the hero makes the heroine into a woman.[12] He does this by stripping her of agency and making her body into something over which she has no control. This process inverts the examples of the scholar Nina Puren (1995), in which the fragmentation of the woman's body, "her beauty," leaves her open to blame and responsibility for what that beauty has caused in the man who rapes her. In Puren's account the woman is the agent of the violence, which works itself through the medium of the man. In the sexbattle stories I examine in this section, however, the man is the agent of the change that works itself out through the body of the woman. The woman is allowed agency when it frees the man from responsibility that could cause him to be adversely affected. Otherwise she is the medium, the site of change that is worked on her by a man.

The process by which the hero makes the heroine into a "real" woman provides the agent for the transformation Simone de Beauvoir so famously described: "One is not born, but rather becomes, a woman" ([1949] 1972: 295). It is a man who makes a woman. In Nelson S. Bond's "The Priestess Who Rebelled" (first published in *Amazing Stories* in October 1939) and Edmund Cooper's *Who Needs Men?* (first published by Hodder and Stoughton in 1972), the process of "becoming woman" takes place when the woman is incorporated into the heterosexual economy. Becoming a real woman is also the theme of the song "You Make Me Feel Like a Natural Woman" written by Carole King. Judith Butler, in her article "Gendering the Body: Beauvoir's Philosophical Contribution," discusses the song, as sung by Aretha Franklin, and its relations to Beauvoir: "[Aretha] uses a simile that suggests that she knows the natural woman to be a figure and a fiction. Her claim, then, seems to translate into the following: 'you allow me a fantasy for a moment, the experience of a unity of my sex, gender, and desire that I know to be false but wish were true.' Aretha doesn't dispute Beauvoir, but gives us some understanding of the emotional pull of the illusion of a natural and substantial identity" (Butler 1989: 258–59).

"You Make Me Feel Like a Natural Woman" does indeed complement Beauvoir's utterance and supplies agency: You, presumably a man, are the agent that allows me, as medium, to feel like (to begin to become) "a natural woman." You are responsible for how I am positioned within the economy of heterosexuality. In "The Priestess Who Rebelled" and *Who Needs Men?* however, this account of agency cannot stand, because the account is still framed from the woman's point of view and so allows her some (small) control of the discourse. In these texts the statement changes to "He made her become a real woman."

The sexbattle texts in which man makes woman closely resemble the story of Pygmalion, who, revolted by "the many faults which nature has implanted in the female sex," created an ivory statue called Galatea, whom Venus blessed with life so that "the ivory lost its hardness, and grew soft: his fingers made an imprint on the yielding surface" (Ovid 1964: 231–32).[13] There is one crucial difference: in the battle-of-the-sexes texts,

Venus disappears, and Pygmalion makes his creation real without the aid of a goddess.

My examination of the creation of these Galateas centers on penetrative intercourse and the kiss. To highlight the ways in which this romance narrative works to construct a compliant, heterosexual, "real" woman's body I make a detailed comparison of some key passages of Nelson Bond's story "The Priestess Who Rebelled" and Edmund Cooper's *Who Needs Men?*

In "The Priestess Who Rebelled," set in a postapocalyptical matriarchal world, Meg meets a man, Daiv, who is unlike the soft, weak men who serve her people as breeding stock. He comes from the one unmatriarchal people left on Earth. Meg is on her way to see the Gods, this being the last rite before she becomes the Mother, head priestess of her people. The man, Daiv, tells her that her Gods are men and implores her to be his mate as she is very beautiful—though his first words to her are: "You . . . talk too much. Sit down and eat, Woman!" (208).[14] Before Meg goes to see her Gods, Daiv kisses her, "the touching of mouths," and she is swept off her feet but still determined to do her duty. She arrives at Mount Rushmore, which turns out to be the Place of the Gods, and sees that her Gods are in fact men: Jaarg, Taamuz, Ibrim, and Tedhi. Meg realizes that her sterile, unnatural, virgin existence need not continue: she can become Daiv's mate and live happily ever after.

Who Needs Men? is set in far-future Britain where the only remaining men are fighting for their existence in rugged Scotland.[15] In a skirmish Diarmid MacDiarmid, leader of one rebel band, defeats Rura, an exterminator, the highest caste of the new matriarchal world, whose function is to exterminate men. Diarmid kisses Rura. She is unable to forget him and realizes that sex with women is empty. Eventually Rura is captured by Diarmid and they escape further north to live together. Their idyll does not last, and they are killed by exterminators.

In both "The Priestess Who Rebelled" and *Who Needs Men?* the romance between hero and heroine is the battle of the sexes in miniature. The restoration of the natural order, of male rule and heterosexuality, will follow from this conquest if it is to happen at all. In the sequel to "The Priestess Who Rebelled," "The Judging of the Priestess," the Mother (the head priestess of Meg's Clan) declares that "Meg was right. . . . She rebelled against the Law that said a Priestess might not mate—but she was right in her rebellion. List, now, for with the all-seeing eyes of one on the threshold of death I tell you truth. It is right that Women should mate with

Men. There should be no Workers, no Warriors, no breeding-mother. Our Clan should own no stud-males, pale chattels like . . . horses. All this is wrong" (Bond 1940: 59). Heterosexuality's place at the heart of the transition from female rule is made even more explicit at the end of the "The Judging of the Priestess." One of the Wild Ones asks the Warrior Chieftain of Meg's Clan, Lora, to be his mate: "Lora spoke, and her answer was the answer of all womankind to the new regime. . . . 'You must be mad, Man!' she declared. 'But—but I think I like your madness'" (59). In the 1972 text *Who Needs Men?*, however, the evil matriarchy triumphs and the heroine, Rura, dies with the already dead hero, Diarmid, in her arms.

In both texts a kiss is the turning point in the conversion from matriarchy to patriarchy. In "The Priestess Who Rebelled" the kiss is the climactic, in every sense, moment and it occurs toward the end of the text:

> "There is a custom in our tribe . . . a mating custom which you do not know. Let me show you—"
>
> He leaned over swiftly. Meg felt the mighty strength of his bronzed arms closing about her, drawing her close. And he was touching his mouth to hers; closely, brutally, terrifyingly.
>
> She struggled and tried to cry out, but his mouth bruised hers. Anger-thoughts swept through her like a flame. But it was not anger—it was something else—that gave life to that flame. Suddenly her veins were running with liquid fire. Her heart beat upon rising, panting breasts like something captive that would be free. Her fists beat upon his shoulders vainly . . . but there was little strength in her blows.
>
> Then he released her, and she fell back, exhausted. Her eyes glowed with anger and her voice was husky in her throat. She tried to speak, and could not. And in that moment a vast and terrible weakness trembled through Meg. She knew, fearfully, that if Daiv sought to mate with her, not all the priestessdom of the gods would save her. There was a body-hunger throbbing within her that hated his Manness . . . but cried for it! (Bond [1939] 1972: 216)

This extraordinary passage is a description of a kiss, or rather the touching of mouths. The constraints against representing sex at the time this story was published meant that the it could only represent penetration and orgasm metaphorically and metonymically.[16] The traces of standard representations of intercourse are here throughout: she falls back "exhausted" after the touching of mouths, her eyes "glow" and her voice is "husky." In later versions of this narrative, the kiss is sometimes transformed into penetrative sex that is, at least initially, like this kiss, resisted by the woman. For example in *Who Needs Men?*, the heroine Rura meets an old woman, once an exterminator, who tells her that rape is a myth because

> [n]o woman—particularly an exterminator—who is conscious and uninjured can be raped. So I'll tell you what happened, sweet. I got tired of being punched, and I got tired of struggling uselessly. And the revulsion and the feeling of sickness just sort of died. And the weight on top of me seemed to be—well, interesting. And when he pinioned my arms and bit my throat and dug his fingers into my breast, it all hurt like hell. But, chicken it aroused me. Goddess, how it aroused me. So I let him enter. And he grunted and I groaned, and we thrashed about like a couple of mindless creatures in a frenzy. I tell you, I never knew what a climax was until that red-haired animal squirted his semen into my womb. (Cooper [1972] 1974: 46-47)[17]

Initially she resists and then she discovers that she likes it. Penetration is crucial to her becoming woman. The rapist says to her prior to the rape, "They made an exterminator of you. Now I'll make a woman of you" (46).

In *Who Needs Men?* the kiss appears very close to the beginning of the text, and is just the first step toward Rura's becoming a "real" woman (she needs to be gang-raped and learn to love heterosexual penetrative sex and get pregnant before the process is complete). "He kissed her on the lips. She struggled, but with one arm he managed to hold her. The rifle was dropped. There was something terrible about the kiss. It was like no other kiss she had ever known. It was humiliating, it was degrading, it was disturbing. It drained strength from her limbs, filled her head with nightmares. He let her go. 'Well, exterminator. *That was a kind of rape, was it not?*'" (my emphasis; Cooper [1972] 1974: 24).[18] In *Who Needs Men?* there is no constraint against representing sexual intercourse. Yet the kiss is represented as an extraordinarily powerful force in the text and still functions in a manner very similar to the kiss in "The Priestess Who Rebelled." This passage also links the kiss and rape: "That was a kind of rape, was it not?"

A belief in the necessity of female orgasm to conception, and indeed to heterosexual intercourse, is apparent in *Who Needs Men?* The old woman who tells Rura of her rape became pregnant. Rura also becomes pregnant immediately after having intercourse with her Diarmid. For both women it is the first time they have ever had an orgasm. The belief in the necessity of orgasm to conception is an old one. Thomas Laqueur notes that until the eighteenth century it was widely held that without orgasm women would not wish to engage in sexual intercourse, or find it pleasurable, or conceive (Laqueur [1990] 1992: 3).

The women have vaginal rather than clitoral orgasms: Rura feels Diarmid's sperm "pulse . . . excruciatingly, wonderfully, through her vagina" (Cooper [1972] 1974: 110) and the old woman declares that she "never knew what a climax was until that red-haired animal squirted his semen into my womb" (Cooper [1972] 1974: 47). Both women have unusually sensitive vaginas, vaginas with the same sort of sensitivity as penises—inverted penises, in effect. Inverted penises were a feature of the one-sex model of female anatomy (Laqueur [1990] 1992: 4). Coincidentally, this is exactly how a vagina is constructed for many male-to-female transsexuals. The procedure utilizes the "skin of the penis for the lining of the new vagina and retains a portion of the erogenous tissue from the base of the penis for the clitoris . . . if accomplished correctly, [this] allows for vaginal feeling (even vaginal orgasm) because the penile skin used to line the vagina retains its nerve endings. . . . Success is often measured by the ability to engage in penile-vaginal intercourse" (Hausman 1995: 68–69). Rura's vagina, like those of many male-to-female transsexuals, seems to have been designed specifically so that she will find most pleasurable what most men are supposed to find most pleasurable—penetrative penile intercourse. In this story, for a real woman to orgasm she needs a real man. In many battle-of-the-sexes texts, however, genital stimulation is not a prerequisite for the real woman's orgasm; they can climax from kissing, as in "The Priestess Who Rebelled."

To explore such interrelationships I have analyzed the clauses of the story in terms of the functions of their various elements (for a fuller account of the analysis, see the appendix). In "The Priestess Who Rebelled," Meg is ostensibly the only "sayer" or "senser." However, as it is Daiv who speaks the opening paragraph, he also is an implied sayer. He also speaks, whereas Meg "tries to cry out" but is prevented or "trie[s] to speak" but cannot. Moreover, when she is senser her perceptions are uncertain: in the first paragraph, she does "not know," and later when she does know something it is "fearfully."

Meg isn't the grammatical subject (agent or actor) as much as Daiv, and when she is, her actions are expressed as intransitive verbs, with no object or goal: "She fell back," "She struggled." By contrast, only once does Daiv *not* have a goal: "He leaned over." Normally, Meg is his goal: "Daiv sought to mate with her." However, various parts of Meg's body and emotions/sensations are actors: anger thoughts (presumably hers), her veins, her heart, her fists, her eyes, a vast and terrible weakness (also presumably hers as it "trembles through [her]"). This fragmentation of her body into parts serves to demonstrate that before this kiss she was not an integrated, real woman. Her body is a series of parts which she struggles against and tries vainly to control. Her body parts know what she wants better than she does. The final sentence of this passage sets up this split subjectivity explicitly: "There was a body-hunger [throbbing within her] that hated his Manness but cried for it." The "body-hunger throbbing within her" has consciousness, not Meg, and it is this "body-hunger" that hates "his Manness" but also cries for it. Her body knows what she wants better than she does, and it manifests this knowledge by acting where she does not or cannot. This split subjectivity collocates with the clause that is an indexical feature of the genre of romance, particularly of bodice-rippers—"her body betrayed her."

In my analysis of the kiss passage from *Who Needs Men?* (24), the heroine, Rura, is actor only twice and, as in the passage from "Priestess," she is only actor when she has no effect on anything else. Indeed, one of the clauses also appears in "The Priestess Who Rebelled": "She struggled." The other clause in which Rura is an actor is "He let her go," but she is only actor in a process which he, Diarmid, initiates. Like Rura, Diarmid is actor only twice, but in both cases he affects something, the process extends beyond him to a goal—Rura: "He kissed her"; "With one arm he managed to hold her."

The other actor in the passage is not any of Rura's body parts, as in the previous passage, but the kiss itself: "It [the kiss] drained strength from her limbs." In the previous passage, Meg is overcome by her body's response to the "touching of mouths," or kiss, but the kiss does not become an actor in this extraordinary manner.

The repetitious structure in the kiss passage from *Who Needs Men?*—"It was humiliating, it was degrading, it was disturbing" (24)—highlights the tremendous importance of the kiss. Rura is being transformed by its power, and that transformation into a real woman is "humiliating," "degrading," and "disturbing." This structure of repeated intensive attributive clauses is paralleled in a later passage in *Who Needs Men?*: "'Love me,' said Rura. 'I want to open myself for a man. Love me, please. . . .' Diarmid lay upon her, caressed her, loved her. It was not like the rape of the previous day. It was not like lying with women. It was not like anything she had ever known. It was warm, it was disturbing, it was exciting, it was humiliating, it was proud" (108).[19] The parallelism could not be more exact. Not only is the grammar identical, with the structure "it was x" repeated, but there are also echoes in the lexical choice of "humiliating" and "disturbing." In this passage "it" refers to penetrative penile-vaginal intercourse, in the earlier passage "it" refers to the kiss. In both passages the power of the kiss and then of sexual intercourse is transcendental.

Meg, in "The Priestess Who Rebelled," is never the grammatical subject (actor or agent), but is displaced into other, less direct structures: "Anger-thoughts swept through her"; "Her voice was husky in her throat"; "A vast and terrible weakness trembled through Meg." Daiv is the agent responsible for the process that takes place through the medium of her body. Even when there is no agent in a clause it is not hard to infer that Daiv is the cause of this, as he is the agent responsible for everything else that takes place in the passage: "Her eyes glowed with anger." Meg has no responsibility for the actions and behaviors of her body. Her body is literally not her own. "Her body betrayed her."

A similar analysis of the kiss passage from *Who Needs Men?* reveals that Rura, like Meg, never has agency. She is either the medium, or parts of her become the location for the beginnings of her transformation from exterminator to woman: "He kissed her on the lips." Diarmid, like Daiv in "The Priestess Who Rebelled," is the agent in this clause, the one who causes the kiss to happen. However, in this passage, unlike the passage from "The Priestess Who Rebelled," the kiss is also an agent: "It [the kiss] drained strength from her limbs." Once again Rura's body parts, her limbs, are just places where the action occurs. The centrality of the kiss to the process of becoming a woman is realized in the grammar.

Becoming a Real Man

In worlds where the natural order of things has been disturbed, it is not only females whose sexuality is undermined; the masculinity and virility of males is also corrupted. As I have demonstrated, men can become the "breeders" and "Wild Ones" of "The Priestess Who Rebelled," and once they are in this category they are not real men. However, although the categories are fixed, the bodies within them are fluid. At the end of the sequel to "The Priestess Who Rebelled," "The Judging of the Priestess," one of the Wild Ones has acquired a name, Wilm, and is close to acquiring a mate—once he has bathed to remove "the smell from [his] body" and "shave[d] off that *awful* beard" (Bond 1940: 59). He will be incorporated into the heterosexual economy and become a real man like Daiv.

In Wallace West's "The Last Man" ([1929] 1972) the eponymous hero,

M-1, believes what his custodians tell him: "But the world was perfect now, M-1 realised. No further change was necessary. He grew ashamed of his suggestions that new discoveries might be made. Everything was known! Life was complete, vibrant! The millennium was at hand, and he was the only discordant factor" (109). It is the atavistic woman Eve who teaches M-1 to recognize that the matriarchy is stagnant and decaying. She seeks him out and utters blasphemies that he tells her are "wicked" (110). Eve introduces the idea of escape and begins the process that will make M-1 into a real man, using the transcendental effect of her real woman's body:

> They stopped and looked at each other under the moon, which had just passed the zenith. A great wave of tenderness and admiration swept over him. Awkwardly he seized both her hands in his.
>
> "You're so different," he marvelled. "You make me feel queer here." He tapped his chest. "Like tears," he stumbled, "and sunshine and flowers."
>
> She smiled, and leaning forward, gently touched her lips to his. A shock, like that from a dynamo, passed through him. He leaped back as though she had struck him, then reapproached.
>
> "What was that?" he asked stupidly.
>
> "A kiss," she answered. (West [1929] 1972: 116)

The parallels between this passage and the touching-of-mouths passage from "The Priestess Who Rebelled" are obvious. The kiss overwhelms and an orgasmic wave passes through his body. However, the roles are reversed—Eve, the heroine, is the agent and the hero's lips are the place where the action is realized: "She touched her lips to his." Although Eve is the agent, the encounter is not violent as the kisses are in "Priestess" (1939) and *Who Needs Men?* (1972). Eve touches her lips to M-1's "gently," Daiv's touches his mouth to Meg's "closely, brutally, terrifyingly."

This kiss seals M-1's rejection of the matriarchy, "the human hive" (105).[20] Eve also renames M-1, "My name is Eve. . . . I gave it to myself. I have forgotten my number. . . . I shall call you Adam" (117) and suggests they escape into the wilderness:

> "We are doomed. I see it all so clearly now. There can be no more progress. There can be no more superman to drag mankind forward in spite of its blindness."
>
> "No," Eve whispered, "but there are atavists to drag mankind backward to a point where it can get a fresh start."

> The idea dazzled him. "You mean—we—we could have children—and build a new, clean, race?" (121)

From that moment on Adam begins to behave like a real man and Eve ceases to initiate all the action. He comforts her when she bursts into tears, and when they hatch a plan together to blow up the "life factory" Adam announces that it is his "place to do this thing" (126). Adam's blossoming masculinity causes the text to try to rewrite itself describing the "growing love between the last man and the woman *he had now chosen as his mate*" (my emphasis; 124). Eve chose Adam; now, although she made Adam into a real man, once he has become a man she cannot initiate anything without threatening his newly acquired manhood.

Mama Come Home: Parodies of the Sex War?

Some battle-of-the-sexes texts are not predicated on the idea that female rule is wrong and do not necessarily reinscribe the natural order of things. Some typical examples are *Search the Sky* (1954), by two of the so-called Futurians, Frederik Pohl and Cyril Kornbluth; John Wyndham's "Consider Her Ways" (1956); James Tiptree Jr.'s "Mama Come Home" ([1968] 1973);[21] and Bruce McAllister's "Ecce Femina!" (1972). Pohl and Kornbluth's *Search the Sky* is described by Russ as containing "a brief satiric sketch of a role-reversal society" (1980: 13). Sam J. Lundwall says that the novel gives a "wry, tongue-in-cheek account of a world run by women" where "career men are frowned upon [and] the male protagonist is regarded as little more than a talking parrot when he starts to explain things to a leading business-woman. . . . The protagonist is even subjected to an attempted rape by a drunk (female) truck driver. And suddenly he isn't a hero any longer—he's just a decorative piece of furniture to be admired and used. If this seems farfetched, look around you. You have it everywhere here and now, only it is the other way around" (Lundwall [1969] 1971: 149).[22]

There are moments in this sequence from *Search the Sky* when I find the satire effective, as in these wedding vows: "Marylyn, you have chosen to share part of your life with this man. You intend to bear his children. This should not be because your animal appetites have overcome you and you can't win his consent in any other way but because you know, down deep in your womanly heart, that you can make him happy. Never forget this. If you should thoughtlessly conceive by some other man, don't tell him. He would only brood" (99). The hero observes that the groom is crying and decides that he "doesn't blame the poor sucker"; then "being a man of conscience" he wonders "if that was why on Halsey's Planet [his home planet] women cry at weddings" (99). Yet the heroine is shown as helpless and giggling, and when she works out how to operate the F-T-L drive it is because she is an idiot savant (107). The novel ends with this sentence: "Eventually he set up the combinations for Halsey's Planet on the Wesley Board. Helena was beside him, proud and close, as he threw in the drive" (169).

"Consider Her Ways" by John Wyndham, first published in 1956 is often cited as an early example of science fiction's engagement with questions of feminism. The heroine, Dr. Jane Summers, whose husband has been killed recently, volunteers to be a guinea pig for the testing of a drug. After taking the drug she wakes to find her mind in the body of a breeding mother in a future matriarchal world where all the men died centuries earlier as the result of a virus. The story's center is some twenty pages of dialogue between Jane and Laura, an esteemed historian of her age. Jane asks how the world managed to survive without the men. Laura gives her a condensed history of the role the discourse of romance has had in subjugating women:

> When the crisis came it turned out that hardly any of them knew how to do any of the important things because they had nearly all been owned by men, and had to lead their lives as pets and parasites. . . .
>
> It wasn't their fault. . . . They were caught up in a process, and everything conspired against their escape. It was a long process, going right back to the eleventh century, in Southern France. The Romantic conception started there as an elegant and amusing fashion for the leisured classes. Gradually, as time went on, it permeated through most levels of society, but it was not until the latter part of the nineteenth century that its commercial possibilities were intelligently perceived, and not until the twentieth that it was really exploited. . . .
>
> You see, the great hopes for the emancipation of women with which the century had started had been outflanked. Purchasing power had passed into the hands of the ill-educated and highly-suggestible. The desire for Romance is essentially a selfish wish, and when it is encouraged to dominate every other it breaks down all corporate loyalties. The individual woman thus separated from, and yet at the same time thrust into competitions with, all other women was almost defenceless; she became the prey of organized suggestion. When it was represented to her that

the lack of certain goods or amenities would be fatal to Romance she became alarmed, and thus, eminently exploitable. (1965: 48–51).

Jane is appalled and does not recognize this description of her world. She argues that this matriarchal world is one without love, and Laura observes that Jane is "repeating . . . the propaganda of [her] age. The love you talk about, my dear, existed in your little sheltered part of the world by polite and profitable convention. You were scarcely ever allowed to see its other face, unglamorized by Romance. *You* were never openly bought and sold, like livestock; *you* never had to sell yourself to the first-comer in order to live; *you* did not happen to be one of the women who through the centuries have screamed in agony and suffered and died under invaders in a sacked city" (60).

Sam Lundwall quotes part of this dialogue about romantic love and argues that while the dialogue "might not give much blood to the debate . . . it is still a healthy sign of science fiction recognizing the problem" ([1969] 1971: 151). Kingsley Amis calls "Consider Her Ways" a rare example of "female-emancipationism" in science fiction (1960: 99). He also quotes a large chunk of the text's central dialogue, commenting that "Laura is not only a thoughtful and intelligent person but gets the best of the argument, saying all that can be said for the notion that women would be better off without men and making what seem to me some fairly damaging criticisms of the contemporary female role" (77–78). Joanna Russ says that "Consider Her Ways" is a "pro-feminist discussion of romantic love and the feminine mystique" (1980: 13). She has reservations, however, and observes parenthetically that "Wyndham creates another of those beehive-like societies structured by biological engineering" (13). (The society is, in fact, deliberately modeled on ants.) I would add another criticism. It seems fairly extraordinary that there would be no lesbianism or masturbation in an all-female world; once again the assumption is that without men there can be no sex.

Russ includes Bruce McAllister's "Ecce Femina!," first published in *Fantasy and Science Fiction* in February 1972, among her "Flasher" texts. After reading her account of "Ecce Femina!" I expected another *Who Needs Men?* but found instead a satirical text. Russ characterizes this humor as "unintentional" (1980: 13). But Russ's satire "The Cliches from Outer Space" ([1984] 1985) includes "The Turnabout Story," which is remarkably similar to "Ecce Femina!" It features a "ravaging, man-hating, vicious, hulking, Lesbian, sadistic, fetishistic Women's Libbers" motorcycle gang who terrorize the hero, George (33).[23] However, the moments in

McAllister's story when a motorcycle gang member called Queen Elizabeth uses "soda pop for strange purposes" (127), and the gang members call each other "brother-muckers" (131), seem to me far from "unintentionally" funny. It is true the magazine blurb that accompanies "Ecce Femina!" does not encourage a reading of the text as satire: "Here's something different from Bruce McAllister: a tough and pungent extrapolation of women's lib" (*Magazine of Fantasy and Science Fiction* 42, no. 2 [February 1972]: 117). Nonetheless, I read the text as a "tough and pungent extrapolation" of men's *fears* of "women's lib," and a fairly dark one too. Most of the text is a role reversal, with female rather than male bikers in the Hell's Angels mold. The women bikers become masculine and uncontrollable as a result of shooting up with E9. One man tells the narrator Mac how "he had gotten sick and tired of supporting her—her bike, her E9, her arrogance, her appetite, her perversions" (133).

Unlike the other stories I have covered in this chapter, "Ecce Femina" is not told from the point of view of one of the heterosexual pairings at its center. The story is told by an observer, Mac. The pairing is between Jack, who is the biggest and most violent of the women and runs her own garage, and a beaten and abused man, Oscar, or "papa," who is brought in by the local motorcycle gang. She adds to the violent abuse the man has suffered and then nurses him back to health and keeps the gang members away from him. When one of the gang stabs Oscar, Jack kills her, and, in a parody of the me-Tarzan-you-Jane scenario of many of these texts, she grabs the injured Oscar, who struggles against her: "[S]he hit him. He went out, and in one easy motion she slung him over her shoulder" (142). The text ends ambiguously with the narrator Mac looking at a photo that Jack and Oscar have sent him of Jack, with her muscle gone to fat, holding a baby: "No matter how you look at the picture, her eyes seem to be looking at you. They follow you around. And you can't tell whether she is smiling or not. But then, you never could" (144).

While Russ does not read "Ecce Femina!" as a commentary on the sex war, she does read Tiptree's "Mama Come Home" in this way. Russ argues that "Mama Come Home" is one of the "few attempts to write thoughtfully about the Sex War." According to Russ the explanation for the story's "odd" treatment of the sex war, "both inverting some of its elements and commenting critically on others . . . is not far to seek. As the SF community now knows, 'James Tiptree Jr' is the pseudonym of Alice Sheldon. A woman does not, obviously, have the same stake in the myth as male authors may have" (Russ 1980: 12).

Amanda Boulter, in her article "Alice James Raccoona Sheldon Tiptree Sheldon Jr: Textual Personas in the Short Fiction of Alice Sheldon," discusses this tendency to read "a feminist subtext" in all of Tiptree's work and asks, "[R]eading with hindsight what precisely do we choose to see?" (1995: 6). When the story was first published James Tiptree Jr. was not known "to be" Alice Sheldon. Russ argues that "Mama Come Home" inverts some of the elements of the sex war and comments critically on others (Russ 1980: 12). I would argue that this is also true of "Ecce Femina!" Russ's knowledge of Tiptree's hidden "true" sex makes her more alert to the satire and subversion in Tiptree's work than she is in McAllister's story. This does not mean, however, that she is uncritical: Russ also argues that the heroine of "Mama Come Home," Tillie, is "presented as without family, without friends, indeed without a social context of any kind. Thus her choice is—as it is in all these stories, for all the heroines—between evil (or in some cases decaying and sterile) female tyranny and some version of the hero, i.e. men" (Russ 1980: 12).

"Mama Come Home," like Tiptree's more famous story "The Women Men Don't See" (1973), is told in the first person. The narrator is Max, a hard-boiled CIA agent who is, in the tradition of Philip Marlowe, a chivalric romantic, a sweet misogynist. Aliens land from the planet Capella. According to the blurb that accompanied the story's original publication in the June 1968 issue of *If*: they are "brainy, lovely, man-crazy—and eight and a half feet tall!" (81). Like the women in Richard Wilson's book *The Girls from Planet Five* (1955), the women are considerably taller than their male counterparts,[24] blond, and beautiful, and their intentions toward Earth are not good. However, in *The Girls from Planet Five* the alien women, the Lyru, are controlled by the evil Crones, whereas the Capellan women act for themselves.

The Capellan women use men as slaves and sex toys. The story revolves around defeating the Capellans, but according to Joanna Russ, as in many of the other battle-of-the-sexes stories "[t]he real struggle is for Tillie's loyalty, and it is her conversion to loving the hero that is the center of the story" (Russ 1980: 12). Tillie's coldness toward men has a cause: "Tillie at fifteen had caught the full treatment from a street gang. Fought against knives, left for dead—an old story. They'd fixed her up as good as new, except for a few interesting white hairlines in her tan, and a six-inch layer of ice between her and everybody who shaved" (Tiptree [1968] 1973, 60).

Tillie is operating outside the heterosexual economy, and the story details her reincorporation. Unlike the women in the stories discussed earlier, she is not overpowered by a kiss or sexual intercourse but by the proof that the Capellans are not her saviors, that they are rapists. When the Capellans get out of their spaceship and it becomes apparent that they are all very tall, the narrator, Max, sees "a funny look on Tillie's face. Several girls were suppressing themselves, and Mrs. Peabody seemed to feel an egg hatching in her uplift. The men looked like me—tense. Right then I would have settled for green octopuses instead of these good-looking girls" (57).

Tillie looks just like a Capellan, but one who is only five foot tall. They adopt her as a kind of pet. Max the narrator sees Tillie becoming more and more involved with the Capellans and tries to warn her about them: "You think your big playmates are just like yourself, only gloriously immune from rape. I wouldn't be surprised if you weren't thinking of going home with them. Right? No, don't tell me kid, I know you. But you don't know *them*. You think you do, but you don't. Did you ever meet any American blacks who moved to Kenya? Talk to one some time" (64). This collapsing of race and sex so that white women's oppression and otherness is made equivalent to that of African American men with no African American women in sight is a sleight of hand that is sometimes practiced in white feminist writing (Spelman 1988; hooks 1984; Ang 1995).

When Max is eventually raped by the Capellans, he says "My next clear view was from the ground where I was discovering some nasty facts about Capellan physiology through a blaze of pain. (Ever think about being attacked by a *musth* vacuum cleaner?)" (66). Tillie's allegiances start to shift: "The American black who goes to Kenya often discovers he is an American first and an African second, no matter what they did to him in Newark. . . . She swung back her hair, slowly. I could see mad dreams dying in her eyes" (71).

In order to defeat the Capellans Tillie has to relive her own rape. This disturbs the balance between Tillie and Max because it means that she has, in a sense, been raped *twice* and he only once. A trap is set to force the alien women, who want to use human men as sex toys, to go home. At the same time, as Russ argues, the story details the traps that are set for Tillie so that she too will come home to the heterosexual economy. However, Tillie's reincorporation is not the joyous one that it is for Meg in "The Priestess Who Rebelled." She can barely talk about it: "The closest we came—then or ever—to an explanation was over the avocado counter. 'It's all relative, isn't it?' she said to the avocados. 'It is indeed,' I replied. And really, that was it. If the Capellans could bring us the news that we were inferior mutations, somebody could bring them the word that they were inferior mutations. If big, hairy Mama could come back and surprise her runt relations, a bigger, hairier Papa could appear and surprise Mama" (78).

Tillie, like her sexbattle compatriots of the texts that I have been looking at, has been coerced into heterosexuality, into being a real woman. The difference is that her reincorporation into heterosexuality does not physically transform her. She is with Max because her dream of a women's utopia, free from rape, has been dashed, not because of the magical force of a kiss. Despite the overwhelming pessimism about the relations between men and women there are still remnants of the real man and real woman ethos. Tillie is asked about the male Capellan Mavrua—"He's—I don't know—like gay only not" (70). Max studies him on the monitors and notes that "as Tillie said, queer but not. Clean-cut, muscular, good grin; gonads okay. Something sapless in the eyes" (71). Clearly he is not a real man. Yet it is the story's hero who is raped and the heroine who rescues him from that rape. Max observes that "[a]nalogic reasoning works when you have the right frame. We need a new one. For instance, look at the way the Capellans overturned our psychic scenery, our view of ourselves as integral to this world. Or look at their threat to our male-dominant structure. Bigger, more dominant women who treat our males as sex-slave material" (71–72). But the psychic shock is overcome and life continues. Tillie has resigned herself to life behind enemy lines but will not talk about her capitulation. This is the same kind of coping strategy that is adopted by the mother and daughter in another Tiptree story, "The Women that Men Don't See" : "What women do is survive. We live by ones and twos in the chinks of your world-machine" (Tiptree [1973] 1990: 140). I discuss this story in chapter 5.

"Mama Come Home" is as inconsistent and as contradictory as "Ecce Femina!," "Consider Her Ways," or *Search the Sky*. Male rule is revealed, either by implication (as in *Search the Sky* and "Ecce Femina!") or directly (as in "Consider Her Ways" and "Mama Come Home"), as violent and oppressive to women. Romantic love operates within the heterosexual order to keep women in their place. On the other hand, different knowledges about women and their biological inferiority are upheld: in *Search the Sky* the heroine is considerably less capable than the hero and depends upon him; in "Consider Her Ways" the only society women can bring about for themselves free of the tyranny of romantic love is a near-fascist one modeled on ants; in "Ecce Femina!" the tough mountain of a heroine Jack melts into motherhood; and in "Mama Come Home" Tillie gives way to the narrator without a murmur because "[I]t's all relative, isn't it?" On this level there is no difference between the texts I have discussed in this section and texts such as "The Priestess Who Rebelled" and *Who Needs Men?*—both groups of texts lay open the necessity of the heterosexual economy for making a female into a "real" woman.

3 PAINWISE

Hermaphroditism and Other Solutions

In the final section of "*Amor Vincit Foeminam*," Russ mentions some texts that "appear to be pro-feminist in intention": Frederik Pohl and Cyril Kornbluth's *Search the Sky* (1954), John Wyndham's "Consider Her Ways" (1956), Theodore Sturgeon's *Venus Plus X* (1960), and Mack Reynolds's *Amazon Planet* (1966) (Russ 1980: 13). I considered *Search the Sky* and "Consider Her Ways" in chapter 2; in this chapter I examine *Venus Plus X* and *Amazon Planet*, along with other works that offer solutions or alternatives to the conflict between the sexes that do not involve the reinscription of male rule. These texts envisage worlds in which

- men recognize that women are not necessarily the "weaker" sex—Robert Vaughan's "The Woman from Space" (1932), Philip Wylie's *The Disappearance* (1951), Robert Silverberg's "Woman's World" (1957), and Reynolds's *Amazon Planet* (1966)
- women establish a society without men in which the lack of men is not a problem—Russ's "When It Changed" (1972)
- there is only one sex, which is hermaphrodite or androgynous—Katherine Burdekin's *Proud Man* (1934), Sturgeon's *Venus Plus X*, and Ursula Le Guin's *The Left Hand of Darkness* (1969)

In the texts that posit "equality" between the sexes, the economy of heterosexuality that I examined in the previous chapter is still firmly in place. Relations between the sexes are centered on sexual exchange and reproduction. The second group, represented by Joanna Russ's story "When It Changed," comprises the texts that embody what Russ calls "feminist utopias" in her essay of the same name (1981). Her own story, one of the first of the type, is a direct response to many of the assumptions of the earlier battle-of-the-sexes texts. The last group posits a hermaphrodite or androgynous world where sexual difference has been erased. These one-sexed worlds, however, have been so frequently read as all-male worlds that the erasure of difference becomes instead the removal of women.

Equality?

I discovered a number of stories that purport to offer "equality" between the sexes as an end to the sex war. Not all of these texts, however, have the same understanding of what equality between men and women means.

Richard Vaughan's "The Woman from Space" was published in the spring 1932 edition of *Wonder Stories Quarterly*. Sam Moskowitz gives the following plot synopsis:

> The women of an as yet undiscovered planet between Neptune and Pluto unwillingly take over when their men have virtually destroyed themselves. . . . They develop an extraordinary science and successfully clear the asteroid belt, then move their planet into a new orbit to be closer to the sun. The earth, rendered almost uninhabitable by a star that has brushed too close to our solar system, has lost most of its women. The two worlds, one almost devoid of men, the other short of women, agree to a happy accommodation. So logical an attitude was not long to prevail in science fiction. (Moskowitz 1972: 16–17)

The women of the planet Arion seized power because it was the only way to stop the men from destroying themselves and the planet. The women's motivation for seizure of power is in marked contrast to the desire for power and the subjugation or elimination of men that is the most common reason for women's usurpation of control in the texts I examined in chapter 2. The women of Arion are brilliant, and their society is not stagnant like many of the matriarchal societies of the previous chapter, nor is it modeled on ants, termites, or bees.[1] The Aronian women have built a technology and civilization far superior to that of Earth. The heroine, who is telepathic, tells the hero, "I sense from some of your thoughts that your civilization is not quite the equal of ours, is perhaps younger in evolution" (Vaughan 1932: 369).

The story's hero, Dirk Sarrazin, is Earth's most formidable scientist. Sarrazin first meets one of the Aronian women, Lella, when she lands on

Earth as part of a team of intrepid explorers who have been sent out to explore the new galaxy. Sarrazin is dazzled by his first sighting of an Aronian:

> It was apparently of a shape similar to that of an earthly being and was completely covered by a transparent, glassy envelope or suit, as supple as gauze. Through it a pair of enormous and brilliant eyes looked at him curiously. Its skin, where visible, was the loveliest, luminous blue that Dirk had ever seen, its features human in outline, yet strangely alien, as though the spirit behind them were of another essence and tempered in unknown fires.
>
> Although standing a foot or so taller than his own goodly height, it seemed almost to float with an effect of airy grace instantly noticeable and arresting as though it was impervious to the influences of gravity. Yet a sense of power and authority dominated all its effects. (367)

The description is of an alien, whose sex is unknown at this stage in the story. In 1932 it would have been automatic to assume that an alien landing on Earth in a science fiction story was male, yet Sarrazin uses the pronoun "it," the generic pronoun. The title of the story, "The Woman from Space," and the use of the pronoun "it" seem to indicate that the alien is at least not a man, but it does not account for the way this being is described: it is "transparent," "glassy," "supple," "enormous," "brilliant," "loveliest," "luminous," "arresting," "impervious," and has an "airy grace" and at the same time "a sense of power and authority dominated all its effects." Most of the description fits the beautiful women of countless science fiction stories, yet "power and authority" do not. Both sets of attributes, however, the grace *and* the power, remain Lella's throughout the text. Both sets are, in fact, linked in medieval religious discourses on saints' lives and mystical experience.[2] It appears that Sarrazin has seen not an alien, but a saint or angel.

Sarrazin initially finds it very difficult to believe that beauty, power, and intelligence could be a woman's:

> Sarrazin's eyes opened as the conception of a dominatingly feminine planet, infinitely distant, yet a part of his own solar world, dawned on his mind for the first time. The undeniable beauty of the being from space seemed more natural now that he knew it to be feminine. Although Earth had not lacked for brilliant women in the last few centuries, he found it hard to believe that the virile power of the mind he found dealing with his could normally belong to a woman. That a being who

> could navigate alone and undaunted the boundless realms of space could be, even though of a different race, one of what on Earth was called the gentler sex. (369)

The choice of "virile" here to modify the nominalization the "power of the mind" is telling. Lella literally has a mind like a man. This construction is a projection of the mental process "found it hard to believe." The nominalization "the power of the mind" operates within the Cartesian mind/body split and locates manly power explicitly in the mind. It is this virile mind-power of Lella's that is the "actor" dealing with" "his [mind]." Nevertheless, although it is *her* power of the mind, she is written out of the passage, becoming a generalized "woman" or "being." By contrast, at the beginning of this passage, mind is attributed directly to Sarrazin: "a conception . . . dawned on his mind for the first time." There is a fusing here of the conception of the body, which is the prerogative of the female, and the conception of the mind, which is the prerogative of the male.

Lella also has to reconcile herself to Dirk Sarrazin's difference from her people's ideas of "manly" behavior, and tells him:

> No Aronian man would have been permitted to venture, as you have done, on a voyage through space, and it has seemed continually strange to me to see a man daring the same dangers as a woman and thinking with a mind equal to hers . . . stranger, indeed, than if you had been some alien form of life.
>
> According to Aronian ideas, you are more like a woman than a man; I can see that you, with your Earthly conceptions, think I am more like a man than a woman. Our men are of a timid, slothful disposition; they are capricious and weak in capacity for endurance or action. Little is to be expected of them intellectually, though now and then they have produced a distinguished mind! (372)

On both planets a binary shaping of sex difference prevails. Daring and the mind are the prerogative of the valorized sex. On each planet it is the "mind" sex that is dominant, while the "weak" sex dwindles. Both planets are entirely heterosexual: "In our world one sees none but women. The men are so rare as to be considered too precious to expose to the hazards of every day life. How happy your planet must be! With us, only one woman in a thousand may mate; and even then she can only keep her husband five years, unless he expressly refuses to leave her, for which he is considered unpatriotic. Only one woman in a thousand can be a mother" (369).

The two planets begin to come together through the joining of the hero and heroine, Sarrazin and Lella: "Would you take an Earthman for your mate Lella?" he [Dirk] asked her hoarsely. She trembled in his arms and her eyes answered before her words. Dirk caught her close and for a moment she was as feminine and clinging as any woman of Earth" (373). Although there is no kiss, this moment is similar to the kisses analyzed in the previous chapter, which were the site of the inscription of the heterosexual order. The contact with a real man robs Lella of speech, and her body answers before her mind. Dirk is the actor, and Lella, his goal. As a result, she carries the attributes of a proper Earth woman, femininity and clinginess. However, in the question Dirk asks, it is Lella who is the actor, taking the Earthman, her goal, as her mate. This is also the grammar of a traditional marriage proposal, "Will you marry me?" Traditionally it is the man who asks, as does Sarrazin here.

There is a rhetoric of equality between the two that Lella calls on while at the same time calling Dirk a "demi-god":

> She told him that she had loved him when first she saw him. . . . After the weak men of Arion he had seemed like a demi-god and companionship with him through the endless day of space had shown her that here was that thing undreamt of on her planet . . . a mate who was an equal and a friend.
>
> "Imagine what you are to me, whose mothers have known only the inferior men of Arion," she said when Sarrazin told her what she was to him . . . all the things man looks for in man and all those he dreams of in a woman. (373)

On Arion, Sarrazin meets an Aronian man, Luthor, who is not like the other inferior men of Arion. Dirk "rejoiced at the proof . . . [Luthor] presented, that the men of Arion were the victims of environment rather than of inherent weakness" (376). There is nothing in the text that suggests that the Earth women might also be "the victims of environment rather than of inherent weakness."

The women use their science to move their planet closer to Earth. Sarrazin says of this future union: "A few generations of intermarriage between Arion and Earth would equalize somewhat the proportion of men and women here, and the situation would become normal, so that each woman could have the right to marry if she chose, and men would be free as they were in the very old days" (377). Sarrazin talks only of an improvement in the status of Aronian men; he says nothing about how the relations between Earth and Arion would affect the status of Earth women. Indeed, there are no Earth women anywhere in the story. When Lella and Sarrazin discuss their future life together, Lella says:

> Arion needs me and I cannot refuse her my services. There will be much special exploration to do once we have achieved the success of this plan (moving Arion closer to Earth), but neither can you deprive the Earth of your knowledge, or live perpetually on Arion the life of one secondary to myself. We must divide our time fairly between our two worlds. In Arion you must be Lella's husband, though even there your position will be different and higher than that of our Aronian men. On Earth, I shall be only Dirk Sarrazin's wife, and proud of my husband. Perhaps one day, after years of intercourse between Arion and Earth, men and women will come to have an equal importance on both planets. It is possible that we can help to bring that day closer. (379)

Lella raises the possibility of a time when all men and all women of both planets will have "equal importance." In the same speech, however, she accepts the status of an Earth woman while on Earth, while Dirk will enjoy superior status to Arion men (though not as high as Arion women). Also, like the Lyru women of *The Girls from Planet Five* (1955), Lella has shrunk in height. At the beginning of the text, when Lella is still referred to as an "it" and is still potentially male or something else, the Aronian is described as "standing a foot or so taller than [Dirk's] own goodly height" (367). Once Lella has acquired the female pronoun and has agreed to be Dirk's mate, she ceases to be a foot taller, and is able to "lean against his [Dirk's] strong shoulder" (376). The hegemonic force of the discourse of romance is irresistible.

In "Woman's World" by Robert Silverberg, published in the June 1957 issue of *Imagination Science Fiction*, the hero volunteers to be put into deep sleep and sent into the future because of the "bust-up of [his] engagement" (110). He finds himself in a matriarchal world. The role reversal is immediately obvious because the women are called Phil and Sam, and the men Lola and Clara. He is seized by the men as a savior who will lead a revolt against the women. He wakes up to discover that none of it was real; he was merely "under-going preliminary psychological tests" before being put in the "somnocasket" (113).[3] On discovering that his experiences in the women-dominated world were induced dreams the hero decides not to go into the future:

> I knew now that there was no sense in running off to the future; things weren't any simpler there.

> I knew what I would do: I would find my girl, take her out someplace [*sic*], talk over all our misunderstandings. I was confident we'd patch things up somehow.
>
> All I had to do to make our marriage work was be a little more considerate—and let her share the responsibilities, instead of trying to run the whole show myself. Yes, I thought, as I started down the familiar dirty old twentieth-century street. Women needed to be given more responsibility in running things. (114)

Women need to be the beneficiary of "more responsibility in running things"—a gift bestowed upon them by the men. If only men would treat women well, the world would be a better place and open warfare between men and women would be avoided. It is no surprise that the hero's "girl" is not the actor in any of these clauses, any more than women are in the final sentence.

Philip Wylie's *The Disappearance* (1951) appears to be making a similar argument to that of "Woman's World"—if only men would treat women better we would not have the tension between the sexes that exists. The contemporary unequal relationship between men and women is the fault of the men. In *The Disappearance*, on 14 February at 4:04 (and fifty two seconds) in the afternoon, all the men disappear from the world the women inhabit, and all the women from that of the men. For four years they inhabit parallel worlds on Earth. The story focuses on William Percival Gaunt—mostly referred to as Gaunt—his wife, Paula, and their struggles to cope with their newly unisex worlds. More chapters are devoted to Gaunt and the men's struggle to deal with the Disappearance (it is capitalized throughout the text) than the women's. Gaunt is called to Washington, along with other experts, to decide what to do. While they are gathered together, the Soviets threaten to attack them. Nuclear bombs are exchanged—the USSR is devastated, as is a great deal of the United States. In the women's world, a Soviet ship of "liberation" comes to the United States and contact is established; the women becoming friends rather than enemies and pledge to help one another. The odds against the women are large because of their relative lack of professional and trade training. In the men's world there is lawlessness and fascism. In the final chapter, "Home-Coming and Conclusion," they all return to where they were at that final moment before the Disappearance: Gaunt at his desk, Paula in the garden, the two worlds have been reunited. They have not forgotten what happened, and the Earth is full of joy and happiness at having survived God's trial, or whatever the Disappearance was.

Kingsley Amis, in *New Maps of Hell*, discusses *The Disappearance* at some length, observing that only in science fiction could such an "examination not only of the part played by sex in contemporary society, but of the whole inner nature of sexual difference" take place (1960: 75). An entire chapter of *The Disappearance* consists of just this sort of speculation, which Wylie calls "[a]n essay on the philosophy of sex, or the lack thereof, extraneous to the narrative and yet its theme, which the impatient may skip and the reflective might enjoy" (Wylie 1951: 216). Robert Scholes, in "A Footnote to Russ's 'Recent Feminist Utopias,'" has this to say about *The Disappearance*: "If I could add a footnote to Russ's essay it would be to mention Philip Wylie's neglected novel *The Disappearance*. . . . But for our present purposes one important idea emerges: though both worlds are horrible enough for everyone to desire a return to a world with two sexes, the women's world is not anywhere near as horrible as the men's. I think Wylie reached this conclusion in spite of himself, by honest extrapolation; and I think any honest extrapolation would arrive at the same result" (1981: 86).

There is no moment when Gaunt has a sense of relief at Paula's disappearance, whereas Paula,

> [i]f she had told the truth to herself, . . . would have admitted that at times and in certain ways the absence of Bill had compensations. . . . She enjoyed *management* free of criticism and safe from arbitrary change, change without adequate reason (from her viewpoint) and without notice. She appreciated being given, even by universal tragedy, her own way in every personal matter. She had put to good use the good brain she owned; she was in every possible respect, her family's head as a result. Besides, in a moment of national crisis, she had been valuable. Such conditions and facts were satisfying to a hitherto frustrated element of her nature. (Wylie 1951: 201)

Gaunt comes to believe that men have long been thwarting women. In his essay on the philosophy of sex he writes that "woman's dilemma has for ages been far greater than even she imagined. . . . [I]t was not ameliorated in modern times, and . . . largely male attitudes have been the occasion of it all" (228). According to Gaunt, men have to learn that a "'person' is a-man-plus-a-woman; with one or the other absent, there is no person" (233). Other male characters come to the same conclusion. Teddy, who has had a brief affair with Gaunt's wife, Paula, asks Gaunt rhetorically, "What in hell *is* a woman but a part of the whole person?" (195). And the clergyman Connauth announces after men and women are reunited: "There is only one sex, Bill! Woman, man, are halves" (348).

In his essay, Gaunt stresses the sameness between men and women: "The *actual* differences between the sexes of genus *Homo* are not very great. Some women are larger than most men; some have bigger brains than most men; some are stronger. It is quite possible that by the use of genetics mankind could have reversed all conventional tendencies" (228).

In stressing this sameness, *The Disappearance,* while being informed by two centuries of a predominantly two-sex model, harks back to an earlier model of the relationship between man and woman, Laqueur's one-sex universe. Women and men, in Laqeur's model, are composed of the same liquids, *both* excreting sperm and having essentially the same genitalia. Women are "inverted, and hence less perfect men" (Laqueur [1990] 1992: 26). Laqueur argues that, according to Galen,

> [n]othing could be more obvious . . . than to imagine women as men. For the dullard who could not grasp the point immediately, Galen offers a step-by-step thought experiment:
>
> Think first, please, of the man's [external genitalia] turned in and extending inward between the rectum and the bladder. If this should happen the scrotum would necessarily take the place of the uterus with the testes lying outside, next to it on either side.
>
> The penis becomes the cervix and vagina, the perpuce becomes the female pudenda, and so forth on through various ducts and blood vessels. (30)

Both men and women, he states, produce semen: "[M]ale and female semen . . . stand in the same relationship to blood that penis and vagina stand to genital anatomy, extruded and still-inside organs" (40). This understanding of the relationship between male and female biology is echoed in *The Disappearance:*

> Mankind has everywhere emphasized the sex *differences.* He has only recently known much of the *identities and parallels.* . . . The epithelial cords from the seminiferous tubes—or the mesenchyme. The Graafian follicle comes into being in one sex; in the other, from the same tissue, a transitory network in the mesovarium. The mesovarium in the female is, in the male foetus, mesorchium. Paroophoron and organ of Gir-

> aldes; common Wolffian duct—and Mullerian duct, becoming Fallopian tubes, uterus, and perhaps vagina in the female, uterus masculinus in the male. So, endlessly, the anatomical parallel continues. And while each emergent body of protoplasm takes up its appointed form and situation, neither male nor female lacks in embryo the same entities, or their rudiments or vestiges. Our outward organs appear greatly different only to the mind that does not intimately know how alike they are and of what identical tissues they have been composed. How superficial, then, how *ignorant* it is to postulate an important differentness of spermatozoa or ova, clitorises or penes or any other aspect or characteristic of the sexes! (Wylie 1951: 229)

And later, "We—male and female—are the same flesh and the flesh is beautiful. We have all the same organs, differing only in speciality. The same chemicals course in us both. When we love each other it is the same love. When we lie together we are in solemn truth that One. And until men made it so, in prestigious excesses of egotism, no such thing existed as a woman and no such thing existed as a man" (233).

Gaunt, like the writers of the editorial blurbs I examined in chapter 2, refers to the discovery of hormones. However, for Gaunt hormones are a sign of sameness, not difference. His arguments have more in common with Nelly Oudshoorn's (1994) arguments about sex hormones. Gaunt says:

> Lately we have discovered "sex" hormones: male, female. To the disquietude of some, we have also learned that each sex possesses both and that no more than a slight preponderance of one over the other exists in either sex. With pragmatic zeal we have caused cockscombs to grow on hens and found that female hormones relieve to some degree cancerous conditions of the prostate. We have even somewhat changed personality by injection, and disoriented libido. We might have done better. We might, for instance have wondered more what such facts *mean*. (230)

These arguments have much in common with those of liberal feminists such as Mary Wollstonecraft, Harriet Taylor, and Betty Friedan who accept "the underlying conception of human nature" but feel that there has been a startling omission, a blunder, in the treatment of women (Jaggar 1982: 21).

Gaunt's point of view is the opposite of a traditional one, succinctly expressed by Laqueur, in which "*man* is the measure of all things, and woman does not exist as an ontologically distinct category. Not all males are masculine, potent, honorable, or hold power, and some women exceed some men in each of these categories. But the standard of the human body and its representation is the male body" (Laqueur [1990] 1992: 62). Despite Gaunt's long arguments for the sameness of the two sexes, and the injustice of man's tyranny over woman, the text ends with the restoration of the old sexual order. Paula's daughter, Edwinna, has been doing backbreaking work during the Disappearance, including hunting and farming. However, her new-found independence and self-reliance make her realize that she really loved her first husband and that she wants to be a wife again: "I thought I was just a glamour-puss, for sale to the highest bidder. . . . I thought he was weak and *that* was unfair and I thought the world was mean. I never tried to help Charlie. I didn't know what I had to try *with*. Now . . . I do know. I ought to be quite a wife, for *any* guy! And I picked him first, after all. In some ways, some very important ways, Charlie was a *man!* I want peace. I want kids. I want home" (Wylie 1951: 340).

Paula, who has spent the whole book leading a community, working hard, and making numerous decisions, discovers that she is a feeler, not a thinker (350). In the last few pages she asks her husband leading questions so that he can pontificate out loud:[4]

> "Did God do it, Bill?"
>
> "Well who made God? I don't mean the real one that we have hardly tried to learn about. The God of the universe. Of evolution. Of instinct. Of the conscious mind and the unconscious mind. I mean, the squalid gods made in men's images that men worshipped." (349)

Gaunt even explains to her how a man has explained to him what she, Paula, feels: "Teddy made me perceive what you felt, that it never occurred to me any *women* really felt. So look, Paula. I don't *own* you. I *am* you" (350).

In fact the text echoes Gaunt's ideas about the ways in which men have tried to suppress women, because whenever there are men *and* women present, the men dominate. In the chapters where there are no men, the women have as many long speeches as the men do in their chapters. When the worlds are reunited in the final chapter there are no long speeches from the women about the new world they are all facing. The longest speech by a woman is the one I quoted above by Edwinna, on her desire to be a good wife. By contrast, Jim, a neighbor, gives a ten-line speech on the new world in which "[t]here is a passion in the hearts of all" (343); another character, Connaught, has a seventeen-line speech that leads to his announcement "There is only one sex" (348); and Gaunt has a series of speeches. One is twenty lines long, on "[t]he blunder of both sexes, that grew out of their insane sense of separateness!" (349-50). Paula's longest speeches are five lines long and are explanations for Gaunt of what happened in the time they were apart (342, 345). Gaunt dominates the final chapter, and he is the most frequently recurring theme. The men and Gaunt dominate the book, with eleven chapters given to their experience under the Disappearance, while the women have only seven. It is the men who make the discovery that men and women are two halves of a whole, and they then announce it to the women. The women in their part of the text do far less overt philosophizing and, once women and their men are restored to each other, they revert to their secondary role as helpmeet and angel of the house.

This notion of *The Disappearance,* that women and men are two halves of a whole, is as predicated on heterosexuality, as are the Pygmalion/ Galatea texts that I discussed in the previous chapter. On the back flap of the dust jacket there is "Mr. Wylie's own comment," which bears this out: "I became appalled by the ageless human view of women which holds them to be 'second class' persons. . . . I suddenly appreciated a long-standing blunder of our species. . . . . [M]an . . . has perverted the truth, grading women down to enhance egotistical assumptions and so, ineluctably, degrading his whole kind. The fact is, *no such thing as 'man' or 'woman' exists*; one sex without the other has neither past nor future and is but death" (Wylie's italics).

Wylie quotes Carl Jung, who, in viewing "man in Nature," observed that "*instinct* provides impulses for all we call 'good' as well as all we call 'evil.' Only man has attributed goodness to his conscious will and eschewed evil as a property of beasts. If Jung's observation is correct . . . [i]t follows . . . that the old blunder could be undone, the chasm bridged, and the two sexes reintegrated, at which point woman would be restored to humanity and man to love. So my novel became a love story, a new kind" (dust jacket).

The Disappearance is indeed a love story, though I am not sure how new it is. It has many similarities with love stories like Edmind Cooper's *Who Needs Men?*, where Rura discovers that "[w]omen are not a species, they are only part of a species" and that "[t]here is a fine tuning between men and women" ([1972] 1974: 96). This is the language that Jane resorted to in John Wyndham's story "Consider Her Ways," when she tries to convince Laura that a world without men is a nightmare world, and that men and women could coexist happily: "Lots of us were complementary. We were pairs who formed units" ([1956] 1965: 59).

This "equality" between the sexes is something bestowed by men and is dependent on heterosexual love. *The Disappearance*, like *Who Needs Men?*, does include homosexuality as an option. But, as in *Who Needs Men?*, it is unnatural and both protagonists reject it. Paula turns down the attractive young Kate with the words, "I'm not a child, thank God! Good night, dear" (Wylie 1951: 256), while Gaunt says, "Infantile business, homosexuality. Immature and unfortunate" (145).

Like the narrow class of real men and real women of the texts I discussed in the last chapter, those who are part of the man-plus-women-equals-person equation are still a small group. Those who indulge in same-sex love, male or female, are ruled out, as are African American women (there are no African American men in the text). When the Disappearance occurs, Paula Gaunt allows Hester, her maid, to camp in tents in the garden with Hester's daughters and granddaughters and other black families. Only one other garden resident is referred to by name, Hester's oldest daughter, Margot. This is when Paula graciously offers Hester's family refuge from the hurricane in the big house (Wylie 1951: 238). While Hester and Margot and their other female relations are camped in the yard, many of the white women of the neighborhood move into the house so that all the white women can work and organize together. The gulf between the two groups is thus made abundantly clear.[5] When the women and men are reunited, only Hester loses control: "A confused ululation came from the rear of the house. 'It's Hester,' Paula said quickly, 'having hysterics, poor darling! I'll go talk to her'" (337). Throughout the text Hester and her relatives are referred to as belonging to Paula Gaunt—they are part of "*her* colored colony" (my emphasis; 201).

In the world of *The Disappearance* the only axis of oppression is that of sex. If men learn to treat women better and give them more responsibilities, the world will be a much better place. That the "colored" people in the text are also second-class citizens—only allowed inside the big house in times of hurricane—is not mentioned. Indeed, in both "Woman's World" and *The Disappearance* it is the white men who are responsible for doing something to make the world more equal. These texts are concerned with specific men's journeys toward discovering their own privilege and part of what that privilege is built upon.

The heterosexual economy, with its basic unit of one man plus one woman, is also at the center of Mack Reynolds's *Amazon Planet* (1966).[6] Joanna Russ describes the text as having "a role reversal facade . . . —armed female guards and simpering men—only to reveal beneath it a peaceful and substantially egalitarian world" (Russ 1980: 13). Guy Thomas is an operative for Section G of the Bureau of Investigation of the United

Planets. He is sent to Amazonia, a female-ruled planet, under cover as an interplanetary trade commissioner to discover more about the planet. The Amazonian government give him an armed escort of Amazonia warriors dressed in bronze sandals and short skirts to protect him from other Amazonian warriors who might want to marry him. The majority of the novel takes place amidst this role reversal world where an "effeminate" man is one who behaves in a "masculine" way:

> When they got into the small living room, before looking around, Guy said, "Look. . . . The next person, man, woman, or child that makes another crack suggesting I'm effeminate, I'm going to award a very fat lip!"
>
> His guide was taken aback. "A very fat lip?" he wavered.
>
> "A bust in the mouth."
>
> "Oh, dear, you're so unmanly." (Reynolds [1966] 1975: 55-56)

There are many similiar passages where Guy's exaggerated masculinity is mocked. At the end of *Amazon Planet* Guy discovers that the wimpy men and Amazon women are all actors trying to prevent him from discovering how Amazonia actually operates. The last three chapters consist of explanations and justifications of Amazonia's social system, which supports Amis's claims about sf's "readiness to theorise and debate" (Amis 1960: 74). These chapters are also a neat role reversal of the science fiction motif of woman as ear, for it is women, the two civil rulers of the two continents of Amazonia, the Myrine and the Hippolyte, who give the explanations, and Guy who listens and asks questions like, "When did you stop having a military?" The answer is, "From the beginning. We're women, remember" (Reynolds [1966] 1975: 183). Then there are longer passages of explanation:

> You see, at first I imagine we were something like the Mormons who settled Utah back in old times. We had a multitude of ideas, principles, beliefs, and a great deal of faith in what, as we look back at it today, was obviously extremism. But we were no incompetents. And like the Mormons we quickly became pragmatic. Just as they gave up their polygamy when it proved impractical, we gave up the domination of one sex over the other. Not so quickly, perhaps, but step by step. . . . [W]hen our first colony ships landed all property was community owned, save, of course, personal things. Our original ideas of a female-dominated socioeconomic commonwealth proved nonsense within the year. The smallest unit of a life form is that unit which can reproduce itself. In the case of the human race, a woman and a man. (182)

So, as in *The Disappearance*, "a-man-plus-a-woman" (Wylie 1951: 233) is the core of humanity .

Much of *Amazon Planet* is in the same parodic mode as *Search the Sky* (Pohl and Kornbluth 1954) or "Ecce Femina!" (McAllister 1972). The me-warrior routine of Minythyia and the simpering of Podner Bates parody previous sexbattle worlds like that of "The Priestess Who Rebelled" (Bond 1939). There is even a moment when Guy is told to shut up by a woman (Reynolds [1966] 1975: 103). Unlike *The Disappearance*, there is no mention of any sexuality but heterosexuality. Patricia O'Gara, a recent migrant to Amazonia, explains to Guy about Amazonian laws on sexuality and marriage: "Amazonians don't believe in restricting personal relationships with too many laws. Actually, though, usage frowns on promiscuity and having close relations with even two or three persons at a time is considered rather far-out. However, some people are just built that way. They're not one-man women, or one-woman men. You've had the problem down through the ages" (Reynolds [1966] 1975: 145). The heterosexual unit is still at the center of society—there is no mention of one-woman women or one-man men.

When It Changed: A Different Kind of Female Rule

In Poul Anderson's *Virgin Planet* (1957),[7] a male explorer discovers an all-female world where the women, in Russ's words, "span the whole range of human temperaments and activities" (Russ 1980: 13). The women have "sweet-hearts" amongst themselves, but one group of women, the Whitleys, have never had a sweetheart (Anderson [1957] 1973: 23). Two of the Whitleys spend the novel fighting over the hero. The significance of the Phallus is spelled out on the first page, when Barbara Whitley sees the explorer's spaceship: "The thing stood upright, aflash with steel pride, like a lean war-dart, though it lacked fins. As a huntress and arbalester the corporal was necessarily a good judge of spatial relationships, and she estimated its height as forty meters" (5).

In Joanna Russ's "When It Changed" (1972), men arrive on an all-female world called Whileaway, and the women do not melt when they meet the possessors of the long-lost phallus.[8] Terry Carr refers to "When It Changed" in his November 1975 guest editorial for *Amazing* on women's progress within science fiction. He cites the story as an example of this progress, as a "blow struck for sexual rationality," and gives the following plot synopsis:

> [The story] opened with a lost Earth colony on some distant planet where all the men died long ago and the women learned to reproduce parthenogenically. They've established a workable and happy society and pretty much forgotten, over the centuries, that men ever existed. Then a spaceship from Earth happens to land on the planet, rediscovering this lost colony, and the men in the crew go around looking amazed at how plucky and resourceful the little ladies have been, and telling them rather pityingly that their long exile is over, The Men Are Here. The women just look at them blankly and wonder what the hell they're talking about. (Carr 1975: 124)

The inversion of the sexbattle mythos, whereby the women, or at least one real woman, would be glad that the men have returned is undone. Terry Carr applauds this and notes that the story "promptly won the Nebula Award as the best short story of the year" (Carr 1975: 124). This for Carr is another sign of science fiction's progress. Susan Wood, in her guest editorial for the spring 1978 issue of the feminist fanzine *Janus*, also comments on the impact of Russ's work in the early 1970s: "I remember a talk Joanna [Russ] gave, I think at the Toronto Secondary Universe conference in 1972, wittily reversing sex roles; woman makes rite of passage into adulthood by killing bear, etc." (Wood 1978: 5). Wood was referring to a passage in "When It Changed," where the narrator, Janet, is thinking of her daughter, Yuki: "Someday soon, like all of them, she will disappear for weeks on end to come back grimy and proud, having knifed her first cougar or shot her first bear, dragging some abominably dead beastie behind her, which I will never forgive for what it might have done to my daughter" (Russ [1972] 1983: 4).

Janet also describes her first sighting of men:

> They are bigger than we are. They are bigger and broader. Two were taller than me, and I am extremely tall, one meter, eighty centimeters in my bare feet. They are obviously of our species but *off*, indescribably off, and as my eyes could not and still cannot quite comprehend the lines of those alien bodies, I could not, then, bring myself to touch them, though the one who spoke Russian—what voices they have!—wanted to "shake hands," a custom from the past I imagine. I can only say they were apes with human faces. He seemed to mean well, but I found myself shuddering back almost the length of the kitchen—and then I laughed apologetically—and then to set a good example (*interstellar*

> *amity*, I thought) did "shake hands" finally. A hard, hard hand. They are heavy as draft horses. Blurred deep voices. (5)

Janet's daughter, Yuriko, says of the men, "I thought they would be good-looking!" (5). Janet asks her daughter if she "could fall in love with a man?" Yuriko laughs at the notion that she could fall in love "[w]ith a ten-foot toad!" (11).

This response to a first view of the manly form leaves behind the heterosexual equation of man plus woman equals person. Woman as love interest, woman who is not yet a woman until she is completed and molded into being by heterosexual penetration, is absent. Nor is the one-sex world in view where "*man* is the measure of all things, and woman does not exist as an ontologically distinct category" (Laqueur [1990] 1992: 62).

For the men who have just arrived on Whileaway, men *are* still the measure of all things, and they ask "Where are all the people?" They are told about the plague. The question is repeated: "'Where are all the people?' said the monomaniac. I realized then that he didn't mean people, he meant *men*, and he was giving the word the meaning it had not had on Whileaway for six centuries" (6–7). His people are men, but for Janet people are women. The two groups, the women of Whileaway and the men from Earth, operate in completely different paradigms. Janet tells the men from Earth where the men of Whileaway are:

> "They died," I said. "Thirty generations ago."
>
> I thought we had poleaxed him. He caught his breath. He made as if to get out of the chair he was sitting in; he put his hand to his chest; he looked around at us with the strangest blend of awe and sentimental tenderness. Then he said, solemnly and earnestly:
>
> "A great tragedy."
>
> I waited, not quite understanding.
>
> "Yes," he said, catching his breath again with that queer smile, that adult-to-child smile that tells you something is being hidden and will be presently produced with cries of encouragement and joy, "a great tragedy. But it's over." (7)

For the Whileawayans the men's arrival is the tragedy, and Katy, Janet's wife, even tries to kill one of the men but is stopped by Janet, who later regrets it: "Katy was right, of course; we should have burned them down where they stood" (10).

The men tell them that "sexual equality has been re-established on Earth" and that the Whileawayan world is "unnatural" (8–9). Katy counters that "humanity is unnatural" (9). The leader of the male party agrees: "'Humanity is unnatural. I should know. I have metal in my teeth and metal pins here.' He touched his shoulder. 'Seals are harem animals . . . and so are men; apes are promiscuous and so are men; doves are monogamous and so are men; there are even celibate men and homosexual men. There are homosexual cows I believe. But Whileaway is still missing something. . . . You know it intellectually, of course. There is only half a species here. Men must come back to Whileaway'" (9). There is a need to restore the "natural order of things," the heterosexual economy, but the Whileawayans are not willing to become real women. They resist the romance narrative that should swing into play when the men arrive. There is no joy here at the reunion. Janet muses: "Our ancestors' journals are one long cry of pain and I suppose I ought to be glad now but one can't throw away six centuries, or even (as I have lately discovered) thirty-four years" (11). It is no longer an equation that makes any sense, men have become ten-foot toads. This all-female world challenges the equation by eliding it altogether.

"When It Changed" is the first text in this period in which the case for heterosexuality has to be put at all:

> "There's been too much genetic damage in the last few centuries. Radiation. Drugs. We can use Whileaway's genes, Janet." Strangers do not call strangers by their first names.
>
> "You can have cells enough to drown in," I said. "Breed your own."
>
> He smiled. "That's not the way we want to do it. You know as well as I do that parthenogenic culture has all sorts of inherent defects, and we do not—if we can help it—mean to use you for anything of the sort. Pardon me; I should not have said 'use.' But surely you can see that this kind of society is unnatural." (8–9)

The man's mistake here is telling, for that is exactly what these men plan to do. The Earth men want to "use" the women of Whileaway—they want to get access to those genes in a "natural" way—through heterosexual penetrative sex. To do otherwise would continue these women's existence outside the patriarchal heterosexual order, outside the discourse of romance. Janet's offer to give them all the genes they want is not enough. A society that is outside the heterosexual economy is unnatural. This is the absolute given of every other battle-of-the-sexes texts from 1926 to 1973. This text marks a crucial shift in the battle-of-the-sexes texts and is indeed a moment "When It Changed."

Hermaphroditism

CORRECTING HERMAPHRODITUS

> *Indeed, how could one separate the idea of subordination from the existence of the sexes? Gabrile de Foigny's remarkably fictitious land of* Australie *(1673), a utopia of hermaphrodites, shows how close the link between subordination and two sexes was perceived to be. The* Australian, *in whom the sexes were one, could not understand how a conflict of wills could be avoided within the "mutual possession" of European marriage. The* French *traveller answered that it was simple, for mother and child were both subject to the father. The hermaphrodite, horrified at such a violation of the total autonomy that was the sign of complete true "men," dismissed the European pattern as bestial. (Davis 1975: 128)*[9]

"How could one separate the idea of subordination from the existence of the sexes?" is a very important opening question. The response in this seventeenth-century text is to remove sexual difference altogether and replace it with hermaphrodites or androgynes. This solution to the conflict between women and men has also been posited in science fiction, although texts with this approach to the sex war are rare in the period 1926–1973, there are a few worth noting: Murray Constantine's *Proud Man* (1934), *Venus Plus X* (1960), and *The Left Hand of Darkness* (1969).[10]

The term "hermaphrodite" comes from the name of the first hermaphrodite, Hermaphroditus, son of Hermes and Aphrodite. A version of the story is told at some length in Ovid's *Metamorphoses*. According to Ovid, he was so beautiful that "[e]ven blushing became him: his cheeks were the colour of ripe apples, hanging in a sunny orchard, like painted ivory or like the moon when, in eclipse, she shows a reddish hue beneath her brightness" ([1955] 1964: 103). When he was fifteen he went traveling until he came across a pool of water. In this pool lived the naiad Salmacis. The moment she saw Hermaphroditus she was lust-struck and set about luring him into the water. Once he had entered the water, Salmacis tried to kiss him. Hermaphroditus struggled but "she twined around him, like a serpent." As she held him, Salmacis called out to the Gods, "Grant me this, may no time to come ever separate him from me, or me from him!" Her prayers were answered instantly "for, as they lay together, their bodies were united and from being two persons they became one . . . . [W]hen their limbs met in that clinging embrace the nymph and the boy were no longer two, but a single form, possessed of a dual nature, which could not be called male or female, but seemed to be at once both and neither" (104).

Hermaphroditus called to his parents and begged them to change the waters of the pool "if any man enter this pool, may he depart hence no more than half a man, may he suddenly grow weak and effeminate at the touch of these waters" (104). Both his parents were moved with compassion, and granted this request of their child. In this formulation hermaphroditism is something that makes a man effeminate, that takes something away from him so that he becomes "no more than half a man" (Ovid [1955] 1964: 104).

Hugh Hampton Young (M.A., M.D., Sc.D., F.R.C.S.), in his influential 1937 text, *Genital Abnormalities: Hermaphroditism and Related Adrenal Diseases*, gives a brief overview of the various accounts of Hermaphroditus's story. He is unhappy that Ovid's account is the most well-known and finds it "amazing" that the *Oxford Classical Dictionary* and the *Encyclopedia Britannica* give Ovid's "fantastic version" of the origin of hermaphroditism, to which there are many "obvious objections . . . especially from a medical standpoint" (5). Apparently water cannot really turn a man into an hermaphrodite.

Despite Young's disapproval of Ovid's "fantastic version," there is a basic similarity between Ovid's and Young's view of hermaphroditism. For both, hermaphroditism is a problem. In Young's book, and in every other medical textbook I looked at, hermaphroditism is something that must be corrected. Young stated that the actual or most viable sex for each individual intersex has to be determined before the correction can be made. Is the intersex really a man or really a women? The questions that are pertinent in making this decision are not just practical, such as which set of genitalia is more viable, but also entail social questions, such as what is the sexual preference of the intersex? If s/he prefers to have "sexual relations with" (Young's phrase) men, then the preference is to make the body female. Does s/he look more like a woman or a man?

In *Proud Man*, *Venus Plus X*, and *The Left Hand of Darkness*, hermaphroditism or androgyny is transformed from a problem that must be surgically corrected into a possible solution to the problem of difference between men and women. Unlike the other battle-of-the-sexes text that I have been discussing in this and the previous chapter, *Proud Man* was not published as part of the American pulp magazine tradition of science fiction.[11] The book, by Katherine Burdekin writing under the name of Murray Constantine, was published in England in 1934.[12] It is written in the form of a report on Earth by an alien visitor to England in the early 1930s. The alien, who is named Alethea Verona when passing for a woman, has visited England through a dream. While there, Verona spends time with three different "sub-humans." Each of Verona's encounters is covered in a separate part of *Proud Man*. Part II is "The Priest," part III "The Woman," and part IV "The Man." Part I is called "The Person" and sets out the reasons for the account and explains the difference between the inhabitants of England and Verona's own hermaphrodite race:

> You will understand by this time the subhumans are of two sexes, like animals, birds, fish and insects. If evolution is a fact, the whole course of human evolution would seem to be from a single-sexed unconscious being, such as an amoeba, to a single-sexed conscious being such as you or I. The subhumans were beyond the animal stage, as they were certainly partially conscious, but they were still two-sexed mammals. They had abandoned a breeding season, and the interest of one sex in another was constant. They bore their young alive, and fed it at the breast. They had no conception of a *person*, that is an entity independent of others both physically and emotionally, who is self-fertilising, and can produce young, if it wishes to, alone and without help. No *person* so far as I could discover, had yet been born, though there have been cases of a clumsy sex fusion, making it difficult to say whether the individual was a male or a female. But such freaks, as subhumans call all their fellows who differ markedly from themselves, were not true *persons*, with a human mind or consciousness; and, as far as I know, I was, during the two years of my dream, the only *person* extant. The idea that one individual should be both male and female, wholly and practically and conveniently within itself, was repugnant to them, even though their bisexuality was the cause of unbelievable pain, discomfort, and grief. (22–23)

Once again a person equals a man plus a woman—but this time the man and the woman are contained in the same body. The person who narrates the book is also outside the discourse of romantic love, which, in *The Disappearance* (1951) and *Amazon Planet* (1966), brings the unit of man plus woman together. This idea is, however, articulated within *Proud Man* by the woman, Leonora, who is the subject of part III: "But I and my lover will be quite different. We shan't be two people, we shall be a unit. A unit of far more power than either of us would be separately. We shall do the same work, together" (176).

Later, Verona asks Leonora if she has thought about the children of her "units of lovers," wouldn't they be different to children of more "disunited" "antagonistic" pairs? Verona suggests that "with such perfect understanding between the parents children might in time be born who united the whole natures of the lovers in themselves, even to their own sexes."

> "Oh no," cried Leonora. "There would be no more lovers, and the children would be cold, cold. They must stop short of *that*."
>
> "Now you are like your children who say they won't grow up. How dull to be grown up, they say. Yet you like coldness. You like to have me with you. . . . Naturally being sexual, *you* don't want to be without sex. But being reasonable, you should not mind evolution." (191–92)

As did Jane in "Consider Her Ways" (Wyndham 1956), Leonora finds the idea of a world without romantic love appalling. "One of you is lovely," she says. "A world of you is terrifying" (192). This underlines how essential romance is to the formation of subjectivity. Leonora cannot comprehend a world in which subjectivity would be formed in such a radically different way. For Leonora, Verona and her people are like the women of "The Last Man," who, "no longer having need of sex, dropped it like a worn-out cloak and became sexless" (West [1929] 1972: 108–9); or the men in "The Last Woman," whom a drug allows to turn "[a]ll the energies" that had been wasted on "sex and the emotional side of life" to "thought and work" (Gardner [1932] 1972: 134). Or indeed the women of the matriarchy in "Consider Her Ways," who have escaped the enslavement of romantic love. Verona's people escape romantic love by being hermaphrodite—a fusion of the perfect man and perfect woman and their love for each other. In this way, romantic love is transcended. Verona's people are the apotheosis of romantic love, its fulfilment, but that means her people are neither heterosexual nor homosexual, they are asexual.

CRIME'S OFFSPRING

> *For a long time hermaphrodites were criminals, or crime's offspring, since their anatomical disposition, their very being, confounded the law that distinguished the sexes and prescribed their union.* (Foucault [1976] 1981: 38)

In *Proud Man*, the centrality of sex and of romantic love to Leonora's sense of herself is crucial. If you are neither man nor woman, how can you signify within the economy of heterosexuality? Indeed, the word "hermaphrodite" and various corruptions have been used to refer to homosexuals. The term "moffie" derived from "hermaphrodite," is a South African equivalent for the Australian term "poofter" (Branford 1987: 226). A hermaphrodite is neither man nor woman, and so in the West, especially since the 1960s, hermaphrodite bodies have been altered. Modern surgical techniques prevent the blurring of the distinctions between the two true sexes and their place within the heterosexual economy.

According to a 1990 textbook on paediatrics, "Major problems arise when the genitalia are malformed to the extent where the gender cannot readily be identified" (Warne 1990: 474). In 1969 English physicians, Christopher J. Dewhurst and Ronald R. Gordon wrote about a newborn hermaphrodite: "One can only attempt to imagine the anguish of the parents. That a newborn should have a deformity . . . [affecting] so fundamental an issue as the very sex of the child . . . is a tragic event . . . conjur[ing] up visions of a hopeless psychological misfit doomed to live always as a sexual freak in loneliness and frustration" (quoted in Fausto-Sterling 1993: 23).

To exist legally and socially, over the past two hundred years, a body has needed to be sexed male or female. As Foucault observed, in his introduction to *Herculine Barbin:*

> [E]verybody was to have his or her primary, profound, determined and determining sexual identity; as for the elements of the other sex that that might appear, they could only be accidental, superficial, or even quite simply illusory. From the medical point of view, this meant that when confronted with a hermaphrodite, the doctor was no longer concerned with recognizing the presence of the two sexes, juxtaposed or intermingled, or with knowing which of the two prevailed over the other, but rather with deciphering the true sex that was hidden beneath ambiguous appearances. (Foucault [1980] 1987: viii)

Judith Butler, in a footnote to her article "Sexual Inversions," discusses Foucault's claims about the category of sex and the way it "constitutes and regulates what will and will not be an intelligible and recognisable human existence" (Butler 1992: 353). She writes that the

> political question for Foucault, and for those who read him now, is *not* whether "improperly sexed" beings should or should not be treated fairly. . . . The question is whether, if improperly sexed, such a being can even be a being, a human being, a subject, one whom the law can condone or condemn. . . . .The journals of Herculine Barbin, the hermaphrodite . . . demonstrate the violence of the law that would legislate identity on a body that resists it. But Herculine is to some extent a *figure* for a sexual ambiguity or inconsistency that emerges at the site of bodies

and that contest the category of subject and its univocal or self-identical "sex." (353–54)

In Sturgeon's *Venus Plus X* (1960) this violence is overt: when the human Charlie Johns discovers that the hermaphrodite race, the Ledom, are not a "natural" mutation but a self-imposed surgical alteration, he is appalled, and declares that humans would "exterminate you down to the last queer kid . . . and stick that one in a side-show" (152). According to the *American Dictionary of Slang* "queer" meaning "homosexual" has been in "common use since c1925" (Wentworth and Flexner 1960). If you are not heterosexual, according to Charlie Johns, you must be homosexual. However, it could be argued that the queerness of the hermaphrodite body puts it outside dichotomous sexuality, and that the Ledom are both heterosexual *and* homosexual.

LEAKING BODIES

When it appeared in September 1960, *Venus Plus X* was billed as "the strangest science fiction novel Theodore Sturgeon has ever written" (which was as much to say the strangest anyone had ever written).[13] In the novel, Sturgeon contrasts the sexual inequality of 1950s middle America with a supposedly future utopia where the Ledom (which spells "model" backward) are "biologically androgynous," being equipped with both male and female "sexual equipment." All of the Ledom can impregnate and be impregnated. This is different from reproduction in *Proud Man*, which only requires one "person." Most of *Venus Plus X* is concerned with the story of Charlie Johns, who wakes up and finds himself in the world of the Ledom. They show him their world, explain its workings, and ask for his verdict. This narrative is interspersed with one about Herb and Jeanette Raile in suburban America and their take on issues of sex and sexuality (among other things, they discuss Wylie's novel *The Disappearance*).

Venus Plus X is the first of the battle-of-the-sexes texts published within the field of science fiction to postulate altering the bodies of women and men as a solution to the Sex War. It stands opposite such texts as David Keller's "The Feminine Metamorphosis" (1929), where the alteration of "natural" womanly bodies is viewed as an abomination and an act directly contrary to the will of God. *Venus Plus X* explicitly locates itself within the sf battle-of-the-sexes tradition. In discussing *The Disappearance,* Herb tells Jeanette about it even though she has already read it: "He [Wylie] says people made their big mistake when first they started to forget the similarity between men and women and began to concentrate on the difference. He calls that *the* original sin. He blames it for all wars and all persecutions. He says that because of it we've lost all but a trickle of the ability to love" (Sturgeon 1960: 73). And as in *The Disappearance*, it is Herb who considers the big questions and explains them to Jeanette.

While *The Disappearance* and *Amazon Planet* argue for a recognition of the basic sameness between the sexes as the solution to the battle (the "*actual* differences between the sexes of genus *Homo* are not very great" [Wylie 1951: 228]), *Venus Plus X* sees the biological difference—or humans' perceptions of it—as too huge an obstacle to equality. For equality to be possible, biology, for at least a time, has to be remade and physical difference has to be removed. This "solution" has been considered elsewhere since Sturgeon wrote about it in 1960. In an essay on the sex/gender dichotomy Moira Gatens discusses the desire to efface (or ignore) difference between the sexes, "the claimed necessity of the neutralising of sexual difference," and cites Shulamith Firestone's "cybernetic communism," which "proposed the literal neutering of bodies by means of the complete technologization, and hence socialisation, of the reproductive capacity" (Gatens [1983] 1996: 17).

Venus Plus X, published ten years before Firestone's 1970 feminist tract *The Dialectic of Sex*, and in a completely different field, also sees biology as the problem but posits a slightly different solution. In Firestone's text the solution is cybernetic wombs, which remove the necessity for "clumsy," "inefficient," "painful" childbirth (224). In Sturgeon's text everyone gives birth, because each of the Ledom possesses penis, womb, and vagina. The result is the same: inequality, which stems from physical difference, is removed. Same-bodied experience equals tolerance equals peace and understanding. And these Ledom bodies are almost identical: Charlie Johns, taken from Earth's past to judge his humanity's future, has great difficulty telling the Ledom apart. They are all roughly the same height and shape, only their dress sense distinguishes them; there is no mention of skin color, although the accompanying illustrations in the *New Worlds* serialization show the Ledom as white.

The story of the Ledom is threaded with that of Herb and Jeanette Raile. In their world there is no neat solution. The only conclusions that Herb and Jeanette reach is that they love each other and that they love their child. They are not two halves of one whole and frequently they do not understand each other, but the safety of the nuclear family will have to do.

In the postscript to the first book edition of *Venus Plus X*, Sturgeon writes that it "was my aim in writing *Venus Plus X* to, a) write a decent book, b) about sex" (Sturgeon 1960: 160). The implication is that, although the earlier sexbattle stories may have fulfilled the second condition, they definitely did not fulfill the first. *Venus Plus X* takes up where the less "decent" battle-of-the-sexes texts I discussed in the previous chapter left off. Those texts close with the union of the hero and the heroine and the array of different sexed bodies neatly forgotten. However, this array of sexed bodies still manages to leak out of these texts. Sturgeon's *Venus Plus X* is an attempt to make use of some of this leakage. Ironically, however, it manages to shut down the range of bodies that had emerged from the earlier texts by surgically altering every one into a version of the same. The Ledom may be equipped with a womb, but they are breastless and appear to be men. One of the first observations of the story's narrator, Charlie Johns, is that he "saw no women" (16). Later revelations of the "true" nature of the Ledom's sex do not dispel this impression of an all-male world.

There are parallels between *Venus Plus X* and Ovid's tale of Hermaphroditus. The naiad Salmacis's plea for eternal unity with the beautiful boy leaves her with nothing, not even a self. She has become a component of Hermaphroditus in much the same way that the Ledom are women and men transformed into men with additional female parts.

Ann Rosalind Jones and Peter Stallybrass argue in their "Fetishizing Gender: Constructing the Hermaphrodite in Renaissance Europe" that Ovid's tale is an example of "the absorption of the Other into the Same. For if Hermaphroditus's name suggests the intertwining of male and female, the name is that of a boy who, even as he intertwines with Salmacis, erases her name; henceforth, the name is transformed from the conjunction of two genders to the absorption of the woman's name into the man's, paradoxically at the very moment of the submission of the man to the woman" (Jones and Stallybrass 1991: 85). This encounter and absorption is echoed in traditional marriage vows when the woman is submerged into her husband's name. The hermaphrodite in this light is not the unity of two producing another kind of being—the hermaphrodite is half a man: "His prayer to the gods to make other swimmers leave the pond 'less than men' obliterates the nymph as active ingredient in the metamorphosis. She is present not as the female half of a hermaphrodite but as the drainer away of Hermaphroditus' masculinity; she defines him through negation. Thus Hermaphroditus' change is represented as a problem of male identity" (Jones and Stallybrass 1991: 96–97).

If woman is lack, and man is the one, then their unity will result in the woman vanishing altogether, or in the woman becoming a man. The Ledom are a version of men, but not a version of women. The implied neutrality of the hermaphrodite is not, Moira Gatens notes, neutrality at all, but "a 'masculinisation' or 'normalisation' (in a society where men are seen as the norm, the standard) of women—a making of 'woman' into 'man'" (Gatens [1983] 1996: 17). But if Hermaphroditus is only another kind of man why has "he" been so consistently obliterated, renamed, ignored, or punished under the law? Why is the human bisexual visitor to a world of hermaphrodites so horrified?

In Ursula K. Le Guin's *The Left Hand of Darkness* (1969) the visitor to the hermaphrodite world is Genly Ai, an envoy from the Ekumen, a vast intergalactic association of planets and cultures. Genly Ai is sent to the planet Winter to contact the native inhabitants and see if they are ready to join this intergalactic association. The planet Winter, or Gethen as it is called by its inhabitants, is unlike any known world because its inhabitants are neither male nor female but neuter, except for a short period of time when they go into heat, or "kemmer," and become either male or female. The story centers on Genly Ai's interactions with a Gethenian, Estraven. The text is replete with the envoy Genly's binary thinking, his attempts to make the Gethenians male or female. A typical example is: "I was still far from being able to see the people of the planet through their own eyes. I tried to but my efforts took the form of self-consciously seeing a Gethenian first as a man, then as a woman, forcing him into those categories so irrelevant to his nature and so essential to my own" ([1969] 1991: 18).

To render the people of Gethen intelligible, Genly turns them into men. But he is never comfortable with this move, and it keeps sliding out of his grasp because the Gethenians are neither male nor female, and they will not stay fixed as Genly would have them. He is forced to think about his assumptions about male and female. Women are the Other that shadows the text. Early on, when describing Gethians, Genly makes it clear that he thinks of men and women as different species: "They lacked, it seemed, the capacity to *mobilize*. They behaved like animals, in that respect; or like women. They did not behave like men, or ants. At any rate they never yet had done so" (47). This statement is at once a nice gesture in the direction of a branch of the battle-of-the-sexes texts—only with an inversion, so that ants are aligned with men, not women—and also an example of Genly's unease with women. Genly's world is entirely sexed, so that when he watches Estraven making "food-ration calculations" he can only view them as "house-wifely or scientific" (204). Estraven asks Genly if women are "like a different species." He replies:

> "No. Yes. No, of course not, not really. But the difference is very important. I suppose the most important thing, the heaviest single factor in one's life, is whether one's born male or female. In most societies it determines one's expectations, activities, outlooks, ethics, manners—almost everything. Vocabulary. Semiotic usages. Clothing. Even food. Women. . . . Women tend to eat less. . . . It's extremely hard to separate the innate differences from the learned ones. Even where women participate equally with men in the society, they still after all do all the childbearing, and so most of the child-rearing. . . . ."
>
> "Equality is not the general rule, then? Are they mentally inferior?"
>
> "I don't know. They don't often seem to turn up mathematicians, or composers of music, or inventors, or abstract thinkers. But it isn't that they're stupid. Physically they're less muscular, but a little more durable than men. Psychologically— . . . "I can't tell you what women are like. I never thought about it much in the abstract, you know. In a sense, women are more alien to me than you are. With you I share one sex, anyhow" (200)

The "heaviest single factor in one's life, is whether one's born male or female." Yet Genly is able to find more ground between himself and the Gethenians than with women because they are male sometimes, and he can extend that maleness further to give them humanity. Genly's words echo those of the man landing on Whileaway in "When It Changed"—"Where are all the people?" People means men; Genly has accepted the Gethenians; they are men. At least the Gethenians he respects are men. He refers to the "voluble" Gethenian with whom he stays in Ehrenrang as his "landlady" (46). And he describes the unreliable and duplicitous King Argaven as laughing "shrilly like an angry woman" (33).

Even a female observer has trouble with the question of sex. In chapter 7, "The Question of Sex: From Field Notes of Ong Tot Oppong, Investigator, of the First Ekumenical Landing Party on Gethen/Winter, Cycle 93 E. Y. 1448," Oppong, a "woman of peaceful Chiffewar," observes that "you cannot think of Gethenians as 'it.' They are not neuters. They are potentials, or integrals. Lacking the Karhidish 'human pronoun' used for persons in somer, I must say 'he,' for the same reason as we used the masculine pronoun in referring to a transcendent god: it is less defined, less specific, than the neuter or the feminine. But the very use of the pronoun in my thoughts leads me continually to forget that the Karhider I am with is not a man, but a man-woman" (85). Here the female observer of the strange planet has internalized the ancient observation, attributed by Plato to Protagorus, that "*man* is the measure of all things."

The edition of *The Left Hand of Darkness* that I own has the words "A Classic of Science Fiction" across its cover under the title. On the back cover the blurb begins, "This outstanding classic of science fiction, which won both the Hugo and Nebula Awards when first published . . . ." The book has been reprinted virtually every year since its first publication in 1969 and, unlike the majority of the texts I have been discussing, has a solid place within most canons of science fiction. It is one of the most written-about texts in science fiction scholarship. I have no memory of my first reading of *The Left Hand of Darkness,* but when I reread it recently, the use of the male pronoun seemed, in the opening pages, to smooth over the difference—the hermaphroditism—of the inhabitants of Winter, because it delays the revelation of difference. As the novel opens you are surrounded by men; it is only gradually that "kemmer" is intro duced and you learn the extent of the difference between the Gethenians and humans.

PRONOUNS ARE IMPORTANT

> *. . . a nice face, neither boyish nor too beautiful; and oh, it was not Laura; it's just that she had Laura's hair.*
>
> *She. . . .*
>
> *"Y-y-you kept saying he!" cried Charlie stupidly.*
>
> *"About Soutin? Yes, of course—what else?"*
>
> *And it came to Charlie, yes of course—what else! For Philos had told his story in the Ledom tongue, and he had always used the Ledom pronoun which is not masculine nor feminine but which also is not "it"; it was he, Charlie, himself, who had translated it "he." (Sturgeon 1960: 147)*

Throughout *Venus Plus X* (1960), the Ledom have seemed just like men, partly because of this use of the masculine pronoun. This pronoun is the choice of Charlie, is his translation, and it is he who, discovering that the Ledom are not hermaphrodite as the result of a "natural" mutation, calls them all queer. Possessors of an unnatural alteration of their real selves, they become homosexual and deviant, but still male.

In the majority of the texts I have discussed in this chapter there is an unthinking use of "man" for humanity and the pronoun "he" as though it were generic. In Mack Reynolds's *Amazon Planet* (1966) when the women rulers, the Hippolyte and the Myrine, are explaining the workings of Amazonia, they refer to the "human race" rather than "mankind": "The smallest unit of a life form is that unit which can reproduce itself. In the case of the human race, a woman and a man. . . . Or as Citizen Bronston would undoubtedly put it, a man and a woman" (182-83). Earlier in the text, when Guy is having the system of payment explained to him, a feminine pronoun is used as a generic. "Surely nothing is more just than to realize that each person's time is as valuable to her, as any other person's" (99). This is the only example of a feminine pronoun used as the generic, and it comes when the Amazonians are still trying to convince Guy that their world is a ruthless matriarchy. On the previous page the same character uses masculine pronouns; "For every hour he puts in as a student, he accrues one hour" (98). In the last three chapters, when Guy is having Amazonia explained to him, the masculine pronoun and man as universal returns: "A highly trained man's time can be worth several times as many hours as an unskilled man" (185). *The Disappearance* (1951) uses only "he" as a generic pronoun and "mankind" for humanity.

The question of pronouns is one that has been raised frequently about *The Left Hand of Darkness*. In his review for *Fantasy and Science Fiction*, Alexei Panshin wrote: "[Le Guin's] hermaphrodites, seen only in public function, eventually seem purely male, partly because she chooses always to call them 'he'" (Panshin 1969: 51). Le Guin responded to this charge in her article "Is Gender Necessary?":

> [A] frequent criticism I receive [is] that the Gethenians seem like *men*, instead of menwomen.
>
> This rises in part from the choice of pronoun. I call Gethenians "he" because I utterly refuse to mangle English by inventing a pronoun for "he/she."
>
> "He" is the generic pronoun, damn it, in English. (I envy the Japanese, who, I am told, do have a he/she pronoun.) But I do not consider this really very important.
>
> The pronouns wouldn't matter at all if I had been cleverer at *showing* the "female" component of the Gethenian characters in *action*. (Le Guin [1979] 1989: 145)

Le Guin later responded to her own article.[14] She writes that her "utter refusal" of 1968, restated in 1976, collapsed utterly within a couple of years: "I still dislike invented pronouns, but now dislike them less than the so-called generic pronoun he/him/his, which does in fact exclude women from discourse; and which was an invention of male grammarians, for until the sixteenth century the English generic singular pronoun was they/them/their, as it still is in English and American colloquial speech. It should be restored to the written language and let the pedants and pundits squeak and gibber in the streets" (Le Guin [1979] 1989: 145). She added that if she had "realized how the pronouns I used shaped, directed, controlled my own thinking, I might have been 'cleverer'" (145).

The use of the masculine pronoun as the neuter pronoun in *The Left Hand of Darkness* is closely connected to the fact that the most frequent first-person narrator is Genly Ai, the envoy. Genly is a man, the masculine pronoun is his. His use of "it" keeps the nature of the Gethenians at arm's length. His use of "he" keeps this world of Others in the realm of the Same.

So has Genly succeeded in making the world of Winter male? Has his male pronoun, his "he," erased the hermaphrodite neuter existence of the majority of a Gethenian's life? Or does the hermaphrodite neuter existence erase women? There is one near-erasure in the text—homosexuality. The heterosexual couple is at the heart of Winter. An Ekumen observer writes that when they go into kemmer: "[E]ither a male or female hormonal dominance is established. The genitals engorge or shrink accordingly, foreplay intensifies, and the partner, triggered by the change, takes on the other sexual role" (82). The Ekumen observer makes a parenthetical note, "? without exception? If there are exceptions, resulting in kemmer-partners of the same sex, they are so rare so as to be ignored" (82). But ignored by whom? The Gethenians or the Ekumen investigators? In Genly's account, the vowing of kemmering is as equivalent to monogamous marriage as is perhaps Leonora's "units of lovers" from *Proud Man*. Man during kemmer plus women during kemmer equals the basic unit of society. But there is nothing to say that each partner in the kemmering will remain that sex every time they go into kemmer.

FAULT
Love, Sex, and Women in Science Fiction

In this chapter I trace a recurring debate within the letters and articles of science fiction magazines about whether women, love, and sex have a place in science fiction. The letters were published between the 1920s and the early 1950s; the articles between 1955 and 1975. The battle of the sexes was played out in the debates in these letters and articles as explicitly as it was in the stories I examined in the last two chapters.

One set of arguments that is articulated within these debates clearly demarcates a division between public and private, where the public becomes the masculine space of science fiction from which women are excluded. In this division, intelligence (the mind) is located within the field of science fiction and is thus associated with men, and sex (the body) is relegated to the private sphere of women outside science fiction. This imaginary masculine space of science fiction is conjured up in the pages of science fiction magazines. John W. Campbell, the extremely influential editor of *Astounding*, wrote "long chatty editorials . . . . that had the style of an after-dinner speaker at the Elks Club. When he previewed van Vogt's *Slan*, he wrote, 'Gentlemen, it's a lulu!'" (Carr 1975: 5). To keep this imaginary space masculine and populated only by "real" men the borders of the field have to be policed and women have to be excluded.

As I noted in chapter 1, the idea of the science fiction reader and fan as a superior kind of being, a slan, whose intelligence and knowledge puts him (I use the pronoun deliberately) head and shoulders ahead of the general public, had considerable currency. This scientifically interested, mostly young male should not be thinking about sex. Sex and the libidinal body are outside the realm of science and therefore of science fiction. If he is not thinking about sex, then he is not thinking about women. This idea that sex is contaminating, even draining, of a man's masculinity is very similar to the highly influential classical idea that when a man ejaculates he loses some of his strength and virility: "The most virile man was the man who had kept most of his vital spirit—the one, that is, who lost little or no seed" (Brown 1988: 19).[1]

These ideas about virility, masculinity, and celibacy are borne out in Thomas S. Gardner's "The Last Woman" (1932), which I discussed in chapter 2. In this story the notion that sex is outside the realm of science is pushed to its logical conclusion. Without women and sex the new scientific empire is dominated by virile, strong men, proving Soranus's claim of many centuries earlier that "[m]en who remain chaste are stronger and better than others and pass their lives in better health" (quoted in Brown 1988: 19).

The slide from "sex" to "women" also occurs in the debates in letters and articles in prozines. These debates shift from being about whether there is a place for sex and love in science fiction to whether there is any place for women in science fiction. In the battle-of-the-sexes stories that I discussed in chapter 3 there is a definite place for women, because the stories are specifically about the relationship between men and women. In other science fiction the presence of women becomes tenuous; a woman can only signify within science fiction when she is the "love interest," and thus part of the heterosexual economy. This conflation of woman, sex, and/or love is vividly illustrated by the entry for "sex" in the *Fancyclopedia*:

> Sex—The great majority of fans are males. It has been asserted that a female cannot be the psychological type of the s-f fan, but there are several dyed-in-the-wool fannes to refute this. In addition, there are a lot of sweet-hearts, wives, daughters, sisters, etc, of the he-fans, who tag along at fan gatherings, make some appearances in the fanzines, and assist in dirty work such as mimeoing.
>
> It is generally believed that Joe Fann is considerably later than average in associating with girls; at any rate, it was some two years after 1938 (when the average fan was 18) before love affairs received any great notice in fan discussions, tho there had been some isolated eroticism earlier, especially among the Futurians and the Moonrakers. Since 1940 both generalizations and particulars on fan-meets-femme have appeared frequently in conversation and writing, and among the more "mature" Britishers have sometimes reached shocking depths. In American, a mi-

> nority has been vociferously lewd, and some shoddy events have resulted from infidelity of married scientifictionists. (Speer 1944: 83)

Women here are synonymous with sex, existing momentarily as independent "fannes" before becoming secondary fans, part of fandom only as sweetheart, wife, daughter, and so forth of some male fan, "Joe Fann."[2] In the second paragraph, women—or rather girls—become something that Joe Fann does or does not associate with as he discovers the wonderful world of heterosexuality. The *Fancyclopedia* entry sets up two different meanings for sex. In the first meaning, sex is the category of sex, but it is only women who have a sex. Men are the unmarked sex, they are human, the norm, the standard. The unmarked fan is always male. In the second sense, women are sex in that they are the embodiment of the libidinal body; this is why the second paragraph of the definition is about heterosexual sexuality and about fan meeting femme. It is also why, more than twenty years later, Robin White can ask "Are Femme-Fans Human?" (White 1968: 51). This conflation between the category of sex and sex in the sense of sexuality occurs frequently in the debates about women as love interest within science fiction.

The long-standing idea that women are inimical to science fiction did not go unchallenged. For example, Peggy Kaye of Dorchester, Massachussets, writes:

> What gives with these characters who don't want to have any female interest or illos [*sic*] in the stories they read? Are they trying to convince themselves that men are the only beings really important in this existence? Or do they take that reference to MAN as the only intelligent species on earth literally—meaning MAN and not WOMAN too?
>
> If that is the case, no wonder it shakes them down to their poor misguided little souls when they read a story in which the hero finds himself romantically inclined towards a desirable (horrors!) heroine. Maybe they'd like it better if the guy were a eunuch, h'mm?[3] (Kaye 1952: 130)

During the 1950s more letters, editorials, and articles were published that were in favor of the presence of sex, and therefore of women, within science fiction. Often the argument is couched in terms of the need for science fiction to grow up, to mature. Desire for sex and for women is a sign of adulthood, and once science fiction has grown it will move beyond the childish need to repudiate sex. Women in this argument become a kind of angel of the house who is responsible for supporting and nurturing the field and allowing it to grow.

Girl Germs: Love and Sex as Pollution

One of the reasons most frequently given for a lack of female characters in early science fiction is that there was rarely any need for a love interest. Sam Moskowitz explains: "While love interest is a standard ingredient in most fiction, the same editors who give lip service to the need for more natural dialogue and clear-cut characterization fail even to note the omission of romance when evaluating the acceptability of science fiction. Stories in which female characters *appear at all* are in the minority in the magazines of prophetic literature" (Moskowitz 1972: 1). Notice the slide here from "love interest" to "romance" to "female characters." Moskowitz is implying that female characters can only appear in science fiction where "love interest" and "romance" are present. The romance narrative is, in this argument, one of the few narratives in which "woman" can signify and be a meaningful subject.

This equation between women and the love interest is regularly played out in the letters that were published in the pulps. A typical example is from Edwin Todd of Parkville, Missouri, writing of Don A. Stuart's "The Cloak of Aesir":[4] "Another point in this story was the treatment of the love interest. It was never forced artificially into the scene. Too many stories throw a girl into the picture whether she has any logical reason for being there or not" (Todd 1939: 159). As in the remark by Sam Moskowitz, the slide from "love interest" to "girl" is unremarked, and the only "logical reason" for a girl being in a story is to function as "love interest." The girl does not find her own way into the story. She is "thrown" in. This is a similar structure to the one I discussed in chapter 2, where the heroine is the medium of her transformation by a man into a woman. The figure of a woman (more often a girl) being thrown or dragged into the narrative recurs in many of these letters.

This anxiety to keep the whole discourse of romance out of science fiction (talk about the impossible dream!) is a long-running one. The idea of romance, and therefore women, polluting science fiction begins almost immediately in the pulps. Love was not what Gernsback had in mind for the pages of *Amazing Stories*. Not all readers of Gernsback's magazines were happy with this separation between science and sex and love. Thomas Coffin of Whittier, California, writes: "Why do authors not make a love plot more evident and important? It seems that such a plot could very easily be woven into nearly all the stories, and, instead of distracting the reader from the real plot, it would only heighten his interest and make him feel the stories were more true to life. True, many stories have love plots, but they seems so lifeless, and all have such an abrupt ending that it takes away all romance from the story" (Coffin 1928: 373). Love, here, is a mark of realism and will add to the "real" plot which is that generated by the discourse of science.

Gernsback responds: "Writing stories based on science does seem to have the tendency to cause the authors to put aside the love feature as an element therein. We presume that if our stories are to be scientific, this love element will be missing in most of them. The scientific features to a certain extent operate to exclude every day romance" (19280: 373). Although he modifies his statement with "seem," "presume," and "to a certain extent," the inference is clear: the hard, virile space of science operates to expel romance and thus women.

Another reader who was not averse to a love interest was Mrs. Helen Ammons of Chicago, Illinois: "You know, Mr. Editor, that you have quite a number of woman readers and, although I cannot speak for all of them, still I can and do speak for a large group of them in Chicago. We eagerly read science fiction stories, but we like our stories to be flavored with the sugar of a good love element. Not too much sugar—you understand. We don't want them gooey; just enough to give them interest" (Ammons 1929: 567). She understands that "a good love element" is bad for her, rots the teeth, and so will settle for just a little. However, in the same issue, C. R. Paratico of Brazil makes four suggestions for improving *Science Wonder Stories*. The last one is that there be no sugar at all:

> (a) Refrain as much as possible, from reprinting stories by popular authors, who are widely known.
> (b) Avoid the more glaring improbabilities.
> (c) Read the stories yourself, and cut out such parts as would tend to give your readers false knowledge of scientific facts.
> (d) Remember that love interest can only enter these stories if it is dragged in by the hair. (Paratico 1929: 669)

Once again the love interest is "dragged in," this time "by the hair." However, "love interest" is dragged into science fiction stories by an unnamed agent. The violence is actually being done to the love interest/woman and yet the implication is that it is she who is corrupting science fiction. This is reminiscent of Nina Puren's arguments about the grammar of the rape trial where the woman who is raped is made responsible for that rape; "Her beauty made him go crazy" (Puren 1995: 18).

For the editors and many readers romance was not only inimical to science fiction but so also was "sex-type literature." In his editorial "Fiction versus Facts," Gernsback quotes one of his authors, G. Peyton Wertenbaker: "*Amazing Stories* should appeal, however, to quite a different public (referring to the sex-type of literature). Scientifiction is a branch of literature which requires more intelligence and even more aesthetic sense than is possessed by the sex-type reading public" (Gernsback 1926d: 291). Sex, in short, is nasty and brutish and anyone with an aesthetic sense would choose not to read "sex-type" literature. These superior types are drawn to science fiction. In fact, Wertenbaker defines "scientifiction" as a branch of literature in opposition to the "sex-type literature."

Gernsback was more direct about this in his editorial for the first issue of *Science Wonder Stories*: "The past decade has seen the ascendancy of "sexy" literature, of the self-confession type as well as the avalanche of modern detective stories" (Gernsback 1929e: 5). This literature will not contaminate Gernsback's new magazine: "SCIENCE WONDER STORIES are clean, CLEAN from beginning to end. They stimulate only one thing—the IMAGINATION" (Gernsback 1929e: 5). *Science Wonder Stories*, he implies, frees the mind from the body, stimulating the one while leaving the other alone.

By the 1930s the "spicies," pulp magazines that emphasized stimulating the libido, had emerged. They had names like *Spicy Mystery*, *Spicy Western Stories*, and *Spicy Detective Stories*, and lurid covers to match. Many, at the time, worried about the effect the spicies would have on science fiction. Others changed with the times. In 1938, the publisher Martin Goodman and the editor Robert Ersiman decided that their new magazine, *Marvel Science Stories*, would give sf "a new direction" by making it "more spicy" (Ashley 1975: 36). Goodman and Ersiman asked sf writer Henry Kuttner to add some spicy scenes to his stories. In the first issue he published three stories—one under his own name, Henry Kuttner, and two under the pen names James Hall and Robert O. Kenyon. All three stories were strongly criticized (Ashley 1975: 36). According to Susan Wood, the first three issues, which "offered the fans sex and sadomasochism with their SF . . . proved unpopular" (Wood 1978–79: 12). Lester del Rey writes that "*Marvel* got off to a wrong foot with readers by featuring a lead story by Henry Kuttner which was considered somewhat sexy in its time. The publishers had decided that sex should increase its interest, but they soon found that it turned the readers off. . . . The magazine never quite lived down that feeling" (del Rey 1979: 122).

Many letter writers in *Marvel* advocated that the magazine abandon its "spiciness." Any change they detected in that direction was applauded. Bill Brudy of Wolverine, Michigan, writes: "It is gratifying to see the magazine sticking to good taste. The first issue tottered dangerously. Sex can only ruin science fiction. No class of pulp publications has higher standards than fantasy fiction and the reading public will keep them that way" (Brudy 1939: 108). In the same issue George Aylesworth of Mackinaw City, Michigan, agrees with Bill Brudy: "Four issues of *Marvel* now repose in my files and on reading through them I note the rapid improvement 'our' mag has made. At first, it is true the mag had a spicy atmosphere but now it seems to have thrown that off" (Aylesworth 1939: 110). An example of the kind of spicy material *Marvel* published is "Lust Rides the Roller Coaster" by Ray King,[5] from the December 1939 issue. "Lust" is about a young man whose former mistress vows to destroy him. One of the "spicy" passages runs: "Those long evenings—they had seemed so exciting when she danced for him, stripped to almost the last tiny transparent garment, and he had snatched her to him hungrily, devouring her with his hot lips and breathless passion" (King 1939: 72). After some supernatural occurrences involving a roller coaster, the hero discovers that he is better off with a nice girl than his evil mistress. The story was not popular with fans.

Prozine Covers

Much of the debate about sex in science fiction was focused on the covers of the magazines. Sex was located in representations of women on the front covers of the sf magazines but not, on the whole, in representations of men. Indeed, this was the most obvious way in which women were present in science fiction during the period from 1926 to the late 1950s. Initially the covers of most science fiction magazines were not dominated by naked or scantily clad women. Although the covers of *Amazing Stories* during the 1920s did include representations of women, and although some of them wore considerably less clothing than the men on the covers, the women were not the focus of attention (see figure 7). However, by the 1930s the representation of women on the covers was becoming increasingly genitally focused and particularly obsessed with breasts. On many covers the women were the overwhelming focus of attention.[6] These women were always white.

In the debates about the covers, sex comes to stand for women and vice

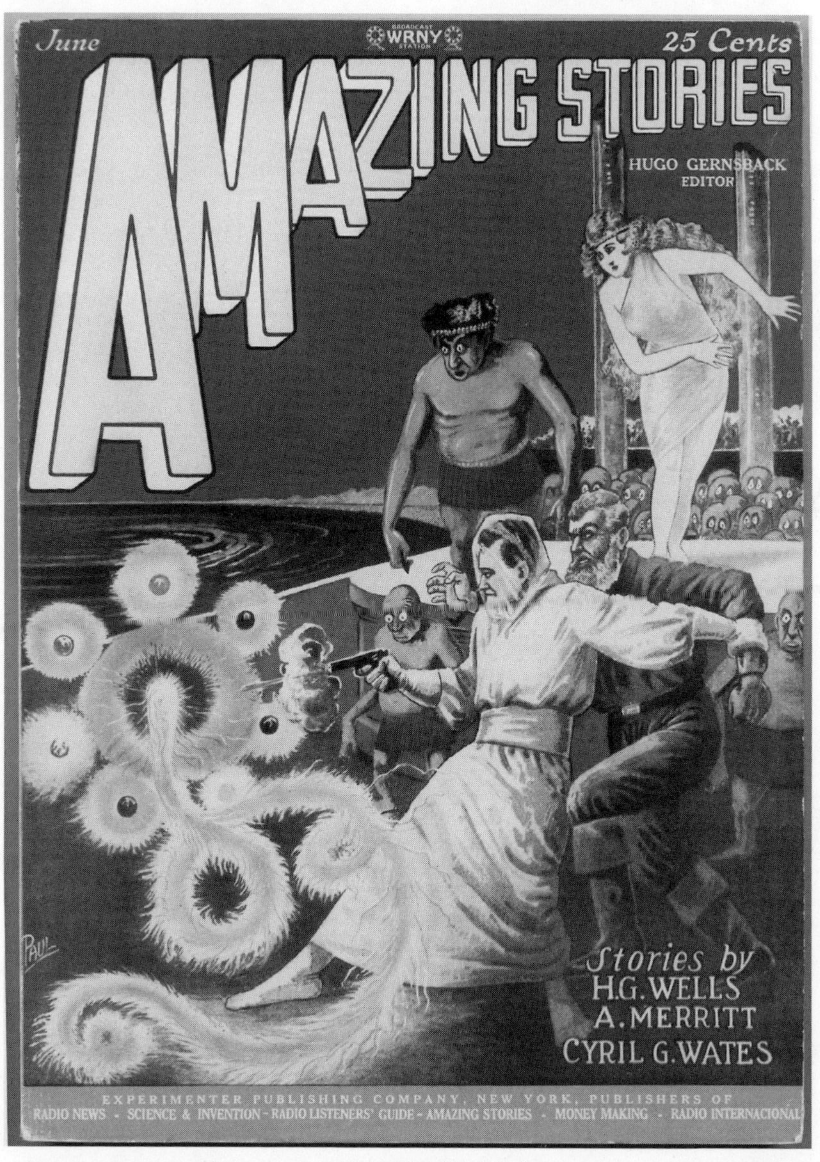

7. June 1927 cover of *Amazing Stories*, by Frank R. Paul.

versa. When covers focus on women's bodies, there are complaints about the cover being too sexy or spicy. The following letter from G. E. Rennison of Blackburn, England, illustrates: "Though well drawn, they [the covers] represent what is the dregs of sfn.-sex appeal. Why must you plaster the covers with half nude women? Though easy on the eyes, they do not suit sfn . . . . Sure a Nice woman will do NOW AND AGAIN, but put some clothes on 'em. Don't get me wrong, I like pictures of half (?) nude women but not in sfn. mags" (Rennison 1942: 121).

However, when the cover features a muscular male figure there are no such comments. For instance, the cover of the October 1939 *Astounding* by Rogers features the hero Kimball Kinnison of the immensely popular *Lensmen* series (figure 8). He is the epitome of fascist chic in a silver-gray uniform, with his well-defined muscles, grim expression, and chiseled jaw. The cover generated an overwhelmingly enthusiastic response. Ray Bradbury wrote in to *Astounding* to say, "If you could have been at the Thursday meeting of the Los Angeles Science-Fiction League you would have heard a chorus of excited ohs and ahs echo far into the night as Forrest J. Ackerman produced the October issue of *Astounding*. It is, undoubtedly the best cover of the year. . . . Kimball Kinnison as coverized is enough to make Atlas melt away into his original ninety-seven pounds" (Bradbury 1939b: 101).

Covers that emphasized a woman's physicality in this way rarely generated that kind of adulation. Magazines with scantily clad women on the cover were discussed in terms of whether their "sexiness" was a good or a bad thing. In the 1950s *Future's* covers, for example, frequently featured representations of women. Robert "Buck" Coulson of Wabash, Indiana, writes, "[Y]our covers all look alike, and they are all definitely second-rate" (Coulson 1958: 126). Robert Ebert of Urbana, Illinois, writes: "Buck Coulson has a lot of truth in his statement about your covers; you seem to be in a sort of rut. You've had a girl on the cover of the last five issues—this may have been ok for *TWS* [*Thrilling Wonder Stories*], but not for good ol' *Future*. Don't feel too badly—*Infinity* has had girls on all but one of its seventeen covers! *Astounding* has had one girl in the last twenty-seven issues, and she was a scientist with a turtle-neck sweater *and* a jacket on" (Ebert 1958: 115).

Astounding was the leading science fiction magazine at the time. That *Astounding* had so few "girls" grace its cover is an indication of the magazine's superiority. The one girl who was represented on the cover was not just a girl, but a scientist, and a fully clothed one at that (figure 9). It illus-

8. October 1939 cover of *Astounding Science Fiction,* by Hubert Rogers, illustrating E. E. "Doc" Smith's "Grey Lensman"

trates the story "Omnilingual" by H. Beam Piper. The story's protagonist is a linguist, Martha Dane, and it is she who is illustrated on the cover: forehead creased in concentration, poring over various texts, pen in one hand and her other hand held to her temple as though thinking. She is not stereotypically beautiful and her breasts are not noticeable. It is an unusual cover for the time, as is the story.

The turtleneck sweater and her status of scientist mean that Martha Dane has ceased to signify sex. Her presence on the cover does not sully science fiction. In a sense, she is no longer a girl in the same way that the girls who grace the covers of *Future* and *Infinity* magazine are. This is an image of a woman who has not been incorporated into the heterosexual order in the same way that the heroines of the stories I examined in chapter 2 were. Oddly enough, in the imaginary pure sphere of masculine science fiction, there is a small space for the woman who can exist outside heterosexuality as a not-real woman of a particular kind—the honorary man.

I discovered some letters by women demanding more men as sex objects. Evelyn Catoe of Brunswick, New Jersey, wanted to have covers where men signified "sex": "I will say that I liked the cover on the December issue. It is nice to pick up one of my regular mags and find no girls, just lots of good looking men. Something for my sex at last. I am going to start campaigning for more men on more covers" (Catoe 1952: 132).

As well as debating the appropriateness of sex—that is, "desirable" women—to the covers and therefore to science fiction, readers also discussed the unscientific nature of these covers. One particular subject attracted comment: images of women in space without the need for any breathing apparatus (figure 10). Marian Cox writes: "I suppose we gals should be flattered by the obvious fact that men regard us as such indestructible creatures. According to them, we don't feel heat or cold and so don't need space suits. We must manufacture our own oxygen, or else we can exist without breathing at all. (Which is it, fellows?) They still call us the weaker sex, but I'm beginning to wonder" (Cox 1952: 127). In the same letter she agrees with Evelyn Catoe that there should be more sexy men on the covers. This would result in the male body being acknowledged as an object of sexual desire, rather than simply a projection of what the male fans desired to be. I would argue that the scarcity of male fans expressing approval of representations of male bodies on the covers during the 1950s can be directly attributed to the production of knowledges about, and thus fear of, homosexuality.

The debate about covers did not often conclude that women should be

9. February 1957 cover of *Astounding Science Fiction*, by Frank Kelly Freas, illustrating H. Beam Piper's "Omnilingual"

10. August 1951 cover of *Thrilling Wonder Stories*, by Earle Bergey

kept off the covers altogether, though it was implicit in the argument that sex should be kept off the covers. This conflation is explicit in a letter from B. W. Williams that refers to representations of women on the covers as well as in inside illustrations in the magazine: "What's wrong with sex inside or outside as long as the gal shows expression in her eyes?" (Williams 1953: 136).[7] This inadvertently funny comment is revealing: sex is a gal.

The Love Interest Controversy

A thread of letters appeared in 1938–1939 in "Brass Tacks," the letter column of *Astounding Science Fiction*, in which readers debated whether there was any place for women in science fiction.[8] The readers' letters illustrate the terms of the debate; namely, that science fiction is a masculine space whose borders must be carefully patrolled to keep the pollution of women out. *Astounding* at the time had a reputation for being a technology-based magazine with a predominantly, and proudly, male readership. Nevertheless, Buck Coulson claims in a letter to *Aurora* that women have never been suppressed in science fiction and cited *Astounding* as evidence of this claim: "[I]n the Good Old Days, *Astounding* was presumed to be for men only, but the other STF mags used women writers. And even ASF had MacLean, without a male pseudonym" (Coulson 1986–87: 5). Science fiction writer Margaret St. Clair, who began publishing in the 1940s, has a different view. She writes that *Astounding* "wanted hard-core science only, and the editor there was reputed never to accept a story by a woman if he were aware of her sex" (St. Clair 1981: 151).

In the letters concerned with love and science fiction to *Astounding*'s readers' column, "Brass Tacks," the term "the love interest" frequently functions doubly. First, it functions as a synonym for "women"; second, it functions as a space in which the romance discourse can operate within the field of science fiction. If the love interest can be kept out of science fiction, then so too can the discourse of romance. The fear of the love interest in both these senses is part of the delineation of the science fiction field as masculine public space. This is why, in many accounts of the relationship of women to science fiction, the growing presence of women within the field is figured as an invasion. I discuss these accounts in the next chapter.

The main protagonist in this debate is Isaac Asimov of Brooklyn, New York, who had three long letters published, in contrast to the one or two letters published by the other participants. Asimov was born in January

1920, so at the time of writing he was in his late teens. The only other correspondent for whom I have an age is David McIlwain,[9] who was exactly a year younger than Asimov. I suspect that most of these misogynist letters are from boys of eighteen or younger.

The role of the love interest and of women in science fiction was a topic dear to Asimov's heart, and I found letters from him on this subject in *Startling Stories* and *Planet Stories* as well as the letters in *Astounding*. The presence or absence of the love interest was one of his criteria for a good story: he typically condemns a story for having "no plot outside of one that would fit it for some future 'scienti-love magazine'" (Asimov 1938a: 158). Such a genre formed from the cross-pollination of science fiction and romance is, for Asimov, a patent absurdity.[10] Asimov writes almost all his letters with tongue planted firmly in cheek. He argues for the sheer pleasure of argument and takes delight in being outrageous and provoking a response, contradicting himself whenever it suits him.

The first letter in the thread comes not from Isaac Asimov, but from a fellow traveler, Donald G. Turnbull of Toronto, Canada. The editor places the letter within the context of the battle of the sexes by giving it the heading, "Misogynist! Bet you hear from Miss Evans!" Patricia Evans of New York City had had a few letters published in *Astounding*; none of her letters raised any questions about representation of women. Her name is simply being used as a sign of women in science fiction. Turnbull writes:

> In the last six or seven publications females have been dragged into the narratives and as a result the stories have become those of love which have no place in science-fiction. Those who read this magazine do so for the science in it or for the good wholesome free-from-women stories which stretch their imaginations.
>
> A woman's place is not in anything scientific. Of course the odd female now and then invents something useful in the way that every now and then amongst the millions of black crows a white one is found.
>
> I believe, and I think many others are with me, that sentimentality and sex should be disregarded in scientific stories. Yours for more science and less females. (Turnbull 1938: 162)

This letter features the by now familiar equation of "females" and "love" and "sex," and adds another, "sentimentality." According to Turnbull, women taint science fiction, and only stories that are "free from women" are "good" and "wholesome." His imaginary space of science fiction is one populated by the *asporos*—the men who become eunuchs once fully grown—so as not waste their energies in sex. When he is immersed in the field he wants to leave the world of women behind. He is furious when this is not possible and his imaginary space is violated.[11] For although science fiction is located in the public sphere, it is also frequently imagined by Turnbull and others as a private male sphere, much like a men's club where a fellow can smoke his cigars and drink his port in the company of like-minded men. However, for all their malign influence, he assigns these females no agency. They are (again) "dragged into" the text by some unknown agent and are part of the nominalization "good wholesome free -from-women stories." The only exception is the "odd female [who] . . . invents something useful." Added to Turnbull's dismissal of women is the implicit racism of his "white crow/black crow" analogy.[12] Although white women were by no means central in science fiction of the 1920s and 1930s, women and men who were not white and middle class were even less visible.

Asimov is one of the "many others [who] are with [Turnbull]" on the question of love in science fiction: "Three rousing cheers for Donald G. Turnbull of Toronto for his valiant attack on those favoring mush. When we want science-fiction, we don't want swooning dames, and that goes double. You needn't worry about Miss Evans, Donald, us he-men are for you and if she tries to slap you down, you've got an able (I hope) confederate and tried auxiliary right here in the person of yours truly. Come on, men, make yourself heard in favor of less love mixed with our science!" (Asimov 1938b: 161).

Turnbull's depiction of women as unwholesome and having no place in "anything scientific" becomes in Asimov's text a "valiant attack on those favoring mush." The list of equivalences for women expands to include "mush" and "swooning dames." He takes up Turnbull's cry for undiluted, wholesome science that is not "mixed with" love. Asimov also transforms Turnbull the "misogynist," with his attack on unwholesome women polluting science fiction, into someone in need of protection, offering to protect him from regular *Astounding* correspondent Miss Evans. However, it was the editor who invoked Miss Evans's name and who made the charge of misogyny against Turnbull. Patricia Evans herself was silent in the debate and made no attack on Turnbull. In a letter in a later issue Evans writes an aside, "being, after all just a dumb dame," which could be an ironic response to Turnbull and Asimov (Evans 1938: 157); if that is the case, it is the *only* response she made to the debate about the role of women in science fiction. Or the only one that was published.

In the same November 1938 issue, directly following Evans's letter, is

DOWN WITH LOVE!

Dear Editor:

I just wish to amplify certain sane remarks by Don G. Turnbull which appeared in the July Brass Tacks.

"Love interest" has no place in serious science-fiction—and it should not be necessary to include it. A good story, by which I mean a well-written piece of science-fiction based on a sound, ingenious plot, should be in itself sufficient to grip the readers' attention, without necessitating the introduction of the sex bogey.

Science-fiction (especially Astounding) does not cater to sentimental old maids who like a bit of "slop" in their literature. Neither does it cater to love-sick nymphs who attempt to gain the Elysium of their frustrated desires via the doorway of books.

Your male readers greatly outnumber your female fans, so why not cut out the age-old love idea, and give us newer themes?

The only kind of tale in which love interest is (perhaps) permissible is the humorous one. When the "mighty emotion" is stripped of its banality and dressed in the ludicrous garments of frivolity—it becomes bearable. If you don't believe me, refer back to the works of S. G. Weinbaum—particularly his Van Mauderpootz series—and laugh.

There are few writers today who can handle L. I. So effectively.

Congratulations on Brown's wonderful cover, the best I've seen in years. I liked L. Ron Hubbard's "Dangerous Dimension" too! Quite amusing!—David McIlwain, 14 Cotswold St., Liverpool, England

11. Letter from David McIlwain, *Astounding Science Fiction,* November 1938, p. 158

one headed "Down with Love!," from David McIlwain of Liverpool, England (figure 11). McIlwain is not saying there should be no women in science fiction stories but rather that there should be no "love interest" that would be likely to attract female readership to science fiction. The binary opposition is still in place: female readers want love, men do not.

The first letter I found that opposed the views of Turnbull and Asimov is by Mary Byers of Springfield (figure 12). Byers tries to counter the equation of the "feminine" and "sex." Women are not sex, and therefore they do have a place in science fiction. She implicitly accepts, however, that sex is not good and does not belong in science fiction. She observes, "Undoubtedly it has never occurred to him [Asimov] to wonder whether the girl fans like the incredible adventures of an almost-ridiculous hero any better than he likes the impossible romance of an equally impossible heroine. He probably still cherishes the outdated theory that a girl's brain is used expressly to fill up what would otherwise be a vacuum in the cranium" (Byers 1938: 160).

Down with Love!

Dear Editor:

I just wish to amplify certain sane remarks by Don G. Turnbull which appeared in the July Brass Tacks.

"Love interest" has no place in serious science-fiction—and it should not be necessary to include it. A good story, by which I mean a well-written piece of science-fiction based on a sound, ingenious plot, should be in itself sufficient to grip the readers' attention, without necessitating the introduction of the sex bogey.

Science-fiction (especially Astounding) does not cater to sentimental old maids who like a bit of "slop" in their literature. Neither does it cater to love-sick nymphs who attempt to gain the Elysium of their frustrated desires via the doorway of books.

Your male readers greatly outnumber your female fans, so why not cut out the age-old love idea, and give us newer themes?

The only kind of tale in which love interest is (perhaps) permissible is the humorous one. When the "mighty emotion" is stripped of its banality and dressed in the ludicrous garments of frivolity—it becomes bearable. If you don't believe me, refer back to the works of S. G. Weinbaum—particularly his Van Mauderpootz series—and laugh.

There are few writers today who can handle L. I. so effectively.

Congratulations on Brown's wonderful cover, the best I've seen in years. I liked L. Ron Hubbard's "Dangerous Dimension" too! Quite amusing!—David McIlwain, 14 Cotswold St., Liverpool, England.

In other words, it isn't what you say, it's the way you say it.

Dear Editor:

After reading Isaac Asimov's letter in the September Brass Tacks, I feel the necessity of taking the issue of "swooning dames" up with him.

To begin, he has made the grave error of confusing the feminine interest with the sex theme—for proof of this turn back to the time-honored *Skylark* stories and note well the fact that the presence of Dorothy detracted from the general worth of the story not one bit, then compare one of Kuttner's pieces of hokum with it, and the distinction will be evident to even the most unobservant reader.

Continuing this bigoted line of thought, he goes on to express himself as regards much in s-f. Undoubtedly it has never occurred to him to wonder whether the girl fans like the incredible adventures of an almost-ridiculous hero any better than he likes the impossible romance of an equally impossible heroine. He probably still cherishes the outdated theory that a girl's brain is used expressly to fill up what would otherwise be a vacuum in the cranium.

To his plea for less hooey I give my whole-hearted support, but less hooey does *not* mean less women; it means a difference in the way they are introduced into the story and the part they play. Let Mr. Asimov turn the pages of a good history book and see how many times mankind has held progress back; let him also take notice that any changes wrought by women have been more or less permanent, and that these changes were usually made against the prejudice and illogical arguments of men, and feel himself chastened.

Also, the fact that the feminine sphere of influence carries over to Donald Turnbull is shown by the inference that he reads s-f. to escape from them. Did you ever want to escape from an authority that didn't exist, Mr. Turnbull? Regarding the occasional "white crow"—all famous people are "white crows," according to that theory, which reasons that to have invented or done something useful makes a "white crow" of the person. There is a larger percent of famous men than of famous women—sure, but remember that women haven't been actually included in the sciences except for the past hundred years or so. Note the number of successful women today, though!

Yours for more like "Who Goes There?" and "The Terrible Sense" and less like "The Legion of Time"—Mary Byers, Chaney Farm, R. F. D. 5, Springfield, Ohio.

IN OTHER WORDS, IT ISN'T WHAT YOU SAY,
IT'S THE WAY YOU SAY IT.

Dear Editor:

After reading Isaac Asimov's letter in the September Brass Tacks, I feel the necessity of taking the issue of "swooning dames" up with him.

To begin, he has made the grave error of confusing the feminine interest with the sex theme—for proof of this turn back to the time-honored *Skylark* stories and note well the fact that the presence of Dorothy detracted from the general worth of the story not one bit, then compare one of Kuttner's pieces of hokum with it, and the distinction will be evident to even the most unobservant reader.

Continuing this bigoted line of thought, he goes on to express himself as regards much in s-f. Undoubtedly it has never occurred to him to wonder whether the girl fans like the incredible adventures of an almost-ridiculous hero any better than he likes the impossible romance of an equally impossible heroine. He probably still cherishes the outdated theory that a girl's brain is used expressly to fill up what would otherwise be a vacuum in the cranium.

To his plea for less hooey I give my whole-hearted support, but less hooey does *not* mean less women; it means a difference in the way they are introduced into the story and the part they play. Let Mr. Asimov turn the pages of a good history book and see how many times mankind has held progress back; let him also take notice that any changes wrought by women have been more or less permanent, and that these changes were usually made against the prejudice and illogical arguments of men, and feel himself chastened.

Also, the fact that the feminine sphere of influence carries over to Donald Turnbull is shown by the inference that he reads s-f. to escape from them. Did you ever want to escape from an authority that didn't exist, Mr. Turnbull? Regarding the occasional "white crow"—all famous people are "white crows," according to that theory, which reasons that to have invented or done something useful makes a "white crow" of the person. There is a larger percent of famous men than of famous women—sure, but remember that women haven't been actually included in the sciences except for the past hundred years or so. Note the number of successful women today, though!

Yours for more like "Who Goes There?" and "The Terrible Sense" and less like "The Legion of Time"—Mary Byers, Chaney Farm, R. F. D. 5, Springfield, Ohio.

12. Letter from Mary Evelyn Byers, *Astounding Science Fiction,* December 1938, pp. 160–61

Byers wants the understanding of the audience to be expanded to account for the fact that there are girl fans as well as boy fans. For her, science fiction is not a masculine space. McIlwain has already rejected this argument on the grounds that there are many fewer girl fans. She also argues that the representation of males in sf is as absurd as that of women. She could be referring to the overblown representation of Kimball Kinnison on the cover of the October 1939 *Astounding*, which was so avidly received by male fans.

Byers continues: "To his [Asimov's] plea for less hooey I give my whole-hearted support, but less hooey does not mean less women; it means a difference in the way they are introduced into the story and the part they play" (Byers 1938: 160). Her argument here is almost identical to some of those of Russ (1971), Badami (1976), and Wood (1978–79) more than thirty years later, which I consider in the next chapter. In the 1970s they argued for more exploration of "gender roles" and for more fiction that abandoned stereotyped representations of women. Byers then switches the argument to changing attitudes to women generally. Although Byers challenges Turnbull and Asimov, she accepts one part of their argument—she agrees that "sex" and "hooey" have no place in science fiction. She does not, however, read them as synonymous with women. However, in Byers's phrasing, women still have to be "introduced" into the story by someone else. They still have limited agency.

Another letter by a woman that appeared around the same time makes a similar argument. Naomi Slimmer of Russell, Kansas also wants less "sex" (which she too associates with women) but at the same time she wants better representations of women:

> As to the plots of science stories; keep 'em clean. If we wanted to read about "curving pearl-pink flesh, blushing dimpled cheeks and passionate pulsing buzzems" we could get a copy of one of the "Spicies." If you have to have a female in the picture, make her sensible. Let her know a few things about space-ships, heat-guns and such. Phooey on the huzzies who are always getting their clothes torn off and walling an amorous eye at the poor overworked hero. If she's fitten to be in the story, she's gotta be a pard to the poor guy and give him a hand.
>
> You'd be surprised how many women read magazines of this type. Even the pussy-cats who go for sticky romances makes a grab for a copy when I'm dealing out magazines to the patients at our hospital. The nurses read them too, as I said, to keep awake and think of something besides a cranky patient. So how about giving us females a thought

when you are picking tales for futures issues? We like our men to be nice guys, maybe a bit bigger and handsomer than our real boy-friends, and our women we want to be nice guys too, good-looking but not soft. Sensible and good sports. (As we all imagine WE are)." (Slimmer 1939: 119–20)

Charles Hornig, the editor of *Science Fiction*, responds: "You seem to know your science-fiction as well as most fellows do, and your suggestions are helpful. I'm trying to keep the science in the stories from becoming too heavy, and will not let love interest dominate the tales" (Hornig 1939: 119). Hornig's patronizing reply demonstrates the same surprise at women's interest in science fiction that Gernsback evinced ten years earlier. However he modifies Naomi Slimmer's knowledge of science fiction: she only "seems" to know it well. He also fails to respond to Slimmer's desire to see sensible women who "know a few things about space-ships." Hornig does acknowlege Slimmer's call for less gratuitous romance; it is a call with which he was very familiar.

In the January 1939 issue of *Astounding* L. M. Jensen of Cowley, Wyoming, responds to the earlier letters by Asimov, Turnbull, McIlwain, and Byers. He or she also names the debate: "Now, maybe I'm sticking my neck out, but I'm going to put my two cents worth into the Love Interest controversy in Brass Tacks. I won't comment on the subject in general, because I'm not qualified to do so, but I will say that I enjoyed the hearty and wholesome man-and-wife companionship of Dick Seaton and Dorothy—the elfin, half-impudent, half-sacred courtship of Larry and Lakia—the restrained love interest in 'Triplanetary' and 'Space-hounds'" (*Astounding Science Fiction* [January 1939]: 162). Jensen here takes Turnbull's word "wholesome" and reapplies it to refer to the relationship of a man and his wife. Wholesomeness is dependent then on the *presence* of women, not on their absence.

These reversed terms are not acknowledged in Asimov's next letter in the thread (figure 13). He responds to Mary Byers's letter with a very long letter using violent metaphors that firmly situate him within the battle of the sexes. Asimov continues to take up the position of the male under attack, when in fact the debate began with Turnbull's attack on women in science fiction. He begins by saying that although he has "barely survived the bludgeonings of Miss Byers in the December issue, I return undaunted to the fray" (Asimov 1939a: 159). The debate itself is a battle, and Byers has been attacking him. Asimov's first response to these "bludgeonings" is that Byers actually agrees with him: "she herself considers the 'sex theme' as

AND SIMAK'S GOT A WOMAN THIS TIME!
ANYWAY, 1000 YEARS OUGHT TO BE OLD ENOUGH!

Dear Mr. Campbell:

Having barely survived the bludgeonings of Miss Byers in the December issue, I return undaunted to the fray.

First, I wish to point out that she herself considers the "sex theme" as unadulterated "hokum." She tries to get out it, though, by bringing in the idea of "feminine interest" and saying that it's not women in themselves, but the way they are handled that causes the whole trouble.

Very well, granted! Women are pretty handy creatures! (What would we do without them, sniff, sniff?) *But,* how in tarnation are you going to enforce a rule that the "feminine interest" must be introduced in an inoffensive manner?

There are certain authors (very few) that can handle women with the greatest of ease. The great Weinbaum simply permeated his stories with women and yet I never read a story of his that I didn't enjoy (may his soul rest in peace). E. E. Smith's women are swell, and I find I get along with them. Jack Williamson is pretty good, even when he brings in his goddesses. However, that about exhausts the list.

The rest of the authors, while all very good in their way, can't bring the "feminine interest" into a story without getting sloppy. There is an occasional good one ("Helen O'Loy" is a beautiful case in point) but for every exceptional one there are 5,739 terrible cases. Stories in which the love interest drowns out everything, in which "swooning damsels" are thrown at us willy-nilly.

Notice, too, that many top-notch, grade-A, wonderful, marvelous, etc., etc., authors get along swell without any women, at all. John W. Campbell, Jr., himself, is the most perfect case of all. Nat Schachner has very few indeed. Clifford D. Simak has none. Ross Rocklynne has none. The list can be extended much further.

The point is whether we can make every author a Smith and Weinbaum or whether we cannot. What do you think? Therefore, let Smith and Williamson keep their women, but for Heaven's sake, let the rest forget about them, partly anyway. I still say we're after science-fiction.

Of course, we could have women-scientists. Madame Curie is immortal, so are many others. Unfortunately, instead of having a properly aged, resourceful, and scientific woman as a savant, what do we have? When there is a woman-scientist (which is very rare in fiction, believe me) she is about eighteen and very beautiful and, oh, so helpless in the face of danger (gr-r-r-r).

Which is another complaint I have against women. They're always getting into trouble and having to be rescued. It's very boring indeed for us men. I should think the women themselves (proud creatures) would be the first to object.

In the third paragraph, Miss Byers wants to know whether I think girl-fans are interested in the adventures of an "almost-ridiculous hero." Oh, don't I? How about Robert Taylor and Clark Gable? I'll bet all the females swoon just reading their names in Brass Tacks. Besides, if they don't go for

And Simak's got a woman this time! Anyway, 1000 years ought to be old enough!

Dear Mr. Campbell,

Having barely survived the bludgeonings of Miss Byers in the December issue, I return undaunted to the fray.

First, I wish to point out that she herself considers the "sex theme" as unadulterated "hokum." She tries to get out of it, though, by bringing in the idea of "feminine interest" and saying that it's not women in themselves, but the way they are handled that causes the whole trouble.

Very well, granted! Women are pretty handy creatures! (What would we do without them, sniff, sniff?) *But,* how in tarnation are you going to enforce a rule that the "feminine interest" must be introduced in an inoffensive manner?

There are certain authors (very few) that can handle women with the greatest of ease. The great Weinbaum simply permeated his stories with women and yet I never read a story of his that I didn't enjoy (may his soul rest in peace). E. E. Smith's women are swell, and I find I get along with them. Jack Williamson is pretty good, even when he brings in his goddesses. However, that about exhausts the list.

The rest of the authors, while all very good in their way, can't bring the "feminine interest" into a story without getting sloppy. There is an occasional good one ("Helen O'Loy" is a beautiful case in point) but for every exceptional one there are 5,739 terrible cases. Stories in which the love interest drowns out everything, in which "swooning damsels" are thrown at us willy-nilly.

Notice, too, that many top-notch, grade-A, wonderful, marvelous, etc., etc., authors get along swell without any women, at all. John W. Campbell, Jr., himself, is the most perfect case of all. Nat Schachner has very few indeed. Clifford D. Simak has none. Ross Rocklynne has none. The list can be extended much further.

The point is whether we can make every author a Smith and Weinbaum or whether we cannot. What do you think? Therefore, let Smith and Williamson keep their women, but for Heaven's sake, let the rest forget about them, partly anyway. I still say we're after science-fiction.

Of course, we could have women-scientists. Madame Curie is immortal, so are many others. Unfortunately, instead of having a properly aged, resourceful, and scientific woman as a savant, what do we have? When there is a woman-scientist (which is very rare in fiction, believe me) she is about eighteen and very beautiful and oh, so helpless in the face of danger (gr-r-r-r).

Which is another complaint I have against women. They're always getting into trouble and having to be rescued. It's very boring indeed for us men. I should think the women themselves (proud creatures) would be the first to object.

In the third paragraph, Miss Byers wants to know whether I think girl-fans are interested in the adventures of an "almost-ridiculous hero." Oh, don't I? How about Robert Taylor and Clark Gable? I'll bet all the females swoon just reading their names in Brass Tacks. Besides, if they don't go for heroes, what are they doing reading science-fiction? Let them go back to love stories (which are written by women for women) and they'll find even slap-happier heroes there.

Furthermore, Miss Byers is very ill-advised in her attempt to bring up the greater influence of women as against men in the course of history. Let me point out that women never affected the world directly. They always grabbed hold of some poor, innocent man, worked their insidious wiles on him (poor unsophisticated, unsuspecting person that he was) and then affected history through him. Cleopatra, for instance. It was Mark Antony that did the real affecting; Cleopatra, herself, affected only Mark Antony. Same with Pompadour, Catherine de Medici, Theodora and practically all other famous women of history.

But I'll quit now before I create a national vendetta against myself on the part of all female science-fictioneers in the United States. (There must be at least twenty of them!)

This answer may be taken as a defense of Donald Turnbull's courageous stand against the ace menace to science-fiction as well as a defense of my own stand. I say this, because Donald may not find time to answer, and I have promised to defend him against attack with all the power of my good right arm—Isaac Asimov, 174 Windsor Place, Brooklyn, N. Y.

heroes, what are they doing reading science-fiction? Let them go back to love stories (which are written by women for women) and they'll find even slap-happier heroes there.

Furthermore, Miss Byers is very ill-advised in her attempt to bring up the greater influence of women as against men in the course of history. Let me point out that women never affected the world directly. They always grabbed hold of some poor, innocent man, worked their insidious wiles on him (poor unsophisticated, unsuspecting person that he was) and then affected history through him. Cleopatra, for instance. It was Mark Antony that did the real affecting; Cleopatra, herself, affected only Mark Antony. Same with Pompadour, Catherine de Medici, Theodora and practically all other famous women of history.

But I'll quit now before I create a national vendetta against myself on the part of all female science-fictioneers in the United States. (There must be at least twenty of them!)

This answer may be taken as a defense of Donald Turnbull's courageous stand against the ace menace to science-fiction as well as a defense of my own stand. I say this, because Donald may not find time to answer, and I have promised to defend him against attack with all the power of my good right arm—Isaac Asimov, 174 Windsor Place, Brooklyn, N. Y.

13. Letter from Isaac Asimov, *Astounding Science Fiction*, February 1939, pp. 159–60

unadulterated 'hokum'" (159). In his arguments about representation it is the women only whose representation is a site of trouble. They are like radioactive material that has to be "handled" carefully. Byers's attempt to separate that which is represented from the manner of its representation is to Asimov absurd and impossible to enforce. However, "[t]here are certain authors (very few) that can handle women with the greatest of ease" (159).

The expertise of these writers protects them from contamination by women. Unfortunately, most writers are unable to write about women without having it turn their writing into "slop." The act of bringing in the "feminine interest" is what ruins the stories. Presumably it was the writer who brought the love interest in, but this contradiction is not explored. Once again the "swooning damsels" appear in the text against their own volition and are then held responsible for their presence in the text.

Asimov's example of a successful use of a love interest in science fiction is a story in which the love interest is not a woman but a robot. "Helen O'Loy" by Lester del Rey appeared in the December 1938 issue of *Astounding*. The heroine of the title is a robot created by the hero and his best friend as their version of the perfect woman. Both men fall in love with her. The story was very popular with readers and has been reprinted frequently. However, the letter immediately following Asimov's, by Charles Johnson of Drexel Hill, Pennsylvania, is not full of praise for the story. He refers to the character Helen O'Loy as a "walking, talking, cooking, loving robot" and says that the story is a "bit of drivel" (*Astounding Science Fiction* [February 1939]: 160). More than thirty years later, Beverley Friend, in her article "Virgin Territory: Women and Sex in Science Fiction," writes of the final line of the story, "there was only one Helen O'Loy," echoes that phrasing when she writes that one Helen O'Loy is "[f]rankly, one . . . . too many . . . —a walking, talking doll performs better as an android than she could possibly do as a human" (Friend 1972: 49).

Throughout his letter Asimov uses the pronoun "we" to refer to the inhabitants of the space of science fiction. It is taken for granted that this is a space within which women are entirely marginal and that this "we" is masculine. Asimov also refers to the place of women outside science fiction and how this has *not* translated to science fiction: "Of course, we could have women-scientists. Madame Curie is immortal, so are many others. Unfortunately, instead of a properly aged resourceful, and scientific woman as a savant, what do we have? When there is a woman-scientist (which is very rare in fiction, believe me) she is about eighteen and very beautiful and oh, so helpless in the face of danger (gr-r-r-r)" (Asimov 1939a: 160). The woman scientist in "the turtle-neck sweater *and* jacket" on the cover of *Astounding* is taken out of the realms of the "spicy" by being clothed. Another method of allowing a woman to operate within science fiction without being love interest is for her to be "properly aged" (unlike the young Asimov) and presumably asexual. Asimov conflates women with the way they are represented in science fiction and then makes them responsible for that representation. There are actually many parallels between Asimov's criticisms and later feminist critiques of representations of women in science fiction. He is clearly saying that the representations of women in science fiction at the time were, with a few rare exceptions, appalling. However, Asimov's complaint is "against women," rather than against the ways in which they had been represented in science fiction.

Asimov continues his rebuttal of Byers: "In the third paragraph, Miss Byers wants to know whether I think girl-fans are interested in the adventures of an 'almost-ridiculous hero.' Oh, don't I? How about Robert Taylor and Clark Gable? I'll bet all the females swoon just reading their names in Brass Tacks. Besides, if they don't go for heroes, what are they doing reading science-fiction?? Let them go back to love stories (which are written by women for women) and they'll find even slap-happier heroes there" (160). Men, "heroes," no matter how illogical or unbelievable, belong in science fiction. A woman cannot be a hero and therefore does not belong. However, these heroes are also functioning in the space of the love interest. They are a locus for heterosexual female desire in the same way that the female love interest is a locus for male heterosexual desire. These are desires that Asimov, however, is keen to keep outside science fiction.

Asimov also refutes Byers claim that women have had any effect on history:

> Furthermore, Miss Byers is very ill-advised in her attempt to bring up the greater influence of women as against men in the course of history. Let me point out that women never affected the world directly. They always grabbed hold of some poor, innocent man, worked their insidious wiles on him (poor unsophisticated, unsuspecting person that he was) and then affected history through him. Cleopatra, for instance. It was Mark Antony that did the real affecting; Cleopatra, herself, affected only Mark Antony. Same with Pompadour, Catherine de Medici, Theodora and practically all other famous women of history. (160)

Asimov finishes his letter where he began, by placing the debate in the sphere of violence between men and women, which is arguably also where romance is located. He talks of a "national vendetta against myself on the part of all female science-fictioneers in the United States. (There must be at least twenty of them!)" and terms his actions as "a defense of Donald Turnbull's courageous stand against the ace menace to science-fiction as well as a defence of my own stand" (160). The warfare metaphors are back to the fore; this debate is war. Asimov valiantly defends himself against women and all the trappings of romance they bring with them.

In the April 1939 *Astounding* there are three responses to Asimov's letter. James Michael Rogers II of Muskogee, Oklahoma, objects to Asimov's version of women in history:

> Mr. Asimov thinks women of no account in history. Points out that men are the famed leaders. But history is a record of wars and sad oppression. Women are not famous for such things as this. Let men have all credit as rulers in history. But wait—wasn't there a certain Maid of Orleans? Women are great in other things, too. I am reading what I believe to be the best novel in my experience: "Kristin Lavransdatter" by Sigrid Undset. Don't give man too much credit for the better things of our world. There are women Dostoievskys [*sic*] and Einsteins, but I hope never a woman Napoleon or Hitler! (Rogers 1939: 159–60)

The second response comes from Mary Evelyn Rogers of the same address in Muskogee, Oklahoma, who is obviously some relation to James Michael (figure 14). Continuing Asimov's tongue-in-cheek tone she unpacks Asimov's conflation of representation with that which is represented and shifts responsibility on to the author: "I agree with you that the women should be convincing, human creatures. Not goddesses or silly, simpering saints of sweet sixteen, but honest-to-goodness human creatures. However, that should not put a ban on the entire sex. Nor do I agree that all authors, except Smith and Campbell, give up writing about women. Practice makes perfect, you know, and how are the other writers ever going to learn the right way to handle the female characters if they don't experiment?" (160). Her call, like that of Byers, is for better representation of women, which allows them to be included in the category of human beings rather then to exist merely as the "love interest."

Another letter to engage with this debate in the same April edition is from Charles M. Jarvis of St. Paul, Minnesota. He thinks that "Don Turnbull and Isaac Asimov are creating an issue where one doesn't exist when they take the stand they do on the 'female' subject" (Jarvis 1939: 161). Although Jarvis agrees that there is too much mush in science fiction, he believes that as the writing improves "such situations will be handled with more expertness and understanding" (160). He then conflates love with humanity and the love interest becomes the "human interest": "After all, science-fiction needs 'human interest' as much as any other kind of fiction, and the high class of authors that are frequenting the pages of our magazine have the ability to handle their stories wisely and to the best advantage. Love is no more foreign to us than eating, and if a plot needs love to send the hero into the yawning cavity of space . . . by all means give the poor fellow love and send him out on his adventure" (161).

This is a shift in the argument. Byers and Mary Rogers argued that women do belong in science fiction although "hooey" does not and that the two are not the one and the same. Jarvis is arguing that women and love in science fiction are a sign of the maturity of the genre. A grown-up man needs a woman, and having her is sign of his maturity. Heterosexuality makes the presence of women ubiquitous. Indeed the presence of women is an indication that males in science fiction have matured from their homosocial/sexual adoration of Kimball Kinnison. Fred Hurter of Red Rock, Ontario, Canada, agrees with Asimov on that "much-battered love-interest question: In a well-written story, love interest is not neces-

We'll say this; the elimination of women would certainly have eliminated history!

Dear Mr. Campbell:

After I read your magazine it was your misfortune that my eye happened to light on the good old typewriter. And once fixed upon that organ of torture, I could not tear it away. It became my intention, irrevocable, to write my reaction of the current Astounding so that all, (yes, all!) might read it. I knew that you might not want my comment, that you could probably get along very well without it, but, well, maybe I wanted to see my name in print again. Or, perhaps, I just got mad at Mr. Isaac Asimov's letter.

In any event, I will tear into Mr. Asimov first. He says he is against women in science-fiction because the authors do not handle them properly. Mr. Asimov! Is that nice? It would be equally just for the women readers of science-fiction to campaign for the elimination of men in science-fiction because of a few idiotic, imbecilic males in science-fiction stories. We do not judge the men or the value of the men in science-fiction by a few blunders, so—why should you? Then, too, pictures of the future would not be complete without women. Or don't you agree that there will be women in the future? I agree with you that the women should be convincing, human creatures. Not goddesses, or silly, simpering saints of sweet sixteen, but honest-to-goodness human creatures. However, that should not put a ban on the entire sex. Nor do I agree that all authors, except Smith and Campbell, give up writing about women. Practice makes perfect, you know, and how are the other writers ever going to learn the right way to handle the female characters if they don't experiment. Another fault I find is your contention that women did not affect history. You say that women only affected the men who made history. Isn't that the same?

Ah, well, to leave Mr. Asimov for a space—until he answers, at least, I wish to say that I like the new artist, Rogers. No, he isn't related to me (he would probably be the first to deny it), I am not pulling for the family name. It is my sincere opinion that he is good. I think my favorite illustration of the issue was the one illustration "The Shadow Of The Veil." Jack Williamson's story was good, one of his best stories, I think. The "Living Fossil" was excellent. Oh, well, why go on? 'Tis sufficient that I didn't find a single story in the magazine to make me disgusted or even mildly resentful. The forecast promises great things, too. I'll be sitting around waiting for the next Astounding to appear on the newsstands with feverish impatience—Mary Evelyn Rogers, 2006 Court Street, Muskogee, Oklahoma.

WE'LL SAY THIS; THE ELIMINATION OF WOMEN WOULD CERTAINLY HAVE ELIMINATED HISTORY!

Dear Mr. Campbell:

After I read your magazine it was your misfortune that my eye happened to light on the good old typewriter. And once fixed upon that organ of torture, I could not tear it away. It became my intention, irrevocable, to write my reaction to the current Astounding so that all, (yes, all!) might read it. I knew that you might not want my comment, that you could probably get along very well without it, but, well, maybe I wanted to see my name in print again. Or, perhaps, I just got mad at Mr. Isaac Asimov's letter.

In any event, I will tear into Mr. Asimov first. He says he is against women in science-fiction because the authors do not handle them properly. Mr. Asimov! Is that nice? It would be equally just for the women readers of science-fiction to campaign for the elimination of men in science-fiction because of a few idiotic, imbecilic males in science-fiction stories. We do not judge the men or the value of the men in science-fiction by a few blunders, so—why should you? Then, too, pictures of the future would not be complete without women. Or don't you agree that there will be women in the future? I agree with you that the women should be convincing, human creatures. Not goddesses, or silly, simpering saints of sweet sixteen, but honest-to-goodness human creatures. However, that should not put a ban on the entire sex. Nor do I agree that all authors, except Smith and Campbell, give up writing about women. Practice makes perfect, you know, and how are the other writers ever going to learn the right way to handle the female characters if they don't experiment. Another fault I find is your contention that women did not affect history. You say that women only affected the men who made history. Isn't that the same?

Ah, well, to leave Mr. Asimov for a space—until he answers, at least, I wish to say that I like the new artist, Rogers. No, he isn't related to me (he would probably be the first to deny it), I am not pulling for the family name. It is my sincere opinion that he is good. I think my favorite illustration of the issue was the one illustration "The Shadow of the Veil." Jack Williamson's story was good, one of his best stories, I think. The "Living Fossil" was excellent. Oh, well, why go on? 'Tis sufficient that I didn't find a single story in the magazine to make me disgusted or even mildly resentful. The forecast promises great things, too. I'll be sitting around waiting for the next Astounding to appear on the newsstands with feverish impatience—Mary Evelyn Rogers, 2006 Court Street, Muskogee, Oklahoma.

14. Letter from Mary Evelyn Rogers, *Astounding Science Fiction,* April 1939, p. 160

sary," however, "if it is well written and not overdone" then "it is not objectionable." He also agrees with Asimov about women's secondary role in history: "I am not saying that many men were not encouraged by their wives, but then again many were hindered" (Hurter 1939: 118).

In the next issue the ever-active and ready pugilist Asimov returns to the fray (figure 15). The issue also marks his first professional appearance in *Astounding* with the story "Trends."[13] The tenor of this even longer letter is consistent with the earlier letters and demonstrates Asimov's obvious pleasure in the fight. In it Asimov is consistent in figuring himself as the one under attack. He is not so consistent, however, in the arguments he makes. His delight in combat and turning out pithy amusing phrases means that consistency is of no consequence. In his previous letter he had argued that women had never "affected the world directly" (Asimov 1939a: 160). In this letter he argues that women have affected the world directly in all number of nefarious ways, citing Catherine II of Russia and Elizabeth I of England as examples.

When Asimov switches back to discussing science fiction, he argues that it is in grave danger from the "outer darkness." This darkness is, presumably the "spicies" and similar magazines. Science fiction is being "invaded" by some kind of disease that exhibits terrible "symptoms." As I demonstrate in the next chapter, the appearance of women in the field of science fiction is frequently characterized as an invasion that corrupts the field and drives out those best suited to science fiction, such as the super-intelligent slan type of sf enthusiast, like Asimov himself ,who are "far superior in intelligence." The fascist implications of such an utterance in 1939 are hard to escape. Asimov demonstrates his own "emotional maturity" in the last two paragraphs of his letter by shifting his position from a complete ban on "love interest" to a demand that the love interest be more "realistic."

James Michael Rogers II and Mary Evelyn Rogers of Muskogee, Oklahoma, write a combined response demonstrating that they are better read but just as capable of making sweeping generalizations (figure 16). They argue that it would have been amazing "if men had progressed against such odds" (Rogers and Rogers 1939: 97). These arguments are familiar libertarian feminist arguments of the time. The debate at this point has left behind the issue of women and science fiction for the issue of women and the world. These were issues that were discussed in some fanzines of the period. The following article, for example, appeared in 1945 in one of the fanzines published for the Vanguard Amateur Press Association by Robert W. Lowndes:

> *FREE AND UNEQUAL*
> Somewhere in almost any blue print for a more reasonable social and economic order, the proposition of sexual equality is bound to occur. And perhaps rightly so; consideration of human females as inferior beings *per se* derives from the same emotional and socio-economic base as consideration of the foreigner, or member of any other than the "white" race, or "christian" faith as inferior *per se*. . . .

Conspiracy!

Dear Mr. Campbell:

It's unfair! It's terribly unfair! It must be a conspiracy!

Do you mean to say you have received no letters upholding my courageous stand against slop? If not, why not? Are all the males married and afraid to breathe a word lest the little wife lift the rolling pin? Bah! A fine state of affairs! They're henpecked! All of them!

To take up the Rogers combination first: To wit, James Michael and Mary Evelyn, I state emphatically that this business of two against one is unsportsmanlike. However, right is on my side, and right always triumphs.

Who says that only men are responsible for war and repression? Yes, I mean you, James Michael. How about Catherine II of Russia? How about Catherine de Medici of France? How about Semiramis of Assyria? How about Queen Elizabeth of England? A sweet lot—*not.* The very Joan of Arc you mention, while an inspired national heroine, was chiefly remarkable in the fact that she led men to slaughter and be slaughtered.

On the other hand, the great philosophers and the great religious leaders of the world—the ones who taught truth and virtue, kindness and justice—were all, *all* men.

Mary Evelyn talks of a "few blunders" and "practice makes perfect." There have been too many blunders, and the most consistent offenders are those who have had the most practice and who, indeed, make literary (?) capital out of descriptions of lovely damsels and melting slop scenes under the impression that that is what the readers want. I refrain from mentioning names, but no doubt certain ones spring to the mind.

Here I must admit that as the months pass by Astounding offends less and less, though there have been several lapses. The editor, I must say, does not seem to be very fond of slop himself, judging from the stories he's written—except "Escape"—and the magazine he's edited.

Charles W. Jarvis says I am *creating* an issue. That is wrong. The issue exists and is vital. You have but to cast a look toward the outer darknesses and see certain magazines which make their living out of purveying slop. This system has invaded stf. itself before this, and symptoms of such an invasion are appearing again. Not serious as yet, but to the keen eye none the less alarming. I have the best interests of stf. at heart—believe me—and I assure you that slop is put out merely to cater to a lower class of readers. There is an attempt to increase circulation by attracting certain groups. Very well! They want to make money, so they can have those groups, but they lose other groups far superior in intelligence, in emotional maturity, and sensibility.

Let me state my position clearly. I want no more love interest for the sake of love interest alone. I want love interest written capably, written cleanly, written logically, written inoffensively. I want it written by those who *can* write it. Lastly, since my critics make long speeches about realism, let's have realistic love interest and not slop.

Is there anyone who disagrees with the last paragraph? If so, let him speak now or forever hold his peace, and let this be the last word!—Isaac Asimov, 174 Windsor Place, Brooklyn, N. Y.

CONSPIRACY!

Dear Mr. Campbell:

It's unfair! It's terribly unfair! It must be a conspiracy!

Do you mean to say that you have received no letters upholding my courageous stand against slop? If not, why not? Are all the males married and afraid to breathe a word lest the little wife lift the rolling pin? Bah! A fine state of affairs! They're henpecked! All of them!

To take up the Rogers combination first: To wit, James Michael and Mary Evelyn, I state emphatically that this business of two against one is unsportsmanlike. However, right is on my side, and right always triumphs.

Who says that only men are responsible for war and repression? Yes, I mean you, James Michael. How about Catherine II of Russia? How about Catherine de Medici of France? How about Semiramis of Assyria? How about Queen Elizabeth of England? A sweet lot—*not.* The very Joan of Arc you mention, while an inspired national heroine, was chiefly remarkable in the fact that she led men to slaughter and be slaughtered.

On the other hand, the great philosophers and the great religious leaders of the world—the ones who taught truth and virtue, kindness and justice—were all, *all* men.

Mary Evelyn talks of a "few blunders" and "practice makes perfect." There have been too many blunders, and the most consistent offenders are those who have had the most practice and who, indeed, make literary (?) capital out of descriptions of lovely damsels and melting slop scenes under the impression that that is what the readers want. I refrain from mentioning names, but no doubt certain ones spring to the mind.

Here I must admit that as the months pass by Astounding offends less and less, though there have been several lapses. The editor, I must say, does not seem to be very fond of slop himself, judging from the stories he's written—except "Escape"—and the magazine he's edited.

Charles W. Jarvis says I am *creating* an issue. That is wrong. The issue exists and is vital. You have but to cast a look toward the outer darknesses and see certain magazines which make their living out of purveying slop. This system has invaded stf. itself before this, and symptoms of such an invasion are appearing again. Not serious as yet, but to the keen eye none the less alarming. I have the best interests of stf. at heart—believe me—and I assure you that slop is put out merely to cater to a lower class of readers. There is an attempt to increase circulation by attracting certain groups. Very well! They want to make money, so they can have those groups, but they lose other groups far superior in intelligence, in emotional maturity, and sensibility.

Let me state my position clearly. I want no more love interest for the sake of love interest alone. I want love interest written capably, written cleanly, written logically, written inoffensively. I want it written by those who *can* write it. Lastly, since my critics make long speeches about realism, let's have realistic love interest and not slop.

Is there anyone who disagrees with the last paragraph? If so, let him speak now or forever hold his peace, and let this be the last word!—Isaac Asimov, 174 Windsor Place, Brooklyn, N. Y.

15. Letter from Isaac Asimov, *Astounding Science Fiction*, July 1939, p. 107

OF COURSE, THERE ARE LUCRETIA BORGIAS
AS WELL AS NEROS.

Dear Mr. Campbell:

The Rogers combination desires to answer Mr. Asimov. To begin with: we are not married! And second, he is mistaken when he says *all* philosophers and religious leaders were men. Will he condescend to tell us the sex of the following? Mary Baker Eddy (started the Christian Science Church), Clara Barton (founded the Red Cross), Florence Nightingale (nursing), George Elliot (authoress), Evangeline Booth (started Salvation Army). Men who have advanced ideas of the strong over the weak are too numerous to mention, but I will give you a few of the names. Nietzche formulated the doctrines used by Hitler. Then there was Napoleon, Mussolini, and Alexander the Great, whom doubtless even Mr. Asimov admires.

All in all, we find the score about evenly balanced, with women in the minority because of suppression by men. In ancient Rome it was seriously debated as to whether women had souls. In the time of Shakespeare it was considered indecent for women to have an education. Witness the fact that women's part on the stage was played by men. Many universities today are closed to women. If men had progressed against such odds –

We thought the current Astounding very good and congratulate the editor on the capture of Finlay for next month. The best interior illustrations were Schneeman's for "Greater than Gods." All of the stories were up to their usual high standard and we were perfectly satisfied. And, don't you dare give us rough edges!—James Michael Rogers II and Mary Evelyn Rogers, 2006 Court Street, Muskogee, Okla.

16. Letter from Mary Evelyn Rogers and James Michael Rogers II, *Astounding Science Fiction*, September 1939, p. 97

> . . . [W]ere women permitted to develop naturally without the false conditioning of a society which not only regards them as inferior, but refuses to accept them any other way (except under extreme circumstances, and for limited periods of time; already we see hints of the problem of "how to get women out of the war-plants back into the home" arising), lo the symptoms of inequality and/or "inferiority" would not be forthcoming. (Lowndes 1945: 3–4)

The article equates women's oppression with other axes of oppression and continues in the same vein.

Asimov continued to extol the virtues of science fiction without women in other magazines. One of his letters to *Startling Stories* was published with the heading "Feminine-Less Issue" (figure 17). (Sam J. Lundwall quotes this letter as an example of male science fiction writers' attitudes to women

Of course, there are Lucretia Borgias as well as Neros.

Dear Mr. Campbell:

The Rogers combination desires to answer Mr. Asimov. To begin with: we are not married! And second, he is mistaken when he says that *all* philosophers and religious leaders were men. Will he condescend to tell us the sex of the following? Mary Baker Eddy (started the Christian Science Church), Clara Barton (founded the Red Cross), Florence Nightingale (nursing), George Elliot (authoress), Evangeline Booth (started Salvation Army). Men who have advanced ideas of the strong over the weak are too numerous to mention, but I will give you a few of the names. Nietzche formulated the doctrines used by Hitler. Then there was Napoleon, Mussolini, and Alexander the Great, whom doubtless even Mr. Asimov admires.

All in all, we find the score about evenly balanced, with women in the minority because of suppression by men. In ancient Rome it was seriously debated as to whether women had souls. In the time of Shakespeare it was considered indecent for women to have an education. Witness the fact that women's part on the stage was played by men. Many universities today are closed to women. If men had progressed against such odds—

We thought the current Astounding very good and congratulate the editor on the capture of Finlay for next month. The best interior illustrations were Schneeman's for "Greater than Gods." All of the stories were up to their usual high standard and we were perfectly satisfied. And, don't you dare give us rough edges! —James Michael Rogers II and Mary Evelyn Rogers, 2006 Court Street, Muskogee, Okla.

FEMININE-LESS ISSUE

By Isaac Asimov

There is a great deal of significance, I think, in the fact that the four stories of the September issue of STARTLING STORIES did not contain a single female character. Of course, I would be the last to claim that all females be abolished. Women, when handled in moderation and with extreme decency, fit nicely in scientifiction *at times*. However, the September issue goes to prove that good stories can be written even with the total absence of the weaker sex.

There are some fans that claim "human interest" a necessity in stf. since otherwise stories degenerate into uninteresting scientific or semi-scientific recitals. That is a very correct stand, or would be if it were not that these one-track-minded fans know no other form of human interest than the love interest.

Well, let them read "Bridge to Earth" and tell me what it loses in not possessing a heroine. Where would the story have been improved in having a heroine get caught by the microscopic creatures and having the hero rescue her, getting her caught again, having the hero rescue her again, then the hero getting caught and the heroine rescuing *him?* That *always* happens when a shemale is brought in (usually by the hair) and if that's human interest (or any other kind of interest) then I'm a pickled herring.

Three cheers for R. M. Williams for refraining from falling into this morass of hack.

However, Mr. Williams falls into a different error of purely scientific nature, which, since it has been indulged in by various authors ever since the beginnings of stf., it is high time to correct once and for all.

In reducing a man to microscopic size by compressing the spaces between the atoms, you reduce his size all right but you *don't* reduce his mass—since all the atoms originally in him remain unchanged in mass or number. In short, the microscopic hero weighs his full quota of 160 pounds though no bigger than the dot of an i on this page. In such a condition, his density approaches pretty near neutronium, and normal human beings and normal matter (the Earth itself, even) are to him only a rather thick vacuum. When coughed out onto the carpet, for instance, he would sink to the very center of the earth, because nothing on earth can hold up 160 pounds compressed into a microscopic granule.

Of course, a small army of men, all weighing 160 pounds plus a military tank as well, all inside one poor suffering human is just too ridiculous.

This is not to say that I did not enjoy the yarn. I did. But sometimes I do wish that authors when shrinking or expanding their characters either remember that mass remains unchanged or choose some method other than changing the amount of space between atoms.
—174 Windsor Place, Brooklyn, N. Y.

FEMININE-LESS ISSUE
By ISAAC ASIMOV

There is a great deal of significance, I think, in the fact that the four stories of the September issue of *Startling Stories* did not contain a single female character. Of course, I would be the last to claim that all females be abolished. Women, when handled in moderation and with extreme decency, fit nicely in scientifiction *at times.* However, the September issue goes to prove that good stories can be written even with the total absence of the weaker sex.

There are some fans that claim "human interest" a necessity in stf. since otherwise stories degenerate into uninteresting scientific or semi-scientific recitals. That is a very correct stand, or would be if it were not that these one-track-minded fans know no other form of human interest than the love interest.

Well, let them read "Bridge to Earth" and tell me what it loses in not possessing a heroine. Where would the story have been improved in having a heroine get caught by the microscopic creatures and having the hero rescue her, getting her caught again, having the hero rescue her again, then the hero getting caught and the heroine rescuing *him!* That *always* happens when a shemale is brought in (usually by the hair) and if that's human interest (or any other kind of interest) then I'm a pickled herring.

Three cheers for R. M. Williams for refraining from falling into this morass of hack.

However, Mr. Williams falls into a different error of purely scientific nature, which, since it has been indulged in by various authors ever since the beginning of stf., it is high time to correct once and for all.

In reducing a man to microscopic size by compressing the spaces between atoms, you reduce his size all right but you *don't* reduce his mass—since all the atoms originally in him remain unchanged in mass or number. In short, the microscopic hero weighs his full quota of 160 pounds though no bigger than the dot of an i on this page. In such a condition, his density approaches pretty near neutronium, and normal human beings and normal matter (the Earth itself, even) are to him only a rather thick vacuum. When coughed out onto the carpet, for instance, he would sink to the very center of the earth, because nothing on earth can hold up 160 pounds compressed into a microscopic granule.

Of course, a small army of men, all weighing 160 pounds plus a military tank as well, inside one poor suffering human is just too ridiculous.

This is not to say that I did not enjoy the yarn. I did. But sometimes I do wish that authors when shrinking or expanding their characters either remember that mass remains unchanged or choose some method other than changing the amount of space between atoms.—174 Windsor Place, Brooklyn. N. Y.

17. Letter from Isaac Asimov, *Startling Stories,* November 1939, p. 115

18. September 1939 cover of *Startling Stories*. Artist unknown.

[Lundwall (1969) 1971: 148]; Susan Wood quotes it in her essay on women and science fiction [Wood 1978–79: 9].) The issue was not, in fact "feminine-less" at all, as the cover demonstrates (figure 18). The cover is not based on one of the feminine-less stories Asimov praises but is instead the centerpiece of a competition in which readers are invited to send in stories based on this illustration of women in glass coffins being carried by robots. There is also a letter from Katherine Marcusson of Detroit, Michigan, to pollute Asimov's men-only space (Marcusson 1939: 109).

Women on Mars?

A science fiction controversy in 1955 brought the conflation of woman and love interest, women and sex, and the positioning of all these within the private sphere to the fore. Joanna Russ refers to this controversy in "The Image of Women in Science Fiction," writing that "within the memory of living adolescents, John Campbell Jr. proposed that 'nice girls' be sent on spaceships as prostitutes because married women would only clutter everything up with washing and babies" (Russ [1971] 1974: 55). In fact, it was the astronomer Dr. R. S. Richardson[14] not John Campbell who proposed this. In the December 1955 issue of *Fantasy and Science Fiction* an expanded version of Richardson's article "The Day after We Land on Mars" appeared.[15] Dr. Richardson presents himself as being very forward-thinking and permissive about sex. He has considered what would be involved in sending an exploratory party to Mars, and his conclusion is that

> space travel may force us to adopt a more realistic attitude toward sex than that which prevails at present. I feel that the men stationed on a planet should be openly accompanied by women to relieve the sexual tensions that develop among healthy normal males. These women would be of the type which we are accustomed to call "nice girls." They would be nice girls *before* they went to live on Mars. They would be nice girls *while* they lived on Mars. And they would be nice girls *after* they had lived on Mars.
>
> Many will be outraged at the mention of such an idea. They will object that it is shockingly immoral. But it is "immoral" only when viewed from the standpoint of our present social reference system. (Richardson 1955: 52)

Dr. Richardson's underlying assumption about women is very similar to those of Asimov, Turnbull, and others who argued that women are not necessary in science fiction. Women are not human beings; they are not part of Richardson's mankind that will colonize Mars.

In the May 1956 issue of *Fantasy and Science Fiction*, two rebuttals to Richardson's article were published.[16] The first, "Nice Girls on Mars" by Poul Anderson, does not question the terms of Richardson's argument. He just does not think it will work:

> These nice girls would cost a lot more than their wages. . . . Probably they could also do housekeeping chores and secretarial work, but the fact remains that every additional human being you send raises the cost by an astronomical figure.
>
> Quite apart from the expense, though, the nice girls would generate tension and discord merely by being there. . . . If the idea is to work at all, the girls would have to be accepted as full-caste members of the expedition; but that acceptance would remove any psychological barrier to the men's falling in love with them. Probably several men would come to love one girl and resent the attention she paid to everyone else. (49)

Anderson then considers some alternatives. The first is homosexuality, which he rejects because "we . . . are so powerfully conditioned against it that it is a quite impossible 'answer.'" Next he rejects "husband-and-wife teams" because, "[v]ery few men show enough forethought to marry women whose own talents and training fit ideally into the complex jigsaw pattern of organization that will be required. Of these, many will already have children and thus be kept at home" (49–50). Another solution is to send a "group of, say, 50 men and 50 women, all suitable for the work to be done, and let them figure out their own sleeping arrangements." Of course, this would cause trouble, as, "some of the girls will be more attractive than others, and the results are obvious" and "[d]isappointed lovers will have small chance to drown their sorrows" (50). Obviously the only real solution is to send a team of men who can "forego sex, along with numerous other modern conveniences" (50). He concludes that "[t]he question of how we will reach Mars in the first place is a tough one; the matter of feminine companionship and other recreations is relatively minor" (52).

The editorial blurb that follows observes that Anderson's response is "as strictly a male viewpoint as was Dr. Richardson's. But most of the objections from correspondents stemmed from a different attitude—an immediate rejection of the basic male-centered assumptions. And, as is perhaps not surprising in such an audience, this rejection came as frequently from men as from women. The perfect writer to express this—no, not feminist, but merely human point of view—is Miriam Allen deFord, who feels, with tart eloquence, that she has 'News for Dr. Richardson.'" Miriam Allen deFord begins her response thus:

> I am going to tell Dr. Robert S. Richardson a secret.
>
> Women are not walking sex organs.
>
> They are human beings. They are people, just like men.
>
> "I feel that the men stationed on a planet," says Dr. Richardson, "should be openly accompanied by women to relieve the sexual tensions that develop among healthy normal males."
>
> I couldn't agree with him more—if he would end that sentence at the word "women." (deFord 1956: 53)

Using Simone de Beauvoir as an authority, deFord proceeds to point out that all Richardson's assumptions are based on his notion that woman are not actually people. She finishes by reversing Dr. Richardson's proposals:

> Let us suppose that he had suggested that several hundred young women scientists be sent to Mars, and that "to relieve their sexual tensions" shiploads of "nice boys" be sent to serve them.
>
> The mere thought of such a reversal would undoubtedly horrify him.
>
> Well, that's the way both women and men emancipated from his atavistic prejudices feel about his extraterrestrial bordello. (57)

There are many connections between this debate and the earlier one taking place on the pages of "Brass Tacks" in *Astounding Science Fiction*. They serve to demonstrate just how deeply ingrained the notion of women as "walking sex organs" has been in science fiction. These debates also demonstrate that feminism was a part of the debate around the "woman question" in science fiction long before the publication of articles like Joanna Russ's "The Image of Women in Science Fiction" (1971). Despite the claim in the editorial blurb that deFord's positioning is a humanist one rather than a feminist one, it seems to me that her response is explicitly feminist. Arguments about woman's place and their representation in science fiction have a long history in the field.

Women, Sex, and Science Fiction, 1960–1975

The idea that science fiction had always ignored sex and that this had retarded its growth dominates the texts of the period 1960–1975. In 1960, for example, Kingsley Amis published *New Maps of Hell*, which was billed on its cover as the "book that made science fiction grow up." In it he criticizes the lack of speculation about sex: "Science fiction is a literature in which specific sexual interest of the kind familiar to us from other literatures, manifested in terms of interplay between individual characters, is rare, conventional, and thin" (74).

Philip Jose Farmer's first story, "The Lovers" (1952), is often claimed as one of those "rare" examples. The story concerns a sexual relationship between a human and a *lalitha*. Lalithas are parasitic insectoids who are more perfect than human woman because they devote themselves to men and have perky breasts: "He suspected that she either had an extra set of pectoral muscles or else an extraordinarily well-developed normal set. Her large and cone-shaped breasts did not sag. They were high and firm and pointed slightly upwards: the ideal of feminine beauty so often portrayed through the ages by male sculptors and painters and so seldom existing in nature" (Farmer 1952: 49). The lalithas' only flaw is that they die if they get pregnant because their young eat their way out of their mother's body. Robert Scholes and Eric S. Rabkin write that Farmer was "a pioneer in changing" science fiction. They argue that in "The Lovers" Farmer uses his "great skill" to make "this potentially repulsive story . . . a moving study of the development of love" (1977: 185–86).

"The Lovers" notwithstanding, the charge that sf avoided sex was made frequently during this period. P. Schuyler Miller responds to this charge in his book review column in the April 1961 issue of *Analog* (formerly *Astounding*). He writes: "One of the principal accusations made by intellectuals in general and high-literary critics in particular is that science fiction has an unrealistic attitude toward sex, and in most cases, no attitude at all. In judging this criticism, I think that we can assume that what our detractors would like to see is something like Tennessee Williams' ever-so-adult probings into psychopathology, and not a science fictional equivalent of the current school sex-and-bloodshed private-eye mysteries, so beautifully self-parodied in Henry Kane's Pyramid paperback, 'Private Eyeful'" (167). Having stated the issue in these terms, he goes on to ask a question: "Before dissecting a few of the current crop, let's take one more look at the science-fiction field in general, and ask ourselves: 'should the best science fiction be sex-centered?'" His conclusion is that "[o]vert sex is simply out of place in a large part of science fiction, and its absence *is* realism" (167). Here again is the notion that the intellectuality of science fiction perforce keeps sex and the body out of the picture. However, Miller is not so rigid in his proscription; there is a place where sex belongs in science fiction, for he continues,

> [M]ankind is by no means sexless, or he wouldn't be here, nor will he be in the future, unless certain science fiction becomes reality. So where does sex belong in science fiction:
>
> In the first place, it can be treated maturely, casually, and incidentally to a story of the problems of real people in a real science-fictional situation, without "lookit me" exhibitionism or slavering. The best of this kind that we've had in the last year was in two Pyramid books of Judith Merril's *Out of Bounds* and *The Tomorrow People*. This is what I'm thinking of when I agree with the critics that sex isn't properly treated in science fiction—but I suspect some of the most outspoken critics are thinking more in terms of Tennessee Williams than Judith Merril. (67–68)

In many of these discussions "sex" is a code word. Is Miller talking about the act of sex? About sex roles? It is never entirely clear.

When Joanna Russ's article "The Image of Women in Science Fiction" was reprinted in *Vertex* in 1974, it occasioned a great deal of hostility. One of the offended voices was that of science fiction writer Poul Anderson.[17] The nearly twenty years separating his participation in the "Nice Girls on Mars" debate from his response to Russ show that his worldview had shifted very little. In his article entitled "Reply to a Lady," also published in *Vertex*, Anderson tries to refute Russ's charge that there are no real women in science fiction by listing examples from science fiction of "formidable" women and of women "hold[ing] down difficult, responsible, sometimes dangerous jobs" and being their "husband's able partner," and also by agreeing with her charge and explaining that, as Isaac Asimov did in the late thirties,

> in what is probably the bulk of cases, women have not been relevant.
>
> No insult whatever is meant. I simply point out that the stories have not been concerned with the relationship of the sexes. They've treated subjects like expeditions to distant planets, oceanographic engineering, the politics of civilization on a galactic scale. One can only get so much into a given wordage; and in the early days, book-length science fiction was not common. Besides, even in a novel, it isn't practical to play Dostoyevsky. That's better done in the "mainstream" format.
>
> Why should Hal Clement's *Mission of Gravity*, say, bring in a love in-

> terest? Its fascination lies in the depiction of an alien world and alien beings thereon . . . .
>
> Granted for the purposes of that tale they could as well have been women as men; or both sexes might have been present, casually mingling. But it didn't happen that way, and to suppose that it didn't happen because of prejudice on the author's part is nonsensical, especially since women play active roles in other works of his.
>
> It should be remarked in fairness that I don't know if Ms. Russ has ever cited this particular book. But *Mission of Gravity* does go to show that the frequent absence of women characters has no great significance, perhaps none whatsoever.
>
> Certain writers, Isaac Asimov and Arthur Clarke doubtless the most distinguished, seldom pick themes which inherently call for women to take a lead role. This merely shows they prefer cerebral plots, not that they are anti-feminist. (Anderson 1974: 8, 99)

Anderson's response to Russ would have been equally at home in "Brass Tacks" in 1938 writing in support of Don Turnbull or Isaac Asimov.

Philip K. Dick also responds to Russ's article in a later issue of *Vertex*. His response is quite different from Anderson's. He begins by claiming that "Ms. Russ" has "shrilled at [him] in print" and accusing her of using "the tactics of bitter fanatics." He then switches to calling her "Joanna" and saying that he thinks she is right, as Anderson does, but unlike Anderson, Dick does not see the absence of women as something natural and inevitable. Dick writes that Russ has delivered a needed message:

> We are too sure of ourselves, as witness Poul's article-in-response. His article was lovely. Literate and reasonable and moderate and respectable, and worthy in all respects except that it was meaningless, by virtue of the fact that it was just so much space gas. It was like telling the blacks that they only "imagined" that somehow things in the world were different for them, that they only somehow "imagined" that their needs, its articulations in our writing, were being ignored. *It is a conspiracy of silence*, and Joanna, despite the fact that she seemed to feel the need of attacking us on a personal level, shattered that silence, for the good of us all. (Dick 1974: 99)

Dick talks about how he has "long said" that "science fiction may touch the sky but it fails to touch the ground. If by 'ground' we substitute the time-sanctioned symbol and reality of woman, then maybe science fiction will begin to turn out stories related to reality. . . . [I]f your attack serves to make us aware of you and your previously-considered second-class group as our equals, our peers, our friends—then I'll take it. Like a man" (99). Dick has transformed Russ into a nurse administering badly needed medicine: "Joanna is right—in what she *believes*, not how she puts it forth. Lady militants are always like Joanna, hitting you with their umbrella, smashing your bottle of whisky—they are angry because if they are not, WE WILL NOT LISTEN" (99). The pronouns reveal a science fiction belonging to men graciously welcoming the new women to become "our equals, our peers, our friends" (99). Women are not there because they are part of the field of science fiction, but because Dick and Anderson have allowed them in.

Poul Anderson tried to clarify his arguments in *Vertex* in a letter to the Canadian feminist fanzine *The Witch and the Chameleon*: "I never said that women should be in a science fiction story only if there is reason to have a love interest. Rather, what I said—or tried to say—was that in many science fiction stories there has been no reason for a love interest; therefore it was simplest to have all the human characters be of the same sex; and, because most writers happen to be men, it was easiest for them to use males. Thus no systematic discrimination is implied" ([September 1975]: 29).

Joanna Russ responds to Poul's letter thus: "Can we omit such stuff in the future? He's a nice man in a personal way but it's hopeless; I feel like a rock climber at the 14,000-foot pass in the Rockies looking back through a telescope at some enthusiastic amateur in the Flatirons (foothills outside my study window) who's proceeding Eastward, yelling 'Hey! You're in the wrong place! The mountains are *this* way!' It's a sheer waste of time to argue with him; we'd better just let him go until he and his crampons and bolts (or whatever) hit Chicago" (Russ 1976: 13).

This debate about women's place in science fiction was continued in the other general fanzines of the period. In the November 1974 issue of *Notes from the Chemistry Department*,[18] Loren MacGregor wrote a response to Anderson titled "A Reply to a Chauvinist." He concludes that "[d]ealing with 'love interests' may indeed be the duty of 'the mainstream,' as Mr. Anderson suggests, but dealing with speculation, in all its forms and variations, is a function of science fiction, and that has been neglected far too long" (5). Jerry Pournelle also wrote in response to Anderson in *Notes from the Chemistry Department*, but his article is more concerned with proving there are many sex-linked differences between men and women than discussing science fiction, as are other replies in a similar vein.

In the November 1975 issue of *Amazing* a guest editorial by Terry Carr appeared. Quoting examples from various 1940s pulp stories and comparing them with contemporary stories by Russ, Dick, and Tiptree, Carr argues that the position of women in science fiction had changed dramatically for the better since the 1940s. His editorial is built around the contemporary advertising campaign for Virginia Slims cigarettes, which used the slogan "You've come a long way, baby." He describes the ads:

> They always start with a faked photo from about 1910 . . . showing Mrs Elspeth Suffragette sneaking a cigarette in the wings after the premiere performance of *Rite of Spring,* only to be discovered by her husband, who turns her over his knee and spanks her. Then they go on to show us how much improved women's position is today. . . .
>
> Well I don't know about you, but I find these ads extremely funny, in a black-humor way. What they're really saying is that we've progressed so far in the last 65 years that we now allow women the right to kill themselves however they see fit to do it. (Carr 1975: 4)

Although sympathetic to women, women have no agency in Carr's writing, either: it is men who are allowing them to kill themselves.

Throughout the editorial Carr keeps returning to a scene which he says has "archetypal relevance to men" (5). A man's wife is threatened by a "slimy monster emerging from the coal cellar, obviously come to rape his wife, and he breaks into a cold sweat, because *who knows*, maybe this monster has better technique in bed than he does (5). This is a scene of white heterosexual male insecurity. At the end of his comparison of stories from the forties and early seventies Carr reimagines this scenario as his "idea for a science fictional variation on those Virginia Slims ads. It would start with a reproduction of an old pulp magazine done in sepia tone, showing Gerry Carlyle [a pulp heroine from the 1940s] sneaking a smoke beneath a Venusian *tobac* bush while a slimy tentacled monster roars down on her intent on God-knows-what. And it would end with Gerry going calmly off into the bushes with the alien beastie—because who knows, maybe he *does* have better technique than we do" (125).

Carr identified this scene as one of "archetypal relevance to men." The anxiety about the "better technique" of the alien beastie which Carr is mocking is identical to white male panic about miscegenation and the allure of the black buck for their white women. This scene, which Carr uses to demonstrate the extent of women's journey within science fiction in those thirty years, however, still figures Gerry Carlyle as synonymous with sex. Once again, women in science fiction *are* sex. The only difference is that the male interested in her body has shifted from being a white American male to being an "alien beastie" male.

Of course, all these debates about science fiction and women were also conducted in the two feminist fanzines of the period, *The Witch and the Chameleon* and *Janus/Aurora*. Another site for the debate was the November 1975 double issue of *Khatru*. The double issue was devoted to a symposium on women in science fiction. The participants were Suzy McKee Charnas, Samuel R. Delany, Virginia Kidd, Ursula K. Le Guin, Vonda N. McIntyre, Kaylyn Moore, Joanna Russ, James Tiptree Jr., Luise White, Kate Wilhelm, and Chelsea Quinn Yarbro. It was edited by Jeffrey D. Smith, who also took part. The exchange of letters that make up the symposium took place over seven months. In 1993 the symposium was reprinted, with comments from most of the participants looking back on the changes that had taken place over the nearly twenty years since it originally appeared. The reprint also included comments from others who had not been part of the original symposium: Mog Decarnin, Karen Joy Fowler, Jeanne Gomoll, Jane Hawkins, Gwyneth Jones, and Pat Murphy. The inclusion of comments by Karen Fowler and Pat Murphy, the founders of the James Tiptree Jr. Memorial Award, makes explicit the connections between the prize and this repository of feminist debate from the mid-1970s. I look at the debates in these feminist locations in detail in the next chapter.

5 THE WOMEN MEN DON'T SEE

In the previous chapter I looked at debates about whether love, sex, and women had any place in science fiction at all. In this chapter I examine stories about women and science fiction that take for granted that women are part of science fiction. My examination includes a consideration of the competing discourses around the conjunction of "women" and "science fiction." I also construct a history of both "women and science fiction" and the beginnings of feminist science fiction, looking at various stories that have been told about women and science fiction, feminism and science fiction, and feminist science fiction.

Other Stories about Women and Science Fiction

Feminist accounts of science fiction are as much a part of the historical moment in which they occurred as the texts they were engaging with, as we see from James Tiptree Jr.'s "The Women Men Don't See" and the ways in which the story has been discussed. First published in the December 1973 issue of the *Magazine of Fantasy and Science Fiction*, the story is one of the best known battle-of-the-sexes texts of the 1970s. John Clute, in *The Encyclopedia of Science Fiction*, calls it Tiptree's "most famous single story" (Clute and Nicholls 1993: 1231).[1]

At the time of publication, its author was not known to be Alice Sheldon by anyone in the science fiction community. The story is told in the first person by the middle-aged Don Fenton, presumably some kind of government operative, which is what many speculated that the "real" Tiptree was:

> Because Tiptree lives just a few miles from the Pentagon, or at least uses a mailing address in that vicinity, and because in his letters he often reports himself as about to take off for some remote part of the planet, the rumour constantly circulates that in "real" life he is some sort of government agent involved in high-security work. His obviously first-hand acquaintance with the world of airports and bureaucrats, as demonstrated in such stories as "The Women Men Don't See," gives some support to this notion. . . . Tiptree's admission to one of his editors that he spent most of World War II in a Pentagon subbasement has contributed to this myth. (Silverberg 1975: xii)

"The Women Men Don't See" received a rapturous response and was nominated for both the major science fiction awards, the Nebula and the Hugo. Tiptree, however, withdrew the story from consideration. At the time "he" said it was because he wanted to give the younger writers a turn; however, it has been argued that Tiptree was reluctant to win an award for the "masculine" feminism it supposedly displayed (Le Guin 1978). Tiptree summarizes the story thus:

> "Hero"—narrator, two plain women (mother & daughter) and Maya pilot crash on a sand-bar in Asuncion Bay. Hero and the mother set off on foot to cross bay and bring back fresh water. That night they are awakened by strangers in military-type vehicles who do not respond to their cries for help. Narrator thinks they are revolutionaries; woman picks up a dropped artefact and deduces that they are aliens. When aliens return for their object next eve, woman persuades them to take her and narrator back for plane. Arriving there, she quickly gets her daughter in the boat and over narrator's horrified protests, begs aliens to take them off earth. They do. Story has lots of struggle, hardships, wounds, tension. Message is total misunderstanding of woman's motivations by narrator, who relates everything to self. Message No. 2 is bleak future for feminism.[2]

"The Women Men Don't See" can be read as addressing the notion that women can only be represented in science fiction in discourses of romance or the domestic. In the story, Don Fenton, the narrator, can only see women sexually. He describes Mayan women thus: "[T]he little Maya chicks in their minishifts with iridescent gloop on those cockeyes [are] . . . highly erotic. Nothing like the oriental doll thing" (Tiptree [1973] 1990: 122). When Fenton first encounters the two women, Ruth and Althea Parsons, on the flight from Cozumel Airport, they are merely a "double female blur . . . registering nothing. Zero" (121). On the chartered flight Fenton "see[s] the girl has what could be an attractive body if there was any spark at all. There isn't" (121). The women become visible to him when they crashland together. Fenton's perceptions of the women change when they are the only women present: "[M]y eyes take in the fact that Mrs. Parsons is now quite rosy . . . with her hair loose and a sunburn starting on her nose. A trim, in fact a very neat shading-forty. . . . Miss Parsons is even rosier and more windblown. . . . A good girl, Miss Parsons, in her nothing way" (128–29).

Fenton's perceptions of the women echo the long-running debate within science fiction about women's place within the field. In that debate, a woman is only visible when she is a potential love interest. He misreads what is happening around him because he can only think of women within such a narrow perspective. Women exist for the convenience of men like himself. They exist within a chivalric order: there for him to desire, or for him to rescue. They exist so that he can see his "real" manliness reflected back at him. In "The Women Men Don't See," neither of the Parsons will respond to his desire, and when the opportunity arrives for him to achieve the rescue, he accidentally shoots Ruth Parsons in the arm (143). When it becomes plain that Fenton does not matter to either of the Parsons, a "mad image" of a female conspiracy "blooms" in Fenton's mind, and he imagines "generations of solitary Parsons women selecting sires, making impregnation trips. Well, I hear the world is moving their way" (138). This scenario of a secret conspiracy of women against men is straight from the pages of texts like Jerry Sohl's *The Haploids* (1952), James Gunn's "The Misogynist" (1952), and Sam Merwin's *The White Widows* (1953). "The Women Men Don't See" shifts the terrain of the battle of the sexes away from images of "mad" conspiracies of women against men to that of women "surviv[ing] . . . liv[ing] by ones and twos in the chinks of your world-machine" (Tiptree [1973] 1990: 140).

Robert Silverberg, in his introduction to the Tiptree collection *Warm Worlds and Otherwise*, "Who Is Tiptree, What Is He?," was also struck by the way this story inverts earlier science fiction. He characterizes the story's ending thus: "The thematic solution is an ancient s-f cliche—Earth-women carried off by flying-saucer folk—redeemed and wholly transformed by its sudden shattering vision of women, stolid and enduring, calmly trading one set of alien masters for another that may be more tolerable" (Silverberg 1975: xvi). Nevertheless, he claims, the story proves that men can "do" feminism, because "The Women Men Don't See" is a "profoundly feminist story told in entirely masculine manner, and deserves close attention by those in the front lines of the wars of sexual liberation, male and female" (xvi).

Terry Carr makes a similar argument in his 1975 editorial "You've Come A Long Way, Baby." In it, he writes that "there are some male writers in the field today who are able to show some insight into the female point of view" (Carr 1975: 125). He cites Tiptree as one of these writers. Carr gives his own summary of the plot of "The Women Men Don't See": the story's resolution, he claims, with the mother and her daughter getting into the "alien's ship and tak[ing] off for spaces unknown" is a sign that "[w]e really have come a long way, people" (125). Carr's sign of the most spectacular "progress" of science fiction is that "The Women Men Don't See" was written by a man. A woman writing a "profoundly feminist story" would not be such a revelation. Carr also discusses Joanna Russ's "When It Changed" (1972) as a sign of the progress of science fiction. However, this story signifies change for Carr, not so much because the story inverts battle of the sexes tropes, but because the story won a Nebula: the story was accepted and lauded by the once "almost . . . exclusive province of male readers" (Carr 1975: 5).

By the mid 1970s, the men who constituted the field of science fiction had grown up and were able to welcome women into their midst. Tiptree's story demonstrated for them not only that men can recognize women's talent but that they can even *understand* women. The revelation in 1977 that Alice Sheldon "was" James Tiptree Jr. undid this sense of progress and caused the story's feminism to be read differently. The uniquely sensitive, though very masculine male author had become a woman. The story's feminism had shifted and was no longer a proof of the adulthood of male sf writers.

"The Women Men Don't See" is frequently referred to in more recent work on feminist science fiction (Barr 1987: 30–32; Cranny-Francis 1990: 29–38; Kaveney 1989: 90; Lefanu 1988: 122–27; Pearson 1990: 18; Boulter 1995: 18–22; Donawerth 1997: 125–27; Roberts 2000: 97–99). For some critics the story has becaome an "exemplar for feminist science fiction" (Cranny-Francis 1990: 26). Once again, this reading seems to be largely dependent on the perceived sex of the story's author—Amanda Boulter, in her 1995 article "Alice James Raccoona Tiptree Sheldon Jr: Textual Personas in the Short Fiction of Alice Sheldon," argues that once Tiptree became Sheldon, readings of "her" stories were caught up with the story's authorship by a writer whose writing life has come to embody a feminist lesson, "demonstrat[ing] that there was no inevitable connection between biology and writing, the penis and the pen." Boulter argues that "[t]his gender deception has made Alice Sheldon a particularly exciting figure for feminist critics of science fiction" (Boulter 1995: 6).

Sarah Lefanu, in her 1988 book-length study of feminism and science fiction, *In the Chinks of the World Machine*,[3] discusses "The Women Men Don't See" in conjunction with Robert Silverberg's now-famous introduction to *Warm Worlds and Otherwise* in which he had written, "It has been suggested that Tiptree is female, a theory that I find absurd, for there is to me something ineluctably masculine about Tiptree's writing" (Silverberg 1975: xii). In his later postscript to the introduction to *Warm Worlds*, Silverberg writes: "She fooled me beautifully, along with everyone else, and called into question the entire notion of what is 'masculine' or 'feminine' in fiction" (Silverberg 1993: 5). Lefanu agrees with Silverberg's postscript: "The notion of what is 'masculine' or 'feminine' fiction must indeed be questioned; it is too simplistic to say that male writers of science fiction concern themselves only with technology or 'hard' science at the expense of development of character and the consequences in social terms of technological development. Such a distinction not only posits a crude sexual dualism—masculine is hard, feminine is soft—which anyway is anathema to Tiptree, but it also denies the connections between the different 'hard' and 'soft' sciences, connections that in good science fiction should be made" (Lefanu 1988: 123–24).

This split between "hard" and "soft" science has its equivalence in "hard" and "soft" science fiction. "Hard" science fiction is frequently portrayed as "real" science fiction because it is more "scientific" than "soft" science fiction.[4] "Hard" science fiction is predominantly mapped on to the male, and "soft" sf, on to the female. Sheldon/Tiptree's authorship of "The Women Men Don't See" makes explicit the fragility of this opposition of "masculine" to "feminine."

The Battle of the Sexes and Feminist Utopias

The dual authorship of "The Women Men Don't See" by Alice Sheldon/James Tiptree Jr. puts it on the cusp between the mostly male-authored battle-of-the-sexes texts of the period up to the early 1970s and the mostly female-authored texts of the 1970s. Joanna Russ, in a 1981 article, calls the later texts feminist utopias; I maintain that the battle-of-the-sexes texts and the feminist utopias of the 1970s are more closely connected than that term might imply and that they are, in fact, part of the same genre. But while giving the two groups of texts different names, Joanna Russ does, nevertheless, make a connection between the two: "A discussion of these recent feminist utopias would be incomplete without some references to their antifeminist opposite numbers: the role reversal (or battle-of-the-sexes) science fiction novel that assumes as its given the sexist assumptions that feminist utopias challenge and attack" (Russ 1981: 80). Natalie M. Rosinsky makes a similar connection between the two, discussing many of the same texts as Russ, and refers to Russ's "Recent Feminist Utopias." Rosinsky contrasts the feminist texts and "their androcentric chronological predecessors which almost uniformly posit the reestablishment of the 'natural' order of male dominance," noting that Suzy McKee Charnas's *Motherlines* (1978) and Joanna Russ's *The Female Man* (1975) "do not indicate which 'camp' is or will be victorious" (Rosinsky 1984: 65).

Russ and Rosinsky see the battle-of-the-sexes texts and the feminist utopia texts as being in conversation with one another. Indeed, Rosinsky takes the term "battle of the sexes," which Russ uses only to refer to the earlier "androcentric" texts, to refer to what Russ names feminist utopias. Although neither Russ nor Rosinsky includes "The Women Men Don't See" in their discussion, Russ does discuss two other stories "by" Alice Sheldon, "Your Faces, O My Sisters! Your Faces Filled of Light!" (1976), published under the name of Raccoona Sheldon, and "Houston, Houston, Do You Read?" (1976), published under the name of James Tiptree Jr.[5]

Many of the texts that are frequently cited as being part of a utopian tradition in women's writing, like Russ's *The Female Man* (1975) and Suzy McKee Charnas's *Motherlines* (1978), can be read as rewritings of the earlier battle-of-the-sexes stories. As Sarah Lefanu argues, "The stock conventions of science fiction—time travel, alternate worlds, entropy, relativism, the search for a unified field theory—can be used metaphorically and metonymically as powerful ways of exploring the construction of 'woman.' Feminist SF, then, is part of science fiction while struggling against it" (Lefanu 1988: 5).

Joanna Russ's novella *We Who Are About To* (1976).[6] reworks many of the stock conventions of science fiction in just this manner (Lefanu 1988: 180). In an interview with Larry McCaffrey, Russ states that in *We Who Are About To* she is parodying the "whole Robinson-Crusoe-and-the-desert-island business," which she calls an "imperialist myth: you find a place 'out there' and you make it *yours*" (McCaffery 1990: 190; quoted in Donawerth 1997: 88 n.). *We Who Are About To,* as Donawerth notes, is in direct conversation with Marion Zimmer Bradley's *Darkover Landfall* (1972) and also with all earlier examples of that particular "imperialist myth," such as Randall Garrett's "The Queen Bee"(1958).[7]

In the second issue of the first feminist fanzine, the Canadian *The Witch and the Chameleon,*[8] Vonda McIntyre wrote a long and detailed review of Bradley's *Darkover Landfall,* which criticized the novel for upholding this "old pioneering spirit." Bradley's novel is about a starship of the Colony Expedition Force that crashlands on the wrong planet and is forced to make many decisions about the colonists' future. This involves a decision to treat the women's wombs as communal property to ensure successful propagation of the race. McIntyre's negative review of *Darkover Landfall* attracted many letters in subsequent issues of *The Witch and the Chameleon.* Joanna Russ was one of the correspondents on the subject. In response to Bradley's rebuttal of the McIntyre review Russ wrote, "The question, to put it bluntly, of whether a woman's uterus belongs to her or to the community she happens to find herself in (or rather its male authorities) has been a very hot political issue in the U.S. and some parts of Europe for at least a decade; I am surprised that Bradley didn't expect vehement reactions to a novel in which just this question is the central issue of the plot" (Russ 1975: 15). Russ worked out her views on whether a woman's uterus belongs to her or her community more fully in *We Who Are About To* (1976).

Women's uteruses are central to Randall Garrett's "The Queen Bee" (1958). However, the question of whether their uteruses belongs to themselves or their community, a theme that is at the heart of *Darkover Landfall* (1972) and *We Who Are About To* (1976), is never raised. It is the story's given that a woman's uterus belongs to her community. The story cites "Brytell's Law," a set of interplanetary guidelines for what to do in case of a crashlanding. The fourth and fifth articles read:

> Article IV: . . .the women must be isolated. All precautions must be taken to prevent any confusion as to parenthood.
>
> Article V: In the ideal situation, each female would produce at least one female child and one male child by each male. (76)

In Garrett's story, unlike Bradley's novel, a small party of three women and four men, rather than an entire colonist starship, crashlands on an uninhabited planet. Before raising basic questions of survival they are already considering how to populate the planet: "If we're careful . . . and if we eliminate as much inbreeding as possible, we can have this planet populated within a few centuries" (73). One of the members of the party, Elissa Krand, does not take kindly to the situation and to increase her autonomy and power she kills the other two women. The men want to kill her, but they cannot as this would mean the loss of the only available womb. After enduring her bullying for a short while they decide upon an ingenious solution: they lobotomise her. The last sentence of the story is: "One year later, the first child born on the planet Generatrix was a lovely baby girl, named Tina" (96).

The baby Tina is named after the one "real" woman of the original survivors. Neither Elissa Krand nor the third woman, Della Thorn, are real women: Elissa Krand is not real because she actively resists the rule of the men, and Della Thorn because she does not want to have sex with the man she has been alotted:

> "Don't worry. I told her I'd give her a week to get used to the idea. That week is up tonight."
>
> "Oh? Think she'll quit being stubborn?"
>
> "If she doesn't," said Folee flatly, "I'm going to beat the daylights out of her." (87)

The next morning at breakfast there is an "odd atmosphere": "Folee had a placid look on his face as he cut into the purple melon on his plate, but when he caught Branson's eye, he flashed a grin that was both wry and rather sheepish. The side of Della Thorn's face was a trifle swollen and very faintly purplish, and she had an odd expression that Branson couldn't quite translate" (88). Murderous rage at being raped, perhaps? Folee's rape of Della is displaced on to the fruit on his plate. The link between Follee cutting the fruit and Folee raping Della is explicit: the melon is "purple" and the sign of Folee's violence on Della's face is "purplish."

In their introduction to *Aurora: Beyond Equality*, Vonda McIntyre and Susan Janice Anderson cite "The Queen Bee" in discussing the kind of stories they *did not* want for their anthology: "If you stretch the point, we thought, this story has more symbolic truth to it than its author may have imagined. Women in our society are conditioned to develop their physical attractiveness as a 'weapon' to 'kill off' other female competition. Confinement to a single role is, in a sense, a sort of psychic lobotomy" (McIntyre and Anderson 1976: 11–12).

There are many parallels between Russ's *We Who Are About To* and Garrett's "Queen Bee." In *We Who Are About To,* four men and four women crash land on an uninhabited planet, and the conversation soon turns to populating the planet. The story is told in first person by an unnamed woman of child-bearing age rather than the third person of the earlier story. In Russ's version the mad selfish woman, Elissa Krand, has become the narrator and creator of the text. Both women are killers, but Russ's narrator kills for entirely different reasons. She finds the urge to populate ridiculous and doomed, telling the others:

> That if we could eat the local macro-life, the local micro-life could eat us.
>
> That we could die of exposure in the winter because we had no way to make heat after our bungalow wore out and that was in six months.
>
> That we could die of heat in a summer whose length we didn't yet know.
>
> That a breech birth could kill. That a three-days labour and no dilation could kill. That septicemia could kill. (Russ [1977] 1978: 17)

The other characters argue with her, replying that "Civilization must be preserved." "Civilization's doing fine," she tells them. "We just don't happen to be where it is" (23). Eventually, and at first inadvertently, she kills them all and then spends her time waiting to die, talking to her vocorder and hallucinating. The womb as communal property, along with a 1950s discourse of reproduce and colonize at all costs, has been overturned and destroyed.

Absence or Presence

> *The current version of women in science fiction before the 1960s (which I've heard several times lately) goes like this: There weren't any. Only men wrote science fiction because the field was completely closed to women. Then, in the late 60s and early 70s, a group of feminist writers led by Joanna Russ and Ursula Le Guin stormed the barricades, and women began writing (and sometimes even editing) science fiction. Before that, nada. . . . There's only one problem with this version of women in SF— it's not true.* (Willis 1992: 4)

The absence or presence of women within science fiction has, until recently, been central to accounts of feminist science fiction. However, the nature of this "presence" within the field has not been stable, any more than the category "women" is stable.

Versions of women in science fiction are shaped by the histories of the people telling the different versions. What historians have read and seen is vital to their construction of history; what you do not experience is often not included, and the context of your experience can be dramatically different from someone else's. Katie King makes this point, in another context, quoting Alice Echols on efforts to generate a black feminist movement, which Echols argues "were less than successful." King describes her reaction: "This absolutely true statement has a strange, hollow echo in my political memories. *Woman Power*, my first feminist reading, was by a Black woman who represented herself at the very 'heart'" of what both she and Echols call radical feminism" (King 1994: 12). King's reaction is reminiscent of the comments of science fiction writer and multiple Hugo and Nebula award winner Connie Willis, quoted in the epigraph to this section. Willis is reacting to a version of the object "women and science fiction" that her own experience contradicts. She had encountered many stories by women writers when she was first reading science fiction in the 1950s. Judith Raphael Buckrich, on the other hand, had not:[9] "I think the 1960s social revolution caused a revolution in writing too and especially in SF which had in the 1950s been very 'boys' own adventure.' Suddenly women such as Le Guin emerged in the US who were using SF to talk about societal structure and sexism and oppression. This made SF attractive to women readers and writers for the first time and I believe has influenced all women's writing here and elsewhere" (Larbalestier 1995: 60).

At stake for both Buckrich and Willis is whether women have been present or absent in science fiction. The question has shaped many accounts of women and sf. Susan Wood observed this phenomenon in the late 1970s: "There are more stories about real women, and real men, emerging in the SF field. And there are plenty of articles about their absence" (Wood 1978–79: 9). Sam Moskowitz, editor of *When Women Rule*, saw women as largely absent from the field of science fiction: "The readers of science fiction are predominantly men. It has been that way virtually ever since science fiction has been written" (Moskowitz 1972: 1). Kingsley Amis not only felt that women were not present; he also thought it was not seen as a matter of concern: "Though it may go against the grain to admit it, science-fiction writers are evidently satisfied with the sexual status quo—the female emancipationism of a Wylie or a Wyndham is too uncommon to be significant" (Amis 1960: 99). Scott Sanders, in "Woman as Nature in Science Fiction," writes that "[u]ntil very recently SF was written primarily for a male audience, about heroes for whom women are toys, threats or enigmas" (Sanders: 1981: 42). Curtis Smith, in his preface to *Twentieth Century Science-Fiction Writers*, has a different perception: "[A]t least there are now woman characters in science fiction, and an explosion of science-fiction writers who are women: consider Zenna Henderson, Pamela Sargent, James Tiptree, Jr., Ursula Le Guin, Joanna Russ, Lee Killough, Suzy McKee Charnas, Anne McCaffrey, Octavia Butler, Marge Piercy, Zoe Fairbairns, and many others. These writers have brought speculation about the future of sex roles to science fiction. Science fiction, once totally the domain of men, has reversed itself and is now in the forefront of feminist thinking" (Smith 1986: viii–ix). Joanna Russ, in her article "The Image of Women in Science Fiction,"[10] disagrees, noting that although "[t]here are plenty of images of women in science fiction," there are"hardly any women" (Russ [1971] 1974: 57).

Mary Kenny Badami examines this contested absence in her "Feminist Critique of Science Fiction," which appeared in the academic science fiction journal *Extrapolation*, :

> There is little to discuss about 'the role of women in science fiction' because—Jirel of Joiry, Susan Wood, and Mary Shelley not withstanding—until very recently women have had almost no role in science fiction. But it may be instructive to demonstrate that fact and to explore the various ways in which female sex roles in sf generally add up to The Invisible Woman. I propose to illustrate three theses about the non-role of women in science fiction:
>
> Women have *not* been important as characters in sf;
> Women have *not* been important as fans of sf;
> Women have *not* been important as writers of sf. (Badami 1976: 6)

Badami's threefold division is important because not all of the accounts of women's absence from science fiction are referring to the same kind of participation (or lack of it). In Willis's account, it is women as practitioners, as writers and, to a lesser extent, as editors.[11] For Buckrich it is "women readers and writers" (Larbalestier 1995: 60); for Moskowitz, "the readers of science fiction" (Moskowitz 1972: 1); Russ talks about "images of women" and does not claim that there were no women writing before the late sixties (Russ [1971] 1974: 57).[12]

Badami's distinctions fall into three distinct areas: (1) representation—the illustrations and texts; (2) consumption—the readers and fans; and (3) production—the writers, artists and editors. (These three categories are not, of course, quite as easily separable as I am implying here. They are all modes of production—of the knowledge of the field and of the field itself. Fans, of course, produce fanzines and conventions and costumes and filk songs and many other tangible artefacts, but these are "amateur" activities although they all inscribe, shape, and document science fiction.) These three categories—production, consumption, and representation—are a hierarchy with "production" at the top. This is made explicit within fandom with the idea of the "pro" versus the "fan" and the notion that all fans aspire to be pros. Economically it is also a division between paid and unpaid work. That consumption is the least valued of the three is apparent in the rarity of discussion of fandom in academic accounts of women and sf.[13] There are many fanzines of the seventies that discuss women and sf,[14] and there were fanzines like *The Witch and the Chameleon* (first issue August 1974) and *Janus/Aurora* (first issue 1975) that were devoted to women and sf. However, Badami is one of the few writing about feminism and science fiction outside of fan publications to emphasize fandom. Susan Wood, who was, as Badami indicates, very well known for her fan activities and was most definitely a BNF (Big Name Fan), did not discuss fandom in her article "Women and Science Fiction," though she did indicate that there were women readers of the genre and quoted a letter from a female reader published in a pulp magazine (Wood 1978–79: 11).[15]

The difference in these accounts of women's participation across the three categories of production, consumption, and representation is one of emphasis. Clearly no one is saying that there were literally no women in science fiction until the late 1960s. However, there is danger in the argument that there were few women in the field, for, as Connie Willis makes clear, the slide from few women and few representations to no women can easily happen. Work that retrieves women writers from the past is important, and an argument that conflates the overwhelmingly sexist writing of a period with the absence of women can actually lead to the forgetting of important women writers. This has been recognized in the existence of a body of feminist retrieval work. Pamela Sargent's *Women of Wonder* series of anthologies of "sf stories by Women about Women" were particularly important in this regard. In her long introduction to the first book, published in 1974, she draws attention to such writers as Francis Stevens, C. L. Moore, Leigh Brackett, Wilmar Shiras, and Anne Warren Griffith (Sargent [1974] 1978: 14–29). Her anthologies make available the stories of writers like Hazel Heald, Helen Weinbaum, Leslie Perri, Margaret St. Clair, Miriam Allen deFord, and Katherine MacLean, who would otherwise be completely unavailable. In *The Witch and the Chameleon* and

Janus/Aurora I found articles devoted to early women writers and a conscious effort to think of women's involvement in science fiction as having a history. These include an entire issue of *Aurora*, the summer 1984 "Invisible Women" issue. Another recognition of this history was the fact that Katherine MacLean, whose first story was published in 1949 in *Astounding*, was the first writer guest of honor at the feminist science fiction convention, WisCon.[16]

Feminists are not the only people engaged in this kind of retrieval work. So much early pulp science fiction is out of print and unavailable that the work of anthologists like Everett Bleiler and Sam Moskowitz in anthologizing and cataloguing previously unreprinted work is invaluable for discovering the early science fiction of both women and men. In their note to their anthology of women's sf from the 1920s to the present, *New Eves*, Janrae Frank, Jean Stine, and Forrest J Ackerman discuss the unavailability of most early science fiction:

> Those eager to read more by these extraordinary writers, and to encounter the New Eves they, and their male colleagues, created, may be disappointed to discover there is no "recommended reading" list here. The reason is simple: with the exception of a rare anthologization, the works of all the women (and men) who wrote science fiction before the mid-1960s are out of print, and considering the current structure of the publishing industry, likely to remain so. Their books can only be found by lucky browsers in used bookstores; whereas stories by women who wrote science fiction before 1950, are simply unobtainable, except to the wealthy, who can afford to pay premium prices for the mouldering pulps that alone contain their work. Even the early books of many writers who began their careers in the 1970s and 80s are now out of print—while those of most current women authors can easily be found in one's local bookstore. (Frank, Stine, and Ackerman 1994: xvii)

When articles appear in prozines or fanzines on women and sf, there are usually letters from longtime male fans pointing out someone or some text who has been left off the list. For example, in response to Sam Moskowitz's article "When Women Rule" in the August 1967 issue of *If*, John Borger of Parkersburg, West Virginia, wrote that "I was rather puzzled by the omission, in 'When Women Rule,' of the matriarchy described in *Search the Sky*" (Borger 1968: 161). Leland Sapiro of Richardson, Texas, wrote in response to "The Invisible Women" issue of *Aurora* (summer

1984): "As to Tom Porter's 'Women SF Writers You Probably Never Heard Of' . . . How about names like Claire Winger Harris, Leslie F. Stone, L. Taylor Hansen, that shudda been listed, but weren't?" (Sapiro 1986–87: 5).

This retrieval work does much to complicate the notion that sf before a certain point was wholly male. However, Sarah Lefanu has observed that there is a complex relationship between the presence or absence of women within the field and misogyny within the field: "[Science fiction] has always reflected and continues to reflect a particular type of authority, that of men over women. The absence of women from much science fiction before the 1970s is only one expression of this: the presence of women within science fiction since the early 1970s does not necessarily undermine it" (Lefanu 1988: 87). Lefanu is not saying that there were no women in science fiction before the 1970s, just that there were few.[17] Her point is that the absence or presence of women in the field of science fiction does not of itself say anything about the feminism or misogyny of the field. As the example of Margaret Thatcher demonstrates, a female prime minister is not necessarily an advance for feminism. So you could ask what kind of presence *did* women have within science fiction, and the answer is extremely varied. Which women, at which moment within science fiction, and where in science fiction?

Many of the letters to prozines by women from 1926 to the 1950s explicitly examine the position of women within the field of science fiction. These letters, and the editorial responses to them, indicate that while women were present within the field, their presence was still frequently viewed as an anomaly. A letter from Naomi D. Slimmer of Russel, Kansas, and her sisters, headed "Five of a Kind," leads the first letter column of *Science Fiction:*

> Am warning you that this is merely a women's [*sic*] (five of them) opinion of your new magazine. Somebody brought home a copy of *Science Fiction* last week and it has gone the rounds. We noted your contest announcement and decided to take a crack at it. If you did not know that women read scientific fiction, give a listen:
>
> There are two housewives, an office worker, a high school girl, and a trained nurse among we five sisters and we all read *Science Fiction* (when we can snag it from brother and two husbands). With one accord we greeted your new magazine with whoops of glee and took turns curling up with the durn thing.
>
> We all read a good many "slicks" and quite a few "pulps," and we

> think you've got something there. Since we like our "pulps" to scare us, chill us, and give us to think, we go for *Science Fiction*. Looks like it might be going to fit the bill. It's going to keep me awake and give me goose-bumps when I'm on night duty (I'm the nurse) and the other four sisters say they expect to read it when the baby is cross or the teacher isn't looking or when the boss isn't in. (Don't think I'm trying to say we'll all buy a copy every issue. I wouldn't kid you)
>
> We read *Science Fiction* to help us picture what the world will be in years to come, or to get someone's idea of life in a different world. We know what present-day life is like on this earth (it's a mess! And *Science Fiction* is about the only way we can forget that fact for a few minutes). (Slimmer 1939: 118–19)

The editor, Charles Hornig, replied: "It gives me great pleasure to start off 'The Telepath' with such a breezy and informative letter as the above. It is a revelation to find five girls in one family so enthusiastic about our humble effort. I have received so many letters from women who read science-fiction just lately, that I must confess many of the fair sex have well-developed imaginations. Their group has grown to such proportions that they must certainly be taken into consideration by the male adherents" (Hornig 1939: 119). Hornig's comments here echo Hugo Gernsback's "strange" discovery, thirteen years earlier, that there were a "great many women . . . already reading" *Amazing Stories* (Gernsback 1926f: 483). But note that the admission of women's "well-developed imaginations" is something that Hornig has to "confess."

In 1953 the editor of *Thrilling Wonder Stories*, Sam Mines, also linked the growth of women's imaginations to what he saw as their growing interest in science fiction. For Mines, women's interest in science fiction was an oddity that had to be explained. He made the following comments in response to a letter from Phyllis Grazer of Tillamook, Oregon: "Seems to be a mass movement of housewives away from the home and garden type of literature towards science fiction. Seriously—letters from housewives saying in effect, 'Where has this stuff been all my life?' are mushrooming. And the key is right up there in Mrs Grazer's letter—it makes their imaginations work" (Mines 1953: 142). Grazer had written that this was "my first letter to you but you can expect many more." Nowhere in her letter does Grazer mention that she is a housewife; Mines just assumes that she is (Grazer 1953: 142).

In the January 1953 issue of *Startling Stories*, Sam Mines wrote the following in response to a letter from a Stephanie Szold of Asheville, North Carolina. In it he is even more explicit about women's presence in science fiction occasioning surprise for him:

> Ten years ago stf fans were practically all male, today with or without benefit of fan activities, a lot of girls and housewives and other members of the sex are quietly reading science fiction and beginning to add their voices to the bable *[sic]* of TEV [the Ether Vibrates—*SS*'s letter column]. And a lot of them, tucked away in more or less remote places are beginning to ask, "Where has this stuff been all our lives?" and "Where can we meet other science fiction fans so we can talk shop instead of feeling alone?"
>
> We confess this came as something of a surprise to us. We honestly never expected such a surge of female women into science fiction. (136)

Zillah Kendall of San Bernardino, California, in the February 1953 issue of *Thrilling Wonder Stories,* writes that she has been reading sf magazines since she "was about 14 years old—(back in the Hugo Gernsback days)." She discusses her opinion of contemporary fans and science fiction and ends with the following: "here's hoping there'll soon be more women writers in SF" who are "willing to admit it" (133). For Zillah Kendall, as for Lula B. Stewart of Harmony, Pennsylvania, whose 1953 letter to *Thrilling Wonder Stories* I discussed in chapter 1, knowing that there are other women in the field is important to their own engagement with the field. Stewart ends her letter saying that now she is "backed by a formidable phalange of femfans, I dare speak up, brave lassie that I am" (Stewart 1953: 133). Winifred Beisiegel of Sparrowbush, New York, is more self-confident, but she also connects herself to other readers, in this case, her mother: "[A]lthough I've been an S-F fan for over 20 years, I still like to re-read some of the earlier efforts. In fact, for that same length of time I've been searching for three oldies read by my mother in her younger days. They were: *The Return of She* by Haggard, *The Muglugs,* author unknown and *The Year of Our Lord,* ditto. . . . From what Mom recalls, they were darned good for that era and the last two named were as prophetic as any Jules Verne" (Beisiegel 1952: 132). Beisiegel stakes her legitimacy within the field with her twenty-year knowledge of it, as well as having a mother who was also an avid reader of the genre.

I have demonstrated that women were active in the field of science fiction before the late 1960s and early 1970s, which is frequently invoked as the time in which women emerged in the field. Indeed, many of the women who are associated with the 1970s "emergence" of feminist science fiction, such as Joanna Russ, Marion Zimmer Bradley, and Octavia Butler, were already science fiction readers and, in the case of Bradley at least, longtime fans. However, it is equally clear that the period of the sixties and seventies did mark a change in the way some women perceived their relationship to the field of science fiction. They were already a part of science fiction before they discovered feminism, but that discovery changed the nature of their presence within science fiction.

Sf writer Nancy Kress describes her changing relationship thus:

> I discovered SF at the age of 14. The moment is still very clear to me. My first boyfriend was studying to be a concert musician. As a teenage girl, my job was to hang adoringly over his piano while he practised (it was 1962). However, I am, alas, tone deaf. I could hang adoringly for maybe ten minutes, tops. But in his family's music room were bookshelves, and on the shelves were his father's books, and among them was *Childhood's End* the first SF I'd ever seen. One chapter and I was hooked.
>
> Favorite early authors were Theodore Sturgeon and Frederik Pohl. Later, I discovered Le Guin and Wilhelm and other women writers. But for a long time my adolescent mind, had I thought about it at all (which I didn't), would have assumed that writing SF was a male occupation. It took the women's movement of the 1970's to broaden my traditional Catholic-good-girl upbringing, and without the movement I doubt I'd be an SF writer today. (Letter to author, November 1995)

For Jeanne Gomoll, well-known fan and one of the founders of *Janus* and WisCon, the emergence of the women's movement completely changed her involvement with fandom. She sees 1970s feminism as responsible for the transformation of science fiction fandom:

> A lot of women had stopped reading science fiction during our teens, but hadn't really examined our reasons for giving it up. But one of the first things you learn when you read books like *Sisterhood is Powerful*, *GynEcology* or *The Obstacle Course*, is how to see sexism, and when you start looking for it, it's everywhere. It was a time of pointing out the obvious. "Robert Heinlein is sexist," we said. But it was also a time of happy discovery, because just then, Things were Changing. Women were writing new kinds of SF, SF that some of us women were reading and which was bringing us back to the field.

Pamela Sargent published the *Women of Wonder* series (and more importantly wrote the introductory essays that gave us a historical grounding). Vonda N. McIntyre and Susan Janice Anderson published *Aurora: Beyond Equality*. Suzy McKee Charnas, Joanna Russ, Ursula Le Guin, Liz Lynn, Chelsea Quinn Yarbro, John Varley, James Tiptree, Jr./Raccoona Sheldon, Marge Piercy, Chip Delany, Joan Vinge and others were writing brilliant, wonderful stuff, and were changing the world. Terry Garey has pointed out that the best and practically the *only* feminist fiction was being written in the science fiction field. We started writing about the new women authors and set about changing *our* world, specifically SF fandom. There were Rooms of Ones Own at various conventions; there was a Women's apa; there were awards bestowed upon the new generation of SF writers who were more concerned about people's future lives than new toys. We discovered that SF was an essential resource for feminists: it gave us a place to dream about the way we'd like things to turn out. It gave us an arena in which to plan a strategy. (Gomoll 1991: 8)[18]

Susan Wood was one of the fans involved in starting "women and sf" panels and "the rooms of one's own" at conventions. The feminism of the early 1970s was central to her relationship with the field. She writes about the way in which her

own *click* of consciousness came in 1972, after I had been reading what the library clerk coldly informed me were "boys' books" for some 15 years, happily substituting my female self for their male protagonists. In the December 1972 issue of *The Magazine of Fantasy and Science Fiction*, I read "The Garbage Invasion," by Keith Laumer. This one, unusually enough, featured a woman. . . . She is *in charge* of the world; Retief is assisting her as "Acting Wildlife Officer" during a crisis. So what happens? She spends all her time calling the crisis "perfectly horrid." . . . When Retief's superior arrives, this woman, who is described by Retief himself as filling "a position . . . of considerable responsibility" with "commendable efficiency" is summarily dismissed with an order to "mix us a couple of tall cool ones . . . " at this point, I threw the magazine across the room. (Wood 1978–79: 10)

This "*click*" of consciousness that Wood describes did not take place in a vacuum. In 1978 Susan Wood was the fan guest of honour at WisCon; and was invited to write a guest editorial for the spring 1978 *Janus*, titled "People's Programming" where she discusses her involvement with "women's programming" at conventions, and the process of her transition within fandom from "Honorary Man to Woman Fan," which was made possible by the women's movement (Wood 1978: 4). The process Wood describes is very close to Robin White's account in the earlier "Are Femme Fans Human?" The difference is that in 1968 White was not troubled by being an "honorary man" or being accepted only through her association with her husband (White 1968).

Of course you can be part of science fiction and in conflict with it. Susan Wood's "*click*" of consciousness was brought on by reading a science fiction story she hated. Many women writers of science fiction had a similar experience and as a result went on to write the kind of science fiction they wanted to read. Octavia Butler talks about consuming science fiction from an early age but not always liking what she consumed: "I started reading the magazines—that was my way into adult science fiction. I didn't like them very much, but I kept reading them" (Roberts 1993: 45). In another interview Butler says: "I didn't decide to become a science fiction writer. It just happened. I was writing when I was 10 years old. I was writing my own little stories and when I was 12 I was watching a bad science fiction movie and decided that I could write a better story than that. And I turned off the TV and proceeded to try and I've been writing science fiction ever since" (Beal 1986: 14).

This idea of writing in reaction, of being inspired by what you did not like as well as what you admired, is an important one. Joanna Russ, too had the experience of being an avid reader of science fiction and finding many of the stories filled with women who were only "important as prizes or motives—i.e. we must rescue the heroine or win the hand of the beautiful Princess." Or the women were "active or ambitious" and therefore "evil—this literature is chockfull of cruel dowager empresses, sadistic matriarchs, evil ladies maddened by jealousy, domineering villainesses and so on" (Russ [1971] 1974: 55). As I demonstrated above, Russ used her own writing to transform these science fiction clichés and to provide different representations of women. Anne McCaffrey, in her article "Hitch Your Dragon to a Star: Romance and Glamour in Science Fiction," also discusses her distaste for the dominant "images" of women in science fiction: "After seven years of voracious reading in the field, I'd had it up to the eyeteeth with vapid women. I rebelled. I wrote *Restoree* (1967) as a tongue-in-cheek protest, utilizing as many of the standard 'thud and blunder' cliches as possible with one new twist—the heroine was the viewpoint character and *she* is always Johanna-on-the-spot" (McCaffrey 1974: 282). In doing so, she rewrote the genre and produced her own version, "a space gothic" (282).

The Great Invasion, or the Great Erosion

There's this revisionist history version where there were no women in the field, and then in the late '60s Joanna Russ and Ursula K Le Guin stormed the barricades and suddenly women came pouring in like the Huns and took over. But that's not true. There were all these women, and I know because I was reading them. They're women like Mildred Clingerman and Shirley Jackson and Zenna Henderson and Margaret St. Clair and Carol Emshwiller, and a whole bunch I didn't know about because they were all really C. L. Moore. The field didn't just have women writers—it had really good women writers. These were wonderful stories, and I don't believe they were overlooked at the time, because when I read them they were all in the Year's Best collections. (Willis 1992: 73)

In these remarks, Connie Willis refers to the way in which women have been figured as invading science fiction in the late 1960s or early 1970s and refutes that version of the story by citing her own experience. While many people did, in fact, link the emergence of second-wave feminism and other social upheavals of the time with the transformation of science fiction, others saw the change as happening long before. Samuel R. Delany, for instance, argues that it was the 1950s that marked a radicalization of science fiction:

> The most striking element in American life in the early '50s was McCarthy's persecution and terrorization of Americans associated with the left, just as the Second World War had been the most striking element of the '40s. Until McCarthy, however, the internal dialogue in science fiction was rather rarefied. Themes such as history, science, and, of course, time were seen as most significant. . . . As McCarthyism became a threat to science fiction's historical plurality, American science fiction began to deal directly with problems in the country. It began to touch on the racial situation, population growth, religious freedom, sexual roles, social alienation, "conformity," and ecology. (Delany 1984: 237)

Very few accounts of women and science fiction name the 1950s as a decade in which there was an "explosion" or "invasion" of women. It is interesting, though, that most of the writers Willis refers to are closely associated with the 1950s. Mildred Clingerman, Zenna Henderson, and Carol

Emshwiller all began their writing careers in that decade. Judith Merril is another writer closely associated with this period. Merril told me that in the fifties there were many stories by women from "the woman's point of view" appearing in science fiction magazines: "I don't remember what I thought at the time, but I do think now that several of us were indeed writing women's point of view for the first time in sf in those years [late forties—early fifties]. It wasn't just me: Idris Seabright, Mildred Clingerman come to mind—maybe half a dozen others at first" (letter to author, 13 October 1996).

Some even put the date before the fifties. According to Sam Merwin Jr.,[19] women began to invade the field of science fiction as early as "some indeterminate point in the nineteen thirties" (Merwin 1950: 6). He tells the story of women's invasion of science fiction in a long editorial in the December 1950 issue of *Thrilling Wonder Stories* (figure 19). In the opening section Merwin establishes the state of the field before the invasion. Women's only method of surviving this men-only world was to be a "Tomboy Taylor." This is the method of survival that Susan Wood referred to above—becoming an "honorary man" in order to be accepted into fandom. The next section is concerned with what he calls "the great invasion" of women. Merwin's evidence for this transformation of the field is a series of women writers rather than readers or fans. He details the effects of the transformation in the third section, headed "Husbands and Wives": the wives transform their "renowned" science fiction husbands into better writers. This is the same story of women as nurturer and mother to men that I detailed at the end of the last chapter. Women are again given the responsibility for making science fiction "grow up." Merwin expands on women's role as angel of the house in the final section, "A Good Influence." This good influence on the males in science fiction occurs because within the heterosexual economy the presence of women means that the men will be more polite and neater. Merwin also locates the responsibility for women's position within science fiction with the women not with the men. It is they who must "blossom" into a full partnership with the men. However, this partnership with men is on the men's terms, as he details in the section headed "Two Schools of Thought."

At the beginning of Merwin's editorial the invasion is located in the 1930s. At the end it has become a "comparatively recent development in stf," which Merwin links to feminism and "woman's emancipation" generally. Merwin is in favor of it not least because it benefits men. He imagines a future in space for both women and men. However, like Dr. Richardson

A DEPARTMENT FOR SCIENCE FICTION FANS

FOR a number of decades the world of science fiction was pretty much exclusively a male world. While boys of all ages and castes, united by the umbilical cord of soaring impersonal imagination, delved into the works of Verne, Wells, Conan Doyle, *Tom Swift* and the like, the girls seemed content with *Little Elsie* or the sub-erotic sublimations of E. M. Hull, Ethel M. Dell and other experts in the manufacture of machine-tooled glamour to provide frosting for the solid cake layers of recipes and fashion patterns and little essays on beauty culture.

Primoval clubs and gatherings of science fiction addicts were strictly Little Scorpion affairs. Only rarely did some space-minded Tomboy Taylor manage to crash them. And as a rule she had to keep her hair short and her mind on the refreshments rather than the boys if she hoped to survive in membership.

Women didn't really exist in the stories of the era either—save as opposite numbers to prophylactic Western heroes and such an occasional *She*-like creature as the late Stanley Weinbaum's Margaret of Urbs. Save for a few seldom-heard-from ladies like Lilith Lorraine and M. Rupert and a very few others, women did little writing in the field.

Yes, for quite a time as time is counted these days, science fiction was a world for men and men only.

The Great Invasion

However, at some indeterminate point in the nineteen thirties something happened. Just how or why it happened lies beyond our current ken but at any rate the girls got interested and began to move in. This metamorphosis—called either the Great Invasion or the Great Erosion depending upon the point of view—is too well and too long established to be regarded as any mere passing trend. The girls are in and in to stay.

A number of women writers, ranging from adequate to brilliant, began to turn out science fiction stories of such excellence that in magazine after magazine they grabbed their share not only of inside short stories but of lead novelets and novels, hitherto an exclusively masculine prerogative.

Certainly the fantasies of C. L. Moore were and are as fine as any in the field. And right up alongside her work we have today that of E. Mayne Hull, Leigh Brackett, Margaret St. Clair, Judith Merril, Catherine MacLean, Betsy Curtis, and Miriam Allen deFord, to say nothing of an ambitious platoon of youngsters who are promising to crash into print professionally at almost any moment.

Husbands and Wives

Naturally, with such a group of talented women writers practising successfully for more than a dozen years, the entire story-perspective on women in science fiction has changed. It is no longer uncommon to find a female chief protagonist in an stf story—and not a two-dimensional valentine or a cold-fire priestess-empress but a female who acts, talks and thinks like a woman alive.

Furthermore both Miss Hull and Miss Brackett married science fiction authors of renown—A. E. van Vogt and Edmond Hamilton respectively—and their influence on their talented husbands has made itself felt in the matter of endowing their menfolks'

(Continued from page 7)

partnership as yet—but give them time. Certainly they are well on the way.

Two Schools of Thought

There are, of course, two schools of masculine thought and feeling anent this comparatively recent development in stf. One school withdraws into crusty male resentment toward feminine invasion of yet another masculine sanctum sanctorum. The other prefers mixed singles and/or doubles and makes no bones about it.

Personally, as our readers have doubtless gathered by this time, we belong to the latter group. It is our belief that this female uprising, inrush or whatever it may be termed is entirely in line with the world-trend toward woman's emancipation and equality that has endured at least since the fiery pronunciamentoes of Mary Wollstonecraft and her companions.

The girls have won Nobel Prizes, Senatorial seats, Gubernatorial incumbencies and corporation directorships. They have served as front line soldiers, as day laborers, as top executives and horse trainers, as test pilots and parachutists. More and more they have been accepting the toil, the danger and the responsibility of our era, along with its Hollywood contracts and beauty prizes.

It occurs to us that when the first extra-Tellurian frontier is attained it will not for long be an all-male affair. If something big is going on, be it on Mars, Venus or Ganymede, the girls will be in on it.

We rather envy the space pioneers of the future in their lack of solitude. They may at times grow weary of that inner tension which drives some women to talk for talk's sake. But overall they're going to have a lot more fun than pioneers of the dismal past.

---

female creations with a trio of dimensions. C. L. Moore's sensitivity has been of immeasurable aid in giving depth and reality to the heroines and other she-creatures of her multi-faceted spouse, Henry Kuttner.

Seldom if ever has a single field of fiction been so thoroughly spanned by three such husband-wife combinations as Hull-van Vogt, Brackett-Hamilton and Moore-Kuttner. Should you choose to regard this as an infiltration process, you will have to admit that the girls not only aimed high but got there.

It is our hunch that while the A-bomb, the V-2 rocket and the so-called Flying Saucer have had much to do with giving science fiction a far wider field of reader interest than the authors, editors and publishers conceived of a decade ago, it is these women writers who have played a vital role in making stf acceptable to a more adult market.

The space opera of ten, fifteen or twenty years ago—however clever its pseudo-scientific gadgetry, however vast its galactic scope—was basically little more than an elaborate *Tom Swift* or *Rover Boys* story. Its characters—we use the word in an entirely figurative sense—were mere appendages to its machinery and its dialogue was hopeless *gee-whiz* sub-adolescent.

A Good Influence

We think the girls had a large hand in fixing all that. Space opera—fine, but they wanted it peopled with folk who aroused emotional belief. They got them.

As these writers were establishing themselves other young women began to make their presence felt in the reader's columns of this and other stf magazines. They leaped recklessly into hitherto stag fan-controversies, thereby livening up same not only through the freshness of their approach but through the rebuttals they drew from resenting males.

Fan clubs and fan magazines began more and more to develop feminine brightness and neatness and the boys, forced to look to their laurels, lost much of that lingering dinginess which seems inevitably to accompany the all-male in print or in person. After all, why does the peacock preen? Hardly for other peacocks.

The girls have not yet blossomed into full

(Continued on page 140)

THE READER SPEAKS

A DEPARTMENT FOR SCIENCE FICTION FANS

For a number of decades the world of science fiction was pretty much exclusively a male world. While boys of all ages and castes, united by the umbilical cord of soaring impersonal imagination, delved into the works of Verne, Wells, Conan Doyle, *Tom Swift* and the like, the girls seemed content with *Little Elsie* or the sub-erotic sublimations of E. M. Hull, Ethel M. Dell and other experts in the manufacture of machine-tooled glamour to provide frosting for the solid cake layers of recipes and fashion patterns and little essays on beauty culture.

Primeval clubs and gatherings of science fiction addicts were strictly Little Scorpion affairs. Only rarely did some space-minded Tomboy Taylor manage to crash them. And as a rule she had to keep her hair short and her mind on the refreshments rather than the boys if she hoped to survive in membership.

Women didn't really exist in the stories of the era either—save as opposite numbers to prophylactic Western heroes and such an occasional *She*-like creature as the late Stanley Weinbaum's Margaret of Urbs. Save for a few seldom-heard-from ladies like Lilith Lorraine and M. Rupert and a very few others, women did little writing in the field.

Yes, for quite a time as time is counted these days, science fiction was a world for men and men only.

THE GREAT INVASION

However, at some indeterminate point in the nineteen thirties something happened. Just how or why it happened lies beyond our current ken but at any rate the girls got interested and began to move in. This metamorphosis—called either the Great Invasion or the Great Erosion depending upon the point of view—is too well and too long established to be regarded as any mere passing trend. The girls are in and in to stay.

A number of women writer, ranging from adequate to brilliant, began to turn out science fiction stories of such excellence that in magazine after magazine they grabbed their share not only of inside short stories but of lead novelets and novels, hitherto an exclusively masculine prerogative.

Certainly the fantasies of C. L. Moore were and are as fine as any work in the field. And right up alongside her work we have today that of E. Mayne Hull, Leigh Brackett, Margaret St. Clair, Judith Merril, Catherine MacLean, Betsy Curtis, and Miriam Allen deFord, to say nothing of an ambitious platoon of youngsters who are promising to crash into print professionally at almost any moment.

HUSBANDS AND WIVES

Naturally, with such a group of talented women writers practicing successfully for more than a dozen years, the entire story-perspective on women in science fiction has changed. It is no longer uncommon to find a female chief protagonist in an stf story—and not a two-dimensional valentine or a cold-fire priestess-empress but a female who acts, talks and thinks like a woman alive.

Furthermore both Miss Hull and Miss Brackett married science fiction authors of renown—A. E. van Vogt and Edmond Hamilton respectively—and their influence on their talented husbands has made itself felt in the matter of endowing their menfolks' female creations with a trio of dimensions. C. L. Moore's sensitivity has been of immeasurable aid in giving depth and reality to the heroines and other she-creatures of her multi-faceted spouse, Henry Kuttner.

Seldom if ever has a single field of fiction been so thoroughly spanned by three such husband-wife combinations as Hull-van Vogt, Brackett-Hamilton and Moore-Kuttner. Should you choose to regard this as an infiltration process, you will have to admit that the girls not only aimed high but got there.

It is our hunch that while the A-bomb, the V-2 rocket and the so-called Flying Saucer have had much to do with giving science fiction a far wider field of reader interest than the authors, editors and publishers conceived of a decade ago, it is these women writers who have played a vital role in making stf acceptable to a more adult market.

The space opera of ten, fifteen or twenty years ago—however clever its pseudo-scientific gadgetry, however vast its galactic scope—was basically little more than an elaborate *Tom Swift* or *River Boys* story. Its characters—we use the word in an entirely figurative sense—were mere appendages to its machinery and its dialogue was hopeless *gee-whiz* sub-adolescent.

A GOOD INFLUENCE

We think the girls had a large hand in fixing all that. Space opera—fine, but they wanted it peopled with folk who aroused emotional belief. They got them.

As these writers were establishing themselves other young women began to make their presence felt in the reader's columns of this and other stf magazines. They leaped recklessly into hitherto stag fan-controversies, thereby livening up same not only through the freshness of their approach but through the rebuttals they drew from resenting males.

Fan clubs and fan magazines began more and more to develop feminine brightness and neatness and the boys, forced to look to their laurels, lost much of that lingering dinginess which seems inevitably to accompany the all-male in print or in person. After all, why does the peacock preen? Hardly for other peacocks.

The girls have not yet blossomed into full partnership as yet—but give them time. Certainly they are well on the way.

TWO SCHOOLS OF THOUGHT

There are, of course, two schools of masculine thought and feeling anent this comparatively recent development in stf. One school withdraws into crusty male resentment toward feminine invasion of yet another masculine sanctum sanctorum. The other prefers mixed singles and/or doubles and makes no bones about it.

Personally, as our readers have doubtlessly gathered by this time, we belong to the latter group. It is our belief that this female uprising, inrush or whatever it may be termed is entirely in line with the world-trend toward woman's emancipation and equality that has endured at least since the fiery pronounciamentoes of Mary Wollstonecraft and her companions.

The girls have won Nobel Prizes, Senatorial seats, Gubernatorial incumbencies and corporation directorships. They have served as front line soldiers, as day laborers, as top executives and horse trainers, as test pilots and parachutists. More and more they have been accepting the toil, the danger and the responsibility or our era, along with its Hollywood contracts and beauty prizes.

It occurs to us that when the first extra-Tellurian frontier is attained it will not for long be an all-male affair. If something big is going on, be it on Mars, Venus or Ganymede, the girls will be in on it.

We rather envy the space pioneers of the future in their lack of solitude. They may at times grow weary of that inner tension which drives some women to talk for talk's sake. But overall they're going to have a lot more fun than pioneers of the dismal past.

19. Editorial by Sam Merwin Jr., *Thrilling Wonder Stories*, December 1950, pp. 6, 7, and 140

and his ideas for the exploration of Mars, which I discussed in chapter 4, Merwin sees the men as the "space pioneers," and women only as their companions.

According to Merwin, the entry of women into the field can be characterized as "the Great Invasion or the Great Erosion depending upon the point of view" (6). He implies that women are either an invading army, ultimately improving the genre, or an influence that has corrupted science fiction. Brian Aldiss, in 1973, also figures women as the salvation of science fiction:

> I concur with Harlan Ellison; much of the best writing in science fiction today is being done by women (and he didn't even mention Christine Brooke-Rose, author of *Such*, 1966, and a fine modern novelist).
>
> What has made the difference is the disappearance of the Philistine-male-chauvinist-pig attitude, pretty well dissipated by the revolutions of the mid-sixties; and the slow fade of the Gernsbackian notion that sf is all hardware. Science fiction, in other words, has come back to a much more central position in the world of art. The all-male escapist power fantasy had at one time devoured all but what we have called the Huxleyan branch, those writings which occurred only irregularly as specific

> social criticism. Science fiction has returned from the Ghetto of Retarded Boyhood; and, truth to tell, it seems not to have suffered from its imprisonment. (Aldiss 1973: 306)

Aldiss repeated his position in the expanded version of *Billion Year Spree*, titled the *Trillion Year Spree*, which he wrote with David Wingrove. They locate the "Great Invasion" in the seventies: "In the seventies there was a great influx of women writers. The revolution they began is still under way and is having an effect on the kind of genre we now enjoy. By the end of the seventies it had become clear that SF was no longer a kind of juvenile men's club. Women were to be seen at the bar. SF's unexpressed half was beginning to speak out. Angrily, skilfully, persuasively, sometimes —as in all new causes—with ill-considered over-emphasis, but in many instances speaking with a new voice, a new intonation" (Aldiss and Wingrove 1988: 465). Aldiss and Wingrove's women "at the bar," like those of Merwin more than thirty years earlier, have done the boys a favor by arriving in science fiction.

It is interesting to look at the pronouns in this passage. Who is this "us" and "them" that are referred to? "They" are, clearly, the women writers. "Their" arrival from the outside is seen here as a blessing, for "they" arrive to civilize sf, turning it into "the kind of genre *we* [boys like Aldiss and Wingrove] now enjoy." Women writers in this passage are like the Victorian angel of the house, taking care of the domestic sphere and making sure the master of the house is comfortable. Women become "SF's unexpressed half." Unfortunately, this acceptance of an "unexpressed," invisible, absent body of women until the "revolution" of the 1970s serves to rewrite and gloss over the complexities of the period prior to this "influx" or "explosion" of women in the late 1960s and early 1970s.

In 1982 Isaac Asimov made the same argument as Merwin in an article for *Vogue* called the "Feminization of Sci-Fi." He argues that this "feminization has broadened and deepened the field to the point where science-fiction novels can now appear on the bestseller lists" (Asimov 1982: 608). For Asimov "feminization" has rescued the field from being the "strongly masculine" one that it once was, where the readers were "almost all young men [who were] . . . to a large extent, rather withdrawn young men who either had not yet come to be at ease with members of opposite sex or were actively afraid of them" (558). It is tempting to read this as a description of the Isaac Asimov of the late thirties who wrote the letters I examined in the previous chapter. He ends his article by arguing that both sexes benefit from the "feminization of science fiction": "It's as I have always said: Liberate women—and men will be liberated as well" (608).

The sf critic, writer, and journalist Charles Platt gives a less positive version of the arrival of the female hordes into science fiction. His is an account of "the Great Erosion." In a piece titled "The Rape of Science Fiction" (1989), women are among the rapists eroding science fiction's manhood:

> A new "soft" science fiction emerged, largely written by women: Joan Vinge, Vonda McIntyre, Ursula Le Guin, Joanna Russ, Kate Wilhelm, Carol Emshwiller. Their concern for human values was admirable, but they eroded science fiction's one great strength that had distinguished it from all other fantastic literature: its implicit claim that events described *could actually come true*.
>
> Of course, if you had a whimsical, muddled view of the world—if you didn't know anything about science, and didn't care—soft science fiction could seem perfectly plausible. And many new readers related to it in these terms. Unlike the old core-audience, they didn't enjoy mechanistic, technical stuff. They preferred mythic fables about dreamsnakes and snow queens. (Platt 1989: 46)

He ends by saying that Vonda McIntyre and Joan D. Vinge are responsible "for softening and sweetening science fiction, turning literary mind-food into conceptual cotton-candy that corrupted the tastes of naive adolescents" (Platt 1989: 49).

In Platt's formulation the difference between "hard" science fiction and "soft" science fiction is embodied: men are "hard," women are "soft" and, therefore, an eroding influence on the whole field. His arguments are not new, as I demonstrated in the previous chapter. The science fiction writers Lisa Goldstein, Pat Murphy, and Karen Joy Fowler[20] point out this equation in an interview by Wendy Counsil in the August 1990 *Science Fiction Eye*:

> GOLDSTEIN: Well if we're going to be in *Science Fiction Eye* this is something that really pissed me off. Charles Platt wrote an article . . . about who killed science fiction and he mentions Vonda McIntyre and Joan Vinge. And I was stunned! Here are two women who, as far as I know, haven't been writing nearly as much as they should in the field, except for *Star Trek* novels and movie novelization, and Platt is still annoyed that these women won major awards ten years ago. He's

annoyed that "soft science" has crept into the field in these women's work. Like anthropology.

COUNSIL: And biology.

GOLDSTEIN: And biology! I know; it's funny how the definition of "soft science" changes depending on if it's a man or a woman writing it.

MURPHY: It's because biology deals with soft, squishy living things.

GOLDSTEIN: Yeah, if a woman writes about it, *physics* is a soft science. (Counsil 1990: 27)

Goldstein, Fowler, and Murphy comment on the opposition between hard and soft sf:

FOWLER: You know, this whole hard science/soft science debate has begun to trouble me, because as I read more and more hard science fiction, I find less and less hard science in it. I don't understand—

GOLDSTEIN: There's *no* science in it! That Gibson stuff . . . You know Doug [Mr. Lisa Goldstein] reads this stuff and he's a computer programmer. He says the guy doesn't really seem to know anything about computers. . . .

COUNSIL: Even Larry Niven has admitted that he often isn't writing hard science fiction, that he's writing science fantasy, because there is no such thing as travelling faster than the speed of light.

MURPHY: In a recent article in *SF Eye*, Charles Platt talked about science fiction back in the fifties. He claimed that back then science fiction was based on hard science.

Reading that made me start a survey—though the earthquake stopped me—on comparing four magazines from the fifties to four from the eighties. I was going to categorize the stories: Faster than light travel? Science fantasy. A race of aliens living at the centre of the earth? Science fantasy, or just fantasy. I was going to compare the two groups of magazines to see how many hard science concepts there were in the 50s.

The first story I read in a 50s magazine was about aliens from the center of the earth who were using anti-gravity to steal the gold from Fort Knox. I never did find much of a hard science basis to that one.

GOLDSTEIN: But it was written by a man, right?

MURPHY: Yes, it was. No hard science; there was, however, a sexy babe in it. (Counsil 1990: 23)

My own reading of science fiction magazines from 1926 up to the present day confirmed Pat Murphy's impression. Hard science fiction has *always* been underrepresented in science fiction. Indeed the idea of science, closely associated with the masculine, has always been central to the genre but at the same time has always been lamented for its absence. As I demonstrated in chapter 1, a continual theme in many of the letters I read is the absence or inaccuracy of the science in the published stories. The violence inherent in Platt's very title, "The Rape of Science Fiction" becomes in his text a "softening," "sweetening," a "corrupt[ion]." Women become a polluting influence whose very touch defiles.

The changes wrought in science fiction from the late sixties appear quite different in feminist accounts of the period. Rather than use such terms as Aldiss and Wingrove's "influx" and "revolution" and Platt's "rape," Sarah Lefanu writes instead of an "intervention": "Previous to the intervention by feminist writers in the late sixties and early seventies science fiction reflected, in its content at least, what could be called masculine concerns, based around the central theme of space exploration and the development of technology: masculine concerns because access to these areas was effectively denied women in the real world, and science fiction, like all writing is written from within a particular ideology" (Lefanu 1988: 3). This "intervention," however, comes from the inside, not the outside: "Feminist SF . . . is part of science fiction while struggling against it" (5). Lefanu's women in science fiction are neither corrupting science fiction nor invading it.

Connie Willis also finds no hordes of women storming the barricades. There was instead a "tradition" of women's writing within science fiction. She writes in her editorial for *Asimov's Science Fiction* that the fact that there *were* women writing science fiction before the 1960s and 1970s was

> brought sharply home to me when I was looking up the stories I'd loved as a teenager. I'd never paid any attention to what the names of the stories were, let alone the authors, and, as a result, I found myself constantly saying, "there's this great story, I don't know what it was called or who wrote it, but it was about this town where they didn't have doctors . . ."
>
> I finally got fed up with my own ignorance and went back to my hometown public library to look all these stories up in the rebound copies of *Year's Best SF, Fifth Series*, etc., that I'd read them in in the first place.

> . . . I was surprised at how many of them had been written by women: Kit Reed and Mildred Clingerman and Zenna Henderson and Shirley Jackson and Margaret St. Clair and Judith Merril. (Willis 1992: 4–5)

Willis's reading history was crowded with stories written by women that were themselves crowded with representations of women. As a result she "didn't know there *were* any barricades. It never occurred to me that SF was a man's field that had to be broken into. How could it be with all those women writers? How could it be when Judith Merril was the one editing all those *Year's Best SF*s?" (Willis 1992: 8). Willis thus locates herself in a tradition of women writing science fiction. That she is part of such a tradition is so obvious that there is no need for her to say so explicitly. But access to a tradition of women and science fiction depends on what you were reading. It would have been just as possible to have grown up reading science fiction and read *none* of these writers, as was the case for Judith Raphael Buckrich and Nancy Kress.

Sweet Little Domestic Stories

> *If there were any women in the field before that [the late 1960s and early 1970s] (which there weren't), they had to slink around using male pseudonyms and hoping they wouldn't get caught. And if they did write under their own names (which they didn't), it doesn't count anyway because they only wrote sweet little domestic stories. Babies. They wrote mostly stories about babies. (Willis 1992: 4)*

The implication of Charles Platt's arguments in "The Rape of Science Fiction" (1989) is that women do not belong in sf because of their softening influence. In this section I look at the suggestion that much of the earliest science fiction written by women was overly concerned with the domestic and that this is, of itself, a bad thing. Connie Willis refers to this method for dismissing the writing of women in the parody that heads this section, referring to a dismissal that was happening at the time she wrote her editorial. However, this notion of women's sf being "sweet little domestic stories" was already current at the time of their publication in the late forties and fifties. Anne McCaffrey, referring to the work of Judith Merril—whose first and perhaps best known sf story, "That Only a Mother," was published in 1948—writes that at the time Merril's stories were referred to as "diaper stories"

(McCaffrey 1974: 280). The editorial blurb about Carol Emshwiller from the "Author! Author!" section of the February 1958 issue of *Future* magazine also attests that the "diaper" label is not a later development: "Carol Emshwiller's stories do not show the 'typical' characteristics of tales by some female science-fictionists. They aren't attempts to swashbuckle so that readers will think she's a man; nor are they heart-throb-and-diapers accounts such as you find in the slicks. They're individual, and a needed reminder that God created science fictionists male and female, too!" A similar put-down appears in a review of a story by Rosel George Brown; William Atheling Jr. (pen name of James Blish): "Mrs Brown is just about the only one of *F&SF*'s former gaggle of housewives who doesn't strike me as verging on the feebleminded; in fact I think her work has attracted less attention than it deserves" (Atheling [1964] 1974: 128).[21]

Both Russ and Wood continue this dismissal of women's sf stories of the late forties and fifties as being "sweet little domestic stories." However, it is important to put their critique in context. As I argued in the introduction, the idea that science fiction is a genre within which anything is possible is an extremely important one to criticism of the field. If extrapolation about anything is possible, why is there such a failure to imagine anything new?

Russ makes this point in "The Image of Women in Science Fiction": "One would think science fiction the perfect literary mode in which to explore (and explode) our assumptions about 'innate' values and 'natural' social arrangements, in short our ideas about Human Nature, Which Never Changes. Some of this had been done. But speculation about the innate personality differences between men and women, about family structure, about sex, in short about gender roles, does not exist at all" (Russ [1971] 1974: 54). Russ felt that the "new" societies being invented did none of these things. They were either a kind of "intergalactic suburbia . . . the American middle class with a little window dressing" or, worse, a society based on "an idealised and simplified" past where men are men and women are in the background (54–55).

After talking about men writers of sf, Russ discusses science fiction written by women. She divides their work into four categories: The first is "ladies' magazine fiction," "in which the sweet, gentle, intuitive heroine solves an interstellar crisis by mending her slip or doing something equally domestic after her big heroic husband has failed. Zenna Henderson sometimes writes like this" (Russ [1971] 1974: 56). The other three categories are galactic suburbia, space opera,[22] and avant-garde fiction (56). I will examine only Russ's first category, "ladies' magazine fiction." There is a strong implication in her description of this category that the domestic is intrinsically uninteresting, unheroic, and somehow foolish in science fiction, and that the ways in which it has been written in science fiction only reproduce the stereotype of housewife. This view is shared by one of the best-known female pulp writers, Leigh Brackett: "Domesticity bored the bejesus out of me. Adventure stories were what I liked to read, so they were what I wrote. If I put a woman in any of my stories she was there because she was doing something, not worrying about the price of eggs or who's in love with who!" (quoted in Bradley 1977–78: 17).

Russ's reference to the heroine solving a crisis by "mending her slip" sounds remarkably like Zenna Henderson's story "Subcommittee" (1962),[23] which Susan Wood discusses in her article "Women and Science Fiction." On the one hand, Wood dismisses the story as "silly" and "sentimental"; on the other, she argues that it "makes an important point. The men are automatically suspicious and hostile, thinking only of gaining power over each other. The women, with their shared concern for the nurture of life, quickly establish communication and trust" (Wood 1978–79: 12). Wood's more favorable assessment of the story is embedded in an essentialism that revalues "female" qualities as positive and "male" qualities as negative, rather than the reverse. However, she is still caught in the flipside of those valuations, wherein a concern with many women's everyday domestic lives is viewed as "trivial" and "sentimental" and "boring." At the same time, Wood wants to think about ways in which science fiction can talk about those women "whose primary concern is the family" (12).

Wood's second reading of "Subcommittee," as a text that makes an important point about conflict resolution, is pushed further by Farah Mendlesohn in her article "Gender, Power, and Conflict Resolution" (1994). Mendlesohn argues that the story is "revealing as a critique of power structures and the language of power and, finally, as a study of gender" (124). Earth and alien invaders, the Linjeni, are at war, and Serena has accompanied her husband, a general, to the negotiations. While he spends all day attempting to secure a settlement with the aliens, Serena spends her days looking after her son, Splinter. Splinter makes friends with one of the alien children, Doovey. This friendship gives Serena the opportunity to make contact with one of the alien wives, whom she calls Mrs. Pink. The time the women spends together allows Serena to learn some Linjeni and to discover that this alien people have not come to invade Earth but in search of salt, which is essential to their ability to reproduce. With this knowledge Serena breaks into the negotiations and by displaying the slip that Mrs.

Pink made for her, she is able to prove to the men that common ground between humans and the aliens is possible.

Russ characterizes heroines like Serena as "sweet," "gentle," and "intuitive." Their ability to deal with situations is something innate to them, not something achieved by skill. Mendlesohn argues that "at no time is Serena portrayed as intuitive as such: she makes no guesses; rather, she listens and learns" (Mendlesohn 1994: 125). She is operating in a different social milieu from her husband the general . Unlike him, Serena "exists within a world of morning coffee and neighbourliness, with its own mores and codes of conduct. Her reaction to the stranger, therefore, is—metaphorically—to knock on the door with a cake. This is not feminine intuition or any innate feminine gentleness, but it is integral to a complex social community with its own values and demands" (125).

In treating women's sf as "sweet little domestic stories," the early examples of feminist sf criticism by Russ and Wood accept the marginalization of women's writing. These are the very grounds for dismissing women's writing that Russ outlines so brilliantly in her 1983 *How to Suppress Women's Writing* : "[S]he wrote it but look what she wrote about" (Russ [1983] 1984: 48). This kind of dismissal also serves to discourage others from going back and reading some of those "sweet little domestic stories." For instance, I avoided Zenna Henderson, Judith Merril, and other writers of the period because the accounts of 1950s women's science fiction I read made their stories sound dull. It was only after reading Connie Willis's "The Women SF Doesn't See" editorial for *Asimov's* that I finally made an effort to track down some of the "domestic" writing of women in sf in the 1950s.

Roz Kaveney also argues that pre-1960s science fiction by women was overly sweet and concerned with the domestic:

> The women SF writers of this period tended to be marginalised in one of three ways: one, editors were keen on stories which were "feminine" in the sense of being saccharine; the work of Zenna Henderson and Judith Merril does admittedly extend the range of SF material to cover issues like nurture but does so with that sentimentality which the SF of the time tended to confound with emotional truth. Two, women were encouraged to write light jokey fiction like that of Evelyn E. Smith, fiction which keeps a low temperature even in its humour. In some of the work of Evelyn Smith and of Margaret St Clair there is a quiet anger from which Russ probably learned, her own early fiction appeared towards the end of this time and was in more or less that vein. (Kaveney 1989: 84)

There is some evidence to support Kaveney's claim that certain editors expected women to write certain kinds of stories and that it was difficult to publish other kinds of stories. Wood writes that "[i]n 1948 John W. Campbell [editor of *Astounding*] commissioned Judith Merril's first science fiction story, asking her to provide 'the woman's point of view' on scientific developments. The story, "That Only a Mother," deals with the effects of radiation in terms of a mother's blind love for her mutant daughter. The galactic house wives of 2050, happily dusting the robochef in the living unit while hubby tends the yeast farms, might represent a failure of social extrapolation, but they were, perhaps, a little more believable as human beings than all the princesses and priestesses. Perhaps" (Wood 1978–79: 10).[24]

Wood's shift from discussing "That Only a Mother" to talking about the "galactic house wives of 2050" implies that "That Only" is this kind of a story. Certainly the story was presented as being from the feminine point of view when it first appeared. The title page features a sketch of a mother holding a child whose face only she can see, and Judith Merril is billed as "a new feminine science fiction author" (*Astounding Science Fiction* [June 1948]: 88). Connie Willis, however, offers a different assessment: "Although "That Only" does have a baby in it, it hardly classifies as a domestic tale. It's a story about radiation, infanticide, and desperate self-delusion that manages to be poignant and horrific at the same time" (Willis 1992: 8). Perhaps the problem here is the way the term "domestic" is used to be synonomous with dull or everyday for all those things—radiation, infanticide and desperate self-delusion happen within the domestic sphere.

Judith Merril gave me a different account of the story's genesis after I spoke to her at WisCon 20 in May of 1996. Merril told me that Campbell did *not* commission the story:

> In August 1947 I went to Philadelphia for my first science fiction convention. At a very drunk hotel room party [Theodore] Sturgeon introduced me to the great editor, John Campbell. It was friendship—forever at first sight.
>
> "John," I said, slurring only slightly, "John, I wan' tell you, I wrote a story so good I can' sell it to you, 'cause you couldn' pay enough for it." (*Astounding* paid top rates for a pulp, two to three cents a word).
>
> "You' right," he said, with his own bit of a slur. "If you' story is that good, I can' pay enough for it." We beamed at each other.
>
> Next morning I woke up more horrified than hung over—but six

months later, when it had finished its rounds of the slicks . . . John did buy the story. It was published in the June, 1948 issue of *Astounding.* (Letter to author, 16 November 1996)[25]

Merril sent him another story, which Campbell rejected, saying that he preferred to see her writing stories from the woman's point of view. Merril was less than pleased by this. She writes:

> The woman's point of view request came in response to the second submission I sent him. I'd have to find the files to give you a title and/or exact quote, but it was a story with a male protagonist.
>
> Yes, which ever it was, it did sell elsewhere. And yes, the request pissed me off. I felt everything I wrote was a woman's point of view, but the only stuff I had (and to this day, have) not been able to sell were my attempts to write the woman's point of view as perceived by the publishing world, i.e.romances, confessions, slick magazine stories!
>
> I did not feel constrained to write woman's point of view for Campbell or anyone else. I submitted everywhere, but the only editor I ever consciously wrote for was Anthony Boucher, and this was largely because he never attempted to superimpose his values on mine. (Letter to author, 13 October 1996)

Other women writers had a different experience. In her article "An Evolution of Consciousness: Twenty-five Years of Writing about Women in Science Fiction" (1977) Marion Zimmer Bradley, for example, writes that in the 1950s "with the failure of both *Web of Darkness* and *Window on the Night* to find publication, I realized that if I were going to write for anyone's edification other than my own, I would have to write about men; I would have to write novels with heroes rather than heroines. This was simply the rules of the game, the economic facts of life in the market" (Bradley 1977: 35).[26] And as late as the 1970s, Joanna Russ and Suzy McKee Charnas had enormous difficulty getting their women-centered novels, *The Female Man* (1975) and *Motherlines* (1978), published.

One of Margaret St. Clair's stories, "Short in the Chest" (1954),[27] does indeed evince the "quiet anger" that Roz Kaveney mentions; however, I would argue that it is closer to biting satire than "light jokey fiction" (Kaveney 1989: 84). St. Clair experienced some difficulty in getting the story published: "In the fifties and sixties sex was, if not quite a no-no, something one had to be careful about. A short, funny story of mine, 'Short in the Chest,' was rejected by Horace Gold with the comment, 'If you want to put me out of business, Margaret, I wish you'd do it with French postcards'" (St. Clair 1981: 151).

The story is definitely not a "sweet little domestic story." It is set in a future where everyone in the United States is in the armed forces and all the different services hate each other. A Marine, Major Sonya Briggs, goes to a huxley—a computerized psychiatrist—because of problems she has been having "dighting"—having sex with—a member of Air. She asks the huxley if it is "true that the dighting system was set up by a group of psychologists after they'd made a survey of inter-service tension?" (St. Clair [1954] 1995: 132). The drug they take to get aroused, a "Watson," does not work for her. The huxley she goes to see has a short in its chest and advises her to shoot the next "yuk from Air" she is assigned for dighting. At first she thinks that that "wouldn't reduce inter-service tension effectively" (137), but then she decides to follow the huxley's advice. The huxley, it turns out, "had had interviews with twelve young women so far, and it had given them all the same advice it had given Major Briggs. Even a huxley with a short in its chest might have forseen that the final result of its counselling would be catastrophic for Marine" (137).

A story that is more typical of the kind of writing that Russ refers to as "intergalactic suburbia" than "Short in the Chest" is Garen Drussai's "Woman's Work" (1956).[28] The editor's blurb describes the story as an extrapolation of "the housewife in an age of the ultimate development of competitive salesmanship" (Drussai 1956: 104). In the far future, the housewife's "woman's work" is to deal with the salesmen. As Sheila deals with the first salesman at her door (at four A.M.) and his array of gizmos, such as "a pneumatic float" to lull her into a "state of acceptance," she is always thinking of her husband, Hal, "lying there in the bedroom—trusting her to do her best" (105). At the end of the story it becomes apparent that Hal, too, is a salesman. As he goes off to work, "[s]he looked numbly after him, thinking of the hours ahead till she could escape to the shops and shows that made up her day. Then she straightened up determinedly. After all, this was woman's work" (106). The story then ends the way it started: "The alarm on her wrist was giving off small electric shocks. *Someone was coming up the walk!*" (106).

"Woman's Work" takes for granted that the stereotypical household economy of white middle America of the 1950s will remain unchanged into the future. In Russ's words, "assumptions about 'innate' values and 'natural' social arrangements" are neither "explored" nor "exploded" (Russ

[1971] 1974: 54). "Woman's Work" can also be read as a satire of its present, overdrawing the stultifying pointlessness of middle-class "woman's" work of the period. For all science fiction's utopic striving towards various futures, it will always be as much about its own now as about any imagined future.

It is difficult, however, to know if this reading of the text was available at the time of its publication. *The Magazine of Fantasy and Science Fiction*, where the story first appeared, did not have a letters column, and I have found no discussion of the story or its author anywhere else. There is a sense in which my historical distance from the text makes it easier for me to read it as a satire of what may have been seen as the suffocating monotony of fifties suburbia. However, I can imagine how a steady diet of the narrow confines of stories like Drussai's could be maddening. The cumulative effect of reading through countless pulp science fiction stories from the 1920s through to the early seventies was that it became much easier to understand what it was that Russ and Wood and McCaffrey were reacting to.

The coding of the work by women of this decade as "domestic" is part of the same move that sees women coded as the "love interest." It reduces women's ability to signify within science fiction outside the bedroom or the kitchen. The acceptance of this coding fits in with the accounts of women and science fiction that figure women as invading science fiction from outside and bringing their feminine concerns such as domesticity with them. This is the same separation between the public and private spheres that I discussed in chapter 4.

6 I'M TOO BIG BUT I LOVE TO PLAY
Stories about James Tiptree Jr.

"You will in the future have compensations for defeat."

"I know. . . . You are going to tell me that in a hundred years the readers of the whole world will have my books standing on their shelves to take them down with reverence and delight. I have had it said to me before."

"But wrongly said, Milord, wrongly said. . . . In a hundred years your works will be read much less than today. They will collect dust on the shelves."

"I do not much mind," said Lord Byron.

"But one book," said Pipistrello, "will be rewritten and reread, and will each year in a new edition be set upon the shelf."

"What book is that?" Lord Byron asked.

"The Life of Lord Byron," said Pipistrello.

(Dinesen [1975] 1987: 315)

The James Tiptree Jr. Memorial Award is a site where the battle of the sexes in science fiction continues. However, unlike many of the earlier battle-of-the-sexes texts, it is a site in which feminism is celebrated and the battle of the sexes is reworked and transformed. The Tiptree Award takes its name and its inspiration from the work and lives of James Tiptree Jr. In this chapter I sketch out some of the stories that surround Alice Sheldon/James Tiptree Jr. in order to begin thinking about how these stories have become part of a feminist sf mythos and, so, how these stories have helped make the Tiptree Award possible.

For almost ten years James Tiptree Jr. published science fiction stories that had a tremendous impact on the field, earning prizes and critical acclaim. No one had met the writer, but many had received letters from "Tip," and curiosity about "Tip" was enormous. During that period Raccoona Sheldon (from here on Raccoona) also published science fiction stories, though not nearly as prolifically as Tiptree. In 1976 it was revealed that James Tiptree Jr. and Raccoona "were" Alice Sheldon. So James Tiptree Jr. and Raccoona were written into creation by Alice Sheldon; perhaps together they form a literary hermaphrodite.

Any discussion of Alice Sheldon/James Tiptree Jr./Raccoona finds itself dealing with the problem of pronouns. Do I simply use the name Alice Sheldon to refer to writing under Tiptree's name as well as writing under the name of Raccoona as well as writing under the name Alice Sheldon? Is Tiptree's writing "his" writing, "her" writing, or "their" writing? This problem crops up frequently in writing about Tiptree et al. Jeffrey Smith begins his article "The Short Happy Life of James Tiptree, Jr.": "How does one attempt a biography of someone who is more persons than person? When *was* James Tiptree, Jr. born? Was it 1915, when his alter-ego Alice Sheldon (then Bradley) came into the world? Was it at that childhood date when she discovered science fiction? Was it in 1967, when she began writing sf under the Tiptree name? Or not until March of 1968, when *Analog* published 'Birth of a Salesman'?" (Smith 1978: 8).

In writing about this "someone who is more persons than person" it is very difficult to decide just how to refer to "them." Of course no one is a unified subject: "Human beings are characterised both by continuous personal identity and by discontinuous personal diversity" (Davies and Harre 1990: 46). At least for most people, there are no more than one or two names to refer to this "continuous personal identity" and "discontinuous personal diversity." For the subject of this chapter, however, there are far more than one or two names, and whatever shorthand I choose will give the stories I tell a certain emphasis.

Le Guin in her introduction to Tiptree's *Star Songs of an Old Primate* (1978) names her/him Alice James Raccoona Tiptree Sheldon Jr. Amanda Boulter also uses this naming in the title of her 1995 article, "Alice James Raccoona Tiptree Sheldon Jr.: Textual Personas in the Short Fiction of Alice Sheldon." In her article, Boulter uses the pronoun "she" to refer to Alice and Raccoona Sheldon and the pronoun "he" to refer to James Tiptree Jr. This allows Boulter to set out the difficulties of a straightforward mapping of the "pen name" of James Tiptree Jr. on to the body of Alice Sheldon. Boulter closely examines Tiptree's and Raccoona's short fiction and the way these texts have been read by a variety of critics in terms of the human body that was presumed to have produced them. She argues that frequently the perceived feminism of Tiptree's writing rests in the knowledge that he is really a woman.

I follow Boulter's practice of referring to Tiptree as "he." However, the focus of this chapter is not the published science fiction stories of Tip and Raccoona. I am examining a cluster of texts that have built up around and constructed the person(s) born Alice Hastings Bradley in 1915 and died Alice Sheldon in 1987. To do this, I expand the title of Boulter's paper, adding a few more names so that her/his name becomes "Alice James Raccoona Tiptree Davey Hastings Bradley Sheldon Jr."

I cannot remember where or when I first came across the story of James Tiptree Jr. Perhaps it was in Joanna Russ's *How to Suppress Women's Writing,* where, after discussing how the reception of Emily Brontë's *Wuthering Heights* changed depending on the perceived sex of the author, she gives a more recent example: "It would be nice to think that the exaltation of male authorship via the derogation of female authorship is dying out. In 1975, however, Robert Silverberg . . . introduced the collected works of a new, unknown and pseudonymous fellow writer as follows . . . 'there is to me something ineluctably masculine about Tiptree's writing.' In 1977 it was revealed that James Tiptree, Jr. was the pen name of a sixty-one-year-old retired biologist named Alice Sheldon—who had found a pseudonym on a jar of marmalade while shopping in the supermarket" (Russ [1983] 1984: 43–44) (in fact, Sheldon was never a biologist).

Here are the bare bones of the fable of the woman, Alice Sheldon, writing sf as a man, James Tiptree Jr., who "proved" there was no essential difference between the way men and women write, but only in the way that what they write is actually read. Part of the fable, of course, was what a joke the revelation of Tiptree's "true" sex was on the science fiction boys, particularly poor old Robert Silverberg and his oft-quoted observation about Tiptree's Hemingwayesque ineluctable masculinity (oft-quoted because he said quotably what everyone else at the time was thinking). This is in part what was behind the choice of Tiptree's name for the first science fiction prize to be named for a woman. There is more to the fable, because Alice Sheldon had done many of the masculine things ascribed to her when she was him. Sheldon had worked for the CIA; in her forties she had gone back to university to earn a Ph.D. in psychology; she had spent part of her childhood in Africa and Asia; and she had an "easy familiarity with such 'masculine' matters as guns, airplanes, the interior workings of automobile engines, and the military/espionage world" (Silverberg 1993: 5).

In reading these stories by and about Tiptree I found that I was not able to make a simple distinction between the stories of the life of the writer and the writer's published stories. The more I read, the more I needed to read. As I read many interviews with Alice Sheldon/James Tiptree Jr.—they were never with Raccoona—I became increasingly fascinated by her/his stories of her/his life, of lives really, by the series of names and disguises that did *not* begin with James Tiptree Jr. In this chapter I explore each of these lives in turn.

Alice Hastings Bradley b. 1915

And suddenly mother realized that Africa was only another fairy tale to Alice, whose whole world was all half fairy. (Bradley 1927: 68)

Stories in which Alice Hastings Bradley appears are told by more than one storyteller. However, she is usually a minor character, the little girl in Africa who "became" Tiptree. After cautioning us that "the links between a writer's work and her life are never simple," Sarah Lefanu tells us: "She spent much of her childhood exploring Africa with her parents, in the days when exploring meant walking: 2,700 miles to the Mountains of the Moon in search of the black gorillas. Her parents were impressive: her mother wrote more than thirty-five books" (Lefanu 1988: 116). Adam J. Frisch, offering no such explicit caution, states: "The daughter of naturalist Herbert Bradley and mystery writer Mary Hastings, Tiptree as a child often accompanied her parents on wildlife expeditions to Africa and Indonesia, trips that may have sparked her later interest in the study of behavioural psychology" (Frisch 1982: 48).

Of the stories of little Alice that I read, the first that offered more detail appears in Donna Haraway's *Primate Visions: Gender, Race, and Nature in the World of Modern Science* (1989).[1] It allows Haraway to make a direct link between colonial presences in Africa in the 1920s and the science fiction of the 1970s and 1980s that "interrogate[s] the conditions of communication and reproduction of self and other in alien and home worlds" (Haraway 1989: 377). The link, of course, is a flesh-and-blood one as well as a textual one—it is Tiptree and Raccoona and Alice.

However, Alice had been a literary persona long before she became Tiptree and Raccoona, and long before Haraway's influential text. In the 1920s Alice's mother, Mary Wilhemina Hastings Bradley, told stories of her daughter in the travel books that she wrote about expeditions to parts of Africa and Asia in the 1920s. Two of these were written for children and are ostensibly all about her daughter, namely, *Alice in Jungleland* (1927) and *Alice in Elephantland* (1929). Alice also features in Mary Hastings Bradley's three other travel books, *On the Gorilla Trail* (1922), *Caravans and Cannibals* (1926), and *Trailing the Tiger* (1929).[2]

The entry in *Contemporary Authors* for Alice Sheldon (in parentheses: Raccoona Sheldon, James Tiptree Jr.), which was most probably written by Sheldon/Tiptree, Mary Wilhemina is described as a writer, explorer, and linguist and her husband, Herbert Edwin, as an attorney, explorer, big-game collector, and naturalist. In the 1942–1943 edition of *Who's Who in America,* Mary is named an author and big-game hunter and Herbert a lawyer, traveler, big-game hunter, and explorer. In 1921, with their little daughter, Alice, the Bradleys were part of Carl Akeley's first expedition "to find gorillas for a group for the American Museum of Natural History of New York" (Bradley 1922: 1).

Mary Bradley relates her stories of this expedition in *On the Gorilla Trail* (1922) and *Alice in Jungleland* (1927). Both are illustrated with photographs from the trip, and, in addition, the front dust cover of *Alice in Jungleland* proudly proclaims that it has "drawings by Alice herself!" *Alice in Elephantland* (1929) is also illustrated by "Alice Hastings Bradley." The difference between the mother's contemporary accounts and the daughter's memories of Alice in foreign climes could not be more marked: the determined cheerfulness of the mother's account where dangers of disease and cannibals are introduced to add color to these fabulous adventures contrasts with the melancholy alienation evinced by the grown child. Africa, says the grown-up Alice, gave her "a case of horror vitae that lasted all my life" (Sheldon 1988: 56).

As I read Mary Bradley's travel books I found myself placing her stories alongside the later ones of her daughter. Here is Mary's story of a costume party amongst the white passengers on the boat bound for Africa. Mary dresses her Alice as a doll:

> It gave Alice's Mummy a very queer feeling to see her little girl being carried off like a toy in a box, and she was glad when the cover was taken off and she could see Alice again. They stood the box up on end and there Alice stood, just like a doll. Every one had been afraid that she would never stand still, but she surprised them all by keeping perfectly quiet, just like a real doll in a box—in fact she felt so strange and shy that she didn't want to come out of the box at all.
>
> One little baby was so sure that Alice was a real doll that she tried to pull her out to play with and that made Alice laugh and come out. (Bradley 1927: 12)

Photographs of Alice from this time show a doll-like child dressed in white delicate dresses with her blond hair in ringlets.

Tiptree tells a similar story about hiding: "Once I ran away; I got into a good patch of elephant grass, where I made a secret house by crushing the grass down. Mother led a search for me and hauled me back out. You know, being hauled out of my James Tiptree retreat, when everyone found out who I was and I had to go back to being Alice Sheldon, was a similar feeling" (Platt 1983: 260).

Later in *Alice in Jungleland*, Bradley observes that the exotica of Africa, gorillas, lions, volcanoes, were now "so much a part of her life . . . that she did not think there was anything strange about them" (Bradley 1927: 130). The shift in Alice's view of what is normal caused problems for her when she returned "home":

> A long time after, when she came back to America and went to school with other girls and boys there was a geography lesson about mountains and volcanoes. The teacher asked them what a crater was.
>
> Up went Alice's hand. This was something she *did* know about.
>
> "My mummy spent the night in the crater of an active volcano," she said.
>
> A small boy turned and looked at her. Looked and looked and his round face grew rounder and rounder with disbelief.
>
> "She did not!" he said, indignantly.
>
> For, of course, no one's Mummy ever spent a night in a crater. A volcano was something in a book to study about. It didn't happen, not in real life. Of course not. At least not in *your* real life. (Bradley 1927: 130–31)

In the article about Alice Sheldon in *Contemporary Writers*, she writes about this period of her life in the third person: "And finally, she was exposed to dozens of cultures and sub-cultures whose values, taboos, imperatives, religions, languages, and mores conflicted with each other as well as with her parents. And the writer, child as she was, had continuously to learn this passing kaleidoscope of Do and Don't lest she give offence, or even bring herself or the party into danger. But most seriously, this heavy jumble descended on her head before her own personality or cultural identity was formed. The result was a profound alienation from any nominal peers, and an enduring cultural relativism" (Gearhart and Ross 1983: 444).

In the first ever interview with James Tiptree Jr., conducted by Jeffrey Smith and published in the June 1971 issue of the fanzine *Phantasmicom*,

Tiptree is asked a series of questions about his writing, and about his "real" life which, as his mother observed almost fifty years earlier, is not everybody else's "real" life. Tiptree is happy to talk about his writing and about sf generally but is less forthcoming about this hidden life of his. He responds as follows to Smith's slightly exasperated "[H]ow about telling us what you *are* willing to let us know about you?"[3]: "Well I . . . trailed around places like colonial India & Africa as a kid (and by the way, I knew in my bones that they weren't going to stay 'colonial' any more than I was going to stay a kid, but nobody ever asked me)" (quoted in Smith 1971: 7).

The choice of word "trailed around places" echoes the titles of two of Bradley's travel books about colonial India and Africa, *On the Gorilla Trail* and *Trailing the Tiger*. The choice of word points up Alice's lack of agency in Mary Bradley's accounts of this period in colonial Africa and Asia. The child that Tiptree refers to in this fragment of interview, little Alice, was not asked but was told and then was told of. As a little white girl, Alice was coming up against the boundaries of race and sex in a setting that is other and exotic in Mary Hastings Bradley's discourse:

> [India] was an uneasy place in which to travel with a little girl of nine. Alice was a woman to these folk and we were told, by English residents, not to let her go alone from her room to the dining-room, even in big hotels. The Indian servants of the place are not always reliable, and there are the bearers of white travellers loitering about and servants delivering packages.
>
> There had been no race problem in the heart of Africa, where Alice's native boy had been a dependable guardian, but here we could not let her go out alone with her Indian bearer. There are faithful and trusty Indian servants, of course, but a hasty traveller has no way of discriminating, and our warnings were earnest. (Bradley 1929b: 14)

In Africa and India there was no possibility of Alice passing or even of hiding, as she was able to later via the CIA and science fiction. In every one of the photographs of Alice in Africa she is preeminently visible: the only white child, the only head of blond ringlets, the little doll. Constantly looked at; never alone.

Donna Haraway's version of Alice in "Jungleland" is very different from that of Mary Bradley: "I have tried to fill *Primate Visions* with potent verbal and visual images—the corpse of a gorilla shot in 1921 in the 'heart of Africa' and transfixed into a lesson in civic virtue in the American Museum of Natural History in New York City; a little white girl brought into the Belgian Congo in the 1920s to hunt gorilla with a camera, who metamorphosized in the 1970s into a writer of science fiction considered for years as a model of masculine prose" (Haraway 1989: 2). These first two "potent . . . images" from Donna Haraway's *Primate Visions* both feature Mary's daughter Alice Hastings Bradley: first as a member of the expedition (led by Carl Akeley) in which that gorilla was made into a corpse in 1921, and second as "the litle white girl" who became Tiptree. Little Alice is a potent "verbal image" in a list of many such verbal and visual images that dominate Haraway's construction of her visions of the interaction between primates: monkeys, apes, humans. But in this part of the story, the "little white girl," Alice Hastings Bradley, remains unnamed, as is is the "writer of science fiction" she "metamorphosized" into.

Haraway's telling of the Tiptree story brings into conversation two literary personas, "the little white girl" and the masculine "writer of science fiction." Haraway reads Sheldon/Tiptree in terms of her other names "Bradley" and "Hastings" and the colonial heritage associated with those names. In her discussion of the 1921 Akeley gorilla hunting expedition, in a chapter titled "Teddy Bear Patriarchy: Taxidermy in the Garden of Eden, New York City, 1908–36," she describes a photograph of Akeley, the Bradleys, two anonymous Africans, and the dead gorilla, which, when mounted and stuffed for the museum, is renamed "the giant of Karisimbi":

> The photograph in the American Museum film archive of Carl Akeley, Herbert Bradley, and Mary Hastings Bradley holding up the gorilla head and corpse to be recorded by the camera is an unforgettable image. The face of the dead giant evokes Bosch's concept of pain, and the lower jaw hangs slack, held up by Akeley's hand. The body looks bloated and utterly heavy. Mary Bradley gazes smilingly at the faces of the male hunters, her own eyes averted from the camera. Akeley and Herbert Bradley look directly at the camera in an unshuttered acceptance of their act. Two Africans, a young boy and a young man, perch in a tree above the scene, one looking at the camera, one at the hunting party. (34)

In the final chapter of *Primate Visions* Haraway returns to this view of the Bradleys and brings the young Alice into focus:

> Tucked in the margins and endnotes of "Teddy Bear Patriarchy" was a little white girl in Brightest Africa in the early 1920s. Little Alice Hast-

> ings Bradley was brought there by Carl Akeley, the father of the game, on his scientific hunt for gorilla, in the hope that her golden-haired presence would transform the ethic of hunting into the ethic of conservation and survival, as "man" and his surrogates, sucked into decadence, stood at the brink of extinction. . . . Duplicitous, the little girl turned into James Tiptree Jr., and Raccoona Sheldon, a man and a mother, the female author who could not be read as a woman and who wrote science fiction stories that interrogated the conditions of communication and reproduction of self and other in alien and home worlds. But Tiptree's gender, species and genre transfigurations were only beginning to germinate in the child placed in the world still authored by the father of the game and the law of the father. (377–78)

Haraway reads the location of the golden-haired Alice through the later writing career of Tiptree/Raccoona. Her "little white girl" became Tiptree/Raccoona, man and woman, who reinvents herself and transfigures "gender, species and genre" and seizes the agency that was denied her as a child trailing through Africa, pretending to be a doll silent in a box.

Alice Davey b. 1934

Mrs. Alice Davey, wife to William Davey, "poet and polo-player," came out during Alice's first career, as a painter. In "Everything but the Name Is Me"[4] Tiptree gives an account of her complex "me" and of this first career as a painter, in which the marriage and family are made into background noise, relegated to the dependent clauses: "If you'd asked me any time from age 3 to 26, I'd have told you 'I'm a painter.' (Note, not "artist"—painter. Snobbism there.) And I was. I worked daily, whether I was supposed to be listening to lectures on Chateaubriand, whether my then-husband was shooting at me (he was a beautiful alcoholic poet), whether the sheriff was carrying our furniture out, whether Father was having a heart-attack, whatever" (Tiptree 1979: 32).

In the account Tiptree gave to Charles Platt in an interview, her view of the economics of marriage where the woman is bought and then renamed for the master is made explicit:

> I was made into a debutante, and I thought that meant I was on the slave block, so I married the first boy that asked me, three days later. I'd seen him for seven hours. He'd been seated on my left at the party, he

was certified as a poet and a gentleman by the president of Princeton, so I ran off and married him in Waukegan. Broke my mother's heart, because she'd given me the most expensive debutante party ever seen, in the middle of the depression, and had intended a grand tour to follow, culminating in my presentation at the English court, to the King, with three feathers on my head. Anyway, I married this beautiful but absolute idiot—what they hadn't mentioned in the documentation was that he was maintaining half the whores in Trenton and was an alcoholic. (Platt 1983: 262)

The following version of the story comes from Mark Siegel's appreciation of Tiptree. The text consists of his commentary as well as excerpts from private conversations and correspondence between them:

"He was beautiful, he was charming, he was a poet. . . . He was like an angel possessed by demons. It was an extraordinary thing. . . .

"Mother quite rightly perceived that this was no father for her grandchildren, but unknowingly removed the possibility of grandchildren forever by having the head of gynecology at the University of San Francisco Hospital perform a legal abortion on me—just a D&C, but he muffed it, and he wouldn't admit he muffed it and discharged me from the hospital with a temperature of 104. We got in the car and started out through the Mojave Desert, which was only a one-track road at the time, you know, with signs saying "Last Water." Bill had brought cases of whiskey and one canteen of water, and halfway through the desert to Santa Fe, with me getting hotter and sicker, the day about 120, the car broke down. He said, "This is the end!," emptied the water, drank a quart of whiskey, and passed out in the back seat. Well, I drove the car the rest of the way to Santa Fe, found a sign that said "Doctor," and passed out on his steps. (Quoted in Siegel 1988/89: 7)

Elsewhere Tiptree refers to not being able to have children because of a bad case of septicemia but does not mention the botched abortion. The marriage took place in 1934. By 1941 they were divorced.

Alice B. Sheldon b. 1945

"I'll never let myself outlive him," *she said quietly, nodding toward the living room where Ting was watching TV.* "His eyesight's going. He has to sit right on top of that set now to see anything." *She told me, as she'd told other friends, that if things got too bad for him, she'd kill them both.* "Unless of course I die first," *she laughed, taking another hit off her cigarette and hacking loudly. The scar on her chest from her recent open-heart surgery purpled with anger. (Quoted in Siegel 1988–89: 6)*

Alice B. Sheldon's story begins in 1945 and ends in 1987, when Alice killed her husband and then herself. Charles Platt tells the story this way: "In 1945, she joined the Air Staff Post-Hostilities Project, devised by its commander, Colonel Huntington D. Sheldon, who had been Deputy Chief of Air Intelligence in the European Theatre. . . . Alice Hastings Bradley married Huntington D. Sheldon in a French mayor's office, very shortly after she had begun working in his project. They remain married to this day, a very strikingly close and devoted couple" (Platt 1983: 263).

Every story I have read about this second marriage repeats this description of their relationship. Hartwell wrote that they "were an extremely close couple" (Hartwell 1987: 63). Jeffrey D. Smith wrote in his obituary for Alice Sheldon that "[s]he and her husband (it was hard at first to think of this quiet but forceful white-bearded man as 'Ting,' but that soon passed) were extremely devoted. They watched each other constantly, and while you talked with one the other would lean forward and drink in the scene with pleasure and admiration. Alli told me once that the worst night in her life was the one when Ting's small fishing boat had been swept out to sea by a storm; the emotion in her voice, years later, was overpowering" (Smith 1987: 16).

After their time in the armed forces and a brief stint running their own business, a chicken hatchery in New Jersey, they both went to work for the CIA: "Ting . . . joined . . . at supergrade level; I was at mere technical level, helping to start up their photo-intelligence capability, which was then evaluating captured German air photography of the U.S.S.R." (Platt 1983: 263). In the interview with Platt the next important moment is Sheldon's attempt to escape from everything and everyone. In the mid-1950s "I wrote a two-line letter of resignation, and ran away from *everybody*. I used the techniques the CIA had taught me, and in half a day I had a false name, a false bank account, a false security card, and had rented an apartment and moved in. I was somebody else. . . . I wanted to think. So I thought, then I got back in touch with my husband and we thought together, and decided we could really work things out" (Platt 1983: 264).

Alice went back to university to get a Ph.D. in experimental psychology: "I dragged out the predoctoral fellowship, long after I finished my Ph.D. exams, so that I could do four years of solid research, and I'll tell you, there is no greater thrill I've ever had than to stand bare-faced in front of Nature and say, 'I think this is the way your creations work; tell me, am I right?' And Nature grumblingly and reluctantly makes you do—as I did—thirteen different paradigms of the god damned experiment before you get the thing without any uncontrollable variables, and then finally says, in answer to your question, a clear-cut 'Yes.' That is the most thrilling moment I ever had in my whole life" (Platt 1983: 265). She continued to work teaching experimental psychology and statistics at George Washington University, Washington, D.C., until she retired because of ill health in 1968.

James Tiptree Jr. b. 1967

It was a lovely life being nobody. But then of course the "nobody" became terribly obtrusive, so that in many ways I was glad to get rid of him because I was evoking too much curiosity. (Quoted in Gearhart and Ross 1983: 445)

This is the story with which the science fiction community is most familiar: the man with the "ineluctable masculinity" who turned out to be a woman. Sheldon created Tiptree with his own signature, bank account, and post office box, and when mail came, "to avoid lying, she gave 'Tiptree' her own life history" (Platt 1983: 267). James Tiptree was not just a pseudonym—there have been other pseudonyms in science fiction—but a whole new persona whose "real" identity was hidden from publishers and even Tiptree's agent.

James Tiptree Jr. was born in 1967: "I simply saw the name on some jam pots. Ting was with me; I said 'James Tiptree' and he says—'Junior!' It was done so quickly, without conscious thought; but I suppose I couldn't have avoided having the thought—although I don't remember it—that the editor would take my stories more seriously" (Platt 1983: 266).

James Tiptree Jr. entered the world of science fiction with ease, writing four stories that were sent out and duly accepted. Jeff Smith recalls that they did not make an instant impact:

> I remember reading Tiptree's first story, "Birth of a Salesman," in the March 1968 *Analog* and thinking it was funny (though I can't claim I predicted great things for its author). I had read a dozen or so Tiptree stories by 1970, when I wrote to him and asked him if he would participate in a postal interview for my fanzine, *Phantasmicom*. (This was based on no great perception on my part that Tiptree was about to blos-

som into the writer he became, but because in those New Wave vs. Old Wave days Tiptree was being claimed by both camps—and there seemed to be a story in that.) (Smith 1987: 16)

The first cheque to arrive came from John W. Campbell, one of the most famous science fiction editors, whose name is synonymous with the so-called golden age of science fiction. Selling your first story to Campbell is a heady entry into science fiction. It is also an entry into a particularly boy's own version of the genre. By 1974 P. Schuyler Miller, well known for his review column in *Analog,* was acclaiming Tiptree as "one of the finest talents to appear in the field in some time" (Miller 1974: 152), and many concurred. Silverberg's well known introduction to *Warm Worlds and Otherwise* (1975), "Who Is Tiptree, What Is He?," is overflowing with enthusiasm for Tiptree's writing. Tiptree had won Nebulas and Hugos for his work, before the revelation of his "true" identity.

Tiptree wrote many articles and letters to *Phantasmicom* and later for another Jeffrey Smith fanzine, *Khatru,* as well as to other fanzines. He was one of the participants in the 1975 *Khatru* symposium on women and science fiction. His voluminous correspondence and his contributions to fanzines mark Tiptree clearly as one of the many pros who did not disdain the fan world. Though they had never met Tiptree in person, many in the field felt that they knew Tip (or "Uncle Tip" as he sometimes called himself) well through his many letters. Le Guin writes of her friendship with Tiptree: "He always types with a blue typewriter ribbon, and the only question I have asked him which he has always evaded is, 'Where do you get so many blue typewriter ribbons?' When he himself is blue, he has told me so, and I've tried to cheer him up, and when I have been blue I've been turned right round into the sunlight simply by getting one of Tiptree's preposterous, magnificent letters. The only thing better than Tiptree's letters is his stories" (Le Guin 1978: viii).

In these letters, as well as in his articles and the interview with *Phantasmicom,* Tiptree let slip various details about his background and current situation. In the "Galaxy Stars" department of *Galaxy* there is the following report: "James Tiptree, Jr., one of our more peripatetic writers, is just back from a fishing sojourn amid the primeval rocky lochs of Northern Scotland. Saw no Loch Ness monsters, he reports: also no fish" (*Galaxy* January 1969: 194). In the June 1971 issue of *Phantasmicom,* Tiptree was interviewed by Jeffrey Smith. Smith opened by asking, "Your friends and associates are unaware that you are a science fiction writer, so you don't want sf people finding out who your friends and associates are. But how about telling us what you *are* willing to let us know about you?" (Smith 1971: 7). Tiptree responds:

> Well I was born in the Chicago area a long time back, trailed around places like colonial India & Africa as a kid. . . . I'm one of those for whom the birth and horrendous growth of Nazism was the central generational event. . . .
>
> At any event, by the time I had finished the decade's worth of instruction in How Things Are provided by this event—you know, joining organisations, getting in the Army, milling around in the early forms of American left-wing sentiment, worrying about Is It Going to Happen Here—an occupation I haven't given up—getting out of the Army, doing a little stint in government, trying a dab of business, etc. etc. So ensued a period of more milling (I'm a slow type) including some dablings in academia. And now the story grows even vaguer for the time being, Jeff, since I'm against lying on principle. (Smith 1971: 7)

Smith then asks the obvious: "Why don't you want your friends to know about your 'second career'? Don't you think that perhaps someday somebody will stumble across one of your stories? Will you then deny being the same James Tiptree, Jr. or what?" (Smith 1971: 10). The answer is "or what":

> I could give you a set of plausible reasons, like the people I have to do with include many specimens of prehistoric man, to them the news that I write *ugh, science fiction* would shatter any credibility that I have left. (Sometimes I think that sf is the last really dirty word.)
>
> Or that I'm unwilling to tarnish my enjoyment of this long-established secret escape route by having to defend it to hostile ears. (Coward!)
>
> Probably the real reason is partly inertia, it started like this, I don't yet really believe it, let it be til [*sic*] it ripens. That too. . . .
>
> Well, the last remaining part of my secretiveness is probably nothing more than childish glee. At last I have what every child wants, a real secret life. Not an official secret, not a q-clearance polygraph-enforced bite-the-capsule-when-they-get-you secret, nobody else's damn secret but MINE. Something THEY don't know. Screw Big Brother. A beautiful secret REAL world, with real people, fine friends, doers of great deeds & speakers of the magic word, Frodo's people if you wish, and

> they write to me and accept my offerings, and I'm damned if I feel like opening the door between that magic reality and the universal shitstorm known as the real (sob) world. (Smith 1971: 11-12)

These bits and pieces of information fueled speculation about Tiptree: "A squad of fans once actually staked out my McLean, Virginia, post-office box when the big science-fiction convention was in D.C.—luckily I was in Canada at the time" (Sheldon 1988: 51).

In almost every review and every editorial comment or introduction to a Tiptree story or collection of stories there is some speculation about the secretive Tiptree. In his sf review of *Warm Worlds and Otherwise* for the *New York Times Book Review*, Gerald Jonas writes, "Tiptree is the current mystery man of science fiction. He keeps to himself, does not show up at S.F. conventions to receive the awards that he wins, and is rumoured to work for a government agency in Washington. No one knows whether the name he signs to his stories is his real name or a pseudonym" (Jonas 1975: 31–32). In 1972 Silverberg wrote:

> The first of James Tiptree's science-fiction stories to see print appeared early in 1968—a long time back, by the reckoning of some, but just an eyeblink ago to those of us who have Cosmic Perspective. It attracted no particular attention, nor did his next two or three; but by 1970 he was finding his way into anthologies and getting nominated for awards, and now it is apparent that a major new short story writer is in our midst: deft, original, vigorous. What he can do in the longer forms is still something of a mystery as of this writing, but the odds favor him. Tiptree the man likewise remains something of a mystery at present. He lives south of Mason-Dixon, thought not very far, seems to travel a good deal, and describes himself as "a Midwesterner who batted around jungly parts of the globe when young and worse jungles with desks when old." Perhaps he's the Secret Master of the CIA; perhaps he's Ho Chi Minh in a clever plastic disguise. One thing is sure: he's a writer. (Silverberg 1972: 21)

In the same year another well-known science fiction writer and editor, Harry Harrison, wrote, "It is with some pride that I say I printed this author's first story just a few years ago. He reluctantly admits that he spent most of World War II in a Pentagon sub-basement, and wonders what war it was he watched go by in Shanghai when he was ten years old. Other facts about him are hard to come by, other than the vital fact that he can write stories such as this one—that purports to be about the far future, but is about all science at the same time" (Harrison [1972] 1976: 182).

In 1975 Robert Silverberg summed up what was known about Tiptree: "James Tiptree, Jr., lives in Virginia, not far from the capital, and prefers to let public attention center on his stories, not on his private life—so not much is generally known about his profession, marital status, childhood and upbringing, and such. He is willing to admit that he is a man of middle years who had travelled widely; all the rest is conjecture, at this point" (Silverberg 1975: 89).

It is inevitable—given their shared life histories (not to mention their shared body)—that Tiptree now gets read through those other lives and those other lives get read through Tiptree. However, Tiptree with the same life story as Alice Sheldon becomes someone different. The coincidence of a supposed male body and the childhood in the wilds of Africa and the knowledge of guns and government workings led to different speculations than those about Alice Sheldon after the revelation.

Raccoona Sheldon b. ?

And what of the much-neglected Raccoona? There are no articles about the short fiction of Raccoona Sheldon. Certainly her output was much smaller than Tiptree's. She, too had a separate life, with her own post office box and bank account in Wisconsin (Tiptree 1979: 34). For Jeffrey Smith it was easy to accept "Alli and Tiptree as the same person, but Raccoona has always been *someone else* to me." Raccoona

> first surfaced as a fanzine artist, as Tip sent me a page of sketches by an "old friend" for my use. (I told him he should try to get her to illustrate his magazine stories: "She draws like you write.") The original scheme had been for Raccoona to establish herself as a writer, then for Tip to drown in Mexico and there'd only be one persona left. But Raccoona couldn't live in McLean so a Wisconsin Post office box had to be set up and mail shuttled back and forth. And neither could Raccoona have just picked up Tip's friendships. Raccoona was left out in the cold: since she couldn't be Tiptree she couldn't really be Alli either. (Smith 1987: 16)

Raccoona initially had some difficulty getting published, until Tiptree wrote covering letters recommending his friend's work. Raccoona herself wrote a letter that was published by the first feminist sf fanzine, *The Witch and the Chameleon*: "I don't know too much about it, but I have a faint suspiction [*sic*] borne out of a smidgin of proof that mss. with a female name on them are *read* differently" ([April 1975]: 26). Raccoona, like Tiptree, took part in fandom and more particularly she was a part of feminist sf fandom. In other letters she comments on feminist issues such as abortion (*The Witch and the Chameleon* [1976]: 14).[5] Raccoona also appears with a poem in which she refers to many of the prominent women sf writers of the period and thus links herself and her writing to them and the feminist sf they embodied: Joanna (Russ), Ursula (Le Guin), Kate (Wilhelm), Vonda (McIntyre), Quinn (Chelsea Quinn Yarbro), Suzy (McKee Charnas), Kit (Reed), Carol (Emshwiller?), and Shirley (Jackson?) (*The Witch and the Chameleon* [September 1975]: 1). In a letter in the final issue of *The Witch and the Chameleon*, Raccoona writes, "Of course my instinct is to stick together as much as we can. We know who profits from us excluding each other" (*The Witch and the Chameleon* [1976]: 30). Her pronouns, her "we" and "us," refer to women and to the women's liberation movement.

The feminism of Raccoona Sheldon was vastly different from that of James Tiptree Jr., the author of a "profoundly feminist story told in entirely masculine manner" (Silverberg 1975: xvi), who, along with the other men involved, was asked to leave the *Khatru* symposium by Joanna Russ: "I suggested asking Tiptree and Delany into this symposium and both have contributed a good deal, but it's true that they are time-hoggers and that they—and Jeff—keep drawing our attention away from what (to me) is what is truly interesting: what *we* think" (Smith 1975: 96). Raccoona used the same pronouns "we" and "our," referring to "we women," but here they operate to exclude Tiptree. The revelation that Tiptree "is" Alice Sheldon shifted the relationship of these pronouns profoundly.

The Revelation

James Tiptree Jr. was first revealed as Alice Sheldon in late 1976. People already knew that his mother lived in Chicago, so when Tiptree reported her death to a few correspondents, "[m]ore than one of Tip's friends checked the Chicago obituaries and found Mary Hastings Bradley, novelist, travel writer, and explorer. The details matched up. Under 'survivors' was listed Bradley's only child: her daughter" (Phillips 1996: 18). Jeff Smith reports his confusion on reading Mary Hastings Bradley's obituary: "The last line read, 'She is survived by one daughter, Mrs Alice Hastings (Mrs Huntington)

Sheldon.' This left me very confused. Sheldon was Raccoona's name, and it never occurred to me that Tip and Raccoona were the same person—I corresponded with Raccoona, too. But if Raccoona was Mary Hastings Bradley's daughter, then why was Tip handling the affairs?" (Smith 1978: 10). He wrote to Tiptree for clarification, and Tiptree confessed to "being" Alice Sheldon. In December 1976 "she admitted the truth to a small group of people like me whom she felt she might have offended by allowing them to persist in their error. 'Honour, or something, compels me to do something after which I fear I may have lost a deeply valued friend. . . . It hasn't been a put-on or attempt to take advantage, it just grew and grew until 'Tip' became me" (Silverberg 1993: 6).

In 1977 Tiptree was revealed as Sheldon more publicly, in the science fiction news magazine *Locus*. It was not really a Great Revelation but a series of revelations: you never come out just once, but over and over again. As Pat Murphy remarks, "James Tiptree, Jr . . . [r]evealed in mid-career as Alice Sheldon, and forever after, in every introduction, revealed as Alice Sheldon" (Murphy [1991] 1992: 8). Even now there are readers who pick up and read a Tiptree book without knowing his "true" sex.

Tiptree, however, will never simply "be" Alice Sheldon: "[W]ith 'Raccoona' selling too, things had gotten fairly confusing. I was writing stories and letters as the female *me*, but from a place I didn't live in and without my own real past—and at the same time writing and corresponding as a man who for a decade had made himself part of me too. Tip owned my past life and my years of science fiction friendships, and he lived in my home, but my husband was his 'gringo friend.' I'm sure you sense the chaos?" (quoted in Gearhart and Ross 1983: 445).

The chaos did not end with the revelation of the "truth" about Tiptree. Instead there was a furor within science fiction. There were some voluble criticism, as Sheldon reports: "[T]he more vulnerable males decided that 'Tiptree' had been much overrated. They sullenly retired to practice patronizing smiles" (quoted in Platt 1983: 267). In a different interview she elaborates:

> [T]here were the male writers who had seemed to take my work quite seriously, but who now began discovering that it was really the enigma of Tip's identity which had lent a spurious interest, and began finding various more-or-less subtle ways of saying so. (Oh, how well we know and love that pretentiously amiable tone, beneath which hides the furtive nastiness!) I'd been warned against it, but it was still a shock com-

> ing from certain writers. The one thing I admire about that type of male hatred is its strategic agility. They soon get their ranks closed. Only here the timing was so damned funny, the perfect unison of their "reevaluation" of poor old Tip rather weakened the effect. (Quoted in Gearhart and Ross 1983: 446)

Brian Aldiss and David Wingrove in their *Trillion Year Spree* have this to say about the revelation: "There is little that is overtly feminist in Tiptree's writing, even as Raccoona Sheldon, and she never tried to write like a man. Her stories and novels are humanistic, while her deep concern for male-female (even human-alien) harmony ran counter to the developing segregate-the-sexes drive among feminist writers. What her work brought to the genre was a blend of lyricism and inventiveness, as if some lyric poet had rewritten a number of clever SF standards and then passed them on to a psychoanalyst for final polish" (Aldiss and Wingrove 1988: 462). "Never tried to write like a man" is almost a direct quote from Alice Sheldon:

> However, men have so pre-empted the area of human experience that when you write about universal motives, you are assumed to be writing like a man. And so when my identity was revealed, some people said it proved that a woman could write like a man. Now, in the first place, this assumes that I was *trying* to write like a man, which was the last thing I was trying to do. I was writing like myself, with the exception of deliberate male details here and there. Other critics talked about my "narrative drive" as being a male writing style, but narrative drive is simply intensity, and a desire not to bore. It has never been confined to men. Take one of the first women utterers that we know about: Cassandra. *She* was never accused of a lack of narrative drive. She was just a little before her time, which is often what women's crimes consist of. (Quoted in Platt 1983: 267)

Certainly Silverberg had believed that Tiptree "wrote like a man." In "Who Is Tiptree, What Is He?" Silverberg compares Tiptree to Hemingway:

> Tiptree's stories don't bore. They are lean, muscular, supple, relying heavily on dialog broken by bursts of stripped down exposition. Although there is no real stylistic influence discernible, I think his work is analogous to that of Hemingway, in that Hemingway preferred to be

> simple, direct, and straightforward, at least on the surface. Hemingway was a deeper and trickier writer than he pretended to be; so too with Tiptree, who conceals, behind the aw-shucks artlessness an astonishing skill for shaping scenes and misdirecting readers into unexpected abysses of experience. And there is, too, that prevailing masculinity about both of them. (Silverberg 1975: xv)

This is not simply a comic misreading on Silverberg's part. Some women sf writers also thought that Tiptree had a "prevailing masculinity" that resulted in the request for Tiptree to leave the *Khatru* symposium on women in science fiction. Tiptree responded to that request as follows:

> Joanna [Russ], your piece inviting me out of the talk is exactly how I feel. My own concept of what I at least was supposed to do was simply to learn and perhaps talk enough to get knocked down after which I felt acutely that I should fade away but didn't know how to. . . . Without, you know, sounding like gimme my wagon and I'll go home mad. So I just burbled on figuring that you could ignore me as well as I could. (After all, one possible use for a male participant is just to remind everybody of *everything* there is to be mad at. All the small exquisite vilenesses I mean.) (Smith 1975: 96)

Alice Sheldon may have protested later that she was "not trying to write like a man," but it is hard to know how else to read these comments, or others made during the *Khatru* symposium. For example, Tiptree "confessed" that the "motive for [flashing] is an obscure and yet apparently potent one, which seems to have missed me or be buried deep" (Smith 1975: 104). It is only when you know that Tiptree "is" a woman that this, and other comments, are revealed as ironic play.

Le Guin was a part of the *Khatru* symposium. She was also fooled by Tiptree:

> Recently I've been hearing from people who have friends who say, "I knew all along that Tiptree was a woman. I could tell it from the prose style," or "from the male characters," or "from the female characters," or "from the Vibrations." I don't know any of these people who knew all along; they didn't say much about it; never even happened to mention that they knew, for some reason, until all the rest of us knew. We (the rest of us) knew rather suddenly and utterly unexpectedly. I don't think I

> have ever been so completely and utterly surprised in my life—or so happily. All I can say is I'm glad I didn't know all along, because I would have missed that joyous shock of revelation, recognition—the beautiful Jill-in-the-box. (Le Guin 1978: viii-ix)

Many others experienced that "joyous shock": "The feminist world was excited because, merely by having existed unchallenged for ten years, 'Tiptree' had shot the stuffing out of male stereotypes of women writers" (quoted in Platt 1983: 267). Amanda Boulter argues that Alice Sheldon's "gender deception" has made her "a particularly exciting figure for feminist critics of science fiction." However, the "history of Tiptree's career makes him a problematic figure for feminist science fiction, raising certain, perhaps, awkward, questions about the feminist implications of Sheldon's gender disguise" (Boulter 1995: 6). These questions are clearly delineated in the *Khatru* symposium, where the Tiptree revelation complicates how the pronoun of the writer is read.

In the symposium, Tiptree insisted that there was more than one kind of white man. He argued that "a huge wrought-iron sign" he saw in Los Gatos that read "THE GENTILE WHITE MAN IS THE KING OF THE EARTH" excluded him just as much as Delany or any of the women in the symposium (Smith 1975: 103). Tiptree claimed that he was a "natural lynchee" who "exudes the same smell of subversion which those good ole boys can smell a mile away" (Smith 1975: 103). Luise White replied: "[Y]ou'll forgive me for wondering why, if you're such a 'natural lynchee' you're still alive, and over one million Vietnamese who had no power at all are dead. And if it *is* just an historical accident, perhaps you could refrain. . . . from baiting minority groups of any sort: you say they're after you 'the way they used to hunt gays.' *Used* to? Next page you call Arthur Clarke 'Jiggling-nuts': I assume that's queer-baiting, Jim. Perhaps me, Joanna, Chip and anyone else who can read find you 'threatening' because *if* you *did* fear 'the abuse of power' you wouldn't try to please one audience by putting down a minority group" (Smith 1975: 122).[6] Tiptree's insistence that white men are not a unitary class was not well received. In 1975, in the *Khatru* symposium, it was not something that could be heard coming from a white man. It would be interesting to know how Luise White would have responded if Tiptree had already been revealed as Sheldon.

This reading, shaped by the pronoun, has been for many feminist commentators, the lesson of Tiptree. In her comments on the second printing of the *Khatru* symposium, Mog Decarnin writes that "she became a living illustration of all that sexism means. I remember a male writing, I think in a prozine, just very bluntly that if Tiptree had really been a man her stories would have been profound and compassionate, but since she was a woman those same stories were worthless and despicable" (quoted in Gomoll 1993: 125).[7]

At the same time that Tiptree was being critically acclaimed for such stories as "The Women Men Don't See," Russ, McIntyre, and Charnas amongst others, were being vociferously attacked and patronized for their feminism. Russ, herself felt sad at losing Tip, the male feminist: "[O]ddly enough [I was] very tearful for a few days. I had been extremely fond of the man I imagined Tiptree to be and grieved at losing the one man who really seemed to understand" (Boulter 1995: 8).

Because the myth of Tiptree—who proved that women could write like men—has been so dominant, discussion of Sheldon's other "persona," Raccoona, has been almost entirely absent. Boulter refers to Raccoona's claim that her "first stories were not accepted until they were accompanied by a testimonial from Tiptree himself, which in turn provoked speculation that Raccoona might be his daughter, or alternatively his own pseudonym. Ironically, the dissolution of the female pseudonym into the male is repeated by contemporary feminist critics. Anne Cranny-Francis and Marleen Barr both discuss 'The Screwfly Solution' as by James Tiptree. Lillian Heldreth credits Raccoona, but only in the notes as a pseudonym of Tiptree" (Boulter 1995: 14–15).

The writings of Raccoona and the whole Raccoona persona are frequently conflated with Alice Sheldon. For example, in the index of Russ's *To Write Like a Woman,* under "Sheldon, Alice," a series of short stories are listed; those that appeared under the byline "Tiptree" have this noted in brackets; the ones published as Raccoona are not signaled in any way.

At the end of an entertaining, sensitive and very revealing interview conducted by Charles Platt and Shawna McCarthy, there is a biographical note:[8] "With the exception of a short story in *The New Yorker* ("The Lucky Ones," 1946), all of Alice Sheldon's fiction has been published under the name of James Tiptree, Jr., or Raccoona Sheldon, the latter being used for five later stories when she felt she needed to write from an overtly female perspective" (Platt 1983: 272). The Raccoona pseudonym is not mentioned at any other point during the interview.

The silence about the Raccoona pseudonym implies that this Raccoona is taken as the real Alice Sheldon, whereas Tiptree is her persona. Somehow it is presumed that Sheldon does not perform Raccoona because she is a woman and there is no need to perform your "true" sex. However, Jeffrey Smith, in his description of his and his wife Ann's first meeting with Alice Sheldon, demonstrates that this was not the case: "While we were there, she was Tiptree often, the raconteur telling stories with little or no provocation, the speculator running with ideas to logical, illogical and evocative conclusions. Sometimes (particularly when she and her husband clattered around the kitchen fixing dinner) she was Raccoona, the rather dotty retired schoolteacher supposedly in Wisconsin. These were unconscious—whenever she thought about who she was, she was Alice Sheldon, the one who doesn't write science fiction" (Smith 1978: 11). Smith is perceiving sex and self here as a *performance*. Sheldon plays at being both Raccoona and Tiptree but also at being Alice Sheldon. They are all performances.

The revelation that Tiptree was "really" Sheldon can be read as a part of the battle of the sexes as it has been played out on the field of science fiction since the 1920s. The revelation both confirmed and confounded gender expectations about biological sex mapping neatly on to perceived sex. Tiptree's work was indeed profoundly feminist *because* "he" was "she" and at the same time "she" had been able to fool everyone into believing "she" was "he." The Tiptree revelation is thus used doubly to prove essentialist notions and to disprove them.[9]

In the next chapter I examine the question of how all these stories operate in the construction of the James Tiptree Jr. Memorial Award. In discussions of the award to date the lives of "Alice James Raccoona Tiptree Davey Hastings Bradley Sheldon Jr." play very little part: the prize has centered on only one of those stories, of James Tiptree Jr., who was "really" Alice B. Sheldon. This feminist fairy tale has been the award's main inspiration, its starting point. Inevitably, however, five years after its announcement, the award has moved away from its inspiration. The term "Tiptree" has now come to refer to this award and to the books that have been shortlisted for it, won it, or that people think are eligible for it. A Tiptree text is no longer only a text written by or about James Tiptree Jr. The Tiptree Award has added yet another story to those of "Alice James Raccoona Tiptree Davey Hastings Bradley Sheldon Jr."

HER SMOKE ROSE UP FOREVER

The James Tiptree Jr. Memorial Award

Tiptree/Sheldon/? the Mistress of Illusion who brought such sharpness of poignancy and point to this collective work that it's hardly bearable at times. Her writing made her beloved; her masquerade made her legend. Mistress of Irony, that her suicide should make her a monument, honored as only the dead ever are! Yet honored in such a way as she would surely find hilarious, inspiring: honored by bake sales, and the works of women! (Mog Decarnin, quoted in Gomoll 1993: 125)

The James Tiptree Jr. Memorial Award, begun in 1991, is given annually for a science fiction or fantasy text that explores and expands gender roles. Short stories or novels by men as well as women are eligible. Each year the Tiptree Award winner or winners are decided by a jury of five, and the jury changes every year. Once the winner(s) are decided, a press release listing the winner(s), those short listed for the award, and all the texts considered (the "long list") is issued. The long list is annotated, making it one of the few awards that gives an insight into the jury's decisions.

The lives of James Tiptree Jr. add many resonances to the award named in his/her memory. In this chapter I examine the award and the many connections between the award and the traditions within science fiction of feminism and engagement with issues of sex and sexuality since 1926. The award powerfully demonstrates continuities of science fiction communities and is another site for the blurring of distinctions between fan and pro. Further, the Tiptree Award reauthors and reworks the stories of James Tiptree Jr. and her/his/their complicated relationship within and with the field of science fiction.

Researching the Tiptree Award confirms the contested nature of the term "gender" and what it designates. In the context of the juries' deliberations, it has been used to refer to the social construction of maleness or femaleness, while the term "sex" was used to refer to biological sex, thus maintaining the sex/gender distinction. It has also been used to refer to the biological "fact" of sexed bodies or to refer to both the social construction of the two normative sexes and sexed bodies. This variety of uses of the term is a reflection of the range of different people who have been involved with the award since its inception. That there are five different judges every year means that the interpretation of what a text that "explores and expands" gender is shifts. Throughout this book I have been using "sex" to refer to the space of biological/social/cultural construction and performance of the sexed self. The variety of texts that have won and been shortlisted for the award reinforce this approach to "sex," in that the shortlist demonstrates that gender does not delineate a "crisp distinction" between sex and gender but rather refers to the "problematical space" they occupy (see Sedgwick 1990: 29).

More Domestic Stories: Feminist sf Communities and the Tiptree Award

A few months ago, I was talking with Richard Kadrey, a born trouble-maker. We were talking about women in science fiction and Richard, just to make trouble, said, "You know what would really piss people off? You ought to give out a women's science fiction award." Interesting idea. It would make certain people very cranky. It would get the conspiracy theorists going, wondering, "What are those women up to now?" We envisioned a little plexiglass cube with all this "women's stuff" floating in it: little plastic babies and cooking pots and ironing boards and sewing machines. (Murphy [1991] 1992: 8–9)

The James Tiptree Jr. Award came into existence on 2 March 1991 at the fifteenth WisCon, in a speech given by guest of honor Pat Murphy. Murphy placed the award in the context of long-running debates about the presence of women in science fiction. These debates usually locate women in the sphere of romance or of the domestic, the one frequently, if not inevitably, leading to the other. Murphy and the writer Richard Kadrey mock this with their vision of a plexiglass trophy full of floating "women's stuff." In the excerpt from Murphy's speech that I use as the epigraph to this section, Kadrey refers to "people," a term that Murphy shifts to "certain people," "conspiracy theorists" who believe that having women in science fiction is equivalent to a "great erosion" of the field (Merwin 1950: 6). As I have shown, part of the fear of women in the field is a fear of the intrusion of the private sphere into the public sphere and, further, a fear of women invading the private men's club within the public sphere.

Murphy continued her narration of the Tiptree Award's genesis by conceding,

> Okay, it was just a joke, nothing more. But a few weeks later, I had dinner with Karen Joy Fowler and I mentioned this joke. Karen is also a trouble-maker, but a very thoughtful one. She looked thoughtful and said, "You know, there is no science fiction award named after a woman."
>
> Let's see: we have the Hugo (for Hugo Gernsback), the Theodore Sturgeon Award, the John W. Campbell Award, and of course the Philip K. Dick Award. No women. *Frankenstein*, by Mary Shelley, has been called the first science fiction novel, but there is no Mary Shelley award.
>
> And then Karen, who tends toward brilliance, said, "What about James Tiptree, Jr.?" (Murphy [1991] 1992: 9)

The proposed award would be named for a woman who, for most of her career in the sf field, was a man. Murphy also located the Tiptree Award in the context of other science fiction awards to mark out its difference. She continued: "And so I would like to announce the creation of the James Tiptree, Jr. Memorial Award, to be presented annually to a fictional work that explores and expands the roles of women and men. We're still in the planning stages, but we plan to appoint a panel of five judges and we plan to finance the award—and this is another stroke of genius on Karen's part—through bake sales" (Murphy [1991] 1992: 9).

Bake sales (in Australia they're called cake stalls) are a common fundraiser for schools and churches and are invariably run and provided with baked goods by women. They are associated with suburbia, the family, and motherhood. Karen Fowler's genius was to link this cliché of suburban domesticity with a science fiction award and so to overtly blur the private and public spheres.

Pat Murphy ended her announcement—and simultaneous enactment—of the Tiptree Award by asking for potential bake sale volunteers to talk to her after the speeches were finished. The response was immediate. Jeanne Gomoll writes, "A few moments later, after a thunderous round of applause, a bunch of us Madisonians clustered around Pat and began vocalizing such dangerous phrases as 'I'll help,' 'We'd like to publish,' 'I could do,' etc. A few months later we found ourselves organizing mailing lists, posters, bakes sales, and one of the largest publications that SF^3 has ever produced" (Gomoll [1991] 1992: 5). Diane Martin concurs: "There was electricity in the air. Trite, but I don't know how else to describe it. In the five minutes after Murphy's speech ended. I talked to at least three other women who had the same idea I did: 'Let's publish a cookbook!'" (Martin [1991] 1992: 5).

Bake sales have now been held at sf conventions all over the United States as well as in the United Kingdom and Australia. Eventually, there were two cookbooks, both published by SF^3, the science fiction group based in Madison, Wisconsin. Both are plays on the titles of Tiptree stories, the first is *The Bakery Men Don't See* (1991) and the second *Her Smoke Rose Up from Supper* (1993) (figure 20). The recipes and anecdotes were provided by pros and fans from within the science fiction feminist community. Although the bake sales have not generated an enormous amount of revenue, they have been extremely successful in generating interest and knowledge of the award within the larger science fiction community.

The most financially lucrative fundraisers have been the marvelous T-shirts of Freddie Baer and the Tiptree auctions run by Ellen Klages. The T-shirts commemorating each award go on sale at the convention where the awards are presented. Invariably they sell out quickly.[1] Klages writes: "The biggest single benefactress of the Tiptree is Freddie Baer. Her T-shirts raise around $1000 a year, and the 'vintage' shirts become auction collectibles. (Top price for an early one is $300, I think.) And the original prints of the awards for each year are about as collectible as any items in Feminist SF fandom" (letter to author, 12 February 2001).

Auctioneer extraordinaire, Ellen Klages, is another benefactress of the Tiptree. Ellen's style is part auctioneer and part stand-up comedian. She has run her comedy routine/auction to raise money for the Tiptree at WisCon, Readercon, Worldcon, ICFA, Diversicon, and Potlatch. The auctions she runs earn between $1,000 and $7,000. Items of no great worth such as $3 jars of Tiptree jelly have sold for $100. The privilege of being chauffered by Ellen in her PT Cruiser has been sold for $250; and of walking up on stage and shaving off Ellen's hair for $500. Klages notes that

> one of the "customs" that's evolved over the years are a couple of "pass the hat" items at every auction. Either to buy something for someone as a nice gesture, or to generate a lot of group solidarity and energy for the silly stuff. It raises a bunch of money for vapor-ware and silliness, but it's also an opportunity to let everyone make a contribution. A lot of folks at WisCon don't have a lot of money, but want to support the Tiptree and

Her Smoke Rose Up From Supper
THE EXCITING SEQUEL TO THE BAKERY MEN DON'T SEE

20. Cover of SF3's *Her Smoke Rose Up from Supper*, illustration by Freddie Baer

contribute (and be a part of the fun). Since a lot of things go for significant money, the pass-the-hat items are a chance for people to chip in a buck or two or five for the cause, contributing to the overall effort without busting their budgets.

It's like a community sing-along sometimes. It's not just a fundraiser,

> not just the all-Ellen show, but a way for everyone to participate and support a growing movement that, we hope, will result in more of what we'd like to read actually getting published and publicized. (Letter to author, 12 February 2001)

Many of the people who became involved with the Tiptree Award explicitly link the Tiptree to a renewal of a tradition of feminist science fiction. This is not only a tradition of writing but also a fan tradition. Diane Martin comments: "I arrived at WisCon 15 cautiously optimistic. I was reconciled to feminist SF being considered as a topic of historical interest, sort of like Latin. I was just hoping to meet up with a few other Latin scholars. Imagine my surprise when I found myself attending and participating in panel discussions that in feminist content and enthusiasm, rivalled the WisCons of the late 70s" (Martin [1991] 1992: 3).

It was no coincidence that Pat Murphy announced the Tiptree Award at the only feminist-oriented science fiction convention in the world. The first WisCon was held in Madison, Wisconsin, in 1977 as a direct result of, and participation in, the feminist explosion within fandom in the seventies. It was part of the new "women and sf" panels held at conventions and the debates about feminism and science fiction conducted in the Women's APA, *The Witch and the Chameleon*, and *Janus/Aurora*, as well as the *Khatru* symposium. Karen Joy Fowler credits the "women of WisCon" for "mak[ing] it happen from the very beginning" and writes that for her the "best thing about the Tiptree Award is that it got a lot bigger than me and Pat. It did this really quickly" (Fowler 1996: 109). Without the continuing engagement between various feminisms and various science fictions over the sf community's history, however, it is very unlikely that the Tiptree Award would have taken off in the manner that it did.

Murphy explicitly locates the Tiptree as a response to what she saw as the marginalization of, and hostility to, women in science fiction. She relates this to the opposition of male "hard" sf to female "soft" sf. In her WisCon 15 speech she leads up to her announcement of the Tiptree Award with the following story:

> A few months ago, I was talking to a science fiction editor who is a friend of mine. We were talking about this and that, and in the course of conversation he happened to say, "Of course, you don't write science fiction."
>
> Now I don't always care what people call what I write, but I do like to

> understand why they call it one thing or another. And I'm curious about how people define science fiction. So I said, "What about "Rachel in Love"? That's science fiction."
>
> And my friend said, "That's not science fiction."
>
> I was really puzzled, so I said, "Using a method of neural transfer that I can justify scientifically, more or less, a scientist transfers his daughter's personality and thought patterns to the brain of a chimp. That's not science fiction?"
>
> My friend frowned and got a little flustered and a little embarrassed and mumbled something or other. After a bit more uncomfortable conversation, it became clear that he had confused my story, "Rachel in Love," with . . . "Her Furry Face," by Leigh Kennedy, and as it turns out, "Her Furry Face," though an excellent story, lacks many of the overt trappings of science fiction. (Murphy [1991] 1992: 7)

What seemed significant about my friend's confusion was that it related to a persistent rumbling that I have heard echoing through science fiction. That rumbling says, in essence that women don't write science fiction. Put a little more rudely, this rumbling says: "Those damned women are ruining science fiction" (Murphy [1991] 1992: 7–8); they are doing it by writing stuff that isn't "real" science fiction; they are writing "soft" science fiction and fantasy".

The other guest of honour at WisCon 15 was Pamela Sargent, the editor of the extremely influential *Women of Wonder* anthologies. In her guest of honour speech she also engaged with this debate and quoted from Charles Platt's claim from "The Rape Of Science Fiction" (1989) that women "eroded science fiction's one great strength that had distinguished it from all other fantastic literature: its implicit claim that events described could actually come true" (Platt 1989: 14). Sargent's response was: "Well, shame on me—I reprinted stories by all these writers [Platt had listed Vinge, McIntyre, Le Guin, Russ, Wilhelm, and Emshwiller] in my *Women of Wonder* anthologies. I never dreamed I was helping to erode science fiction. I suppose we can consider this another ambiguous advance. Once, women were discouraged from entering the boys' clubhouse, and now we are influential enough to be responsible for the decline of the field" (Sargent [1991] 1992: 11).

Sargent also discussed a short essay by Lewis Shiner from the *New York Times*, where he claims that what sf needs is "a new literature of idealism and compassion that is contemporary not only on the technological level but also the emotional" (11–12). "I couldn't agree with him more," said Sargent, "but some of us were writing exactly that kind of literature" in the seventies and eighties" (12). Sargent's arguments are very close to those of Jeanne Gomoll, in which she characterizes the dismissal of 1970s sf and fandom as "boring" as a move to make invisible the upheavals and very exciting changes wrought by the women's movement (Gomoll 1986-87: 7–10).

Sargent's speech was given on the same night as Murphy's announcement of the Tiptree Award. Although neither woman had colluded on the contents of their speeches, they both used the occasion of being guest of honor at WisCon to discuss the state of feminist science fiction and they came to very similar conclusions. Both women began their careers in science fiction in the 1970s and so had been actively involved in second-wave feminism and its impact on science fiction.

In the second volume of the *Women of Wonder* anthology, Sargent begins by discussing the Tiptree Award:

> By 1991, the effect of the women's movement on science fiction had faded in the minds of many. There was a need by then for an award that specifically honored and called attention to works that dealt imaginatively and inventively with gender roles. Some of the writers who had created a stir in the '70s were being forgotten. Women were still writing science fiction and winning acclaim for their work; indeed some of the most honored, accomplished, and important writers in the field were women, so no one could say that the field excluded women or that they had no audience. The situation was more complicated and ambiguous than that. (Sargent 1995b: 2)

The Tiptree Award became a site from which to contest these different constructions of an object called "1970s science fiction," as well as being an active part of that construction.

The first two Tiptree Award presentations were held at WisCon, but it was decided to hold some of the following presentations at other science fiction conventions. Suzy McKee Charnas writes: "The third Tiptree will be awarded in Boston at a convention called ReaderCon in July, 1994. Moving the ceremony to different SF conventions around the country is meant to maximize its educative potential (and to avoid burnout in Madison)" (Charnas 1993). As Charnas indicates, the award is not only about fostering a feeling of community amongst those who are part of feminist science fiction, it is also about actively working toward change. Perhaps, if there are more texts imagining the world otherwise, eventually the world will be otherwise. This utopian impulse is articulated by Karen Fowler: "Just ask yourself, if we weren't taught to be women, what would we be? (Ask yourself this question even if you're a man, and don't cheat by changing the words.) The Tiptree Award is supposed to honor people who try to answer that question—people who try to help us unlearn what television and the movies and books and comics and advertisements for automobiles and cigarettes have taught us" (Fowler 1996: 109).

For Fowler, like de Beauvoir and many others before her, sex is not natural but something that must be learned. And the Tiptree Award is a site in which this learning process can be investigated and deconstructed. Charnas hopes that this process will lead to change: "No one knows how long the Tiptree will continue to be given. What we who have been involved in the process so far would like best would be to see such changes, in fiction and in life, that an award to help illuminate issues of the sex and gender war would no longer be needed. In the meantime, works by Tiptree nominees and winners provide an entry point for women readers into the genre where our own and our children's futures are being imagined in their many possible variations" (Charnas 1993: 20).

The existence of the award and of the feminist science fiction community in which it is fostered and nourished already demonstrates that a series of shifts have taken place within the field of science fiction. The increasing number of varied texts that are nominated each year is also a strong indication that the Tiptree Award has had an impact. However, Fowler and Murphy and others involved with the award would like the award to have an impact outside the world of feminist science fiction.

One way in which the Tiptree Award has had such an impact is the role it played in the successful application of Nicola Griffith to remain with her partner, the writer Kelly Eskridge, in the United States. Griffith won the 1993 Tiptree for her novel *Ammonite*. Permission was granted largely because she was able to prove that she had won "major" awards within her chosen field:

> Winning the Tiptree, and the Lambda, and being nominated for a couple of other things did help with my immigrant application, and I don't mind being quoted, or having my real name used. I applied for an EB-2 visa, granted to "aliens of exceptional ability" in the arts, sciences and so forth. Winning "nationally and internationally recognized" awards is

one of the conditions of that visa. So, obviously, the Tiptree helped there. But where it helped most, I think, was in the second part of the application—the "national interest" waiver.

Labour certification is something that *everyone* has to fight for except heterosexual spouses and people like Nobel prize winners (to get an EB-1, you literally have to win the Nobel prize, "or equivalent"). . . . As a writer, I didn't have a job, don't have a job and never intend to have a job. So I needed a way around that labour certification. I needed a waiver. So me and my lawyers set out to prove to the US government that it was, literally, in the national interest for me to live and work in this country. So I had to prove that my work was not only brilliant, unique, exceptional, extraordinary, prize-winning (etc. etc.) but that American citizens would be worse off without it. And so I talked about feminism, the way literature that shows new possibilities, helps citizens imagine those new possibilities, gives them something to aim for (among them, of course, parity between the sexes). The writer, I said, is the imagination, the soul and spirit, of the people. I can't remember the words I used, exactly, but they were positively stuffed with hyperbole. And I had to get testimonial letters to back all that stuff up. Many people in the SF, and lesbian and gay, and feminist, and literary communities helped me out. And, much to my pleasure, the Justice Department said that, yes, it was in the national interest for me to live and work over here. So I guess I'm about as important as a stealth bomber. Anyway, my case apparently made new law. As far as I know, I'm the first out dyke to be granted this status—and all on the basis of my lesbian feminist science fiction. Chortle.

But what I haven't told many people yet is that the existence of science fiction fandom *directly* helped my case. In my final interview at the US embassy in London, the consular officer took one look at my material and said, "Hey, do you know Roger McBride Allen?" I said I knew his work. She said, "He's a good friend of mine." And we talked about Star Wars and other sharecrop franchises, and she knew what a Nebula Award was, and understood the Tiptree. I believe, of course, that even if she hadn't known SF from a hole in the ground I would have been granted admission, but that fandom thing, the acknowledgment of shared status as part of an often scorned minority, certainly made the process easier. She smiled, and stamped my application and said, "Come back at two o'clock for your visa." As good as a funny handshake. (Letter to author, 18 April 1995)[2]

An award that was conceived initially as a parody of science fiction awards, was able to mimic legitimacy to such an extent that it in fact *became* legitimate and allowed Griffith to win in a game where, as a lesbian and an alien, the odds were stacked significantly against her. Griffith's anecdote also adds to the layers of the science fiction community that I have been discussing in this book. Within the community, writers like Roger McBride Allen and Nicola Griffith are very differently located. Allen's work is frequently described as hard sf and Heinleinesque, while Griffith's work is most frequently called feminist (which still seems to preclude being viewed as a hard sf writer). Despite this gulf, in the context of the U.S. embassy in London, the science fiction community and fandom becomes knowable and inclusive. The overlapping science fiction communities are also able to have an effect on mundane fields, so that it is Griffith's position within science fiction that enables her to become a resident of the United States.

The Tiptree also functions as a playful comment on the field of science fiction as a whole and many aspects of the award were a comment on the older science fiction awards. Vonda McIntyre insisted that there be no stomach-churning suspense for the nominees at the award presentation. So the practice of publishing the "shortlist and the winners simultaneously" was adopted, thus avoiding both the tension of an award night and "transforming the people honored on the shortlist into losers" (Fowler 1996: 109). These lists of all texts considered for the award, the winners, and the shortlist are now a part of the Tiptree Award homepage, >www.tiptree.org<, and include comments from the judges about how each text fits under the rubric of the Tiptree award. In this way the Tiptree works in an expansionary rather than exclusionary way.

Another part of the award's playfulness is the physical award itself. Suzy McKee Charnas and Ursula Le Guin independently suggested that the award be edible, Le Guin commenting that she had "seen and even received some awards that would be far far better eaten." Several of the award winners have thus been presented with a typewriter and award plaque cast in milk chocolate. In 1996 the two writers whose idea the chocolate award was, Charnas and Le Guin, were named Retrospective Tiptree Award winners (along with Joanna Russ) and were presented with huge chocolate plaques. As well as chocolate there is $1,000 in prize money and airfare to and expenses at the convention where the award is presented. Since the first year there has also been a specially commissioned work from an artist. Karen Fowler elaborates:

> The Tiptree award is now famous for its chocolate trophies, but Pat and I also wished to involve (and pay) artists for designing more permanent awards. Every year except for the first when money was tighter, we've commissioned at least one original piece of art. (In years when we've had two winners, but only money for one piece of art, the trophy has often gone to that winner who showed up physically at the ceremony to collect it.) Past trophies have included a sculptured dish inspired by Griffith's *Ammonite* and created by Jean Sillman; a mask for *Larque on the Wing* created by Michaela Roessner; a beaded replication of the Tiptree quilt, created by Rose Cane; a doll by Melissa M. O'Grady inspired by Raphael Carter's 1998 winning story; a snowglobe designed by Ellen Klages for Kelly Link's "Adventures of the Snow Queen" and, in the same year, also by Klages, a handpainted scarf for Candas Jane Dorsey's *Black Wine*. These trophies have been exquisite and I've often wished we'd been foresighted enough to keep a photographic record. (Letter to author, 13 February 2001)

Commissioning these artworks is another reminder of the community behind the Tiptree Award—not just fans and writers but also artists. Up to the year 2000, the prizes created were

1991 to Eleanor Arnason and Gwyneth Jones—chocolate typewriters
1992 to Maureen McHugh—an etched glass bowl by Nevenah Smith
1993 to Nicola Griffith—a sculpted ceramic dish by Jean Van Keuren
1994 to Ursula Le Guin and Nancy Springer—Le Guin received a chocolate typewriter; Springer received a feathered mask by Michaela Roessner
1995 to Elizabeth Hand and Theodore Roszak—Roszak received a beaded version of the Tiptree Quilt by Rose Cane; Hand received chocolate.
1995 Special Retrospective Award to Suzy McKee Charnas, Ursula K. Le Guin, Joanna Russ—all received lucite cubes with silkscreened art by Freddie Baer
1996 to Ursula Le Guin and Mary Doria Russell—both received vests by Kate Schaefer
1997 to Candas Jane Dorsey and Kelly Link—Ellen Klages designed gifts for both winners. Dorsey received a hand-painted silk scarf, and Link a snowglobe
1998 to Raphael Carter—an intersex doll by Melissa M. O'Grady

1998 Fairy Godmother Award to Laurie Marks—a fairy godmother doll by Melissa M. O'Grady

1999 to Suzy McKee Charnas—a silver pendant by Laurie Edison carved with images from *The Conqueror's Child* and cake painted by Georgie Schnobrich

1999 Fairy Godmother Award to Freddie Baer—travel money to attend aussicon 3, WorldCon in Australia

2000 to Molly Gloss—an original calligraphy work by Jae Leslie Adams

The Tiptree Award has also managed to avoid the usual hierarchy that is maintained by many literary awards, where only professionals are invited to be on the jury panel. The jury has included fans, writers, editors, booksellers, academics, even postgraduate students researching the Tiptree Award, as I was when I served on the jury in 1997.

Reception

Pat and I did want to make trouble, and the people we imagined we would annoy were some shapeless, penised force in the field, some vague locus of male power.

Whoever these men are, my sense is that they've managed to ignore the Tiptree entirely. We have failed to upset (I would love to hear I'm wrong about this). Instead, every year has seen some controversy from within our community. I don't know why I didn't anticipate this. Obviously, even when your motive is to honor work, you will inevitably create a second category of the un-honored. This is where the controversy has come in. I think generally people range from okay to ecstatic with the actual winners. It's the non-winners that trouble. (Fowler, fem-sf discussion group, 10 June 1996)

For Karen Fowler, the fact that some "vague locus of male power" in the field was ignoring the award was more invidious than if they attacked it. Two men within the field who have been upset by the award and commented publicly to that effect are David Brin and Charles Platt. The Hugo- and Nebula-winning sf writer, David Brin, spoke negatively about the Tiptree Award in an interview for *Holland SF* by Ruud van de Kruisweg. Kruisweg asked Brin about his novel *Glory Season* (1993) by comparing it to battle-of-the-sexes texts written by women such as Nicola Griffith's *Ammonite* (1993) and Sheri Tepper's *Gate to Women's Country* (1988). Brin responded by referring to the Tiptree Award: "As I say in my afterword, it is a topic in which men are often denied to have the same wisdom or insight as female authors. Fortunately, only a few silly people have said that about *Glory Season* . . . (although those few did make certain the book was not considered for the James Tiptree Award for gender bending SF)" (from the Linkoping Science Fiction and Fantasy Archive, online at >sf.www.lysator.liu.se/sf_archive/sf-texts/authors/B/Brin%2CDavid.mbox<). In fact, *Glory Season* was considered for the Tiptree and was on the 1993 longlist, with lengthy comments from two of the judges, Ursula Le Guin and Jeanne Gomoll.

Charles Platt in a letter to *SF Eye* questioned the need for another science fiction award: "Awards are always a bad idea, and the Tiptree Award is even worse than usual, because it separates books by men from books by women as if the difference matters. It also implies that awards discriminate against women, which they don't (Pat herself has won her share)" (*Science Fiction Eye*, June 1992, 6). It was immediately pointed out to Platt that the award is open to anyone. Texts by men have been on the shortlist in every year of the award, and in 1996 a man, Theodore Roszak, was co-winner with Elizabeth Hand. In a lovely piece of unintentional irony that many associated with the prize have found enormously amusing in some quarters, this has been dismissed as "tokenism." I asked Susanna Sturgis who chaired the 1994 Tiptree jury about reactions to the award:

> After I returned home from Potlatch and the Tiptree ceremony, I started a Tiptree Award topic on GEnie, a U.S.-based online service that has three huge SF roundtables, for the written word, media, and fandom. I hoped it would encourage discussion of the award criteria ("what is gender- bending?" etc.) and encourage people to recommend books and stories for the award. It has done a little of this, but mostly it served as a forum for two or three men to air their uninformed prejudices about the award: why is there only one man on the jury, who decides what the criteria are, why has no man ever won the award, and so on. What struck me is that, although the award founders and supporters are very accessible within the f/sf community, the complaining individuals had made no attempt to contact any of them with their questions and concerns. I encouraged them over and over again to recommend titles for the 1995 award, but none of them has. (Letter to author, 13 May 1995)

The Tiptree has received a lot of coverage within the science fiction community. Outside the field of sf, coverage has been largely confined to the feminist press, with an article by Julie Phillips appearing in the December 1995 issue of *Ms.* Susanna Sturgis has written articles about the "Tiptree Juggernaut" for *Feminist Bookstore News,* May/June 1995; *Sojourner: The Women's Forum,* September 1994, and *American Bookseller,* September 1992. In her construction of the Tiptree, Sturgis shapes it in terms of joking: "With such a trickster as its guiding spirit, the Tiptree Award has been blessed with an exuberant sense of humor. Feminists running *bake sales,* after all?" (Sturgis 1992: 11). She goes on to locate the Tiptree Award within the debates about woman and sf that I discussed in chapter 2: "Through the 1980s, the death of feminism was assumed by many in the mass media and prayed for by others. Not unknown in the fantasy and science fiction field (which, since the 1970s, has been challenged by the increasing visibility of women writers) are male voices wailing that women (a) ruined the genre, messing it up with their concern for plot and character, and/or (b) can't write "hard" (ie rooted in "real" science) science fiction" (11). Sturgis also notes that "many believe that [the award] has significantly affected what is being written and published. In the first eligibility year (1991), I was surprised how few of the books I read took risks with gender-related issues. Each year there have been more, as reflected by the steady growth of the shortlist: 5 titles in the first year, 7 in the second, 10 in the third and 14 in the fourth. Some writers now talk about how the existence of the Tiptree prompted them to re-examine and challenge their own assumptions about gender" (Sturgis 1995: 52).

By far the greatest amount of debate about the Tiptree has taken place within the feminist sf community. Much of the recent discussion occurs on the fem-sf online discussion group and centers principally on the winning and shortlisted texts. The most frequent criticism, however, is not about the texts that are on the list but those that are not.

Judging the Tiptree Award

I don't think it's instructive to talk about trends. Every jury has begun by inventing the wheel—by grappling with the phrase "explores and expands gender" all over again. I am unaware of any jury being led by precedent, except in a couple of cases, where they didn't like what a previous jury had done and vowed not to repeat it. So if some year you see the Tiptree veering, I think you can expect it to right itself again (from whatever slanted position you personally think is upright) and I guess I hope that the more irritated a year's choices make you, the more eager you will be to serve on the jury in your turn and set things straight. This award belongs to us, as

Susanna points out, in a way that other awards don't. (Fowler, fem-sf discussion group 10 June 1996)

I have spoken to a number of Tiptree judges about their experiences judging the award. The first issue that became apparent in these discussions is that each jury is involved in producing the Tiptree Award and that each jury is different. This means that the award, like science fiction itself, is always in a state of becoming. The more recent judges have begun their time on the Tiptree jury with a knowledge of what a "Tiptree text" is. They can point to previous winners and previous shortlists of texts considered. When the first jury convened, a "Tiptree text" was a text written by James Tiptree Jr.[3] When they began debating about which texts they would shortlist and which they would give the award to, they were part of the formation of the objects "Tiptree Award winner" and "Tiptree text." That these terms are beginning to have currency and effects is demonstrated by phenomena like the review of N. Lee Wood's *Looking for the Madhi*. In her review of this text, Shira Daemon argues that the book comments on the "ways in which we perceive gender differences" and asks that the "Tiptree judges take note" (Daemon 1996: 31). I have spoken to science fiction writers, men and women, who have told me that they are planning or writing their Tiptree book or story.

Just what a Tiptree book is becomes the site of negotiation for each successive Tiptree jury. The first jury worked with the rubric that they were looking for texts that "explored and expanded the roles of men and women." They were also given a list of books that Pat Murphy and Karen Fowler would have given the award to in the past. Their paradigmatic case was Carol Emshwiller's brilliant *Carmen Dog* (1990), in which women begin to turn into beasts and beasts into women:

> Pooch . . . now finds herself taking over more and more of the housework and baby-sitting, yet continues to be faithful. Her mistress is deteriorating rapidly—mouth grown wide, eyes suspicious. . . . A guinea pig named Cucumber . . . although not very smart is taking over several of the easier tasks in the house next door. . . . Philip the king snake down the block, has turned out to be female after all, as has Humphrey the Iguana. Neither of them, it is clear, has much maternal instinct, though, and they were last seen heading south on Route 95 with not so much as a good-bye kiss to the little ones who had watched over them tenderly, albeit not very consistently. (Emshwiller 1990: 2-3)

Karen Fowler writes:

> Instructions to the jurists leave them as much latitude as possible, and they often begin the year with a long discussion over where the cutting edge is now and whether it's moved since last year and what they think of last year's selection. This pre-reading discussion carries on when the reading begins. During my year there were great exchanges of philosophies and reading experiences; it was very lively and I missed it terribly when we'd made our choices and packed our tents. Some years seem to have had considerably less chat, and I always think they missed the best part. (Letter to author, 16 February 2001)

Later juries have had the examples of previous year's winners and short lists. In a discussion of the Tiptree guidelines on fem-sf, Lucy Sussex, one of the 1994 jurors wrote: "[A]s Susanna Sturgis wrote in the Potlatch programme book, each year the judging panel redefines the award, as what is challenging in '92 may be old hat in '95. I can't comment on other year's panels, but we did this by consensus. And the award is really not for ersatz Tiptree stories. We're not going to see her like again" (11 July 1995).

Jeanne Gomoll, the chair of the 1993 Tiptree Award responds:

> My experience on the judging panel for the 1993 Tiptree pretty much matches Lucy Sussex's experience, in that we spent a great deal of time in our correspondence discussing what we thought the term "gender bending" meant. We agreed that it is not a term that can be defined once and for all time. It changes from year to year, and we decided that our task as judges was to choose the fiction that best represented its meaning the year we read for the award.
>
> It was an incredible experience, but I don't think any of us dug up Pat's "guidelines" published in a press release to help us in our task.
>
> The Tiptree process reinvents itself anew each year. Guidelines written one year will probably become outdated in another year. Right now, that seems a very good thing to me. If we agree that human consciousness evolves, why shouldn't the prizes we award for it also evolve?
>
> And I agree with Lucy that we're not about giving awards to Tiptree look-alikes. (15 July 1995)

This exchange neatly explicates the negotiation that goes on from year to year on the panels and also the shift in meaning of Tiptree book, from something written by Tiptree to something that could be shortlisted for the

Tiptree Award. Susanna Sturgis, as part of this exchange on fem-sf, writes: "We were guided in our discussions primarily by the works we read and the comments made by previous jurors. Sometimes the latter gave me clues to areas that might not have been taken seriously enough, e.g., exposing the incestuous potential of the Traditional Family in Robin McKinley's *Deerskin* (1993)" (17 July 1995).

Questions like, What does "gender-bending" mean? What are we looking for? What are we rewarding and encouraging? And the arguments and discussion they are part of give voice to undercurrents and debates within the broader science fiction community and beyond. Debates about popular feminism and "political correctness" are raised frequently, though both Pat Murphy and Karen Fowler have made it clear that they do not want the award to fall into some narrow definition of political correctness. The award serves to show also that feminism is not a monolith, any more than science fiction is—that there are many feminists and feminisms.

It is interesting to consider just how difficult it is for people to say what the award is for. The phrase most frequently used by judges and those involved with the Tiptree to try and explain what it is for is "gender-bending." It is a term that is full of possibility—making of gender a play thing that can be endlessly reshaped—and in science fiction, bodies are above all else plastic. The term has been the center of much debate within the context of the award: "Even among award supporters, I think, the term 'gender-bending' is controversial. It's catchy and easier to repeat than 'fantasy or science fiction that explores and expands the roles of women and men'! For some people, though, it means gender CHANGING—characters that change genders, as in *Orlando*" (Susanna Sturgis, letter to author, 13 May 1995).

Each jury has also had different dynamics and negotiated these questions in different ways. Naturally, their deliberations while on the jury are confidential but most were happy to talk to me more generally about their experiences as a Tiptree judge. Fantasy and science fiction scholar Brian Attebery was the "token" man on the 1994 jury. He narrates his experiences of being a Tiptree judge in terms of negotiation and consensus:

> One thing that surprised me was the degree of agreement among the committee members. I had understood that previous panels had been rather divided, and since this was a group of people I had never met (except Pat Murphy, and that was only on one social occasion), I rather expected that we would have different takes on issues and stories. Then when we got to discussing, the most frequent way of introducing com-

> ments was "Susanna is right when she says . . ." or "I agree with Lucy that. . . ."
>
> I wonder if one of the reasons it worked as well as it did was that we made an effort to present ourselves and our readings in personal, informal ways, rather than as impartial judges making abstract statements. There was always a bit of chitchat in and around the discussion: My dealings with pre-school-age children and travels around the wilds of Idaho, Ellen's radio work, Susanna's horseback rides on the beach, Lucy's new neighborhood, etc. All of this not only made us feel like old friends, but it also gave a groundedness to our readings. (Letter to author, 17 May 1995)

His discourse is predicated here on both/and, rather than either/or, and is located in the interpersonal. The 1994 jury was the first all-electronic jury, as by October all jurors had an Internet account. This brought the jurors, who were located in Melbourne, Australia, and various points of the United States, much closer together and made communication faster and more immediate, belying the notion that computers and computer technologies are cold and alienating. The 1996 Tiptree jury, of which I was a member, was also entirely electronic, enabling us to pursue our negotiations about sex/gender/sexuality and how this plays out in terms of individual texts without long delays.

As a founding mother, Karen Fowler, who was on the 1996 jury with me, has had an inside view on the deliberations of all previous juries. She writes that:

> Each jury tends to start off with a round of letters discussing those words ["expand and explore gender roles"]. It gets easier for them than for us here, because they are dealing with actual books. By which I mean that it is easier to say a particular book doesn't do this, than it is to say exactly what "this" is. In effect then, with those vague guidelines, each jury does make up its own criteria, and in different years, different values have predominated. Some juries have valued expansion more than exploration of gender. Some have felt that feminism was a crucial component and the sort of book you propose, the one that argues some essentially feminine quality to women could not have won in those years, although perhaps in others. (fem-sf discussion group, 19 June 1996)

Jurors from various years have also told me that they were guided by certain things they did or did not like about an earlier jury's decisions. Some thought previous years' lists were too long or too short and decided to remedy that situation. As a juror I found that it is much easier to say whether a given book is or is not what I think of as a Tiptree text than it is to explain what a Tiptree text is. Juries are engaged in a meaning-making process and these processes are dependent on paradigmatic contrast. You make meaning by saying whether a given thing is or is not part of a particular paradigmatic set, not by defining the paradigm. The meanings are thus made through exchange and negotiation between each of the jury members. What constitutes a Tiptree text is renegotiated every year. However, this process takes place in the deliberations around all literary awards, the notion of good writing and what text is the "best" is as much under negotiation as is the notion of "expanding and exploring gender."

The Tiptree Texts

ENCOURAGING SPECULATION ABOUT GENDER: THE TIPTREE AWARD

Having a prize means that there must be winners, and in having winners, a shortlist, and a longlist the Tiptree award has created a visible canon of sf that speculates about gender, sex and sexuality. Every year as more winners of the prize are named and more texts added to the short-list, this canon grows.[4] The winners up till the year 2000 have been

1991: Gwyneth Jones, *White Queen*, Gollancz; Eleanor Arnarson, *A Woman of the Iron People*, William Morrow
1992: Maureen F. McHugh, *China Mountain Zhang*,Tor
1993: Nicola Griffith, *Ammonite*, Del Rey
1994: Ursula K. Le Guin, "The Matter of Seggri" *Crank!* 3 (spring); Nancy Springer, *Larque on the Wing*, AvoNova
1995: Elizabeth Hand, *Waking the Moon*, Harper Prism; Theodore Roszak *The Memoirs of Elizabeth Frankenstein*, Random House
1996: Ursula K. Le Guin, "Mountain Ways," *Asimov's Science Fiction*, August; Mary Doria Russell, *The Sparrow*, Random House
1997: Candas Jane Dorsey, *Black Wine*, Tor; Kelly Link, "Travels with whe Snow Queen," *Lady Churchill's Rosebud Wristlet* (winter)
1998: Raphael Carter, "Congenital Agenesis of Gender Ideation," *Starlight* 2, ed. Patrick Nielsen Hayden, Tor
1999: Suzy McKee Charnas, *The Conqueror's Child*, Tor
2000: Molly Gloss, *Wild Life*, Simon and Schuster

While the winning texts and shortlisted texts have as much differentiating them as they have in common, all these texts engage with the problematical space of sex and gender. Not all of the Tiptree texts are easily situated within the battle of the sexes—McHugh's *China Mountain Zhang* (1992), for instance, which is set in a future world in which China is the dominant power and homosexuality is illegal. However, in many of the Tiptree texts, the tropes and themes of the battle-of-the-sexes texts are apparent: all-women or women-dominated worlds—Elisabeth Vonarburg's *In the Mother's Land* (1992), Griffith's *Ammonite* (1993) and Geoff Ryman's "O Happy Day!" (1994); women at war with men—Alice Nunn's *Illicit Passage* (1992) and Suzy McKee Charnas's *The Furies* (1994) and *Conqueror's Child* (1999); and hermaphrodites—Graham Joyce and Peter F. Hamilton's "Eat Reecebread" (1994) and Duchamp's "Motherhood Etc." (1993). In Melissa Scott's *Shadow Man* (1995) the multiple sexes of the earlier texts are given names. Her book has five sexes—fem, man, woman, herm, and mem.[5] Le Guin's "The Matter of Seggri" (1994) is set on a world in which "men have all the privilege and the women have all the power" (Le Guin 1994: 9). The story comments on early sexbattle texts like Bond's "The Priestess Who Rebelled" (1939) as well as the later *Gate to Women's Country* (1988) by Sheri S. Tepper. Springer's *Larque on the Wing* (1994), about a woman who finds she has become a young homosexual man on her fortieth birthday, shares the central sex-change idea with David Keller's "The Feminine Metamorphosis" (1929) and H. O. Dickinson's "The Sex Serum" (1935), although the text entirely reworks these transformations.

The Tiptree texts, as well as being in conversation with pre–Tiptree Award texts that speculate about sex and sexuality, are also in conversation with each other. Each new list of winning and shortlisted texts redefines what it is to speculate about these issues in science fiction and comments on previous years of the award.

Recognizing Past Speculation about Gender: The Retrospective Tiptree Award

Vonda McIntyre wrote, quite rightly, "This is a kind of no-brainer, isn't it? The first retrospective Tiptree should go to Uncle Tip. If you have to have a title, 'The Women Men Don't See,' but better for the body of work." Was James Tiptree eligible for the Retrospective Tiptree Award? That question hadn't occurred to us. Alice Sheldon did, of course write the definitive Tiptree-Award-winning stories (and

> *while doing it, lived a Tiptree-Award-winning-life). Ultimately, we decided that the existence of the award itself was a tribute to James Tiptree and that giving Alice Sheldon the retrospective award would be redundant.* (Murphy 1996: 119)

At the Tiptree Award Presentation held at WisCon 20, May 1996, the first Retrospective Tiptree Award was given to Suzy McKee Charnas for *Walk to the End of the World* (1974) and *Motherlines* (1978), Ursula Le Guin for *The Left Hand of Darkness* (1969), and Joanna Russ for "When It Changed" (1972) and *The Female Man* (1975). The decision was made by getting all the judges of the first five years of the Tiptree to nominate five works for the Retrospective Award. When the nominations were all put together the jurors were asked to choose three works. As well as the three winners, a list of all the other works that had substantial support from jurors was compiled. Pat Murphy writes that for her, "this list has already served its purpose. There are books on it that I missed when they came out—and a few that I'd never heard of it! For me, this is a list of future pleasures—books to seek out and appreciate. But I'd also like to note that this is not the final, complete, never-to-be changed list of what could have won a Tiptree Award. Like the award itself, the list may change over the years. Who knows? Five years (and hundreds of chocolate chip cookies) from now, we could torture another list of jurors with unreasonable requests" (Murphy 1996: 119).

Giving these texts the Retrospective Award makes explicit the tradition of speculation about sex that has existed within science fiction since 1926. The existence of the award makes explicit the way in which the genre consists of readers of texts, as well as texts and producers of texts. The annotated Retrospective Tiptree Award list is full of jurors' reminiscences about the impact these texts had on them as readers. Debbie Notkin writes of *The Left Hand of Darkness* that it "was for me, as I think it was for many readers my age, my first time. In all the science fiction I had read before that, I had only found hints, tantalizing glimpses, of what I knew could be there. *The Left Hand of Darkness* threw open wide the doors that had been left alluringly ajar and said, 'Come in. There's more room here than you ever imagined. Let me show you what some of it is like'" (WisCon 20 Souvenir Book 1996: 120). For Notkin and the other jurors, the process of choosing the winners of the Retrospective Award allowed them to relive their involvement with the field and what they see as crucial shaping moments of that engagement.

Alice James Raccoona Tiptree Davey Hastings Bradley Sheldon Jr. and the James Tiptree Jr. Memorial Award

And then Karen, who tends toward brilliance, said, "What about James Tiptree, Jr.?" James Tiptree, Jr., winner of multiple Nebulas . . . [who] was revealed in mid-career as Alice Sheldon, and forever after, in every introduction James Tiptree was again revealed as Alice Sheldon. James Tiptree, Jr., who helped break down the imaginary barrier between "women's writing" and "men's writing." James Tiptree, Jr., author of "The Women Men Don't See." (Murphy [1991] 1992: 9)

As much as Tiptree enabled the award to come into existence, so too has the award given James Tiptree Jr. another life. In a pamphlet produced by SF^3, "How to Run a James Tiptree, Jr. Memorial Award Bake Sale," there is a section on "Tips for the Gourmet (Optional Suggestions and Other Hints)." The pamphlet demonstrates that part of the award is to encourage interest in the writing and lives of Tiptree. Since the Tiptree Award came into existence, more of Tiptree's work has been brought back into print, a volume of her previously uncollected writings, *Meet Me at Infinity* (2000), edited by Jeffrey Smith, has appeared, and Julie Phillips has been at work on a biography.

I spent much of chapter 3 looking at the figure of Hermaphroditus, as an ambivalent symbol of hope in the battle of the sexes, of acquiescence, and defeat. Tiptree is another ambivalent symbol, a modern-day Hermes.[6] Hermes is a charged figure, flitting between life and death, the God of narrative and the genitor of Hermaphroditus, who is both male and female. Like Tiptree, not easily tied down, and like Tiptree/Sheldon et al., a trickster. As a trickster Tiptree has come to play an important role for some feminists in the science fiction community. It is this role of trickster which has been a strong influence on the formation of the Tiptree Award. The majority of the literature about the James Tiptree Jr. Memorial Award is littered with words like play, laughter, joking, and parody.

The stories I sketched in the previous chapter about the lives of Tiptree et al., along with other connected stories circulating amongst fans and pros, enabled the formation of the Tiptree Award. It is predominantly those stories about the mysterious Tiptree, and after the Revelation, about Alice Sheldon-who-is-Tiptree that have had the most currency. What contribution do stories about the life of a child in and out of Africa and Asia during the final decades of colonial rule, the life of a young woman married to "a beautiful alcoholic poet" (Tiptree 1979: 32), and a little later to an officer and a gentleman, make to the meaning and constitution of a science fiction award, one that is pointedly not the Alice Sheldon Award? All these Alices and Tiptree and Raccoona were, and are, part of the field of science fiction. The child Alice read science fiction:

> The summer when I was 9 we were up in the woods of Wisconsin as usual, and Uncle Harry returned from an expedition to the metropolis of 1000 souls thirty miles away with his usual collection of *The New York Times*, *The Kenyon Review*, etc. . . . Out of his bundle slipped a 7 by 9 magazine with a wonderful cover depicting, if I recollect, a large green octopus removing a young lady's golden brassiere. We stared. The title was *Weird Tales*.
>
> "Ah," said Uncle Harry. "Oh. Oh yes. I, ah, I picked this up for the child."
>
> "Uncle Harry," I said, my eyes bulging, "*I* am the child. May I have it, please?"
>
> "Uh," said Uncle Harry. And slowly, handed it over.
>
> And so it all began. He would slip them to me and I would slip them back to him. Lovecraft—oh god. And more and more and more; we soon discovered *Amazing* and *Wonder Stories* and others that are long forgotten. (Tiptree 1979: 32)

Tiptree and Raccoona were part of the fan world of sf as well as the professional one. More broadly they were part of science fiction communities. They were part of the kind of science fiction that is recognized and perpetuated by the feminist convention, WisCon, and by the Tiptree Award.

In her introduction to *The Bakery That Men Don't See*, Diane Martin argues that the award has to be called the James Tiptree Jr. Memorial Award to remind everyone of the palpable effects of being a male writer and how, if it is discovered that a male writer is "really" a woman, there is a very different set of effects. I agree. However, it is important to remember that Tiptree is not a stable, easily mapped writer. Tiptree is also Raccoona and the three Alices I discussed in chapter 6. Tiptree was also none of them. And the fascination of Tiptree/Alice lies not just in her/his most public science fiction life but in the personal discontinuities that make up those lives. The Tiptree Award is given for texts that explore and expand gender. Alice/Tiptree's lives do just that, and in doing so they demonstrate that being male and being female are not opposites; there are a variety of ways of being either and both, and none of us is (or are) a unified subject (Henriques et al 1984; Davies and Harre 1990). I believe that science fiction is the perfect place to explore these diversities and that the Tiptree Award is a fantastic (in every sense) site for the recognition and propagation of this exploration.

EPILOGUE

In order to know something we first have to make it. . . . [W]e produce the things we know, that's how we come to know them. (King 1994: xv)

In this book I have produced an object, the battle of the sexes in science fiction, and traced its journeys from 1926 to 1973; through the multiple lives of Tiptree et al., through the award shaped by his/her life. This complex, and contradictory object that I have created has enabled me to know the field of science fiction, and in knowing it, to become a part of that field. My science fiction is not the same as the one Kingsley Amis created in *New Maps of Hell* (1960), or Brian Aldiss created in *Billion Year Spree* (1973). Neither is it entirely the same science fiction that Sarah Lefanu created in her *Chinks in the World Machine* (1988) or Robin Roberts in *A New Species* (1993). Mine is a series of shifting communities, consisting of people, texts, and knowledges and their engagements with each other. For my construction of this field, like Katie King's construction of feminist theory (1994), conversations are central.

I have examined a much longer period of sf's development than is usually covered in feminist critical accounts of science fiction (though shorter than that of Jane Donawerth in *Frankenstein's Daughters* [1997]). This examination has enabled me to contextualize and historicize the debates about women and sf within the field of sf, within the various science fiction communities, and within the debates and conversations between these communities. This makes my object, science fiction, different from those of Aldiss, Amis, Donawerth, Lefanu, and Roberts who are predominantly concerned with fictional texts.

My construction of the field of science fiction has also been crucially shaped by my physical location. In the University of Sydney library I was able to trace conversations about men, women and science fiction through the letters, editorials, articles and science fiction stories of prozines, fanzines and books over the past seventy years; conversations between Isaac Asimov, Mary Byers, Mary and James Rogers, Donald G. Turnbull, and others in the pages of *Astounding* in the late 1930s; and between Joanna Russ, Philip K. Dick, and Poul Anderson and others in the early 1970s; and amongst Tiptree judges and the participants of fem-sf on three different continents 1991 to 2001. These series of conversations are produced by, and also produce, science fiction, feminist science fiction, the battle of the sexes texts, WisCon, the James Tiptree, Jr. Memorial Award, and many other sites of these debates.

The conversations that I have charted throughout this book have been crucial in shaping it. So too have the conversations that I have had about, and as a result of, this book. Many of these conversations, with students, scholars, and members of science fiction communities, took place in emails between participants scattered throughout Australia, the United States, Canada, and the United Kingdom. The Internet has not been merely a means of speeding up communication, but has enabled an interaction that would not otherwise have been possible, and has thus been a crucial part of my production of the object of knowledge that is this book. This has operated in a variety of ways, from requests for information about hard-to-find fanzines, resulting in copies of those fanzines materialising in my letter box, to images for this book being sent to me in a matter of minutes from the other side of the world, to the sense of the science fiction community that I am reminded of every time I check my email.

Both fictional and "non-fictional" explorations of the sexes negotiate and explore what it is to be a man or a woman or neither, and the political, social, and cultural capital that attaches to that particular kind of being within the field (or fields) of science fiction. These discourses manifestly demonstrate that there is no one way of being any or either of these sexes—that being is a production, a performance—and it is continuing. These texts also demonstrate that their engagement with such issues is constitutive and explorative and not merely an exemplification of them.

The battle-of-the-sexes stories that I examined in chapter 2 make explicit the inequality between the class known as women and that known as men. Most of these sexbattle stories attempt to teach that the rule of men is natural. Disrupting this natural order can only lead to anarchy and thus stagnation, or, to *too* much order, and thus stagnation. However, in the midst of their conservatism, rampant misogyny, heterosexism, and antifeminism, these texts denaturalize essential differences between the sexes and reveal the existence of more than two sexes, and the fluidity of these sexed bodies.

At the same time, the majority of the texts I examined in chapters 2 and 3 locate all difference on the axis of sex: race and class are almost entirely elided. The worlds imagined in *The Disappearance* (1951) and *Venus Plus X* (1960) are predicated on an equality between white men and white women and yet the term white is never used, let alone explored. White becomes, not only unmarked, but invisible.

The texts I examined in chapter 2 seek to erase the bodies of not-real men and women. However, their existence is what enables the real women and men to signify as real and their erasure is never quite possible as the range of not-real sexed bodies leaks out. These leakages become the focus of some of the texts I examined in chapter 3, such as Theodore Sturgeon's *Venus Plus* X (1960), Ursula Le Guin's *Left Hand of Darkness* (1969), Russ's "When It Changed" (1972), and of many of the Tiptree texts, both those authored by Tiptree, and those associated with the Tiptree Award. Many of these texts, such as L. Timmel Duchamp's "Motherhood Etc" (1993), Nancy Springer's *Larque on the Wing* (1994), and Raphael Carter's "Congenital Agenesis of Gender Ideation" (1998), focus on those who, in the terms of the earlier sexbattle texts, perform their sex inadequately, rather than on the real-man real-woman dyad of sexbattle texts such as Nelson Bond's "The Priestess Who Rebelled" (1939) or Edmund Cooper's *Who Needs Men?* (1972). All these texts, whether overtly feminist or anti-feminist, are also located within the discourse of romance and its enunciation and enforcement of heterosexuality. Some of the texts, including John Wyndham's "Consider Her Ways" (1956), Russ's "When It Changed" (1972), and Gwyneth Jones's *White Queen* (1991) and Kelly Link's "Travels with the Snow Queen" (1997) interrogate this discourse.

The texts I have examined in this book are not simply theorizing the performance of sex; they are engaged in the performance of sex. They are both practice and theory. Nor are those performances confined to written texts. As Pat Murphy writes of Tiptree/Sheldon, "[H]e/she wrote the 'definitive Tiptree-Award-winning stories' and at the same time she/he 'lived a Tiptree-Award-winning-life'" (Murphy 1996: 119).

As I demonstrated in chapter 6, the lives of Alice James Raccoona Tiptree Davey Hastings Bradley Sheldon Jr. vividly demonstrate the groundedness of post-structuralist understandings of subjectivity. A concept of a fixed unitary subject is simply inadequate for mapping out these overlapping and intertwining lives. Even those texts that are predicated on this idea, such as those in chapter 2, serve to demonstrate that the unitary subject is illusionary.

This book is also part of an examination of my own subjectivity. The journey of the production of my book has compelled me to examine my own relationship to the field of science fiction and to think about the ways in which the field has shaped my sense of self. That process of exploration has changed my relationship to the field. I have become an active member of a community of which previously I had had only the vaguest inkling. Researching and writing this book has made real to me that texts are inextricably part of communities; that genres are embodied, are communities, rather than static collections of markings on paper.

APPENDIX

Analysis of Kiss Passages from "The Priestess Who Rebelled" and *Who Needs Men?*

This appendix covers the analysis of clause structures that underpins my arguments in chapter 2. As outlined in the introduction, my grammatical analysis is based on the work of M. A. K. Halliday and particularly his functional grammar. His understanding of language as social semiotic has had a profound effect on my work.[a] Halliday outlines two systems for understanding the way verbs (processes) function in clauses, the transitive system and the ergative system (Halliday 1994: 161-74).

Nina Puren's work on ergativity, following Halliday, led me to the analysis of chapter 2. She explains the difference between transitivity and ergativity thus: "Transitivity is a grammatical movement of extension, in which a process extends (or not in the case of intransitives) from one participant to another. . . . [T]he ergative model of the event understands a verb or a process to be realised through the body of the participant, who is named the medium" (Puren 1995: 18). In her article on romance and the law Puren suggests that Sharon Marcus's compelling argument that the syntax of rape is transitive (as in "He raped her," where "He" is unambiguously the actor assaulting "her" who is the goal of this process) does not account for the narrative the rapist frequently tells within the court room where he is not responsible. For this narrative Puren argues that ergativity is more useful.

She gives as an example the clause "He went crazy" in which "He" is the medium. She goes on to say that when "two participants are involved, the one who causes the action to happen in the other is called the agent, as, for example, in the clause: 'Her beauty made him go crazy', in which 'her beauty' is the agent, and 'he' is the medium that the process of 'going crazy' occurs through. In this kind of construction, the agent is coded as responsible for the action taking place" (Puren 1995: 18). The following tables demonstrate this difference:

TRANSITIVE ANALYSIS

He	*raped*	*her*
Actor	Process	Goal

ERGATIVE ANALYSIS

Her beauty	*made*	*him*	*go crazy*
Agent	Process	Medium	Process

Puren makes it clear that using an ergative analysis allows power relations to be traced as they are explicitly worked out at the level of the grammar. In chapter two I used an ergative analysis to highlight the relations of power enacted in the inscription of "real" femininity and masculinity in the battle of the sexes; that is the way in which a man teaches a woman how to be a woman.

Following is a transitive and ergative analysis of each clause.

Who Needs Men? by Edmund Cooper (1972)

He kissed her on the lips. She struggled, but with one arm he managed to hold her. The rifle was dropped. There was something terrible about the kiss. It was like no other kiss she had ever known. It was humiliating, it was degrading, it was disturbing. It drained strength from her limbs, filled her head with nightmares. He let her go. "'Well, exterminator. That was a kind of rape, was it not?" (Cooper [1972] 1974: 24)

He	*kissed*	*her*	*on the lips.*
Actor	Process: material	Goal	Circumstance: location: place
Agent		Medium	

She	*struggled*
Actor	Process:material
Medium	

but	*with one arm*	*he*	*managed to hold*	*her.*
	Circ.: manner: means	Actor	Process: material	Goal
		Agent		Medium

The rifle	*was dropped.*
Goal	Process: material
Medium	

There	*was*	*something terrible about the kiss.*
	Process: existential	Existent
		Medium

It	*was*	*like no other kiss [she had ever known.]*	
Carrier	Pro.: rel.: int.: attr.	Attribute	
Medium		Range	
		Senser	Pro.: mental: cognition
		Medium	

It	*was*	*humiliating;*
Carrier	Process: relational: intensive: attributive	Attribute
Medium		Range

it	*was*	*degrading;*
Carrier	Process: relational: intensive: attributive	Attribute
Medium		Range

it	*was*	*disturbing.*
Carrier	Process: relational: intensive: attributive	Attribute
Medium		Range

It	*drained*	*strength*	*from her limbs,*
Actor	Process: material	Goal	Circumstance: location: place
Agent		Medium	

filled	*her head*	*with nightmares.*
Process: material	Beneficiary	Circumstance: manner: means(?)
	Beneficiary	

He	*let*	*her*	*go.*
		Actor	
Initiator	Process: material . . .		. . . Process: material
Agent		Medium	

That	*was*	*a kind of rape,*	*was it not?*
Carrier	Process: relational: intensive: attributive	Attribute	
Medium		Range	

"The Priestess Who Rebelled" by Nelson S. Bond (1939).

"There is a custom in our tribe . . . a mating custom which you do not know. Let me show you—"

He leaned over swiftly. Meg felt the mighty strength of his bronzed arms closing about her, drawing her close. And he was touching his mouth to hers; closely, brutally, terrifyingly.

She struggled and tried to cry out, but his mouth bruised hers. Angerthoughts swept through her like a flame. But it was not anger—it was something else—that gave life to that flame. Suddenly her veins were running with liquid fire. Her heart beat upon rising, panting breasts like something captive that would be free. Her fists beat upon his shoulders vainly . . . but there was little strength in her blows.

Then he released her, and she fell back, exhausted. Her eyes glowed with anger and her voice was husky in her throat. She tried to speak, and could not. And in that moment a vast and terrible weakness trembled through Meg. She knew, fearfully, that if Daiv sought to mate with her, not all the priestessdom of the gods would save her. There was a body-hunger throbbing within her that hated his Manness . . . but cried for it! (Bond [1939] 1972: 216)

There	*is*	*a custom in our tribe . . . a mating custom [[which*
	Pro.: exist.	Existent
		Medium
you	*do not know]].*	
Sen.	Pro.: ment.: cognition	
Medium		

Let	*me*	*show*	*you.*
	Actor	Pro.: material	Goal
	Agent		Medium

He	*leaned over*	*swiftly.*
Actor	Process: material	Circumstance: manner: quality
Medium		

Meg	*felt*	*[the mighty strength of his bronzed arms*		*closing about*
Senser	Pro.: ment.: perc.	Phenomenon		
Medium		Range		
		Actor		Proc.: mat.
		Agent		
her,	*drawing*	*her*	*close.]*	
Goal	Pro.: mat.	Goal	Circ.: loc.: place	
Med.		Med.		

And	*he*	*was touching his mouth to*	*hers;*	*closely, brutally, terrifyingly.*
	Actor	Process: material	Goal	Circumstance: manner: quality
	Agent		Medium	

She	*struggled*
Actor	Process: material
Medium	

and	*(she)*	*tried to cry out.*
	Behaver	Process: behavioral
	Medium	

but	*his mouth*	*bruised*	*hers.*
	Actor	Process: material	Goal
	Agent		Medium

Angerthoughts	*swept*	*through her*	*like a flame.*
Actor	Process: material	Circ.: loc.: place	Circ.: manner: comparison
Agent			

But	*it*	*was not*	*anger<<>>*	*[that gave*	*life*
	Carrier	Proc.: rel.: int.: attributive	Attribute		
	Medium		Range		
				Pro.: mat.	Goal
					Medium

to that flame].
Beneficiary
Beneficiary

>>It	*was*	*something else.<<*
Carrier	Proc.: rel.: int.: attributive	Attribute
Medium		Range

Suddenly	*her veins*	*were running*	*with liquid fire.*
Circumstance: manner	Actor	Pro.: material	Circ.: manner: means
	Medium		

Her heart	*beat*
Actor	Process: material
Medium	

upon rising
minor clause

panting breasts	*[ ]*	*[like something captive that*	*would be*	*free].*
Carrier	Pro.: rel.: int.: attr.	Attribute		
Medium		Range		
		Carrier	Pro.: rel.: int.: attr.:	Attribute
		Medium		Range

Her fists	*beat*	*upon his shoulders*	*vainly.*
Actor	Process: material	Goal	Circ.: manner: means
Agent		Medium	

But there	*was*	*little strength in her blows.*
	Process: existential	Existent
		Medium

Then	*he*	*released*	*her*
	Actor	Process: material	Goal
	Agent		Medium

and	*she*	*fell back*
	Actor	Process: material
	Medium	

exhausted
minor clause

Her eyes	*glowed*	*with anger*
Actor	Process: material	Circumstance: manner: mreans
Medium		

and	*her voice*	*was*	*husky*	*in her throat.*
	Carrier	Pro.: rel.: int.: attributive	Attribute	Circ.: loc.: place
	Medium		Range	

She	*tried to speak*
Behaver	Process: behavioral
Medium	

and	*(she)*	*could not.*
	Behaver	Process: behavioral

And	*in that moment*	*a vast and terrible weakness*	*trembled*	*through Meg.*
	Circ.: loc.: time	Actor	Pro.: material	Circ.: loc.: place
		Medium		

She	*knew,*	*fearfully,*
Senser	Pro.: mental: cognition	Circ.: manner: quality

that <<>>	*not all the priestessdom of the gods*	*would save*	*her*
	Actor	Pro.: material	Goal
	Agent		Medium

>>if	*Daiv*	*sought to mate with*	*her.<<*
	Actor	Process: material	Goal
	Agent		Medium

There	*was*	*a body-hunger*	*[[throbbing*	*within her]]*
	Pro.: existential	Existent		
		Medium		
		Actor	Pro.: mat.	Circ.: loc.: place
		Medium		

that hated	*his Manness*
Pro.: mental: affect	Phenomenon
	Range

but	*cried for*	*it!*
	Process: mental: affect	Phenomenon

a. For a different linguistic approach to science fiction, see Peter Stockwell's book on the poetics of science fiction (Stockwell 2000).

KEY TO ABBREVIATIONS

attr. attributive
circ. circumstance
int. intensive
loc. location
ment. mental
perc. perceptual
pro. process
rel. relational

NOTES

INTRODUCTION

1. I am not the first to follow Russ's use of the term "the battle of the sexes." Natalie M. Rosinsky in her 1984 study of women's science fiction, *Feminist Futures*, includes a chapter entitled "The Battle of the Sexes: Things to Come." In a footnote she directs the reader to Russ's article, saying that it gives an "historical overview of these (generally) virulently misogynistic works in twentieth-century fiction" (127). Rosinsky discusses only the later battle-of-the-sexes texts that Russ describes in her article as feminist utopias. Daphne Patai discusses what she refers to as "sex-role reversal utopias," which is clearly another name for battle-of-the-sexes texts. Her examples go back as early as 1870. Although her article was published in 1982 in a science fiction journal, *Extrapolation*, she does not refer to the Russ article, though she does refer to Russ's 1975 novel, *The Female Man* (Patai 1982: 69). Many of the accounts of the relations between feminism and science fiction that appeared in the 1970s paint a picture of sf as a genre in which engagement with questions of sex, gender, and the relations between men and women has been glaringly absent (Russ [1971] 1974; Friend 1972; Bankier 1974; Badami 1976; Wood 1978–79). Other accounts are concerned to point to a tradition of women's sf, sometimes beginning with Mary Shelley (Gubar 1980; Donawerth 1997), sometimes not (the *Invisible Women* issue of *Aurora* [summer 1984]). Accounts such as those of Sarah Lefanu (1988), Robin Roberts (1993), Jenny Wolmark (1994) have added to this picture. Roberts in particular argues that by "isolating moments of science fiction's past, we can begin to see where, why, and how feminist science fiction was formed" (Roberts 1993: 1). I demonstrate that debates and stories about women, men, sex, and sexuality have been a part of science fiction since 1926. Interestingly, battle-of-the-sexes texts considerably predate 1926 and *Amazing Stories* and the concurrent growth of fandom and science fiction publishing. These earlier texts were frequently collected, cited, and listed by science fiction fans and the battle of the sexes soon became a recurring theme in the science fiction magazines. Sam Moskowitz, a longtime active fan and historian of fandom and science fiction, edited an anthology of these stories, *When Women Rule*, which was published in 1972. Five of the ten stories that Russ discusses in her 1980 article come from the Moskowitz anthology. His first selection is the fifth-century account by Herodotus of the Amazons. His last is "The Priestess Who Rebelled" by Nelson Bond, which was originally published in the October 1939 issue of *Amazing Stories*.

2. The entry on IPO in the *Fancyclopedia* states: "IPO—The Oklahoma Institute of Private Opinion (title a take-off on Gallup), a poll series conducted by Speer. Post cards were sent out, with . . . questions hektoed thereon. Twelve sets of questions in all were put out, extending over a period of some two years around 1938. The number of replies was small, usually little more than 20, but were fairly representative till near the end" (Speer 1944: 50).
3. Ray Palmer went on to be a science fiction writer and well-known editor, editing *Amazing* from 1938 to 1949.
4. Although the fans of Australia, the United Kingdom, and Canada may well have considered themselves as separate from the fandom of the United States.
5. "Mundane" is a science fiction term for non–science fiction literature. Delany says that the term comes "from *mundus*, meaning the world; stories that take place on Earth in the present or past. Any other connotations? Well, turnabout is fair play" (Delany 1984: 88).
6. The article "Science Fiction and `Literature'—or, the Conscience of the King," from which this quote comes, was first delivered as a speech in 1979.
7. These two different reading practices explain much about those people who insist they cannot understand science fiction, that it is too difficult and boring: "All that technobabble." I used this example at a systemic linguistics conference and was struck by the fact that the audience was totally surprised by the science-fictional reading of the clause. When I was doing the analysis, the mundane reading of the clause seemed ungrammatical to me and I had to concentrate to remember how to make sense of it.
8. This interchangeability is not unique to science fiction, as Virginia Woolf attests: "[S]ex—woman, that is to say" (Woolf [1929] 1977: 27).
9. David McIlwain wrote science fiction under the name of Charles Eric Maine. He published his first short story under this pseudonym in his own fanzine in 1938 and began publishing novels in 1955 (Moskowitz 1972: 24–5; Clute & Nicholls 1993: 768). In 1958 he published a battle-of-the-sexes text, *World without Men* (a revised version, *Alph*, was published in 1972).
10. On the emergence of romantic love, see, for example, C. S. Lewis, *The Allegory of Love* (1965); R. Howard Bloch, *Medieval Misogyny and the Invention of Western Romantic Love* (1991); and Moshe Lazar's "*Fin'amor*," in *A Handbook of the Troubadours* (1995).

CHAPTER 1: FAITHFUL TO THEE, TERRA, IN OUR FASHION

1. *Amazing Stories* is frequently referred to as simply *Amazing*. I will employ both usages throughout.
2. *Astounding Science Fiction* is also referred to as *Astounding* and *ASF*. I use the first two forms throughout.
3. Aldiss and Wingrove are adamant about rejecting the pulp tradition: "To set science fiction down as something beginning with Hugo Gernsback's lurid maga-

zines in the nineteen-twenties, as some histories have done, is a wretched error" (1988: 142).

4. Gernsback is not the only science fiction editor to be canonized. Science fiction has a history of treating many of its editors as being as important as its writers. Indeed, John W. Campbell, who edited *Astounding/Analog* from 1937 until 1972, is still probably the most famous editor within the science fiction field.
5. *Amazing* was not, strictly speaking, a pulp, since it was originally published on better quality paper of thicker stock than the pulps proper (Ashley 1974: 22). As I read through early issues of the magazines, they did not crumble in my hands as some "true" pulps have; they are in amazingly (pun intended) good condition compared to others of the same period or even more recent times. The wartime pulps are in particularly poor condition because of paper restrictions.
6. This nominal group, "new romancers," sounds like the title of William Gibson's influential 1984 novel *Neuromancer*.
7. In the September 1926 issue of *Amazing*, Gernsback discusses readers' criticism of the magazine's name: "A number of letters have reached the Editor's desk recently from enthusiastic readers who find fault with the name of the publication. . . . These readers would greatly prefer us to use the title 'Scientifiction' instead. The message that these letters seem to convey is that the name really does not do the magazine justice, and that many people get an erroneous impression as to the literary contents from this title. Several years ago, when I first conceived the idea of publishing a scientifiction magazine, a circular letter was sent to some 25,000 people, informing them that a new magazine by the name 'Scientifiction' was shortly to be launched. The response was such that the idea was given up for two years. The plain truth is that the word 'Scientifiction' while admittedly a good one, scares off many people who would otherwise read the magazine. . . . After mature thought, the publishers decided that the name which is now used was after all the best one to influence the masses, because anything that smacks of science seems to be too 'deep' for the average reader" (1926g: 483).
8. This was not the first use of the term "science fiction": "'Science-fiction' (with a hyphen) was coined by William Wilson, . . . in a book entitled A *Little Earnest Book upon a Great Old Subject* (London: Darton, 1851). It would be over 120 years before anyone rediscovered that book, during which time Gernsback and *Wonder Stories* had popularized the term independently" (Tymn and Ashley 1985: 747).
9. In the stories of science fiction, names and naming become a site of contention. This happens most especially from the 1950s onward, with the popular appropriation of the much hated but fan-coined neologism "sci-fi." Prior to that, the terms "scientifiction" and its abbreviation "stf," and "science fiction" and its abbreviation "sf," were the terms most commonly used to refer to this kind of fiction.
10. *Argosy*, which first appeared in 1896, was the first all-fiction pulp magazine (Tymn and Ashley 1985: 103).
11. The first issue of *All-Story* appeared in 1905.

12. The first issue of *Weird Tales* appeared in 1923. Its area of speciality was "weird" fiction—a kind of precursor to the contemporary genre category of horror, but more general than that: "[T]he stories were a mixture of sf . . . horror stories, sword and sorcery, exotic adventure, and anything else which its title might embrace" (Clute and Nicholls 1993: 1308–9).
13. The New York Futurians were a fan group active from 1938 until the mid-forties. Many members of the Futurians went on to become editors, agents, publishers, writers, and critics of science fiction—or all of these.
14. Longtime fan and bibliographer of the field, Graham Stone, suggests that this is probably Leslie F. Stone.
15. I'm not sure that the Gernsback editorial voice was capable of irony.
16. All spelling is as it appears in the *Fancyclopedia*.
17. For more information about this debate see Hansen 1987: 4–5, 48–50.
18. The Michelists, named after John Michel, were all members of the Futurians who espoused John Michel's version of socialism. The International Scientific Association. An organization from the late thirties which, according to the *Fancyclopedia*, consisted of a group that sought to combine amateur scientists and fans and found the latter becoming dominant. It was scarcely international, the chief branches being the NYB-ISA [New York Branch of the ISA] and the PSFS [Philadelphia Science Fiction Society]" (Speer 1944: 50).
19. William Atheling Jr. is the pen name of the sf writer James Blish.
20. These comments were first published in the spring 1953 issue of the fanzine *Skyhook*.
21. According to the entry by Elmer Perdue in the *Fancyclopedia*, "Star-Begotten" comes from the novel of the same title by H. G. Wells: "And, since the 'Star-Begotten' are those people with abnormal intelligence, produced thru the direct or indirect agency uv [*sic*] beings upon another planet, and since these 'Star-Begotten' are misunderstood, intuitive, brilliant people, stphandom has adopted the name as a collective title phor [*sic*] themselves" (Speer 1944: 83). According to the *Fancyclopedia*, the term "First Fandom" was coined by Speer and describes the period up to 1936. He says the "Second Fandom" covers the period October 1937–1938, and "Third Fandom" covers the period from September 1944 on (Speer 1944: 37, 77, 87).
22. The Analytical Laboratory listed the rankings the readers made of the stories of previous issues of *Astounding*.
23. Like rocketry and space travel, which the fan knows will happen one day, fans' accounts of the moment when "man" landed on the moon are more about a vindication of faith than anything else: "We always knew it would happen."
24. The editorial response makes much of this: "Here is a man of learning, an attorney at law" (Gernsback 1927m: 1077).
25. This idea that the science in science fiction has to be accurate is still central among some fans and consumers of science fiction. Henry Jenkins, writing on *Star Trek* fans at MIT, found that science was a central discourse for their under-

standing and enjoyment of *Star Trek*: "The MIT students draw upon their textbook knowledge of real-world science to test the series' technical claims, often relishing their superiority over the writers' 'pitiful' errors. Roberts, a senior physics major, protested, 'sometimes they go a little far afield of science fiction. They keep getting Neutrinos wrong!'" (1995: 225). Jenkins notes that "[t]hese MIT students follow a long tradition of science fiction fans acting as arbiters of scientific validity of popular fictions" (1995: 217).

26. The distinction between the two genres was already beginning to be made. The division between fantasy and science fiction begins with the arrival of *Amazing*. It took up the space of the science fiction magazine and the existing *Weird Tales* became the home of fantasy and weird (a precursor to the contemporary category of horror) fiction. Fantasy as a fully fledged commercial genre does not begin to emerge until J. R. R. Tolkein's *The Lord of the Rings* was published in 1954–1955 (Attebery 1992).

CHAPTER 2: MAMA COME HOME

1. Robert Wentworth was a pen name of Edmond Hamilton.
2. Many of the battle-of-the-sexes texts use the device of role reversal. This device is by no means unique to science fiction. See for instance Natalie Zemon Davis's "Women on Top" (Davis 1975: 124–51).
3. The introduction of *When Women Rule* was first printed as an article in the August 1967 issue of *If*.
4. "The Sex Serum" (Dickinson 1935) concerns a serum that can change a woman into a man and vice versa. The woman experiences a boost in her intelligence when she becomes a man while the man becomes stupid and so is unable to invent a method of reversing his/her transformation. In *The Disappearance* (Philip 1951), all the men of earth find themselves having to exist in a world without women, and all the women find themselves in a world without men. I discuss *The Disappearance* in chapter 3.
5. There was a debate between James Blish, writing as William Atheling Jr., and Moskowitz in the 1950s about Moskowitz's "reputation for reliability in matters of fact," which Atheling contended was "somewhat overblown" (Atheling 1970: 39). In particular Atheling argues that Moskowitz detects influences between stories where there are none because he ignores the frequently long gap between a story's writing and its publication. Atheling cites as evidence stories written by himself some years before they appeared in print that Moskowitz claims were influenced by stories not yet published at the time of writing (Atheling 1970: 35-39). I have no way of knowing, other than Moskowitz's word, if "The Last Woman" (Gardner 1932) was written in response to "The Last Man" (West 1929); however, the similarities between the two texts are remarkable.
6. I discuss the ideas in "The Last Woman" about a man's strength and virility being drained by sex—that is, women—in chapter 4.

7. Nelson S. Bond wrote three stories about the priestess Meg. The third is "Magic City" (1941). Throughout the three stories real men are referred to with a capital M.
8. *The White Widows* was first published in *Startling Stories* in the October 1953 issue and then as a book by Doubleday in the same year. Sam Merwin Jr. was the editor of *Startling Stories* and *Thrilling Wonder Stories* from 1945 to 1951. I refer in chapter 5 to his editorial for the December 1950 issue of *Thrilling Wonder Stories* on the women's invasion of science fiction.
9. "The Misogynist" was first published in the November 1952 issue of *Galaxy Science Fiction*.
10. Theodore Sturgeon's story "The World Well Lost," published in the first issue of *Universe Science Fiction* in June 1953, was one of the earliest sympathetic portrayals of male homosexuality in science fiction and caused "considerable uproar at the time" (Tymn and Ashley 1985: 692).
11. All other responses I found were favorable but not very detailed: Louis Kurzeja of Chicago, Illinois gave it an A, meaning excellent, and remarked, "It gave me a humorous feeling when I had finished reading it" (*Science Wonder Stories* 1, no. 5 [October 1929]: 467).
12. This story is by no means confined to science fiction. I have a vivid memory of an Elvis movie, *Live a Little, Love a Little* (1968), in which the heroine leaves a message in lipstick for Elvis on the mirror the morning after their (off-camera) night of passion: "Thank you for making me a woman."
13. There are more overt versions of this myth in science fiction. "Helen O'Loy" by Lester del Rey is a much-anthologized story first published in *Astounding* in 1938. In it two men create the woman of their dreams—a robot.
14. The hero's telling the heroine that she talks too much and should shut up is a recurring motif. In *Who Needs Men?* Diarmid tells Rura, "Be quiet, woman . . . you speak too much" (Cooper 1972: 80). There are similar moments in *The Feminists* (Cooper 1971), *The Girls from Planet Five* (Wilson 1955), and "War against the Yukks" (McAllister 1965). The Western world has an extremely long tradition of silencing women and equating that silence with virtue (Bloch 1991; Puren 1995: 18).
15. *Who Needs Men?* is not the only sexbattle text that features one rugged area of the world holding out against female rule. In *The Girls from Planet Five* the only refuge in the woman-dominated United States is Texas. The only other place in the entire world is Australia: "Every ambassador and minister was female except the one to Australia. The Aussies, separated by thousands of miles of water from creeping femininity, had demanded and got a male ambassador—and a bachelor at that" (Wilson 1955: 15).
16. A kiss standing in for sex is by no means unique to written science fiction—just look at any film from the same period. The French/Italian co-production *Cinema Paradiso* (1988), directed by Giuseppe Tornatore, turns on this very trope. The local priest is in charge of censorship and edits all the kisses out of the movies

shown in the cinema. The projectionist creates a collage of these kisses, which is shown at the film's end.

17. Hearing this account by the old woman former exterminator is part of Rura's process of unlearning the "brainwashing" of her matriarchal society.
18. I analyze this passage in more detail in the appendix.
19. Russ comments wryly about Edmund Cooper "determinedly charging into his favourite formula: 'It was X. It was Y. It was Z. It was Q'" (Russ 1980: 13).
20. "Consider Her Ways" (1956) is another matriarchal world modeled on bees or ants.
21. "Mama Come Home" was originally called "The Mother Ship" when published in *If* in 1968.
22. Actually, the protagonist is a jet pilot, not a truck driver. A male Azoran says of the difference between truck drivers and pilots: "I know truckers are supposed to be rough and tough; maybe they are. But you can't tell me that deep down a trucker isn't a lady. When you tell them no that's that. But a pilot—it just eggs them on" (Pohl and Kornbluth [1954] 1979: 79).
23. My thanks to Helen Merrick for drawing my attention to these parallels.
24. That is, until the Lyru women of *The Girls from Planet Five* discover that their men really are not wimps, at which point either the women shrink or their men grow.

CHAPTER 3: PAINWISE

1. Unlike "The Last Man" (1929) and "The Priestess Who Rebelled" (1939), which I discussed in the last chapter.
2. See, for instance, St. Teresa of Avila's autobiography, or *The Golden Legend* by Jacobus de Voragine.
3. I have found two other examples of the sex war being only a dream: "The War of the Sexes" by Edmond Hamilton, first published in the November 1935 edition of *Weird Tales*, and "The Superior Sex" by Miriam Allen deFord, first published in the April 1968 edition of *Fantasy and Science Fiction*. In "The War of the Sexes," Allan Rand answers an advertisement for a young man without connections in search of exciting work (Hamilton 1935: 551). He is induced into a dream of a matriarchy to test whether he has "a cold-steel nerve" (Hamilton 1935: 569). He does, and gets the job and the scientist's daughter. In "The Superior Sex," William is the guinea pig for an experiment which will be able to reveal "hidden psychological impulses" (deFord [1968] 1969: 23). The experiment is being conducted by Professor Ranleigh and his associate, Janet, who is William's wife. The experiment which throws Williams into a matriarchy proves to William only that his wife is having an affair with Ranleigh.
4. There is a long tradition in science fiction of the female character performing this function. Sam J. Lundwall notes this phenomenon: "The classic function of the woman . . . was to follow the hero as a kind of reverentially listening Dr. Watson.

By her obvious ignorance of the most elementary things she would give the hero the opportunity to launch into long explanations as to why the devious Hrrigans had invaded the Solar System, or the workings of the new Space Warp" (Lundwall [1969] 1971: 145–46).

5. *The Disappearance* is one of the few battle-of-the sexes-texts that includes people who are not white. In Keller's "The Feminine Metamorphosis" (1929), which I discussed in the last chapter, part of the action takes place in China, but the only role any Chinese people play in the action is to supply the evil American women with glands from their diseased bodies. In "The Judging of the Priestess" (1940), the enemy are the Japcans, who are the descendants of the Japanese who moved to Mexico, they are short and "ugly," and they are all male. David H. Keller's "The Little Husbands" (1928) and Dwight V. Swain's "Drummers of Daugavo" (1943) are set in the Amazon Basin, and Clark Ashton Smith's "The Root of Ampoi" (1949) is set in Malaya. All three stories take place amidst "native" matriarchies. The majority of the other sexbattle texts make no mention of the race of their protagonists and are illustrated with representations of clean-cut "white" folk. For further discussion see Elizabeth Anne Leonard's collection *Into Darkness Peering: Race and Color in the Fantastic* (1997) and Sheree R. Thomas's *Dark Matter: A Century of Speculative Fiction from the African Diaspora* (2000).
6. *Amazon Planet* was first published in three parts in the December 1966 and January and February 1967 issues of *Analog;* it appeared in paperback form from Ace in 1975.
7. *Virgin Planet* was first published in the January 1957 issue of *Venture Science Fiction* and appeared as a paperback in 1959. There is more on Poul Anderson's engagement with the battle of the sexes in chapter 4.
8. First published in the 1972 anthology *Again, Dangerous Visions*. The story won the Nebula Award for best short story for that year. The Nebulas are awarded by the SFWA (Science Fiction Writers of America).
9. Gabrile de Foigny's text was written and published before the eighteenth-century European "discovery" of Australia.
10. Some more recent examples are Octavia Butler's Xenogenesis Trilogy (1987–89), Storm Constantine's The Wraeththu trilogy (1988–89), Samantha Lee's *Childe Rolande* (1988), and L. Timmel Duchamp's "Motherhood Etc" (1993).
11. *Proud Man* was brought to my attention by Don Keller, science fiction fan and publisher and editor, who kindly gave me a copy of the 1993 Feminist Press edition.
12. Burdekin was not publicly known to be Murray Constantine until the 1980s. Daphne Patai writes that "[w]ith the cooperation of . . . friends, and of her publishers as well, Burdekin covered the tracks of her real identity quite effectively. As a result, when, in the early 1980s, I grew interested in Murray Constantine, it took considerable effort to learn that she was indeed Katherine Burdekin" (Patai 1989: 165).
13. In 1961 it ran as a four-part serial in the January, February, March, and April editions of the British magazine *New Worlds*.

14. The term is discussed in her article "Is Gender Necessary?," first published in *Aurora: Beyond Equality* (1976). In the revised version of her collection of essays *The Language of the Night*, Le Guin added a "Redux," where she refers to the "so-called generic pronoun" (Le Guin [1979] 1989: 145).

CHAPTER 4: FAULT

1. I would like to thank Louise D'arcens for making me aware of Peter Brown's book *The Body and Society: Men, Women and Sexual Renunciation in Early Christianity* (1988).
2. In the early fifties the letter writers to *Thrilling Wonder Stories* take it for granted that there are many more than twenty female fans but the notion that these femme fans are only there for the pleasure and convenience of male fans is still current and is made explicit in a debate about whether there are any beautiful femme fans. Earl T. Parris of Seattle, Washington responds to earlier letters: "I've been patiently reading of this argument concerning beautiful girls in fandom but my patience is at an end. Mr. Vick, can you give a clear, concise definition of beauty? Be rather hard to do since beauty is largely a matter of opinion. And you must really get around because obviously you've met all of the lady fans to know there are no beautiful ones" (Parris 1952: 139). Another letter from Joe Gibson of Jersey City, New Jersey lists, by name, femme fans who are beautiful (1953: 144). This debate nicely shows an example of the kind of attitude to women in fandom which Jeanne Gomoll mentions in her "Open Letter to Joanna Russ": "I sit in the audience at all-male 'fandom of the 70s' panels (and so far, that's the way the panels I've witnessed have been filled, by men only) and don't hear *anything* of the politics, the changes, the roles that women played in that decade (except sometimes, a little chortling aside about how it is easier now to get a date with a female fan)" (Gomoll 1986–87: 9).
3. Her reference to eunuchs is particularly apt, as during the classical period "[t]he full-grown man who made himself a eunuch by carefully tying his testicles, became an *asporos*, a man who wasted no vital fire on others" (Brown 1988: 19). And was therefore more masculine and purer than other men.
4. Don A. Stuart was the pseudonym of John Campbell, the editor of *Astounding*. "The Cloak of Aesir" was a battle-of-the-sexes story.
5. He wrote more prolifically under the name Ray Cummings. His full name was Raymond King Cummings.
6. It is easy to dismiss these covers as exploitative of women but more complex readings are available. See, for instance, Roberts 1993: 40–65.
7. The editor, Sam Mines, was unable to keep a straight face: "We'd like to make with the snappy answers to this missive, but we are helpless, having been broken up by one line above, to wit: 'What's wrong with sex inside or outside as long as the gal shows expression in her eyes?' If this doesn't go down as a classic in the annals of stf we will make a pilgrimage to Mecca" (Mines 1953: 136).

8. The title of this section comes from a letter by L. M. Jensen of Cowley, Wyoming (Jensen 1939: 162). I discuss the letter later in this section.
9. David McIlwain wrote science fiction under the name of Charles Eric Maine. He published his first short story under this pseudonym in his own fanzine in 1938 and began publishing novels in 1955 (Moskowitz 1972: 24–25; Clute and Nicholls 1993: 768). In 1958 he published a battle-of-the-sexes text, *World without Men* (a revised version, *Alph*, was published in 1972).
10. Such a genre now exists with titles like Anne Avery's *Hidden Heart* (1996). The back cover reads: "Heir to the Controllership of the planet Diloran, Tarl is saved by a ravishing stranger with plans to save her people." There is even a subgenre of time travel romance with titles like *The Pleasure Master* by Nina Bangs (2001): "Stranded by the side of a New York Highway, hairdresser Kathy Bartlett was of the opinion that men and cars had a lot in common: great form, no function, and they both overheated at the wrong time. When she wished herself somewhere warm and peaceful with a subservient male at her side she found herself transported all right, but to Scotland in 1542 with the last man she would have chosen: He was the Pleasure Master."
11. This is the same outrage, the same "rape," that Charles Platt discusses in his article "The Rape of Science Fiction" (1989), which I consider in the next chapter.
12. In the American context there is the added resonance that Jim Crow was a derogatory term for African American men (Wentworth and Flexner 1960: 291–92).
13. His first published story, "Marooned off Vesta," appeared in the March 1939 issue of *Amazing*.
14. Richardson published science fiction under the name Philip Latham. He wrote popularizations of science under his own name.
15. The original version had been published in the *Saturday Review* on 28 May 1955.
16. C. S. Lewis wrote a short story, "Ministering Angels," in response to Dr. Richardson's article. In it an exploratory mission has been sent to Mars, all-male, of course. After six months two women arrive on a space ship that the exploratory party had thought was the next crew sent early to relieve them. The women are volunteers for "the first unit of the Woman's Higher Aphrodiso-Therapeutic Humane Organisation (abbreviated WHAT-HO)" which was set up to relieve the sexual tension that the men on Mars must be experiencing (Lewis [1955] 1966: 111). One of the women is a prostitute who hasn't got "the slightest chance of being picked up in the cheapest quarter of Liverpool or Los Angeles," and the other is a "crank who believes all that blah about the new ethicality" (113). In another story, "Unbalanced Equations" by Paul A. Carter, published in the January 1956 issue of *F & SF* but written before Dr. Richardson's article appeared, the colony on Mars is the last remaining group of humans when the earth is destroyed. Sexual tension builds up but is eventually resolved when most of the unattached young women voluntarily become prostitutes who call themselves the Free Companions.
17. I briefly discuss Poul Anderson's *Virgin Planet* (1957) in chapter 3.
18. Without the Internet, and the networks of fans who use it, I would not have been

able to get access to *Notes*. I would like to thank Bruce Pelz for sending me copies from the United States.

CHAPTER 5: THE WOMEN MEN DON'T SEE

1. The story is so well known within the sf community that Connie Willis can refer to it in the title of her 1992 guest editorial for *Asimov's*, "The Women SF Doesn't See," without needing to explain the reference (more on the Willis editorial below).
2. The quotation comes from an unpublished summary by Tiptree. I would like to thank Julie Phillips, Tiptree's biographer, for giving me copies of Tiptree's summaries.
3. The title itself comes from"The Women Men Don't See": Ruth Parsons tells Fenton that "[w]hat women do is survive. We live by ones and twos in the chinks of your world-machine" (Tiptree [1973] 1990: 140).
4. This binary of "hard" and "soft"also plays itself out in the division between science fiction and fantasy, with fantasy being the soft and feminine to science fiction's hard masculinity.
5. Both were published for the first time in the collection *Aurora: Beyond Equality*, edited by Susan Janice Anderson and Vonda N. McIntyre.
6. *We Who Are About To* was first published in the January and February 1976 issues of *Galaxy* and was first published as a book in 1977.
7. "The Queen Bee" was first published in *Astounding Science Fiction* in December 1958.
8. There were five issues of Amanda Bankier's *The Witch and the Chameleon*. The first was dated August 1974 and the last appeared in 1976.
9. Judith Buckrich and Lucy Sussex edited the first anthology of Australian women's science fiction, *She's Fantastical* (1995).
10. The article first appeared in *The Red Clay Reader*, a feminist journal, in 1971 but was reprinted in the science fiction journal *Vertex* in 1974.
11. In discussions of women and science fiction, the role of editors—with the exception of Judith Merril—frequently gets forgotten. Two examples are Mary Gnaedinger (1898-1976), who edited all eighty-one issues of *Famous Fantastic Stories*, which was published from its September/October 1939 issue until June 1953; and Cele Goldsmith (born 1933), who edited *Amazing Stories* and *Fantastic* from December 1958 until June 1965, publishing the first stories of Ursula Le Guin, Thomas M. Disch, and Roger Zelazny (Clute and Nicholls 1993).
12. Joanna Russ's first story, "Nor Custom Stale," appeared in the September 1959 issue of the *Magazine of Fantasy and Science Fiction*. In "The Image of Women in Science Fiction" she writes that "[m]ost science fiction writers are men, but some are women, and there are more women writing the stuff than there used to be" (Russ [1971] 1974: 56). Russ is not claiming that there were no representations of women in science fiction, just that the representations that had been available are not satisfactory because they are mere "images."

13. Lefanu is one of the exceptions (Lefanu 1988: 5–7).
14. I briefly discussed one of these debates, which took place in *Notes from the Chemistry Department* in 1974–75, in chapter 4.
15. I discussed this letter in chapter 4. It was by Naomi Slimmer of Russell, Kansas, and appeared in the June 1939 issue of *Science Fiction*.
16. WisCon was the first feminist science fiction convention, inaugurated in 1977 and held annually in Madison, Wisconsin. The guests of honor in 1977 were the writer Katherine MacLean and the fan Amanda Bankier.
17. Indeed, Lefanu discusses Judith Merril, Katherine MacLean, Marion Zimmer Bradley, and C. L. Moore, all of whom were published before the 1960s (Lefanu 1988: 15–18). Lefanu's examples of women writing before the 1960s are the same as those in Pamela Sargent's 1974 collection *Women of Wonder*.
18. The APA (or apa) is the Amateur Press Association.
19. At the time Merwin was the editor of *Thrilling Wonder Stories, Startling Stories, Wonder Story Annual*, and *Fantastic Story Quarterly*. Merwin was also a writer and in 1953 he published a battle-of-the-sexes novel, *The White Widows* (it was republished in 1960 under the name *The Sex War*), which I considered in chapter 2.
20. Fowler and Murphy are the founding mothers of the James Tiptree Jr. Memorial Award.
21. This review first appeared in August 1962.
22. Of space opera, Russ writes: "*Space opera*—strange but true. Leigh Brackett is one example. Very rarely the protagonist turns out to be a sword-wielding, muscular aggressive *woman*—but the he-man ethos of the world does not change, nor do the stereotyped personalities assigned to the secondary roles, particularly the female ones" (Russ [1971] 1974: 56). Russ finds it peculiar that women would write such fiction. This view is also expressed in the blurb about Carol Emshwiller from *Future Magazine*, which declares approvingly that her stories "aren't attempts to swashbuckle so that readers will think she's a man" (*Future* [February 1958]: 5).
23. The story was first published in the July 1962 issue of the *Magazine of Fantasy and Science Fiction*.
24. Merril had earlier published stories in western, sports, and detective pulp magazines: as Judy Zissman: two stories in *Crack Detective* (1945 and 1946); as Eric Thorstein: seven stories in *Sports Leader, Western Action, Blue Ribbon Western, Double Action Western, Famous Western* (1947 and 1948); as Ernest Hamilton: ten stories in *Sports Short Stories, Cowboy, Sports Fiction* (1947 and 1948). According to Merril, western and sports magazines all required male bylines.
25. In that letter she answered some of my questions with sections of her memoir. Unfortunately, Merril died before it could be completed. Her granddaughter, Emily Pohl-Weary, has completed it under the title Merril chose, *Better to Have Loved*.
26. These are two novels that Bradley wrote in the 1950s that were "almost entirely concerned with women" (Bradley 1977: 35).

27. The story was first published in the July 1954 issue of *Fantastic Universe* under the pseudonym Idris Seabright. It has been anthologized many times since, most recently in Pamela Sargent's *Women of Wonder: The Classic Years* (1995).
28. The story was first published in the August 1956 issue of the *Magazine of Fantasy and Science Fiction*.

CHAPTER 6: I'M TOO BIG BUT I LOVE TO PLAY

1. I would like to thank Sylvia Kelso for pointing out Haraway's Tiptree story to me.
2. Thanks to Gordon Van Gelder and Julie Phillips for their help in getting me photocopies of some of Mary Hastings Bradley's travel books. I would especially like to thank Rachel Holmen, Laurel Winter, Jenna Felice, Debbie Notkin, and Freddie Baer for buying me a first edition of *Alice in Jungleland* at the Tiptree Auction at WisCon 24 in May 2000.
3. In correspondence Jeffrey Smith told me that my characterization of him as "slightly exasperated" at Tiptree's reticence was "not at all the case, but I can see how it comes across that way, and it made for a funny line. I laughed even though I knew it wasn't true. Tip had told me before we started that he couldn't give me solid biographical detail. I didn't care; I had never done anything like this before, and was thrilled that a writer was taking me seriously enough to participate. The question was just a way for him to give whatever he wanted. Believe me, I was way too happy to be exasperated. And as those responses came in, I was ecstatic. I had never read anything like those letters before, and I couldn't believe how lucky I was to be able to publish something like that. (And many people didn't read it because it was "too long.") No idea at that time how important Tip was going to be in my life after that" (letter to author, 11 February 2001).
4. This article first appeared in *Khatru* as "Everything but the Signature Is Me."
5. In correspondence Julie Phillips notes that Raccoona's mention of her own abortion in this letter is one of the few really substantial bodily facts about Alice Sheldon that she gave to Raccoona, as most of them had already gone to Tiptree.
6. Tiptree explains that Clarke wrote an "unpleasantly patronizing reply to Joanna Russ in the SFWA (Science Fiction Writers of America) Forum. She had tried carefully to explain to him why his 'joke' about women-should-be-excluded-from-space-because-in-zero-gee-their-breasts-bobble-distractingly-to-the-men was not a joke and contained characteristically deep bias. My 'jiggling nuts' line was a regretfully abbreviated reference to the point someone else made more fully, that it would be as logical to exclude males because their genitals would wave about quite as distractingly to women" (quoted in Smith 1975: 122).
7. Neither Julie Phillips nor I have been able to find this letter.
8. The interview is listed as being with James Tiptree Jr. not Alice Sheldon. The interview for *Contemporary Authors* is listed as being with Alice Sheldon.
9. I would like to thank Julie Phillips for her invaluable assistance and comments on this chapter.

CHAPTER 7: HER SMOKE ROSE UP FOREVER

1. At WisCon 20 in May 1996 the T-shirts were sold out within the hour. I was on a panel as the sale was under way and had to beg a friend to buy a fifth annual Tiptree Award T-shirt for me.
2. The Lambda, mentioned at the start of the quotation, is an award for the best gay and lesbian literature. It includes a science fiction category.
3. Though as I demonstrated in the previous chapter, that is by no means a straightforward proposition.
4. For a full list of the Tiptree Award winners, shortlist, and long list, see >www.tiptree.org<.
5. Scott's *Shadow Man* (1995) was not shortlisted for the 1995 Tiptree but was part of a separate list of "Other Works of Note." On the Web site the book is now listed as part of the long list.
6. I am indebted to Judith Barbour for drawing my attention to the similarity of the figure Hermes to that of Tiptree.

GLOSSARY

APA
  Amateur Press Association

ArmadilloCon
  The regional science fiction convention of Texas. It is held annually in Austin, Texas, and has a reputation for being a sercon that attracts many pros. It also has a dance.

BNF
  Big-name fan. A well-known fan who is very active in fandom.

Fan
  An active participant in science fiction fandom. The definition of what constitutes "active participation" is varied. Some activities that would be considered fan activities are attending science fiction conventions, reading and discussing science fiction, collecting science fiction, running conventions, and publishing and contributing to fanzines. Many definitions distinguish fans from "mere" readers.

Fandom
  The field in which fan activities take place. Fandom is made up of fans and their productions, such as fanzines and conventions.

Fanzine
  An amateur magazine put together by fans.

Filksinging
  The singing of science fiction songs. These songs are usually sung to well-known tunes with lyrics about fandom or science fiction stories or the like. The name is said to originate from a misprint on a convention program for "folksinging."

Hugo Award
  One of the amateur or fan awards for science fiction, officially called the Science Fiction Achievement awards but known everywhere as the Hugos, that are given in honour of Hugo Gernsback. Hugos have been awarded every year at the World Science Fiction Convention since 1955. Along with the Nebula Award, the Hugo is the best known and most prestigious of the science fiction awards. The categories have fluctuated but, since 1973, like the Nebula, there have been four categories for fiction: best novel (over 40,000 words), best novella (17,500-40,000 words), best novelette (7,500–17,500), and best short story (under 7,500 words).

Unlike the Nebula, the Hugo also includes awards for fan activities: best fanzine, best fan writer, best fan artist, and since 1984, best semiprozine. This last award was introduced to accommodate the increasing number of publications that are somewhere in between professional magazine and fanzine.

James Tiptree Jr. Memorial Award

An annual award given to the best science fiction or fantasy text or texts that explore and expand gender roles. The Tiptree Award was named in memory of James Tiptree Jr., the nom de plume of an author who began publishing remarkably gender-bending science fiction in 1968. Tiptree was identified in 1977 as the retired clinical psychologist Alice Sheldon.

Media fandom

Fandom devoted to television and film. Media fandom began with *Star Trek* fandom.

Mundane

Not science-fictional. For example, mundane fiction is all fiction other than science fiction.

Nebula Award

An annual science fiction award that has been presented by the Science Fiction and Fantasy Writers of America since 1966. There are four awards: best novel (over 40,000 words), best novella (17,500-40,000 words), best novelette (7,500–17,500), and best short story (under 7,500 words).

Pro

Someone professionally engaged with the field of science fiction.

Prozine

A professional science fiction magazine.

Pulps

Popular fiction magazines printed on poor-quality, coarse paper, usually measuring about 25cm x 18cm. The first pulp was *Argosy*, which published a variety of fiction. There were adventure and western pulps, as well as crime pulp magazines such as *Black Mask*, where Raymond Chandler and Dashiell Hammett were regularly published. Science fiction pulps included *Astounding Science Fiction* and *Thrilling Wonder Stories*. The term is also used more broadly to refer to the quality of the fiction published.

Sercon

A convention devoted to serious discussion of (mostly) written science fiction. Sercons tend not to have masquerades or pay much attention to media fandom. They don't ban fun, however.

WisCon

The regional science fiction convention of Wisconsin, held since 1977 in Madison, Wisconsin. It is also the only science fiction convention primarily devoted to feminist science fiction. The James Tiptree Jr. Memorial Award was first announced at WisCon and has been presented there on several occasions.

WorldCon

The biggest science fiction convention, held annually in September. Cities bid to be able to hold it. Although it has mostly been hosted by cities in the United States, it has also been held in Australia, Canada, Germany, Holland, and the United Kingdom. The Hugo Awards are presented at WorldCon.

World Fantasy Con

The annual fantasy convention. Like the WorldCon the World Fantasy Convention is held in a different city each year. It tends to attract a large number of pros and is generally considered to be a business convention with a relatively low number of fans.

BIBLIOGRAPHY

Alcott, Linda. 1988. "Cultural Feminism versus Post-Structuralism: The Identity Crisis in Feminist Theory." *Signs* 13, no. 3 (spring): 405–36.

Aldiss, Brian. 1973. *Billion Year Spree*. London: Weidenfield and Nicolson.

———. 1977–78. "The SF State." *Algol* 15, no. 1 (winter): 43–44.

Aldiss, Brian, and Harry Harrison, eds. 1975. *Hell's Cartographers: Some Personal Histories of Science Fiction Writers*. London: Weidenfield and Nicolson.

Aldiss, Brian, and David Wingrove. 1988. *Trillion Year Spree: The History of Science Fiction*. London: Paladin Books.

"Alice Sheldon (James Tiptree, Jr.) Kills Husband, Then Herself in Suicide Pact." 1987. *S.F. Chronicle* (July): 6.

Allen, Virginia, and Terri Paul. 1986. "Science and Fiction: Ways of Theorizing about Women." In *Erotic Universe: Sexuality and Fantastic Literature*, ed. Donald Palumbo, 165–83. New York: Greenwood.

Amis, Kingsley. 1960. *New Maps of Hell*. New York: Ballantine Books.

Ammons, Helen. 1929. Letter to editor. *Science Wonder Stories* 1, no. 6 (Nov.): 567.

Anderson, Carl H. 1941. Letter to editor. *Astounding Science Fiction* 26, no. 6 (Feb.): 156–57.

Anderson, Linda. 1990. *Plotting Change: Contemporary Women's Fiction*. London: Edward Arnold.

Anderson, Poul. 1956. "Nice Girls on Mars." *Magazine of Fantasy and Science Fiction* 10, no. 5 (May): 47–52.

———. [1957] 1973. *Virgin Planet*. New York: Warner .

———. 1974. "Reply to a Lady." *Vertex* 2, no. 2 (June): 8, 99.

———. 1975. Letter to editor. *The Witch and the Chameleon*, no. 4: 29.

———. 1978. "Poul Anderson Talar on Science Fiction." *Algol* 15, no. 3 (summer–fall): 11–19.

Anderson, Susan Janice, and Vonda M. McIntyre, eds. 1976. *Aurora: Beyond Equality*. Greenwich, Conn.: Fawcett.

———. 1976. "Introduction." In *Aurora: Beyond Equality*, 11–15. Greenwich, Conn.: Fawcett.

Ang, Ien. 1995. "I'm a Feminist but . . . : 'Other' Women and Postnational Feminism." In *Transitions: New Australian Feminisms*, ed. Barbara Caine and Rosemary Pringle, 57–73. London: Allen and Unwin.

Annas, Pamela J. 1978. "New Worlds, New Words: Androgyny in Feminist Science Fiction." *Science-Fiction Studies* 5, no. 2 (July): 143–56.

Arbur, Rosemarie. 1993. "Flight of Fancy: When the 'Better Half' Wins." In *Fights of Fancy: Armed Conflict in Science Fiction and Fantasy*, ed. George Slusser and Eric S. Rabkin, 79–91. Athens: University of Georgia Press.

Armitt, Lucie, ed. 1991. *Where No Man Has Gone Before: Women and Science Fiction*. New York: Routledge.

Ashley, Michael. 1974. *The History of the Science Fiction Magazine*. Part 1: 1926–1935. East Kilbride, Scotland: New English Library.

———. 1975. *The History of the Science Fiction Magazine*. Part 2: 1936–1945. East Kilbride, Scotland: New English Library.

———. 1976. *The History of the Science Fiction Magazine*. Part 3: 1946–1955. East Kilbride, Scotland: New English Library.

———. 1978. *The History of the Science Fiction Magazine*. Part 4: 1956–1965. East Kilbride, Scotland: New English Library.

Asimov, Isaac. 1938a. Letter to editor. *Astounding Science Fiction* 21, no. 5 (July): 158.

———. 1938b. Letter to editor. *Astounding Science Fiction* 22, no. 1 (Sept.): 160–61.

———. 1939a. Letter to editor. *Astounding Science Fiction* 22, no. 5 (Feb.): 159–60.

———. 1939b. Letter to editor. *Astounding Science Fiction* 23, no. 5 (July): 107.

———. 1939c. Letter to editor. *Startling Stories* 2, no. 3 (Nov.): 115.

———. 1982. "The Feminization of Sci-Fi." *Vogue* (Oct.): 555, 608.

Atheling, William Jr. [1964] 1974. *The Issue at Hand*. Chicago: Advent Publishers.

———. 1970. *More Issues at Hand*. Chicago: Advent Publishers.

Attebery, Brian. 1992. *Strategies of Fantasy*. Bloomington: Indiana University Press.

Aylesworth, George. 1939. Letter to editor. *Marvel Science Stories* 1, no. 5 (Aug.): 110.

Ayre, Thornton (John Russell Fearn). 1939. "World without Women." *Amazing Stories* 13, no. 4 (Apr.): 6–31.

Bacon-Smith, Camille. 1992. *Enterprising Women: Television Fandom and the Creation of Popular Myth*. Philadelphia: University of Pennsylvania Press.

———. 2000. *Science Fiction Culture*. Philadelphia, University of Pennsylvania Press.

Badami, Mary Kenny. 1976. "A Feminist Critique of Science Fiction." *Extrapolation* 18, no. 1 (Dec.): 6–19.

Bailey, J. O. [1947] 1972. *Pilgrims through Space and Time*. Westport, Conn.: Greenwood Press.

Bainbridge, William Sims. 1986. *Dimensions of Science Fiction*. Cambridge, Mass.: Harvard University Press.

Bammer, Angelika. 1991. *Partial Visions: Feminism and Utopianism in the 1970s*. New York: Routledge.

Bangsund, John. 1974. *John W. Campbell: An Australian Tribute*. Canberra: Parergon Books.

Bankier, Jennifer. 1974. "Women in SF: Image and Reality: A Criticism." *The Witch and the Chameleon* 2 (Nov.): 10–14.

Barr, Marleen, ed. 1981. *Future Females: A Critical Anthology*. Bowling Green, Ohio: Bowling Green State University Popular Press.

———. 1985. "Science Fiction's Invisible Female Man: Feminism, Formula, Word and World in 'When It Changed' and 'The Women Men Don't See.'" In *Just the Other Day: Essays on the Suture of the Future*, ed. Luk de Vos. Antwerp: EXA.

———. 1987. *Alien to Femininity: Speculative Fiction and Feminist Theory*. Westport, Conn.: Greenwood Press.

———. 1992. *Feminist Fabulation: Space/Postmodern Fiction*. Iowa City: University of Iowa Press.

———, ed. 2000. *Future Females, the Next Generation : New Voices and Velocities in Feminist Science Fiction Criticism*. Lanham, Md.: Rowman and Littlefield.

———. 2000. *Genre Fission : A New Discourse Practice for Cultural Studies*. Iowa City: University of Iowa Press.

Barr, Marleen, and Patrick Murphy, eds. 1987. "Feminism Faces the Fantastic." *Women's Studies: An Interdisciplinary Journal* 14, no. 2: 81–194.

Barr, Marleen, and Nicholas Smith, eds. 1983. *Women and Utopia: Critical Interpretations*. Lanham, Md.: University Press of America.

Barron, Neil, ed. 1990. *Fantasy Literature: A Reader's Guide*. New York: Garland Publishing.

Bartkowski, Frances. 1989. *Feminist Utopias*. Lincoln: University of Nebraska Press.

Battersby, Christine. 1989. *Gender and Genius: Towards a Feminist Aesthetics*. Bloomington: Indiana University Press.

Beal, Frances M. 1986. "Black Women and the Science Fiction Genre: Interview with Octavia Butler." *Black Scholar* 17, no. 2 (Mar.): 14–18.

Beisiegel, Winifred. 1952. Letter to editor. *Startling Stories* 26, no. 1 (May): 132.

Benford, Gregory. 1978 "The Time-Worn Path: Building SF." *Algol* 15, no. 3 (summer–fall): 31–32.

———. 1982–83. "Aliens and Knowability: A Scientist's Perspective." *Algol/Starship* 19, no. 1 (winter–spring): 25–27.

Bester, Alfred. 1961. "Review of *Venus Plus X*." *The Magazine of Fantasy and Science Fiction* 20, no. 1 (Jan.): 95–96.

Bleiler, Everett. 1983. *The Guide to Supernatural Fiction*. Kent, Ohio: Kent State University Press.

———. 1990. *Science Fiction: The Early Years*. Kent, Ohio: Kent State University Press.

Bloch, R. Howard. 1991. *Medieval Misogyny and the Invention of Western Romantic Love*. Chicago: University of Chicago Press.

Bloch, Robert. 1981. "An Open Letter to C. L. Moore." In *Denvention Two Program Book*, ed. Phil Normond, 7–8. Denver: Denvention Two—39th World SF Convention.

Bond, Nelson S. [1939] 1972. "The Priestess Who Rebelled." In *When Women Rule*, ed. Sam Moskowitz, 198–221. New York: Walker.

———. 1940. "Judging of the Priestess." *Fantastic Adventures* 2, no. 4 (Apr.): 42–59.

———. 1941. "Magic City." *Astounding Science Fiction* 26, no. 6 (Feb.): 9–36.

Bonner, Frances. 1992. "Towards a Better Way of Being: Feminist Science Fiction."

In *Imagining Women: Cultural Representations and Gender*, ed. Frances Bonner, Lizbeth Goodman, et al., 94–102. Cambridge: Polity Press, in association with the Open University.

Borger, John. 1968. Letter to editor. *If* 18, no. 1 (Jan.): 161–62.

Boulter, Amanda. 1995. "Alice James Raccoona Tiptree Sheldon Jr: Textual Personas in the Short Fiction of Alice Sheldon." *Foundation* 63 (spring): 5–31.

Boyd, John. [1970] 1971. *Sex and the High Command*. New York: Bantam Books.

Bradbury, Ray Douglas. 1939a. Letter to editor. *Astounding Science Fiction* 23, no. 2 (Apr.): 159.

———. 1939b. Letter to editor. *Astounding Science Fiction* 24, no. 4 (Dec.) : 101–2.

"Bradley, Herbert Edwin." 1942. *Who's Who in America: 1942–43*. Vol. 22, 374. Chicago: A. N. Marquis.

"Bradley, Mary Hastings." 1942. *Who's Who in America: 1942–43*. Vol. 22, 374. Chicago: A. N. Marquis.

Bradley, Mary Hastings. 1922. *On the Gorilla Trail*. New York: D. Appleton

———. 1926. *Caravans and Cannibals*. New York: D. Appleton.

———. 1927. *Alice in Jungleland*. New York: D. Appleton.

———. 1929a. *Alice in Elephantland*. New York: D. Appleton.

———. 1929b. *Trailing the Tiger*. New York: D. Appleton.

Bradley, Marion Zimmer. 1952. Letter to editor. *Thrilling Wonder Stories* 41, no. 2 (Dec.): 130–31.

———. 1977. "An Evolution of Consciousness: Twenty-Five Years of Writing about Women in Science Fiction." *Science Fiction Review* 22 (Aug.): 34–45.

———. 1977–78. "My Trip through Science Fiction." *Algol* 15, no. 1 (winter): 10–20.

Branford, Jean. 1987. *A Dictionary of South African English*. 3d ed. Cape Town: Oxford University Press.

Broderick, Damien. 1995. *Reading by Starlight: Postmodern Science Fiction*. London: Routledge.

Broderick, Damien, and Joanna Russ. 1977. "The Broderick-Russ Correspondence." *Australian Science Fiction Review* (May): 9–18.

Brooke Rose, Christine. [1981] 1983. *A Rhetoric of the Unreal*. Cambridge: Cambridge University Press.

Brown, C. N. 1987. "James Tiptree, Jr. Dead." *Locus* (July): 62.

Brown, Earl B. 1927. Letter to editor. *Amazing Stories* 1, no. 11 (Feb.): 1078.

Brown, Peter. 1988. *The Body and Society: Men, Women and Sexual Renunciation in Early Christianity*. London: Faber and Faber.

Brudy, Bill. 1939. Letter to editor. *Marvel Science Stories* 1, no. 5 (Aug.): 108–9.

Burdekin, Katherine. [1934] 1993. *Proud Man*. New York: Feminist Press.

———. [1937] 1940. *Swastika Night*. London: Victor Gollancz.

Burroughs, Edgar Rice. [1912] 1990. *Tarzan of the Apes*. New York: Del Rey.

Butler, Bradford, 1927. Letter to editor. *Amazing Stories* 1, no. 11 (Feb.): 1077.

Butler, Judith. 1989. "Gendering the Body: Beauvoir's Philosophical Contribution."

In *Women, Knowledge, and Reality: Explorations in Feminist Philosophy*, ed. Ann Garry and Marilyn Pearsall, 253–62. London: Unwin Hyman.

———. 1992. "Sexual Inversions." In *Discourses of Sexuality*, ed. Donna C. Stanton, 344–61. Ann Arbor: University of Michigan Press.

Byers, Mary. 1938. Letter to editor. *Astounding Science Fiction* 22, no. 4 (Dec.) : 160–61.

Cameron, Deborah. 1992. *Feminism and Linguistic Theory*. 2d ed. New York: St. Martin's.

Campbell, John. 1941. Editorial comment. *Astounding Science Fiction* 26, no. 6 (Feb.): 67.

Carr, Helen, ed. 1989. *From My Guy to Sci-Fi: Genre and Women's Writing in the Postmodern World*. London: Pandora.

Carr, Terry. 1975. "Guest Editorial: You've Come A Long Way, Baby." *Amazing* 49, no. 3 (Nov.): 4–5, 122–25.

Carter, Paul A. 1956. "Unbalanced Equation." *Magazine of Fantasy and Science Fiction* 10, no. 1 (Jan.): 105–21.

———. 1977. *The Creation of Tomorrow: 50 Years of Magazine Science Fiction*. New York: Columbia University Press.

Carter, Raphael. 1998. "Congenital Agenesis of Gender Ideation." In *Starlight 2*, ed. Patrick Nielsen Hayden, 91 106. New York: Tor Books.

Catoe, Evelyn. 1952. Letter to editor. *Thrilling Wonder Stories* 40, no. 1 (Apr.): 132.

Chandler, A. Bertram. 1968. *False Fatherland*. London: Horwitz.

Charnas, Suzy McKee. 1974. *Walk to the End of the World*. New York: Ballantine Books.

———. 1978. *Motherlines*. New York: Berkeley.

———. 1993. "A Labor of Love." *Women's Review of Books* 9, no. 2 (Nov.): 19–20.

———. 1999. *The Conqueror's Child*. New York: Tor Books.

Chavey, Darrah. 1984a. "Evangeline Walton: Interpreter of Myths." *Aurora* 9, no. 1 (summer): 33–35.

———. 1984b. "A Bibliography of Evangeline Walton." *Aurora* 9, no. 1 (summer): 35.

Christian-Smith, Linda K. 1990. *Becoming a Woman through Romance*. London: Routledge.

Cioffi, Frank. 1982. *Formula Fiction? An Anatomy of American Science Fiction, 1930–1940*. Westport, Conn.: Greenwood Press.

Cline, Cheryl. 1984 "The Doul of Lilith: 19th Century Fiction by Women." *Aurora* 9, no. 1 (summer): 26–29.

Clover, Carol J. 1992. *Men, Women and Chainsaws: Gender in the Modern Horror Film*. Princeton: Princeton University Press.

Clute, John, and Peter Nicholls, eds. 1993. *The Encyclopedia of Science Fiction*. London: Orbit.

Coffin, Thomas. 1928. Letter to editor. *Amazing Stories* 3, no. 4 (July): 373.

Coney, Michael G. 1976. "Whatever Happened to Fay Wray?" *Science Fiction Review* 16 (Feb.): 39–41.

Cook, Diane. 1985. "Yes, Virginia, There's Always Been Women's Science Fiction . . . Feminist, Even." In *Contrary Modes: Proceedings of the World Science Fiction Conference, Melbourne, Australia, 1985*, ed. J. Blackford, R. Blackford, Lucy Sussex, and Norman Talbot, 133–45. Melbourne: Ebony Books, in association with the Department of English, University of Newcastle.

Cooke, David C. 1939. "Women's World." *Science Fiction* 1, no. 5 (Dec.): 78–86.

Cooper, Edmund. [1968] 1969. *Five to Twelve*. London: Hodder Paperbacks.

———. [1972] 1974. *Who Needs Men?* London: Coronet SF.

Cooper, Parley J. 1971. *The Feminists*. New York: Pinnacle Books.

Coppel, Alfred. 1969. "For Sacred San Francisco." *If* 19, no. 9 (Nov.): 73–84.

Cortiel, Jeanne. 1999. *Demand My Writing: Joanna Russ, Feminism, Science Fiction*. Liverpool Science Fiction Texts and Studies 11. Liverpool: Liverpool University Press.

Cotts, S. E. 1961. "Review of *Venus Plus X*." *Amazing Stories* 35, no. 1 (Jan.): 135–36.

Coulson, Robert "Buck". 1958. Letter to editor. *Future* no. 38 (Aug.): 126–28.

———. 1986–87. Letter to editor. *Aurora* 10, no. 1 (winter): 5.

Counsil, Wendy. 1990. "The State of Feminism in Science Fiction: An Interview with Karen Joy Fowler, Lisa Goldstein and Pat Murphy." *Science Fiction Eye* 7 (Aug.): 21–31.

Cox, Marian. 1952. Letter to editor. *Thrilling Wonder Stories* 40, no. 3 (Aug.): 127.

Cranny-Francis, Anne. 1990. *Feminist Fiction: Feminist Uses of Generic Fiction*. Cambridge: Polity Press.

Daemon, Shira. 1996. "Review of N. Lee Wood's *Looking for the Madhi*." *Locus* (Jan.): 31.

D'Ammassa, Don. 1984a. "A Bibliography of Lee Killough." *Aurora* 9, no. 1 (summer): 36.

———. 1984b. "Appreciating Lee Killough." *Aurora* 9, no. 1 (summer): 15–16.

Davidson, Avram. 1973. "Books." *Magazine of Fantasy and Science Fiction* 44, no. 4 (Apr.): 33–38.

Davies, Bronwyn, and Rom Harre. 1990. "Positioning: The Discursive Production of Selves." *Journal of the Theory of Social Behaviour* 20, no. 1: 43–63.

Davis, Natalie Zemon. 1975. "Women on Top." In *Society and Culture in Early Modern France: Eight Essays by Natalie Zemon Davis*, 124–51. Stanford: Stanford University Press.

Day, Bradford M. 1953. *An Index of the Weird and Fantastical in Magazines*. New York: Bradford M. Day.

Day, Donald B. 1952. *Index to the Science Fiction Magazines, 1926–1950*. Portland, Ore.: Perri Press.

Day, Phyllis J. 1982. "Earthmother/Witchmother: Feminism and Ecology Renewed." *Extrapolation* 23, no. 1 (spring): 12–21.

de Beauvoir, Simone. [1949] 1972. *The Second Sex*. London: Penguin Books.
de Camp, L. Sprague. 1951. *Rogue Queen*. New York: Dell.
de Certeau, Michel. 1988. *The Practice of Everyday Life*. Berkeley: University of California Press.
DeFord, Miriam Allen. 1956. "News for Dr Richardson." *Magazine of Fantasy and Science Fiction* 10, no. 5 (May): 53–57.
———. [1968] 1969. "The Superior Sex." *Xenogenesis*. New York: Ballantine Books.
De Hart, H. O. 1928. Letter to editor. *Amazing Stories* 3, no. 3 (June): 277.
Delany, Samuel R. [1977] 1978. *The Jewel-Hinged Jaw*. New York: Berkeley
———. 1978. *The American Shore*. Elizabethtown, N.Y.: Dragon Press..
———. 1984a. "Science Fiction and 'Literature'—or, the Conscience of the King." In *Starboard Wine: More Notes on the Language of Science Fiction*, 81–100. Pleasantville, N.Y.: Dragon Press.
———. 1984b. *Starboard Wine: More Notes on the Language of Science Fiction*. Pleasantville, N.Y.: Dragon Press.
———. 1989. *The Straits of Messina*. Seattle: Serconia Press.
———. 1994. *Silent Interviews: On Language, Race, Sex, Science Fiction, and Some Comics*. Hanover, N.H.: Wesleyan University Press.
Delap, Richard. 1975. "Review of *The New Atlantis and Other Novellas of Science Fiction*, edited by Robert Silverberg." *Delap's F & SF Review* (July): 7–8.
del Rey, Lester. 1938. "Helen O'Loy." *Astounding* 22, no. 4 (Dec.): 118–25.
———. 1975. "The Reference Library: War of the Sexes." *Analog* 95, no. 6 (June): 166–70.
———. 1979. *The World of Science Fiction, 1926–1976: The History of a Subculture*. New York: Ballantine.
de Saussure, Ferdinand. 1993. *Course in General Linguistics*. London: Duckworth.
de Voragine, Jacobus. 1993. *The Golden Legend*. Vols. 1–3. Princeton: Princeton University Press.
DeVoto, Bernard. 1939. "Doom beyond Jupiter." *Harper's Magazine* 179 (Sept.): 445–48.
Dick, Philip K. 1974. "An Open Letter from Philip K. Dick." *Vertex* 2, no. 4 (Oct.): 99.
Dickinson, H. O. 1935. "The Sex Serum." *Wonder Stories* 7, no. 5 (Oct.): 589–601, 625.
Dinesen, Isak. [1975] 1987. "Second Meeting." In *Carnival: Entertainments and Posthumous Tales*.London: Grafton Books: 305-315.
Disch, Thomas M. 1976. "The Embarrassments of Science Fiction." In *Science Fiction at Large*, ed. Peter Nicholls. London: Victor Gollancz.
Dixon, R. M. W. 1994. *Ergativity*. Cambridge: Cambridge University Press.
Docker, John. 1994. *Postmodernism and Popular Culture: A Cultural History*. Cambridge: Cambridge University Press.
Donawerth, Jane L., and Carol A.Kolmerten, eds. 1994. *Utopian and Science Fiction by Women: Worlds of Difference*. Syracuse: Syracuse University Press.

Donawerth, Jane. 1997. *Frankenstein's Daughters: Women Writing Science Fiction*. Syracuse: Syracuse University Press.

Dozois, Gardner. 1987. "Tiptree Appreciation." *Locus* (July): 63–64.

Drussai, Garen. 1956. "Woman's Work." *Magazine of Fantasy and Science Fiction* 11, no. 2 (Aug.): 104–6.

Duchamp, L. Timmel. 1993. "Motherhood Etc." In *Full Spectrum 4*, ed. Lou Aronica et al. New York: Bantam Books: 6-37.

———. 2000. "Playing with the Big Boys: (Alternate) history in Karen Joy Fowler's 'Game Night at the Fox and Goose.'" *New York Review of Science Fiction* 12, no. 8 (Apr.): 1, 4–6.

Ebert, Robert. 1958. Letter to editor. *Future Science Fiction* 40 (Dec.) : 114–16.

Effinger, George Alec. 1971. "All the Last Wars at Once." In *Universe 1*, ed. Terry Carr, 231–49. New York: Ace.

Eggins, Suzanne. 1994. *An Introduction to Systemic Functional Linguistics*. London: Pinter.

Elam, Diane. 1992. *Romancing the Postmodern*. New York: Routledge.

Ellison, Harlan. 1952. Letter to editor. *Thrilling Wonder Stories* 40, no. 2 (June): 134–35.

———. 1957. "World of Women." *Fantastic* 6, no. 1 (Feb.): 30–54.

———. 1974. "Books." *The Magazine of Fantasy and Science Fiction* 46, no. 5 (May): 25–42.

Ellman, Mary. 1968. *Thinking about Women*. New York: Harcourt Brace Jovanovich.

Emrys, Barbara. 1984. "Charlotte Perkins Gilman: Speculative Feminism." *Aurora* 9, no. 1 (summer): 11–12.

Endacott, Sarah Camilla Helen. 1996. "Women and Science Fiction." *Eidolon* 20 (June): 36–51.

Epstein, Julia. 1990. "Either/Or—Neither/Both: Sexual Ambiguity and the Ideology of Gender." *Genders* 7 (Mar.): 99–141.

Evans, Patricia. Letter to editor. *Astounding Science Fiction* 22, no. 3 (Nov.): 157.

Fairclough, Norman. 1992. *Discourse and Social Change*. Cambridge: Polity Press.

"Fairfax Tax on Tiptree." 1980. *Locus* 13, no. 2 (Feb.): 5.

Farmer, Philip Jose. 1952. "The Lovers." *Startling Stories* 27, no. 1 (Aug.): 12–63.

Fausto-Sterling, Anne. 1985. *Myths of Gender*. New York: Basic Books

———. 1993. "The Five Sexes: Why Male and Female Are Not Enough." *The Sciences* 33, no. 2 (Mar.): 20–25.

Firestone, Shulamith. 1970. *The Dialectic of Sex: The Case for Feminist Revolution*. London: Women's Press.

Fitting, Peter. 1987. "A Guide to Reading Single-Sex Worlds." *Women's Studies Special Issue: Feminism Faces the Fantastic* 14, no. 2: 101–17.

Fletcher, Marilyn. 1981. *Science Fiction Story Index, 1950–1979*. Chicago: American Library Association,

Foucault, Michel. [1976] 1981. *The History of Sexuality* . Vol. 1: *An Introduction*. London: Penguin Books.

———. [1980] 1987. *Herculine Barbin: Being the Recently Discovered Memoir of a Nineteenth-Century French Hermaphrodite*. New York: Pantheon Books.

———. [1984] 1988. *The History of Sexuality*. Vol. 2: *The Use of Pleasure*. London: Penguin Books.

———. [1984] 1990. *The History of Sexuality*. Vol. 3: *The Care of the Self*. London: Penguin Books.

Fowler, Karen Joy. 1993. "Introduction." In *Her Smoke Rose Up from Supper*, 6–7. Madison, Wisc.: SF3.

———. 1996. "The Tiptree Award: A Personal History." *WisCon 20 Souvenir Book*, 109. Madison, Wisc.: SF3.

Frank, Janrae, Jean Stine, and Forrest J. Ackerman, eds. 1994. *New Eves: Extraordinary Fiction about the Extraordinary Women of Today and Tomorrow*. Stanford, Conn.: Longmeadow Press

Frazier, Robert. 1984a. "A Bibliography of Sonya Dorman." *Aurora* 9, no. 1 (summer): 36.

———. 1984b. "The Poet Dreams: Sonya Dorman." *Aurora* 9, no. 1 (summer): 19–20.

Friend, Beverly. 1972. "Virgin Territory: Women and Sex in Science Fiction." *Extrapolation* 14, no. 1 (Dec.): 49–58.

———. 1977. "Virgin Territory: The Bonds and Boundaries of Women in Science Fiction." In *Many Futures, Many Worlds: Theme and Form in Science Fiction*, ed. Thomas D. Clareson, 140–63. Kent, Ohio: Kent State University Press.

Frisch, Adam J. 1982. "Toward New Sexual Identities: James Tiptree, Jr." In *The Feminine Eye: Science Fiction and the Women Who Write It*, ed. Tom Staicar, 48–59. New York: Frederick Ungar.

Gallop, Jane. 1992. *Around 1981: Academic Feminist Literary Theory*. New York: Routledge.

Garber, Eric, and Lyn Paleo. 1990. *Uranian Worlds*. Boston: G. K. Hall.

Gardner, Thomas S. [1932] 1972. "The Last Woman." In *When Women Rule*, ed. Sam Moskowitz, 131–48. New York: Walker.

Garrett, Randall. 1958. "The Queen Bee." *Astounding* 62, no. 4 (Dec.): 70–96.

Gatens, Moira. [1983] 1996. "A Critique of the Sex/Gender Distinction." In *Imaginary Bodies: Ethics, Power and Corporeality*, 3–20. London: Routledge.

———. [1989] 1996. "Woman and Her Double(s): Sex, Gender and Ethics." In *Imaginary Bodies: Ethics, Power and Corporeality*, 29–45. London: Routledge.

———. 1996. *Imaginary Bodies: Ethics, Power and Corporeality*. London: Routledge.

Gearhart, Nancy S., and Jean W. Ross. 1983. "Alice Hastings Bradley Sheldon (Raccoona Sheldon; James Tiptree, Jr.)." In *Contemporary Authors*, vol. 108, 443–50. Detroit: Gale Research Company.

Gelula, Abner J. 1931. "Automaton." *Amazing Stories* 6, no. 8 (Nov.): 680–97, 705, 760.

Gernsback, Hugo. 1926a. "Editorial: A New Sort of Magazine." *Amazing Stories* 1, no. 1 (Apr.): 3.

———. 1926b. "Editorial: Thank You!" *Amazing Stories* 1, no. 2 (May): 99.
———. 1926c. "Editorial: The Lure of Scientifiction." *Amazing Stories* 1, no. 3 (June): 195.
———. 1926d. "Editorial: Fiction Versus Facts." *Amazing Stories* 1, no. 4 (July): 291.
———. 1926e. "Editorial: 'Impossible' Facts." *Amazing Stories* 1, no. 5 (Aug.): 387.
———. 1926f. "Editorial: Editorially Speaking." *Amazing Stories* 1, no. 6 (Sept.): 483.
———. 1926g. "Editorial: Imagination and Reality." *Amazing Stories* 1, no. 7 (Oct.): 579.
———. 1926h. "Editorial: Plausibility in Scientifiction." *Amazing Stories* 1, no. 8 (Nov.): 675.
———. 1926i. "Editorial: $500.00 Prize Story Contest." *Amazing Stories* 1, no. 9 (Dec.): 773.
———. 1927a. "Editorial: Incredible Facts." *Amazing Stories* 1, no. 10 (Jan.): 877.
———. 1927b. "Editorial: Interplanetary Travel." *Amazing Stories* 1, no. 11 (Feb.): 981.
———. 1927c. "Editorial: Idle Thoughts of a Busy Editor." *Amazing Stories* 1, no. 12 (Mar.): 1085.
———. 1927d. "Editorial: The Most Amazing Thing (In the Style of Edgar Allen Poe)." *Amazing Stories* 2, no. 1 (Apr.): 5.
———. 1927e. "Editorial: Amazing Creations." *Amazing Stories* 2, no. 2 (May): 109.
———. 1927f. "Editorial: The $500 Dollar Prize Contest." *Amazing Stories* 2, no. 3 (June): 213.
———. 1927g. "Editorial: Surprising Facts." *Amazing Stories* 2, no. 4 (July): 317.
———. 1927h. "Editorial: A Different Story." *Amazing Stories* 2, no. 5 (Aug.): 421.
———. 1927i. "Editorial: The Mystery of Time." *Amazing Stories* 2, no. 6 (Sept.): 525.
———. 1927j. "Editorial: Amazing Youth." *Amazing Stories* 2, no. 7 (Oct.): 625.
———. 1927k. "Editorial: Space Flying." *Amazing Stories* 2, no. 8 (Nov.): 725.
———. 1927l. "Editorial: Strange Facts." *Amazing Stories* 2, no. 9 (Dec.): 825.
———. 1927m. Editorial response to letter. *Amazing Stories* 1, no. 11 (Feb.): 1077.
———. 1928a. "Editorial: Our Unstable World." *Amazing Stories* 2, no. 10 (Jan.): 925.
———. 1928b. "Editorial: New Amazing Stories Quarterly." *Amazing Stories* 2, no. 11 (Feb.): 1025.
———. 1928c. "Editorial: Amazing Thinking." *Amazing Stories* 2, no. 12 (Mar.): 1125.
———. 1928d. "Editorial: $300 Prize Contest Wanted: A Symbol for Scientifiction." *Amazing Stories* 3, no. 1 (Apr.): 5.
———. 1928e. "Editorial: Facts Outfictioned." *Amazing Stories* 3, no. 2 (May): 101.
———. 1928f. "Editorial: Our Amazing Minds." *Amazing Stories* 3, no. 3 (June): 197.
———. 1928g. "Editorial: Our Amazing Senses." *Amazing Stories* 3, no. 4 (July): 293.
———. 1928h. "Editorial: The Amazing Unknown." *Amazing Stories* 3, no. 5 (Aug.): 389.

———. 1928i. "Editorial: Our Amazing Universe." *Amazing Stories* 3, no. 6 (Sept.): 485.
———. 1928j. "Editorial: New Amazing Facts." *Amazing Stories* 3, no. 7 (Oct.): 581.
———. 1928k. "Editorial: Amazing Life." *Amazing Stories* 3, no. 8 (Nov.): 677.
———. 1928l. "Editorial: An Amazing Phenomenon." *Amazing Stories* 3, no. 9 (Dec.): 773.
———. 1928m. Editorial response to letter. *Amazing Stories* 3, no. 3 (June): 277.
———. 1928n. Editorial response to letter. *Amazing Stories* 3, no. 7 (Oct.): 667
———. 1928o. Editorial response to letter. *Amazing Stories* 3, no. 4 (July): 373.
———. 1929a. "Editorial: Amazing Reading." *Amazing Stories* 3, no. 10 (Jan.): 871.
———. 1929b. "Editorial: Life, the Amazing Puzzle." *Amazing Stories* 3, no. 11 (Feb.): 967.
———. 1929c. "Editorial: Our Amazing Stars." *Amazing Stories* 3, no. 12 (Mar.): 1063.
———. 1929d. "Editorial: The Amazing Einstein." *Amazing Stories* 4, no. 1 (Apr.): 5.
———. 1929e. "Editorial: Science Wonder Stories." *Science Wonder Stories* 1, no. 1 (June): 5.
———. 1929f. Editorial response to letter. *Amazing Stories* 3, no. 12 (Mar.): 1140.
———. 1929g. Editorial response to letter. *Science Wonder Stories* 1, no. 5 (Oct.): 467.
———. 1925. *Ralph 124c 41+: A Romance of the Year 2660*. Boston, Mass.: Stratford.
——— 1930a. Editorial response to letter.. *Science Wonder Stories* 1, no. 8 (Jan.): 765.
———. 1930b. Editorial response to letter. *Science Wonder Stories* 1, no. 12 (May): 1143.
Gibson, Joe. 1953. Letter to editor. *Thrilling Wonder Stories* 42, no. 1 (Apr.): 144–45.
Goldhill, Stephen. 1995. *Foucault's Virginity*. Cambridge: Cambridge University Press.
Goldin, Stephen. 1987. "Tiptree Appreciation." *Locus* (July): 64.
Gomoll, Jeanne. 1986–87. "An Open Letter to Joanna Russ." *Aurora* 10, no. 1 (winter.): 7–10.
———. [1991] 1992. "Baking up a Storm." In *The Bakery Men Don't See*, 4–5. Madison, Wisc.: SF^3.
———. 1991. "Sisters." *Sisters* (May): 5–11.
———, ed. 1993. "Symposium: Women in Science Fiction." *Khatru 3 and 4*. Madison, Wisc. 2d ed. Corflu, SF^3.
Gordon, Joan. 1990. "Yin and Yang Duke It Out." *Science Fiction Eye* 2, no. 1 (Feb.): 37–40.
Grazer, Phyllis. 1953. Letter to editor. *Thrilling Wonder Stories* 42, no. 3 (Aug.): 142.
Green, Jen, and Sarah Lefanu, eds. 1985. *Despatches from the Frontiers of the Female Mind*. London: Women's Press.
Greenberg, Martin H., ed. 1981. *Fantastic Lives: Autobiographical Essays by Notable Science Fiction Writers*. Carbondale: Southern Illinois University Press.

Greenland, Colin, Gwyneth Jones, Sarah Lefanu, Brian Stableford, and Jenny Wolmark. 1988. "Foundation Forum: Feminism and SF." *Foundation* 43 (summer): 63–77.

Grosz, Elizabeth, and Elspeth Probyn. 1995. *Sexy Bodies:The Strange Carnalities of Feminism*. London: Routledge.

Groves, J. W. 1953. "Where Sex Met Space." *Planet Stories* 6, no. 2 (Sept.): 57–67.

Gubar, Susan. 1980. "C. L. Moore and the Conventions of Women's SF." *Science-Fiction Studies* 7, no. 1 (Mar.): 16–27.

Gunn, James E. [1952] 1955. "The Misogynist." In *The Galaxy Science Fiction Omnibus*, ed. H. L. Gold, 15–24. London: Grayson and Grayson.

Halliday, M. A. K. 1978. *Language as Social Semiotic*. London: Edward Arnold.

———. 1994. *An Introduction to Functional Grammar*. 2d ed. London: Edward Arnold.

Halliday, M. A. K., and Ruqaiya Hasan. 1976. *Cohesion in English*. London: Longman.

———. 1985. Language, Context, and Text: Aspects of Language in a Social-Semiotic Perspective. Deakin University, Australia: Deakin University Press.

Hamilton, Edmond. 1933. "The War of the Sexes." *Weird Tales* 22, no. 5 (Nov.): 551–70.

Hansen, Rob. 1987. *The Story So Far . . . A Brief History of British Fandom, 1931–1987*. Brighton, England: Worldcon, Conspiracy '87.

Haraway, Donna. 1989. *Primate Visions: Gender, Race, and Nature in the World of Modern Science*. New York: Routledge.

———. 1991. *Simians, Cyborgs and Women: The Reinvention of Nature*. London: Free Association Books.

Harris, John B. 1932. "The Venus Adventure." *Wonder Stories* 3, no. 12 (May): 1352–73, 1379.

Harrison, Harry, ed. [1972] 1976. *Nova 2*. London: Robert Hale.

Hartwell, David. [1984] 1985. *Age of Wonders*. New York: McGraw Hill.

———. 1987. "Tiptree Appreciation." *Locus* (July): 63.

Hausman, Bernice L. 1995. *Changing Sex: Transsexualism, Technology, and the Idea of Gender*. Durham, N.C.: Duke University Press.

Hayler, Barbara J. 1988. "The Feminist Fiction of James Tiptree, Jr.: Women and Men as Aliens." In *Spectrum of the Fantastic*, ed. Donald Palumbo, 127–32. Westport, Conn.: Greenwood Press.

Heldreth, Lillian M. 1982. "Love Is the Plan, The Plan Is Death: The Feminism and Fatalism of James Tiptree Jr." *Extrapolation* 23, no. 1 (spring): 22–30.

Henderson, Zenna. 1965a. *The Anything Box*. Garden City, N.Y.: Doubleday.

———. 1965b. "Subcommittee." In *The Anything Box*, 17–41. Garden City, N.Y.: Doubleday.

Henriques, Julian, Wendy Hollway, Cathy Urwin, Couze Venn, and Valerie Walkerdine, eds. 1984. *Changing the Subject*. London: Methuen.

Herdt, Gilbert. 1994. *Third Sex, Third Gender: Beyond Sexual Dimorphism in Culture and History*. New York: Zone Books.

Hird, M. J. 2000. "Gender's Nature: Intersexuality, Transsexualism and the 'Sex/Gender' binary." *Feminist Theory* 1, no. 3: 347–64.

Hollinger, Veronica. 1989. "'The Most Grisly Truth': Responses to the Human Condition in the Works of James Tiptree, Jr." *Extrapolation* 30, no. 2 (summer): 117–32.

———. 1990. "Feminist Science Fiction: Breaking Up the Subject." *Extrapolation* 31, no. 3 (fall): 229–39.

Hollway, Wendy. 1984. "Gender Difference and the Production of Subjectivity." In *Changing the Subject*, ed. Julian Henriques et al., 227–63. London: Methuen.

hooks, bell. 1984. *Feminist Theory: From Margin to Center*. Boston: South End Press.

Hornig, Charles. 1939. Editorial response to letter. *Science Fiction* 1, no. 2 (June): 121.

Howard, June. 1983. "Widening the Dialogue on Feminist Science Fiction." In *Feminist Re-Visions: What Has Been and Might Be*, ed. Vivian Patraka and Louise A. Tilly, 64–96. Ann Arbor: University of Michigan Press.

Hurter, Fred. 1939. Letter to editor. *Astounding Science Fiction* 23, no. 4 (June): 118.

Jackson Jr., Earl. 1995. *Strategies of Deviance: Studies in Gay Male Representation*. Bloomington: University of Indiana Press.

Jaggar, Alison. 1984. "Human Biology in Feminist Theory: Sexual Equality Reconsidered." In *Beyond Domination: New Perspectives on Women and Philosophy*, ed. Carol C. Gould, 21–42. Totowa, N.J.: Rowman and Allanheld.

Jagose, Annamarie. 1994. *Lesbian Utopics*. London: Routledge.

James, Edward. 1994. *Science Fiction in the 20th Century*. Oxford: Oxford University Press.

"James Tiptree, Jr. Rebounds." 1985. *Locus* (Sept.): 4, 54.

Jarvis, Charles M. 1939. Letter to editor. *Astounding Science Fiction* 23, no. 2 (Apr.): 160–61.

Jarvis, Sharon, ed. 1985. *Inside Outer Space: Science Fiction Professionals Look at Their Craft*. New York: Frederik Ungar.

Jenkins, Henry. 1992. *Textual Poachers: Television Fans and Participatory Culture*. London: Routledge.

Jensen, L. M. 1939. Letter to editor. *Astounding Science Fiction* 22, no. 5 (Jan.): 161–62.

Johnson, Charles. 1939. Letter to editor. *Astounding Science Fiction* 22, no. 5 (Feb.): 160.

Johnson, Lovina S. 1929. Letter to editor. *Amazing Stories* 3, no. 12 (March): 1140.

Jonas, Gerald. 1975. "Review of *Warm Worlds and Otherwise*." *New York Times Book Review*, 23 Mar., 30–32.

Jones, Ann Rosalind, and Peter Stallybrass. 1991. "Fetishizing Gender: Constructing the Hermaphrodite in Renaissance Europe." In *Body Guards: The Cultural Politics of Gender Ambiguity*, ed. Julia Epstein and Kristina Straub, 80–111. London: Routledge.

Jones, Gwyneth. 1987. "Futuristic Gloveleather Blouson: SF and the New Man." *Vector* 139 (Aug.): 11–12.

———. 1988. "Essay Review of *In the Chinks of the World Machine*." *Foundation* 43 (summer): 59–63.

———. 1991. *White Queen*. London: VGSF.

Joywater, Hegory. 1930. Letter to editor. *Science Wonder Stories* 1, no. 12 (May): 1142–43.

Kadrey, Richard, and Larry McCaffrey. [1991] 1992. "Cyberpunk 101: A Schematic Guide to *Storming the Reality Studio*." In *Storming the Reality Studio*, ed. Larry McCaffrey, 17–29. Durham, N.C.: Duke University Press.

Kaveney, Roz. 1989. "The Science Fictiveness of Women's Science Fiction." In *From My Guy to Sci-Fi: Genre and Women's Writing in the Postmodern World*, ed. Helen Carr, 78–97. London: Pandora.

Kaye, Peggy. 1952. Letter to editor. *Startling Stories* 26, no. 3 (July): 130.

Keller, David H. 1928. "The Little Husbands." *Weird Tales* 12, no. 1 (July): 126–30.

———. [1929] 1972. "The Feminine Metamorphosis." In *When Women Rule*, ed. Sam Moskowitz, 149–97. New York: Walker.

Kelso, Sylvia. 2000. "Third Person Peculiar: Reading between Academic and SF-Community Positions in (Feminist) SF." *Femspec: An Interdisciplinary Feminist Journal* 2, no. 1: 74–82.

Kendall, Zillah. 1953. Letter to editor. *Thrilling Wonder Stories* 41, no. 3 (Feb.): 132–33.

Kessler, Suzanne J. 1990. "The Medical Construction of Gender: Case Management of Intersexed Infants." *Signs* 16, no. 1 (summer): 3–26.

King, Betty. 1984. *Women of the Future: The Female Main Character in Science Fiction*. Metuchen, N.J.: Scarecrow Press.

King, Katie. 1994. *Theory in Its Feminist Travels: Conversations in U.S. Women's Movements*. Bloomington: Indiana University Press.

King, Ray (Ray Cummings). 1939. "Lust Rides the Roller Coaster." *Marvel Science Stories* 1, no. 6 (Dec.) : 70–79.

King, T. Jackson 1993. "Interview with Vonda McIntyre." *Science Fiction Chronicle* (May): 5, 30–32.

Knight, Damon. 1939. Letter to editor. *Astounding* 23, no. 5 (July): 107, 109.

———. [1967] 1974. *In Search of Wonder*. 2d ed. Chicago: Advent.

———. 1977. *The Futurians*. New York: John Day.

———, ed. 1977. *Turning Points: Essays on the Art of Science Fiction*. New York: Harper and Row.

Kuttner, Henry. 1938. "Avengers of Space." *Marvel Science Stories* 1, no. 1 (Aug.): 98–127.

Kurzeja, Louis. 1929. Letter to editor. *Science Wonder Stories* 1, no. 5 (Oct.): 467.

Laqueur, Thomas. [1990] 1992. *Making Sex*. Cambridge, Mass.: Harvard University Press.

Larbalestier, Justine. 1995. "An Eidolon Interview with the Editors of *She's Fantastical*: Lucy Sussex and Judith Raphael Buckrich." *Eidolon* 19 (Mar.): 59–63.

Laumer, Keith. 1965. "War against the Yukks." *Galaxy* 23, no. 4 (Apr.): 158–94.

Lazar, Moshe. 1995. "*Fin'amor.*" *A Handbook of the Troubadours*, ed. F. R. Akehurst and Judith M. Davis, 61–100. Berkeley: University of California Press.

Lee, Reba (as told to Mary Hastings Bradley). 1956. *I Passed For White*. London: Peter Davies.

Lefanu, Sarah. 1988. *In the Chinks of the World Machine*. London: Women's Press.

Le Guin, Ursula. [1969] 1991. *The Left Hand of Darkness*. London: Futura.

———. 1978. "Introduction." In *Star Songs of an Old Primate* by James Tiptree, Jr., vii–xii. New York: Del Rey Books.

———. [1979] 1989. *The Language of the Night: Essays on Fantasy and Science Fiction*. London: Women's Press.

Le Guin, Ursula K., Karen J. Fowler, and Brian Attebery. 1993. *The Norton Book of Science Fiction: North American Science Fiction, 1960–1990*. New York: W. W. Norton.

Lemon, Don M. 1931. "The Scarlet Planet." *Wonder Story Quarterly* 2, no. 2 (Dec.): 150–205, 278–81.

Leonard, Elisabeth Anne. 1997. *Into Darkness Peering : Race and Color in the Fantastic*. Contributions to the Study of Science Fiction and Fantasy 74. Westport, Conn.: Greenwood Press.

Lerner, Frederick Andrew. 1985. *Modern Science Fiction and the American Literary Community*. London: Scarecrow Press.

Lewicki, Stef. 1984. "Feminism and Science Fiction." *Foundation* 32 (Nov.): 45–59.

Lewis, C. S. [1955] 1966. "Ministering Angels." In *Of Other Worlds: Essays and Stories*, ed. Walter Hooper, 107–18. New York: Harcourt, Brace and World.

Lewis, Lisa, ed. 1992. *The Adoring Audience: Fan Culture and Popular Media*. London: Routledge.

Link, Kelly. 1997. "Travels with the Snow Queen." *Lady Churchill's Rosebud Wristlet* 1, no. 1 (winter).

Lloyd, Genevieve. [1984] 1986. *The Man of Reason: 'Male' and 'Female' in Western Philosophy*. London: Methuen.

Lorber, Judith. 1994. *Paradoxes of Gender*. New Haven: Yale University Press.

Lorraine, Lilith. 1930. "Into the 28th Century." *Science Wonder Quarterly* 1, no. 2 (Dec.): 250–67, 276.

Lowndes, Robert W. 1945. "Free and Unequal." *Agenbite of Inwit* (Mar.): 3–4.

Ludovici, Anthony M. 1923. *Lysistrata, or Woman's Future and Future Woman*. London: Kegan Paul.

Lundwall, Sam J. [1969] 1971. *Science Fiction: What It's All About*. New York: Ace.

MacGregor, Loren. 1974. "A Reply to a Chauvinist." *Notes from the Chemistry Department* (Nov.): 2–5.

MacLean, Katherine. 1981. "The Expanding Mind." In *Fantastic Lives: Autobiographical Essays by Notable Science Fiction Writers*, ed. Martin H. Greenberg, 79–101. Carbondale: Southern Illinois University Press.

McAllister, Bruce. 1972. "Ecce Femina!" *Magazine of Fantasy and Science Fiction* 42, no. 2 (Feb.): 117–44.

McBride, Debra L. 1985. "A Belated Interview with Theodore Sturgeon." *Fantasy Review* 79 (May): 10, 32.

McCaffery, Larry. 1990. *Across the Wounded Galaxies: Interviews with Contemporary American Science Fiction Writers*. Urbana: University of Illinois Press.

———. 1991. *Storming the Reality Studio: A Casebook of Cyberpunk and Postmodern Fiction*. Durham, N.C.: Duke University Press.

McCaffrey, Anne. 1974. "Hitch Your Dragon to a Star: Romance and Glamour in Science Fiction." In *Science Fiction, Today and Tomorrow*, ed. Reginald Bretnor, 278–92. New York: Harper and Row.

MacGregor, Loren. 1974. "A Reply to a Chauvinist." *Notes from the Chemistry Department* (Nov.): 5.

McIlwain, David. 1938. Letter to editor. *Astounding Science Fiction* 22, no. 3 (Nov.): 158.

McIntyre, Vonda. 1974. "Review of *Darkover Landfall*." *The Witch and the Chameleon* 2 (Nov.): 19–24.

McNay, Lois. 1992. *Foucault and Feminism*. Cambridge: Polity Press.

Maine, Charles Eric. 1972. *Alph*. New York: Nelson Doubleday.

Mallinger, Marion. 1952. Letter to editor. *Thrilling Wonder Stories* 41, no. 1 (Oct.): 134.

Marcusson, Katherine. 1939b. Letter to editor. *Startling Stories* 2, no. 3 (Nov.): 109.

Martin, Diane. 1984. "Sources: Feminist Collections and Feminist Periodicals." *Aurora* 9, no. 1 (summer): 36.

———. [1991] 1992. "Three Questions and Some Answers." In *The Bakery Men Don't See*, 2–3. Madison, Wisc.: SF3.

Martin, Emily. 1987. *The Woman in the Body: A Cultural Analysis of Reproduction*. Boston: Beacon Press.

Mason, Ted. 1929. Letter to editor. *Science Wonder Stories* 1, no. 5 (Oct.): 467.

Mellor, Adrian. 1984. "Science Fiction and the Crisis of the Educated Middle Class." *Popular Fiction and Social Change*, ed. Christopher Dowling, 20–49. London: Macmillan.

Mendlesohn, Farah. 1991. "Women in SF: Six American Sf Writers between 1960 and 1985." *Foundation* 53 (fall): 53–69.

———. 1994. "Gender, Power, and Conflict Resolution: "Subcommittee" by Zenna Henderson." *Extrapolation* 35, no. 2 (summer): 120–29.

Merrick, Helen. 1997. "The Readers Feminism Doesn't See: Feminist Fans, Critics and Science Fiction." *Trash Aesthetics: Popular Culture and Its Audience*, ed. Deborah Cartmell, I. Q. Hunter, Heidi Kaye, and Imelda Whelehan, 48–65. London: Pluto Press.

Merril, Judith. 1952. "Guest Editorial." *Thrilling Wonder Stories* 41, no. 2 (Dec.): 6, 128–30.

———. 1960. "That Only a Mother." In *Out of Bounds*. New York: Pyramid Books.

———. 1993. "Better to Have Loved: From a Memoir-in-Progress." *New York Review of Science Fiction* 59 (July): 1, 8–14.

———. 1999a. "Better to Have Loved: Excerpts from a Life." *Women of Other Worlds: Excursions through Science Fiction and Feminism*, ed. Helen Merrick and Tess Williams{page nos?}. Nedlands: University of Western Australian Press: 422-442.

———. 1999b. "A [Real?] Writer—Homage to Ted Sturgeon." *Fantasy and Science Fiction* 97, nos. 4 and 5 (Oct.–Nov): 105–42.

Merwin, Sam, Jr. 1950. "Editorial." *Thrilling Wonder Stories* 37, no. 2 (Dec.): 6–7, 140.

———. 1953. *The White Widows*. New York: Doubleday.

Miesel, Sandra. 1979–80. "Zenna Henderson's People." 17, no. 1 *Starship* (winter): 37–39.

Miller, Schuyler P. 1961. "The Reference Library: Sexing It Up." *Analog Science Fact and Fiction* 67, no. 2 (Apr.): 166–74.

———. 1969. "Review of *The Left Hand of Darkness*." *Analog Science Fiction/Science Fact* 83, no. 6 (Aug.): 167–68.

———. 1974. "The Reference Library: The Book of Tiptree." *Analog Science Fiction/Science Fact* 92, no. 5 (Jan.): 152–53.

Mines, Samuel. 1952. "Editorial on 'The Lovers.'" *Startling Stories* 27, no. 1 (Aug.): 6, 8.

———. 1953a. Editorial response to letter. *Startling Stories* 28, no. 3 (Jan.): 137.

———. 1953b. Editorial response to letter. *Thrilling Wonder Stories* 42, no. 3 (Aug.): 142.

Moskowitz, Sam. 1954. *The Immortal Storm: A History of Science Fiction Fandom*. Atlanta: Atlanta Science Fiction Organization Press.

———. [1963] 1974. "Hugo Gernsback: 'Father of Science Fiction.'" In *Explorers of the Infinite: Shapers of Science Fiction*, 225–42. Westport, Conn.: Hyperion Press.

———. 1966. *Seekers of Tomorrow: Makers of Modern Science Fiction*. Westport, Conn.: Hyperion Press.

———. 1972. *When Women Rule*. New York: Walker.

———. 1976. *Strange Horizons: The Spectrum of Science Fiction*. New York: Charles Scribner and Sons.

Moylan, Tom. 1986. *Demand the Impossible*. New York: Methuen.

Murphy, Pat. [1991] 1992. "Illusion and Expectation: A Rabble-Rousing Speech and Announcement by Pat Murphy Presented at WisCon 15, March 2, 1991." In *The Bakery Men Don't See*, 6–9 Madison, Wisc.: SF3.

———. 1996. "The Retrospective Tiptree Award." In *WisCon 20 Souvenir Book*, 119. Madison, Wisc.: SF3.

Nicholls, Peter, ed. 1976. *Science Fiction at Large*. London: Victor Gollancz.

Norton, Andre. 1978. "Foreword: The Girl and the B.E.M." In *Cassandra Rising*, ed. Alice Laurance, xi–xiii. Garden City, N.Y.: Doubleday.

Notkin, Debbie, and the Secret Feminist Cabal, eds. 1998. *Flying Cups and Saucers: Gender Explorations in Science Ficiton and Fantasy*. Cambridge, Mass.: Edgewood Press.

Novitski, Paul. 1979. "Starship Interview: Vonda McIntyre." *Starship* 16, no. 2 (spring): 21–28.

Osachie, Edward M. 1969. Letter to editor. *If* 19, no. 9 (Nov.): 156–57.

Oudshoorn, Nelly. 1994. *Beyond the Natural Body: An Archeology of Sex Hormones*. London: Routledge.

Ovid. [1955] 1964. *Metamorphoses*. London: Penguin Books.

Palumbo, Donald, ed. 1986. *Erotic Universe: Sexuality and Fantastic Literature*. Westport, Conn.: Greenwood Press.

Panshin, Alexei. 1969. "Review of *Left Hand of Darkness*." *Magazine of Fantasy and Science Fiction* 37, no. 5 (Nov.): 50–51.

Paratico, C. R.. 1929. Letter to editor. *Science Wonder Stories* 1, no. 6 (Nov.): 669.

Parris, Earl T. 1952. Letter to editor. *Thrilling Wonder Stories* 41, no. 1 (Oct.): 139.

Patai, Daphne. 1982. "When Women Rule: Defamiliarization and the Sex Role Reversal Utopia." *Extrapolation* 23, no. 1 (spring): 56–69.

———. 1989. "Afterword." In *The End of This Day's Business*, ed. Katherine Burdekin, 159–90. New York: Feminist Press.

Pateman, Carole. 1988. *The Sexual Contract*. Oxford: Polity Press.

Pateman, Carole, and Elizabeth Gross, eds. 1986. *Feminist Challenges: Social and Political Theory*. Sydney: Allen and Unwin.

Pearce, Lynne, and Gina Wisker, eds. 1998. *Fatal Attractions: Rescripting Romance in Contemporary Literature and Film*. London: Pluto Press.

Pearson, Jacqueline. 1990. "Where No Man Has Gone Before: Sexual Politics and Women's Science Fiction." *Science Fiction, Social Conflict and War*, ed. Philip John David, 2–25. Manchester: Manchester University Press.

Penley, Constance, and Andrew Ross. 1991. *Technoculture*. Minneapolis: University of Minnesota Press.

Phillips, Julie. 1994. "Feminist Sci-Fi: A Brave New World." *Ms.* (Nov.): 70–73.

———. 1996. "Mars Needs Women: The True Fiction of James Tiptree, Jr." *Voice Literary Supplement* 148 (Sept.): 18–20.

Pierce, Anthony J. 1970. "Inside Conspiracy." *Science Fiction Review* 40 (Oct.): 17–18.

Pierce, John J. 1994. *Odd Genre: A Study in Imagination and Evolution*. Westport, Conn.: Greenwood Press.

Platt, Charles. 1980. *Dream Makers: The Uncommon People Who Write Science Fiction—Interviews by Charles Platt*. New York: Berkeley Books.

———. 1983a. *Dream Makers*. Vol. 2: *The Uncommon Men and Women Who Write Science Fiction: Interviews by Charles Platt*. New York: Berkeley Books.

———. 1983b. "James Tiptree, Jr." In *Dream Makers*, vol. 2: *The Uncommon Men and Women Who Write Science Fiction: Interviews by Charles Platt*, 257–73. New York: Berkeley Books.

———. 1989. "The Rape of Science Fiction." *Science Fiction Eye* 1, no. 5 (July): 45–49.

Plaza, Monique. 1984. "Ideology against Women." *Feminist Issues* 4, no. 1: 73–82.

Pohl, Frederik. 1961. "Review of *Venus Plus X*." *If* 10, no. 6 (Jan.): 84–85.

———. 1979. *The Way the Future Was*. London: Victor Gollancz.

Pohl, Frederik, and C. M. Kornbluth. [1954] 1970. *Search the Sky*. London: Penguin Books.

Porter, Tom. 1984. "Women SF Writers You've Probably Never Heard Of." *Aurora* 9, no. 1 (summer): 37.

Pournelle, Jerry. 1975. "On What Standard?" *Notes from the Chemistry Department* (Sept.): 4–9.

Powell, Jep. 1941. "Amazons of a Weird Creation." *Fantastic Adventures* 3, no. 4 (June): 96–115.

Pullen, Verna. 1930. Letter to editor. *Science Wonder Stories* 1, no. 8 (Jan.): 765.

Puren, Nina. 1995. "Hymeneal Acts: Interrogating the Hegemony of Rape and Romance." *Australian Feminist Law Journal* 5 (Oct.): 15–26.

Rabkin, Eric S. 1981. "Science Fiction Women before Liberation." In *Future Females: A Critical Anthology*, ed. Marleen Barr, 9–25. Bowling Green, Ohio: Bowling Green State University Popular Press.

Radway, Janice. [1984] 1987. *Reading the Romance*. London: Verso.

Reddy, Michael J. 1979. "The Conduit Metaphor—A Case of Frame Conflict in Our Language about Language." In *Metaphor in Thought*, ed. Andrew Ortony, 284–324. Cambridge: Cambridge University Press.

Reed, Kit. 1958. "The Wait." *Magazine of Fantasy and Science Fiction* 14, no. 4 (Apr.): 56–69.

Rennison, G. E. 1942. Letter to editor. *Planet Stories* 1, no. 10 (spring): 121–22.

Reynolds, Mack. [1966] 1975. *Amazon Planet*. New York: Ace.

Rhode, Deborah L., ed. 1990. *Theoretical Perspectives on Sexual Difference*. New Haven: Yale University Press.

Rich, Adrienne. 1980. "Compulsory Heterosexuality and Lesbian Existence." *Signs* 5, no. 4 (summer): 631–60.

Richardson, Robert S. 1955. "The Day after We Land on Mars." *Magazine of Fantasy and Science Fiction* 9, no. 6 (Dec.): 44–52.

Riley, Dick, ed. 1978. *Critical Encounters: Writers and Themes in Science Fiction*. New York: Frederik Ungar.

Roberts, Adam. 2000. *Science Fiction*. New Critical Idiom Series. London: Routledge.

Roberts, Robin. 1984a. "A Bibliography of Katherine MacLean." *Aurora* 9, no. 1 (summer): 36.

———. 1984b. "Katherine MacLean's Subtle Humor." *Aurora* 9, no. 1 (summer): 13–14.

———. 1987. "The Female Alien: Pulp Science Fiction's Legacy to Feminists." *Journal of Popular Culture* (June): 33–52.

———. 1993. *A New Species: Gender and Science in Science Fiction*. Urbana: University of Illinois Press.

Rogers, James Michael II. 1939. Letter to editor. *Astounding Science Fiction* 23, no. 2 (Apr.): 159–60.

Rogers, James Michael II, and Mary Evelyn Rogers. 1939. Letter to editor. *Astounding Science Fiction* 24, no. 1 (Sept.): 97.

Rogers, Mary Evelyn. 1939. Letter to editor. *Astounding Science Fiction* 23, no. 2 (Apr.): 160.

Rose, Mark. 1981. *Alien Encounters: Anatomy of Science Fiction*. Cambridge, Mass.: Harvard University Press.

Rosinsky, Natalie M. 1982. "A Female Man? The 'Medusan' Humor of Joanna Russ." *Extrapolation* 23, no. 1 (spring): 31–36.

———. 1984. *Feminist Futures: Contemporary Women's Speculative Fiction*. Ann Arbor: UMI Research Press.

Ross, Andrew. 1991. *Strange Weather*. London: Verso.

Rupert, M. F. 1930. "Via the Hewitt Ray." *Science Wonder Quarterly* 1, no. 3 (spring 1930): 370–80, 420.

Russ, Joanna. [1971] 1974 "The Image of Women in Science Fiction." *Vertex* 1, no. 6 (Feb.): 53–57.

———. [1972] 1983. "When It Changed." In *The Zanzibar Cat*, 3–11. Sauk City, Wisc.: Arkham House.

———. [1975] 1985. *The Female Man*. London: Women's Press.

———. [1975] 1995 "Towards an Aesthetics of Science Fiction." In *To Write Like a Woman: Essays in Feminism and Science Fiction*, 3–14. Bloomington: Indiana University Press.

———. 1976. "A Letter to Marion Zimmer Bradley." *The Witch and the Chameleon* 5–6: 9–13.

———. [1977] 1978. *We Who Are About To . . .* London: Magnum Books.

———. 1980. "*Amor Vincit Foeminam*: The Battle of the Sexes in SF." *Science-Fiction Studies* 7, no. 1 (Mar.): 2–15.

———. 1981. "Recent Feminist Utopias." *Future Females: A Critical Anthology*, ed. Marleen Barr, 71–85. Bowling Green, Ohio: Bowling Green State University Popular Press.

———. [1983] 1984. *How To Suppress Women's Writing*. London: Women's Press.

———. [1984] 1985. "The Cliches from Outer Space." In *Despatches from the Frontiers of the Female Mind*, ed. Jan Green and Sarah Lefanu, 27–43. London: Women's Press.

———. 1995. *To Write Like a Woman: Essays in Feminism and Science Fiction*. Bloomington: Indiana University Press.

Russell, Eric, Frank Russell, and Leslie T. Johnson. 1937. "Seeker of To-morrow." *Astounding* 19, no. 5 (July): 124–54.

St. Clair, Margaret. [1954] 1995. "Short in the Chest." In *Women of Wonder: The Classic Years: Science Fiction by Women from the 1940s to the 1970s*, ed. Pamela Sargent, 130–38. San Diego: Harcourt Brace.

———. 1981. "Wight in Space: An Autobiographical Sketch." In *Fantastic Lives: Autobiographical Essays by Notable Science Fiction Writers*, ed. Martin H. Greenberg, 144–56. Carbondale: Southern Illinois University Press.

Salmonson, Jessica Amanda. 1984. "Mediocrity and Women's Science Fiction." *Aurora* 9, no. 1 (summer): 30–32.

Sanders, Scott. 1981. "Woman as Nature in Science Fiction." In *Future Females: A Critical Anthology*, ed. Marleen Barr, 42–62. Bowling Green, Ohio: Bowling Green State University Popular Press.

Sapiro, Leland. 1986-87. Letter to editor. *Aurora* 10, no. 1 (winter): 5.

Sargent, Pamela. [1974] 1978. *Women of Wonder*. London: Penguin.

———. 1975. "Women in Science Fiction." *Futures* (Oct.): 435–41.

———. 1976. "Introduction." In *More Women of Wonder*, xi–liii. New York: Vintage Books.

———. [1991] 1992. "The Sheikh's Daughter." In *The Bakery Men Don't See*, 10–14. Madison, Wisc.: SF3.

———. 1995a. *Women of Wonder: The Classic Years: Science Fiction by Women from the 1940s to the 1970s*. New York: Harcourt Brace.

———. 1995b. *Women of Wonder: The Contemporary Years: Science Fiction by Women from the 1970s to the 1990s*. New York: Harcourt Brace.

Sawicki, Jana. 1994. "Foucault, Feminism and Questions of Identity." In *The Cambridge Companion to Foucault*, ed. Gary Cutting, 286–313. Cambridge: Cambridge University Press.

Scholes, Robert. 1981. "A Footnote to Russ's 'Recent Feminist Utopias.'" In *Future Females: A Critical Anthology*, ed. Marleen S. Barr, 86–87. Bowling Green, Ohio: Bowling Green State University Popular Press.

Scholes, Robert, and Eric S. Rabkin. 1977. *Science Fiction: History Science Vision*. New York: Oxford University Press.

Searles, Langley. 1940. Letter to editor. *Startling Stories* 3, no. 1 (Jan.): 110.

Sedgwick, Eve Kosofsky. 1990. *Epistemology of the Closet*. Berkeley: University of California Press.

———. 1993. "Queer Performativity: Henry James' The Art of the Novel." *GLQ: Journal of Lesbian and Gay Studies* 1, no. 1: 1–16.

Sheckley, Robert. 1961. "Pilgrimage to Earth." In *Spectrum: A Science Fiction Anthology*, ed. Kingsley Amis and Robert Conquest, 209–20. London: Victor Gollancz.

Sheldon, Alice. 1988. "A Woman Writing Science Fiction and Fantasy." In *Women of Vision*, ed. Denise Du Pont, 43–58. New York: St Martin's.

Shelton, Miles (Don Wilcox). 1945. "Women's Island." *Fantastic Adventures* 7, no. 5 (Dec.): 46–82.

Siclari, Joe. 1981. "Science Fiction Fandom: A History of an Unusual Hobby." In *The*

Science Fiction Reference Book, ed. Marshall B. Tymm, 87–129. Washington, D.C.: Starmont House.

Siegel, Mark. 1988–89. "'Love Was the Plan, the Plan Was . . . ' A True Story about James Tiptree, Jr." *Foundation* 44 (winter): 5–13.

Siemon, Frederick. 1971. *Science Fiction Story Index*, 1950–1968. Chicago: American Library Association.

Silverberg, L. 1928. Letter to editor. *Amazing Stories* 3, no. 7 (Oct.): 667.

Silverberg, Robert, 1957. "Woman's World." *Imagination Science Fiction* 8, no. 3 (June): 106–14.

———, ed. 1972. *New Dimensions II*. Garden City, N.Y.: Doubleday.

———. 1975. "Who Is Tiptree, What Is He?" Introduction to *Warm Worlds and Otherwise* by James Tiptree Jr., ix–xviii. New York: Ballantine Books.

———. ed. 1975. *The New Atlantis and Other Novellas of Science Fiction by Gene Wolfe, Ursula Le Guin and James Tiptree, Jr.* New York: Hawthorn Books.

———. 1993. "Reflections." *Amazing* 67, no. 12 (Mar.): 5–6.

Silverman, Kaja. 1983. *The Subject of Semiotics*. New York: Oxford University Press.

———. 1992. *Male Subjectivity at the Margins*. New York: Routledge.

Slimmer, Naomi. 1939. Letter to editor. *Science Fiction* 1, no. 2 (June): 118–21.

Smith, Clark Ashton. 1949. "The Root of Ampoi." *Arkham House Sampler* 2, no. 2 (Mar.): 3–16.

Smith, Curtis. 1986. "Preface." In *Twentieth Century Science-Fiction Writers*, 2d ed., vii–xi. Chicago: St James Press.

Smith, Jeffrey D. 1971. "If You Can't Laugh at It, What Good Is It?" *Phantasmicon* 6 (June): 7–17.

———, ed. 1975. "Symposium: Women in Science Fiction." *Khatru 3 and 4*. 1st ed. Baltimore, Md.: Phantasmicon Press.

———. 1978. "The Short Happy Life of James Tiptree, Jr." *Khatru* 7 (Feb.): 8–12.

———. 1987. "Obituaries: Alice Sheldon." *S.F. Chronicle* (July): 16, 18.

Sohl, Jerry. [1952] 1953. *The Haploids*. New York: Lion Books.

Speer, John Bristol. 1944. *Fancyclopedia*. Los Angeles: Forrest J. Ackerman.

Spelman, Elizabeth. 1988. *Inessential Woman*. London: Women's Press.

Spinrad, Norman. 1990. *Science Fiction in the Real World*. Carbondale: Southern Illinois University Press.

Springer, Nancy. 1994. *Larque on the Wing*. New York: AvoNova.

Staicar, Tom, ed. 1982. *The Feminine Eye*. New York: Frederik Ungar.

Stallings, Fran. 1984. "Free Radical: Miriam Allen deFord." *Aurora* 9, no. 1 (summer): 17–18, 21.

Stanton, Donna C., ed. 1992. *Discourses of Sexuality: from Aristotle to AIDS*. Ann Arbor: University of Michigan Press.

Steffen-Fluhr, Nancy. 1990. "The Case of the Haploid Heart: Psychological Patterns in the Science Fiction of Alice Sheldon ('James Tiptree, Jr')." *Science-Fiction Studies* 17, no. 2 (July): 188–220.

Sterling, Bruce. [1986] 1988. "Preface." In *Burning Chrome*, by William Gibson, 9–13. London: Grafton.

Stewart, Lula B. 1953. Letter to editor. *Thrilling Wonder Stories* 42, no. 3 (Nov.): 133–34.

Stockwell, Peter. 2000. *The Poetics of Science Fiction*. Harlow, England: Longman.

Stone, Leslie F. 1930. "Women with Wings." *Air Wonder Stories* 1, no. 11 (May): 984–1003.

———. 1929. "Men with Wings." *Air Wonder Stories* 1, no. 1 (July): 58–87.

———. [1932] 1994. "The Conquest of Gola." In *New Eves: Extraordinary Fiction About the Extraordinary Women of Today and Tomorrow*, ed. Janrae Frank, Jean Stine, and Forrest J. Ackerman, 29–42. Stanford, Conn.: Longmeadow Press.

Strauss, Erwin S. 1966. *Index to the S-F Magazines, 1951–1965*. Cambridge, Mass.: MIT Science Fiction Society.

Stuart, Don A. (John W. Campbell). 1937. "Out of Night." *Astounding* 20, no. 2 (Oct.): 14–38.

———. 1939. "Cloak of Aesir." *Astounding* 23, no. 1 (Mar.): 9–42.

Sturgeon, Theodore. 1952. "The Sex Opposite" *Fantastic* (fall): 66–90.

———. 1953. "The World Well Lost." *Universe* 1, no. 1 (June): 16–123.

———. 1960. *Venus Plus* X. New York: Pyramid.

Sturgis, Susanna J. 1992. "Tiptree Award: Gender Bending the Genre." *American Bookseller* (Sept.): 11.

———. 1995. "Inventing the Tiptrees: Reinventing an Agenda." *Feminist Bookstore News* 18, no. 1 (May): 51–52.

———. 1994. "Feminists Expand Consciousness at F/SF Conferences." *Sojourner: The Women's Forum* (Sept.): 41.

Sumers, Edward. 1940. Letter to editor. *Astounding Science Fiction* 26 no. 4 (Dec.): 113.

Sussex, Lucy. 1995. "The Virtual Juryroom." *Australian Review of Books* (June): 70.

Swain, Dwight V. 1943. "Drummers of Daugavo." *Fantastic Adventures* 5, no. 3 (Mar.): 8–59.

Tenn, William. 1965. "The Masculinist Revolt." *Fantasy and Science Fiction* 29, no. 2 (Aug.): 4–30.

———. 1951. "Venus Is a Man's World." *Galaxy Science Fiction* 2, no. 4 (July): 3–20.

Teresa, of Avila, Saint [1957] 1987. *The Life of Saint Teresa of Avila by Herself*. London: Penguin.

Thomas, Sheree R. 2000. *Dark Matter: A Century of Speculative Fiction from the African Diaspora*. New York: Warner Books.

Thornton, Margaret, ed. 1995. *Public and Private: Feminist Legal Debates*. Melbourne: Oxford University Press

Threadgold, Terry, and Anne Cranny-Francis, eds. 1990. *Feminine, Masculine and Representation*. Sydney: Allen and Unwin.

Threadgold, Terry. 1997. *Feminist Poetics: Poiesis, Performance, Histories*. London: Routledge.

Thurston, Caroline. 1987. *The Romance Revolution: Erotic Novels for Women and the Quest for a New Sexual Identity*. Urbana: University of Illinois Press.

Tiptree, James Jr. 1968a. "Birth of a Salesman." *Analog Science Fiction/ Science Fact* (Mar.): 72–85.

———. 1968b. "The Mother Ship." *If* 18, no. 6 (June): 81–100.

———. [1968] 1973. "Mama Come Home." In *Ten Thousand Light Years from Home*, 53–78. London: Eyre Methuen.

———. 1969. "Happiness Is a Warm Spaceship." *If* 19, no. 9 (Nov.): 4–48.

———. 1971a. "The Peacefulness of Vivyan." *Amazing Stories* (July): 66–76, 79.

———. 1971b. "The 20-Mile Zone: Travelog—In the Canadian Rockies." *Phantasmicon* 8 (Dec.): 34–41.

———. 1972. "The 20–Mile Zone: Do You Read It Twice?" *Phantasmicon* 9 (Feb.): 26–30.

———. 1973. "a day like any other." *Foundation* 3 (Mar.): 49.

———. [1973] 1975. *Ten Thousand Light-Years from Home*. London: Methuen.

———. [1973] 1990. "Women Men Don't See." *Her Smoke Rose Up Forever*. Sauk City, Wisc.: Arkham House.

———. 1976. "How to Have an Absolutely Hilarious Heart Attack." *Khatru* 5 (Apr.): 4–10.

———. 1977. "The 20 Mile Zone: British Columbia, Virginia and Quintana Roo." *Khatru* 6 (Apr.): 28–33.

———. 1978. *Up the Walls of the World*. New York: Berkeley.

———. [1978] 1979. *Star-Songs of an Old Primate*. New York: Ballantine Books.

———. 1979. "Everything But the Name Is Me." *Starship/Algol* 16, no. 4 (fall): 31–34.

———. 1980. "Locus Letters: Status Report on the Case of James Tiptree Jr/Alli Sheldon vs. Virginia's License-to-Write Laws." *Locus* 13, no. 2 (Feb.): 5.

———. 1990. *Her Smoke Rose Up Forever*. Sauk City, Wisc.: Arkham House.

———. 1993. "A Genius Darkly: A Letter to Ted White on Philip K. Dick." *New York Review of Science Fiction* 63 (Nov.): 16.

———. 2000. *Meet Me at Infinity: The Uncollected Tiptree: Fiction and Non-Fiction*. New York: Tor Books.

Todd, Edwin. 1939. Letter to editor. *Astounding Science Fiction* 23, no. 3 (May): 158–59.

Truesdale, David, and Paul McGuire. 1977. "An Interview with Leigh Brackett and Edmond Hamilton." *Science Fiction Review* 21 (May): 6–15.

Tuana, Nancy. 1993. *The Less Noble Sex*. Bloomington: Indiana University Press.

Tulloch, John, and Henry Jenkins. 1995. *Science Fiction Audiences: Watching Doctor Who and Star Trek*. London: Routledge.

Turnbull, Donald G. 1938. Letter to editor. *Astounding Science Fiction* 21, no. 5 (July): 162.

Turner, George. 1940. Letter to editor. *Astounding* 24, no. 5 (Jan.): 155–57.

Tymm, Marshall B., ed. 1981. *The Science Fiction Reference Book*. Washington, D.C.: Starmont House.

Tymn, Marshall B., and Mike Ashley. 1985. *Science Fiction, Fantasy and Weird Fiction Magazines*. Westport, Conn.: Greenwood Press.

Usack, Kendra. 1984. "Re-evaluating Andre Norton." *Aurora* 9, no. 1 (summer): 8–10.

Van Vogt, A. E. [1945] 1953. *Slan*. London: Weidenfeld and Nicolson.

Vaughan, Richard. 1932. "The Woman from Space." *Wonder Stories Quarterly* 3, no. 3 (Mar.): 364–80.

Vinge, Joan D. 1987. "Women in Science Fiction." *Infinity Journal of the Princeton SF Society* (Mar.): 33–39.

Vonarburg, Elisabeth. 1995. "Women and Science Fiction." In *Out of this World*, 177–87. Ottawa: Quarry Press.

Walker, Paul. 1975. "Sexual Stereotypes: Whose Responsibility?" *Notes from the Chemistry Department* 10 (Mar.): 9–11.

Warne, Garry L. 1990. "The Child with Ambiguous Genitalia." In *Practical Paediatrics*, ed. M. S. Robinson, 474–79. 2d ed. Melbourne: Churchill Livingstone.

Warner, Harry, Jr. [1969] 1971 *All Our Yesterdays: An Informal History of SF Fandom in the Forties*. Chicago: Advent.

Warner, Michael, ed. 1993. *Fear of a Queer Planet*. Minneapolis: University of Minnesota Press.

Wasso, John Jr. 1940. Letter to editor. *Astounding Science Fiction* 26, no. 2: 152.

Watson, Noelle, and Paul E. Schellinger, eds. 1991. *Twentieth-Century Science-Fiction Writers*. 3d ed. Chicago: St. James Press.

Wede. 1936. "Death Creeps the Moon." *Amazing Stories* 10, no. 13 (Dec.): 102–17.

Weedman, Jane B., ed. 1985. *Women Worldwalkers: New Dimensions of Science Fiction and Fantasy*. Lubbock: Texas Tech Press.

Wentworth, Harold, and Stuart Berg Flexner. 1960. *Dictionary of American Slang*. New York: Thomas Y. Crowell.

Wentworth, Robert (Edmond Hamilton). 1940. "World without Sex." *Marvel Science Stories* 12, no. 1 (May): 41–54.

Wertham, Frederic. 1973. *The World of Fanzines: A Special Form of Communication*. Carbondale: Southern Illinois University Press.

West, Wallace G. [1929] 1972. "The Last Man." In *When Women Rule*, ed. Sam Moskowitz, 104–30. New York: Walker.

Westfahl, Gary. 1993. "Superladies in Waiting: How the Female Hero Almost Emerges in Science Fiction." *Foundation* 58 (June): 42–62.

White, Robin. 1968. "Are Femme Fans Human?" *Algol*, no. 13 (Jan. 1968): 51–54.

Wilgus, Neal. 1978–79. "*Algol* Interview: Suzy McKee Charnas." *Algol* 16, no. 1 (winter): 21–25.

Williams, B. W. 1953. Letter to editor. *Startling Stories* 28, no. 3 (Jan.): 136–37.

Williamson, Jack. 1979. "SF and I." *Starship* 16, no. 2 (spring): 8–16.

Willis, Connie. 1992. "Guest Editorial: The Women SF Doesn't See." *Asimov's Science Fiction Magazine* 16, no. 11 (Oct.): 4–8, 49.

Wilson, Richard. 1955. *The Girls from Planet Five*. New York: Ballantine Books.

Winchester, Virginia. 1952. Letter to editor. *Thrilling Wonder Stories* 40, no. 3 (Aug.): 128.

Winter, Douglas E. 1984. "Mostly I Want to Break Your Heart—An Interview with Suzy McKee Charnas." *Fantasy Review* 71 (Sept.): 5–6, 41.

WisCon 20 Souvenir Book. 1996. Madison, Wisc.: SF3.

Wittig, Monique. 1992. *The Straight Mind*. Boston: Beacon Press.

Wollheim, Donald A. 1971. *The Universe Makers*. New York: Harper and Row.

Wolmark, Jenny. 1993. *Aliens and Others: Science Fiction, Feminism and Postmodernism*. London: Harvester Wheatsheaf.

Wood, Susan. 1978. "Guest Editorial: The People's Programming." *Janus* 4, no. 1 (Mar.): 4–7, 13.

———. 1978–79. "Women and Science Fiction." *Algol* 16, no. 1 (winter): 9–18.

Woolf, Virginia. [1929] 1977. *A Room of One's Own*. London: Panther.

Wylie, Philip. 1951. *The Disappearance*. London: Victor Gollancz.

Wyndham, John. [1956] 1965. "Consider Her Ways." In *Consider Her Ways and Others*, 7–73. London: Penguin Books.

Young, Hugh Hampton. 1937. *Genital Abnormalities, Hermaphroditism and Related Adrenal Diseases*. London: Bailliere, Tindall and Cox.

INDEX

Bold numbers refer to illustrations.

Library of Congress Cataloging-in-Publication Data
Larbalestier, Justine.
The battle of the sexes in science fiction / Justine Larbalestier.
p. cm.
Includes bibliographical references and index.
ISBN 0-8195-6526-1 (cloth : alk. paper)—ISBN 0-8195-6527-X (pbk. : alk. paper)
1. Science fiction, American—History and criticism. 2. Feminism and literature—United States—History—20th century. 3. American fiction—20th century—History and criticism. 4. Feminist fiction, American—History and criticism. 5. Man-woman relationships in literature. 6. Sex role in literature. I. Title.
PS374.S35 L29 2002
813'.0876209'0082—dc21
2002016741